DON'T LOOK AWAY

Leslie Kelly

Leslie Kelly

ISBN-13: 978-1484140024
ISBN-10: 1484140028

Dedicated with love to Bruce. Thank you so much for always believing in me, supporting me, encouraging me, and loving me. I might have been alive if I'd never met you...but I'd certainly never have *lived*.

Leslie Kelly

Books in the Veronica Sloan Series

Don't Look Away
Don't Ever Stop

PROLOGUE

Washington, D.C.
July 4, 2022

Leanne Carr tried to keep her eyes open throughout her murder.

She didn't scream—that was pointless. This part of the sub-basement was completely deserted, dark and cavernous. Security teams had swept the area clean twenty-four hours ago in preparation for today's event, not even allowing the round-the-clock construction workers access. Then they'd locked down the whole site.

Just her misfortune that she had a high enough security clearance to get around the lockdown. Because the measures used to keep unauthorized people out had done a magnificent job of trapping her in. With a psychopath.

She would have fought if she could. But that had been impossible once her attacker, dressed all in black, had stuck a metal device on her upper arm, sending a million frissons of electric pain rocketing through her. After that, Leanne had been able to do nothing more than lie on the cold concrete floor, every muscle in her body still twitching. Helpless. Useless. Watching groggily as he began to cut her clothes away, piece by piece, not seeming to care if he occasionally took chunks of her skin along with them.

Strange, the cutting didn't hurt as much as she would have expected. Maybe because she was still feeling the reverberations of shock from the weapon he'd used to stun her. Maybe because her mind had begun to remove itself from this situation.

Maybe because she was already dead.

No, not dead. She wasn't experiencing the expected agony of the knife, and the images before her eyes weren't making sense in her brain. *Darkness, just darkness.* But her other senses hadn't completely failed her. She could smell something peculiar. Medicinal. Metallic. Probably blood, which she could also taste on her lips from the first, shocking blow to her face.

Leanne could also still hear enough to know the world continued to turn outside this private corner of hell. Above the hiss of his deep, even breathing, which was driving her mad with its absolute normalcy, came the faint whomp-whomp of powerful rotor blades passing far overhead.

Helicopter.

In her mind, she heard the rest of what must be going on. The voices of carefully-screened, hand-picked reporters calling out pre-approved questions. The college marching band chosen from among thousands of applicants for the honor of playing the national anthem. The patriotic onlookers cheering through their tears, just as each song and every speech was scripted to make them do.

The moment had arrived, the big event she'd been helping to coordinate for the past several months. Funny how little it mattered now, in the last moments of her life.

There was also one more sound slowly building in Leanne's head which finally drove all other thoughts away. With every nerve ending that came limping back to life, only to experience another kind of pain, the noise grew louder.

It was the sound of her moans. Which, she had no doubt, would eventually become screams.

But not dead yet, she reminded herself, though she knew she soon would be. Probably not as soon as she'd like given the way her attacker, so silent but for his breathing, so deliberate in his movements, looked beneath his mask. She could just make out the curve of his mouth behind a draping of black fabric that covered his entire head. He—possibly she?—was smiling.

No. Death would not come soon enough.

"Please."

That was all she could manage. Leanne herself, however, wasn't sure what she was asking. Please let her go? Please let her die? Please let this not be happening?

He ignored her. She tried to focus on anything that could be used to identify him—the shade of his skin, any identifying marks, just as she had been trained to do. But he was well-covered. Hopefully there would be something. Maybe the darkness wouldn't prevent the investigators from finding some clue she didn't even recognize

He began to scrape the tip of the knife over her body in long, deliberate sweeps. Slow. Almost erotic, as though he were caressing her.

The sensations built in intensity as her nerve endings limped back to life and transmitted the messages of pain to her weary brain. A thin trail of fire traced the blade's route across her shoulder, around her neck, between her breasts, down her stomach. Until it reached her bloody thighs and moved between them.

It was tempting to let go. To shut her eyes and wait for it to be over. But the certainty of her impending murder kept her eyelids from falling, even though her mind wasn't fully processing everything she saw. She couldn't, as a matter of fact, process much of anything except the glittering silver of the weapon, tightly clenched in a black-gloved hand.

Suddenly, a brilliant light came on, shining right in her face, blinding her. She groaned, clenching her eyes shut.

It didn't matter. Even if she could no longer see what was happening, after this was all over, someone else would examine the pictures in her mind.

And would catch her murderer.

Chapter 1

"This is gonna take forever."

Detective Veronica Sloan glared out the windshield of her car, mentally cursing the heat, and the crowd. Though traffic in the nation's capital was always a bitch, the lines to get through the Pennsylvania Avenue checkpoints were longer than usual on this wickedly hot summer morning.

A queue of pedestrians wound from each of the heavily-guarded entrances, through Lafayette Park, all the way to H Street. Throngs of other people milled around them, selling cold drinks, packaged food or souvenirs. Some held protest signs, some formed prayer circles.

A bunch of them blocked the damn road.

On any day there would be discontent. On this particularly sweltering July one, tempers were flaring. Hers not the least of them.

In the time it had taken to crawl two blocks in the unmarked sedan, she'd seen one woman faint, two fights break out, and a group of children sprawl on the sidewalk in exhaustion. Flag-draped rednecks glared at Japanese tourists—the slanty-eyed foreigners just as unwelcome as the burqa-wearing ones in their minds. Everyone sweated and cursed and bitched and shouted.

But they didn't leave. Morbid curiosity always ensured they wouldn't leave once they'd made it this far.

She could have roared in on full emergency response, dispersing the crowd spilling into the street with her siren and her horn. She didn't. Because if the people heard about the murder, they might get a little itchy. Might start stampeding, in fact. Washington was quick to panic these days. And she didn't particularly want to add any boot-crushed grandmas from the Midwest to her already backbreaking caseload.

"Christ, I think there are as many people in line now as there were yesterday for the rededication."

Ronnie glanced over at her partner, Mark Daniels, who looked as impatient as she felt. The cynic in her couldn't help saying, "Yeah, but this is nothing compared to the crowds who lined up to gawk at the rubble that first year."

No, it definitely wasn't. As soon as the military had begun to allow visitors to view the destruction wrought in October of 2017, D.C. had become the hottest tourist destination in the world. People had clamored for the chance to say they had seen the site of the worst terrorist attack in history.

Goddamn ghouls.

"I guess you're right." He leaned back in the seat, crossing his arms over his brawny chest and closing his eyes. "Wake me up when we get there."

She laughed softly. "Who was she?"

Her partner didn't bother looking up. "A stripper from the Shake And Bake. I always thought it would be fun to be the pole for a walking pair of jugs, but I think I'm gettin' too old for that stuff."

He wasn't even forty. Nowhere near old, in brain or brawn, though his weary tone hinted at his recent late nights. Daniels had been edgy lately, pushing limits, taking risks. She couldn't say why. Nor could she say she wasn't worried about him.

"Hard living. You'd better slow down."

"Look who's talking."

"Hey, my ass isn't hanging off a bar stool seven nights a week. And the only poles I see are the ones holding up the lights in the park where I run."

Mark's lips twitched a little, though his position never changed. "I keep telling you Ron, a body's only got so much runnin' in it. You better save it for our visits to the East Side. One of these days when you're chasing some banger, you're gonna run out of run."

Ahh, Daniels wisdom. What would she do without her daily dose of it?

Ronnie didn't have time to wonder, because they'd finally reached the turn-off for heavily barricaded 17th Street. Ignoring the glares of the pedestrians who grudgingly got out of the way, she turned and drove past a picket line of armed soldiers dressed in urban fatigues.

This was the only vehicular route into or out of the north quadrant of the area once called the National Mall. An area that had, just yesterday, in a ceremony full of as much pomp and ceremony as could be accomplished behind a wall of bulletproof glass, been rededicated by the president as Patriot Square.

The place had another name on the street. Just as most New Yorkers still called the 9/11 site Ground Zero, most people around here called this The Trainyard.

"Stop the car," a stern voice ordered as she slowly cruised

toward the iron-and-barbed-wire fence. The voice had come out of one of the dozen body-armor wearing troops fronting the gate, every one of whom had a weapon aimed directly at her face. Talk about a welcoming committee.

Eight years ago, when she'd been just a rookie cop and the U.S.—more than a decade after 9/11—had seemed relatively safe, a flashed badge would have gotten her past any roadblock. Times were different now. Much different. So without a word, she threw the car into park, killed the engine, and put her hands up.

"Let's go," she told her partner.

Daniels put his hands up, too, and opened his eyes. The bags under them spotlighted his weariness, not to mention his hangover. Ronnie was seriously going kick his butt later for showing up on the job in such a pathetic state, especially on a day like today, which was shaping up to be a really shitty one. Bad enough on any normal day when they were rounding up the latest gang-enforcer or Pure V dealer, Pure V being the hottest new street drug, a cheap variation of Vicodin. But it was much worse now, when they had to come to this side of town and undergo a thorough inspection.

After they had been given the nod by the sergeant in charge, they stepped out into the bright sunshine, and were each immediately approached by different security teams.

"Sloan, D.C. Police," she said as soon as one of the men reached her, his weapon still trained on her head. Another soldier stood directly behind his left shoulder, and a third was holding the leash of a thick-chested, sharp-toothed K-9.

Never lowering his semi-automatic, the first soldier held out his other hand. She passed over her badge and photo I.D., then moved away from the car for a thorough search. Both of the vehicle, and of her.

He examined her badge. The gun came down. But he didn't holster it.

His mouth barely moving, and his face expressionless, he asked, "Weapon?"

She nodded. "Glock. Rear holster." Ronnie knew better than to reach back and offer it up herself, which was why she hadn't made any proactive move toward it before exiting the car. Her head would have been a slushy pile of brain and bone on the sidewalk the second these hard-nosed troops had seen a weapon in her hand.

"Take off your jacket."

She did, glad to lose the extra weight of the dark, city-issued clothing. Ronnie missed the way she had dressed during her early years as a detective—the pre-2017 days of wearing street clothes on the job. But the way the whole country demanded confirmation and re-confirmation of every person's identity, she figured it wasn't surprising that every cop now had to be in uniform. All the way up to the Chief of the National Department of Law Enforcement.

"Spread."

Assuming a customary position, she went completely still, arms extended at her sides, legs apart. Without saying a word, the men got to work. One of the soldiers removed the 9 mm and spare clip off her back and stepped away to examine them. Another appeared out of nowhere with a digital scanner. He passed it over her upper arm like it was a can of beans at the grocery store, looking for the microchip that was implanted in the arm of every law-abiding American citizen.

The non-law-abiding ones didn't like them so much.

Neither did the civil rights fanatics who had been among the loudest screaming against the idea several years ago when the government had first tried to get its citizens to voluntarily submit to implantation.

Glancing at the data on the tiny screen, the soldier nodded toward the sergeant. "Identity confirmed. Sloan, Veronica Marie, born Arlington, Virginia, January 5, 1993."

One step closer. But still not done.

Clipping a state-of-the-art, super-powerful sensor to his hand, the sergeant moved in beside her. He was so close she could feel his breath on the side of her face and smell the sausage he'd had for breakfast.

"Don't move." He bit the words out from a jaw so tight it could have been used to crack a walnut.

She was tempted to promise she wouldn't, but that would constitute moving her mouth and she really didn't want to get shot or clubbed today. So she just stood there waiting for him to finish.

Showing no emotion, he ran the miniscule device over her entire body, his hand less than a centimeter away from her clothes. If he got any kind of thrill off of scraping his palm across her nipples, he at least had the courtesy not to show it.

The metal detector trilled as it passed over her holster, the button of her pants, the microchip implanted in her arm, the hook of her bra, even the metal eyelets of her shoes. It also gave a soft beep as it moved near her right temple, which made him pause for a moment, double-check the reading, and tug her hair out of the way to study the side of her head. He obviously saw nothing...the incision had been tiny and right up against her hairline.

"If you check my records, you'll see a code for that," she explained, risking the mouth move.

The soldier stared at her, then stepped away to glance at his scanner screen. He might be curious about why she was authorized to proceed into highly secure areas when she obviously had some kind of unexplained metal in her head, but he was professional enough to not ask.

After a moment, he stepped back. His stare shifted to her face. A beat. Then he moved on.

"Clear," he said as he stepped back for the next part of the inspection.

The K-9 had just finished in the car. He now made quick work of sniffing her crotch, her ass, and anywhere else he could stick his nose to make sure she wasn't wired to blow herself up with some kind of bomb stuck into a body orifice.

It'd happened.

When the dog was done, another soldier finished the job the old-fashioned way, feeling her up so thoroughly, she wished he had at least bought her a cup of coffee first. She didn't suspect he'd appreciate the smart-ass comment, so she kept her mouth shut. These guys had a tough job to do, and she, for one, wasn't going to say anything to make their lives any harder. Or to piss them off.

"You're authorized to proceed, Detective Sloan," the sergeant said, returning her I.D. as the other guard returned her weapon. "You know the way?"

Tucking the I.D. in her pocket and her 9mm into its holster, she thought about his question.

Did she know the way?

Why was that such a difficult one to answer? She had been born and raised right across the Potomac, just a few miles from here. She'd attended Georgetown University and currently lived a block away from Rock Creek Park. This was her town.

But the answer to his question was no. She hadn't been on these streets in a long time. Most Washingtonians stayed clear of this quadrant, the wounds still too raw, even after nearly five years.

Not that she was about to admit that. So she took a guess. "The old security entrance off State?"

He replied with a brief nod, then stepped away, watching every move she made as she re-entered the car. Daniels got in on the other side, buckled up and muttered, "Jesus, I think that private just squeezed my dick harder than the stripper did last night."

She had to grin. "Yeah. Join the club."

Driving through the slowly opening gates, still under the watchful eye of the troops, she barely noticed Mark's evil chuckle. "Join the club, huh? So, you telling me some of the guys at the precinct are right about what you've really got in your pants?"

"Screw you," she shot back, her voice holding no heat.

She wasn't really offended by her partner's jab. Ronnie knew better than anyone that a lot of the men she worked with hated her guts. First, because she'd turned a lot of them down. Second because she had made detective when some of the guys she'd gone to the academy with were still writing tickets. Third because most of them knew she could not be intimidated.

Fourth, most recently, because Ronnie had made it onto the Optical Evidence Program Investigative Squad—O.E.P.I.S.. If testing went well, members of the newly formed, national-level unit would someday be in place in every law enforcement agency in America. For now, however, it was virgin territory. Only five-hundred investigators had been chosen from the entire country—a one-to-ten ratio to the five-thousand test subjects who'd had devices implanted in their brains as part of the Optical Evidence Program. So it was a highly sought-after assignment, even though few people actually knew the full scope of the experiment. Ronnie getting in hadn't earned her a lot of friendly thoughts back at the squad. Or in the whole D.C.P.D. Not that she cared. And not that it seemed to matter a bit, since she had yet to actively work on that kind of case.

Maybe today.

The thought flashed through her mind, like it did every time she was personally called out on a case. So far, it hadn't happened. But today could be different. Considering she and her partner were heading out of their jurisdiction, by special request, and given where the victim had been found, this really could be the day. As a rush of nervous excitement shot through her, Ronnie took a deep breath to disguise it from Daniels.

She should have known his mind was still a few steps back. In her pants.

"You know, just in case you forgot, partner, I'm here for you in any old way you need, including giving testimony about how much of a woman you are."

Her eyes narrowed. "Cut it. We're past that shit."

"I know, I know," Mark said, his voice low. No longer laughing. "Can't say I don't think about it, though."

"Stick to your strippers, Daniels. One freebie a life is all I give."

Her words weren't exactly true, since she still occasionally had a sex-only date with an old lover, just as a mutual stress reliever. But Daniels didn't know that. Nor would he. Because though he laughed and mouthed-off and flirted with her, deep down she knew—had always known—that he'd never stopped thinking about what had happened between them that October day in 2017. The entire world had changed in one sweep of the minute hand on a clock and they'd fallen into each other's arms to sob over the horror of it. They'd reached out to grab anything that felt human and alive. She'd needed a pair of arms around her shoulders and he'd needed a pair of legs around his waist and they'd both needed to fuck away the reality of the day.

It was a miracle their partnership had survived the crazy, unexpected sex in the squad car. Maybe if she hadn't fallen right out of public hell into personal one, with the discovery of just how *much* she and her family had lost in the tragedy, it would have been a problem. But because of that, Mark had segued right into concerned partner and friend, so they'd skipped the whole we-had-sex-and-what-are-we-going-to-do-about-it bullshit.

Ronnie was incredibly grateful they'd moved past it, and wouldn't let anything happen to disrupt their partnership again. Not even Mark's seemingly inexhaustible need to try to get under the skirt of any woman in his line of sight.

Besides, if she ever did take him up on it, he'd probably back up so fast his ass would come out his stomach. No way would Daniels risk their working partnership, not when it was so good, the pair of them having the highest case-closing percentage in the precinct.

"This is weird, like science fiction weird."

She thought for a minute Daniels was still talking about *them*. But seeing the way he'd craned forward in his seat to stare out the reinforced windshield, she knew what he really meant.

Because it *was* weird. Surreal, almost, to drive into what had once been a bustling, traffic-laden area overflowing with tourists and politicians, buses, dog-walkers—and see no pedestrians. No cars. No vending trucks hawking ice cream or cheap souvenirs of the good old U.S. of A. made in the good old Republic of China.

Now there were primarily military vehicles and soldiers. Bulldozers and front-end loaders buzzed around the dozen construction sites dotting the entire area surrounding the reflecting pool. Overlooking all was a long, raised, enclosed, horizontal tube through which thousands of tourists passed every day, making the pilgrimage. A bunch of them were in there now, looking like bug-eyed fish in a tank as they stared through the Plexiglas while slowly rolling along the flat people-movers.

Science-fiction-like indeed. Sometimes, she still couldn't quite believe this wasn't a post-apocalyptic dream from which she'd awaken to find the country she'd known early on the morning of October 20, 2017.

Slowing for her turn, she spared a glance ahead and up, unable to prevent a gasp at the close-up, head-on view of the Washington Monument.

Her stomach rolled and rebelled. Her whole body clenched and she blinked several times to convince her brain she could handle it. She'd seen the structure as it was being rebuilt, catching glimpses of it out of the corner of her eye from across the Potomac when she went down to Virginia to visit her mother. She just hadn't been this close in so long. Not since that day.

Here…this was the place where her world had died. Everyone had one particular place that tortured them about 10/20. This was hers.

It was beautiful, though, she had to concede that. Tall, straight, inspiring. Ringed by American flags and fronted by a big, new bronze plaque from yesterday's ceremony, it was brilliantly pale against the cloudless, blue summer sky.

The structure proudly proclaimed that monuments could be rebuilt and America could not be kept down. As the organizers of yesterday's patriotism-personified Independence Day event had hoped, the simple obelisk was a vibrant symbol of all that was right with this country.

Still, she hated it. Loathed it with every fiber of her being.

She had to look away, concentrating on the site coming into view as she turned left onto State. It was a cement monster, rising out of the barren ground, encircled by scaffolding and surrounded by bulldozers and other heavy equipment. Taller on each end, with months worth of work still to be done in the center, it gave the appearance of an enormous, open-jawed beast, ready to snap up and devour anything above it, from a low-flying plane to an entire nation's dreams.

The east side—the only portion of the structure not completely destroyed in the blasts—was farthest along. Congress had decided to repair and re-build from that point, rather than demolish what was left of the famous landmark and start from scratch. They said it was to maintain a link to the historic past. Personally, Ronnie figured seeing the last of it torn down would have been bad for public morale or something like that.

Whatever the reason, when all of this was finished, the east wing would be the famous one, the historical one. Not the west wing.

"It hurts to look at it," Daniels whispered, sounding serious for a change, almost wounded.

She nodded silently, understanding his reaction, and mirroring it. Because even after almost five years, seeing the decimated remains of the White House, where the president of her country had died, was still painful beyond imagination.

Chapter 2

"She's been dead for about eighteen hours."

Ronnie didn't really need the young, inexperienced-looking Secret Service Uniformed Division officer standing with them at the crime scene to tell her that. Any one-day rookie on the D.C.P.D. could figure out how long the victim had been dead. It took a simple swipe of a hand-held scanner across the upper right arm of any law-abiding citizen to get the basics. Name. Age. Address. Criminal record. Vital statistics. Time of death. Right on down to doctor's name and a list of allergies.

She wondered if this woman's mentioned an allergy to big fucking knives.

"So you have found her ID chip?"

The kid nodded. "It took a while, but we got it."

Excellent. The mandated Citizen Identification Program might have caused riots when the government had tried to initiate it for all Americans during the crazy, violent days before 10/20/17, or B.D.C. as a lot of people called it. But Ronnie, as a cop, had been all for it. And *after* 10/20, the protests had pretty much disappeared. Everyone had numbly stood in line to let some government nurse stick a needle as thick as a kindergartner's neck in their arm and inject them with the chip.

After all, who didn't want their remains identified if they were the next to be attacked? If the things were good enough to be used for dogs and cats since the nineties, proponents had argued, why not people?

She wondered if there would have been more protests had the average guy on the street known Uncle Sam was going to use that data chip in his arm to track so much more than his name and vital statistics. Things like where he went on vacation, since the chips had replaced passports two years ago. How much money he made, since they were routinely used to identify customers in any financial transaction. Even how often he went to the can while on the job, that whole bodily function element.

No, they weren't perfect. But for the most part, Ronnie

appreciated the nasty little buggers because they sure made a cop's job easier. Though, she had to admit, in this case it might have been tricky scanning the victim's chip. Because Ronnie wasn't entirely sure which part was the upper right arm.

God, what a mess.

"Have you requested a full data printout on her?" she asked, trying to remember if the young Special Agent had introduced himself as Bailey or Boyle. She had barely spared him a glance when he'd greeted her and Daniels at the bottom of the stairs and led them around the edges of this death chamber. Being in the sub-basement of the under-reconstruction White House was distracting enough, even without the murder they'd come here to investigate.

"Yes, of course." The guy stiffened, getting defensive, like a porcupine flaring his quills. Or like a federal officer who had to let mere city cops onto his turf. Ha, like anybody had ever considered the Uniformed Division guys anything more than private security guards for the White House back when it had actually been in use.

So much for every person in law enforcement being part of one big happy family now, all crammed together in the same department of the federal government. Given the way his lips were clamped shut, she suspected Bailey/Boyle hadn't gotten that memo, and that he wasn't happy about this situation.

Well, wasn't that just too bad for him. Ronnie somehow suspected the poor woman lying in pieces all around them wouldn't appreciate some agency asswipe slowing down the investigation of her murder because he wanted to protect his territory.

"So, uh, Agent Boyle, where might the report be?" Ronnie spoke slowly, her annoyance rising at having to lead him through what should be a routine report. He practically was a kid, so young and fresh she could almost smell the detergent used at the Glynco academy on his uniform. And he was standing here, mute, taking up space instead of going into the basics like any street cop would have done within ten seconds of her arrival on scene.

"It's Bailey." His jaw tightened even more. "The data's being downloaded right now. It'll be finished and printed out within a few minutes." Clearing his throat, he added, "The chip was a little...dented. And dirty. It had to be cleaned up—couldn't get it to connect wirelessly at first."

Reminding herself of the lectures she always got from her lieutenant to play nice or risk alienating someone she wished would be nice back, Ronnie eased her rigid stance and gave old-fashioned law enforcement camaraderie one more shot. "Pretty ugly one, isn't it?"

Bailey, probably in his early-to-mid twenties, jerked his head up and down in one quick nod. Something flashed in his eyes— nervousness, maybe even panic—which told her he had been holding himself together by sheer force of will.

So maybe he wasn't merely playing king-of-the-playground with his stiffness and his attitude. Maybe the kid was just too raw and fresh to be able to deal with this kind of scene without feeling...*something*. Any rookie would.

Ronnie quickly adjusted the thought—anyone with an ounce of humanity would be feeling something.

She had never witnessed this kind of carnage in a non-terrorist-related crime before. And there was a vast difference between seeing the mangled intestines of a suicide bomber strewn across the hood of a Hyundai and seeing the results of an up-close-and-personal torture session in the basement of the White House.

Whoever this woman was, Ronnie just prayed the sick bastard had killed her before he'd gotten really serious with his knife. Deep down, though, she greatly feared the victim hadn't died quickly. This level of mutilation must have taken a long time, meaning the killer had planned enough in advance to know he wasn't going to be disturbed.

So he wouldn't have rushed.

Special Agent Bailey cleared his throat and blurted out, "The victim's name was Leanne Carr."

"Did you know her?" she asked, remembering Bailey had mentioned he was stationed here at the site.

His throat bobbed as he visibly swallowed. "A little. She seemed nice."

Niceness, unfortunately, wasn't effective as a defense mechanism against murderous rage. Being liked was all well and good, but Ronnie would take a Glock and a black belt over <u>nice</u> any day.

"Sometimes you just have to wonder if there is no afterlife at all, and we're already in hell," Bailey murmured, his voice breaking a little bit.

Ronnie nodded. "I'm sure she thought she was."

"I don't even want to think about what she must have gone through." Bailey said, his tone and demeanor confirming he was on the edge of losing it.

Ronnie couldn't help feeling for him. The rookie obviously

hadn't seen enough carnage to harden him to it and this was one wicked trial by fire. It wasn't that the seasoned investigators, like the other Secret Service officers who had greeted them outside and led them down to Bailey, didn't find it just as horrific. But they were better at hiding their instinctive reactions. They were able to shove their emotions way down inside, if only for a little while. Long enough to get the job done.

Eventually, however, even the most hardened among them had to take those feelings out of the deepest recesses of their minds and give them life. It was imperative to let them go before the bottled memories drove them insane.

Every cop was the same, including Ronnie. Late tonight, when she was alone, she'd mourn for this poor woman and allow herself to feel some genuine heartbreak for her. Some anger. Some humanity. Daniels would probably get drunk to try to wipe out the mental image of her last moments. Until then, however, it was time for them to do their job, spending another day being spat upon by the ugliest, green phlegm of life.

"I've never seen anything like it," Bailey admitted. His voice was steady, though his eyelids flickered a couple of times as he surveyed the scene from the corner of the room, where they all stood. "Except maybe in some movie that seemed too gruesome to ever really happen."

Her respect for him went up a notch. At least he was holding himself together, despite the way the crime was getting under his skin, and the fact that he'd known the victim, however slightly.

Deciding to give the man a break because she'd been so hard on him at first, Ronnie glanced at her watch. "Look, I really hate to be a nuisance, but would you mind going for the report now? This one's going to come with a lot of heat and I'd like to know what I'm involved with as soon as possible."

Bailey's half-frown said he wasn't sure how to take her dismissal. She certainly didn't have any jurisdiction over the case—yet. So Ronnie gave him a smile and lowered her voice as if asking for a favor rather than ordering him to get out. "To tell you the truth, I'm not familiar with the layout of this place at all. We were brought straight here and dumped on you. I'd hate to take a wrong turn into a secure area while trying to find the base of operations. Honestly, if you don't mind, you'd be doing me a huge favor."

The tactic worked.

"Sure," he said, looking visibly relieved at being able to get away for a while, without feeling sent off like an errand boy. God only knew why men had been created needing their pride stroked more than their cocks.

"We set up the terminal and communication area in a room a couple of levels up," Bailey said. "The full work-up from her arm chip—criminal record, medical and dental records, and background check—should be finished printing by now. I'll go wait for it and bring it back to you." He was practically bouncing on his goes to get going.

Ronnie didn't blame him for being relieved at the break. It would be nice to grab some fresh air that didn't taste like construction dust and smell like blood. "That would be great."

Without another word, Bailey spun around and walked back the way they had entered, giving the lumpy mass closest to the stairs a wide berth. He kept his eyes front, feet pistoning across the cement floor as if he didn't trust himself not to puke if he let his gaze shift the wrong way. That he hadn't so far was a testament to his future in law enforcement.

"Wow, Ron, if I didn't know better, I'd say you just acted like a girl."

She shot right back. "Aww, sorry, partner, was I stepping on your toes?"

"You finally admittin' I'm prettier than you?"

She grunted. "You're about as pretty as a brick wall."

"Well aren't we a pair, then, since most people'd agree you're built like a brick..."

"Shut up, moron."

Impossible to rile, as usual, Daniels merely held up a hand, palm out, in truce. "Kidding. You handled that really well. The kid looked like he was about to lose his breakfast all over the vic." Looking around, he clarified. "Or some of her. You got him outta here just in time and had him ready to thank you for ordering him around."

"It's not an easy way for anyone to start the morning," she said, rubbing at her temple where a slight headache had begun to pulse. "I don't blame him for being glad to escape."

She looked around, still trying to wrap her mind around what had happened. And where it had happened. This part of the building was in its early stages—already serving its purpose as a solid foundation, but not yet finished off or even divided into smaller rooms. There wasn't a wall or nook in sight. Just bare floor, cavernous hallway, some heavy construction tools stacked in a corner, and body parts. Lots of those.

Shaking his head in bemusement, Daniels looked around the crime scene as well and whistled. "Sweet Jesus Christ in a catamaran, what a mess."

"Definitely."

"Want to wager a guess as to why you'n me seem to be the only ones looking ready to dive in? Where the hell's the forensics team?"

She had no idea. Strange. Very strange.

"And where's the blood? Doesn't look like there's enough for something so...drastic."

The question had already crossed Ronnie's mind. Because in a scene with as much carnage as this one, she would have expected to see all six quarts of the woman's blood puddled on the floor. But there wasn't much, except small amounts pooled around each internal organ, limb or other unidentifiable body part, and thin lines of it spider-webbing across the cement floor.

Another member of the Secret Service team, who'd been securing the perimeter, joined them right outside the yellow Crime Scene tape he'd just finished putting up. "It's down there."

Glancing in the direction he pointed out, Ronnie spotted a rusty drain grate about eighteen inches from a large, sinew-covered mass. Then she blinked, because the grate couldn't be rusty. The White House reconstruction had only begun eight months ago, after years of political fighting over the project. Some money-conscious lawmakers had wanted to raze the site and turn it into a garden of mourning since no president would ever be allowed to live in a publicly-accessible location like this one again. But a lot of the country wanted the building, whether the number one guy was going to live there or not. And they'd staged a national referendum to get it.

Nice to know her fellow Americans had rediscovered their spines.

"I assume that's the victim's blood making it look rusty?" she asked the man.

He nodded. "Down the pipes it went. Under the ground."

They all thought the same thing. The spot under *this* ground was particularly damned.

Daniels shook his head. "What kind of sick, twisted mind would think to do something like this? Here, of all places?"

"Actually, a sick, twisted mind is about the only logical explanation I can come up with right now," Ronnie said.

Because it had to take one warped person to commit murder

near the exact spot where the first explosions had rocked the White House that day.

Now, after years of investigation and Congressional hearings, everyone knew how the deeply-imbedded terrorists had done it. That they had found a way to get below the sub-basement via maintenance access tunnels for the Metro system running around and beneath the National Mall. They'd been inside the damn walls, using the White House's security and secret tunnel system. They'd had volunteers working on the construction of the controversial Deep Underground Command Center, which was supposed to make the president and the White House safer and had instead given access to prime bombing spots to the nation's enemies.

But back then? Well, nobody had conceived that several sleeper cells in existence since before even the 2001 attacks had been placing their people in the D.C. Metro Transit Authority, the park service, the food service. They'd been tour guides, construction workers, maintenance workers at major monuments and docents at national museums. They'd worked in the White House itself.

And they had been patient. So *very* patient. Working, living normal lives, raising families. Yet still digging tunnels wide enough for a man with chemicals and explosives and detonators to crawl through, day after day, month after month. Building. Preparing. Stockpiling.

God in heaven, she really was standing within feet of where the whole thing had started.

"You Sloan?"

Ronnie didn't even have to see him to know she was finally being approached by a senior security officer. His you're-pissing-in-my-soup tone said it all. Steeling herself to not fall into any power battles with another department, she turned to greet him. "Yes. And my partner, Detective Daniels."

She wasn't sure if the Feds would make an issue over Daniels's presence, since, according to the dispatcher, Ronnie had been the only one mentioned by name. But new nationwide regulations said officers in every branch were supposed to stick with a partner while on duty. Not only, unfortunately, to watch each other's backs, but also to watch each other.

One of the 10/20 terrorists had been a cop. Another had posed as one.

The real cop had been the one in charge of taking out the Capitol Building but, thankfully, had screwed up and only wiped-out a men's bathroom. The ineptitude of the terrorist-slash-D.C.P.D. officer, not to mention the Congress=toilet thing, had eventually made for some late-night talk show jokes...when America had started laughing again. Maybe sometime around 2019.

"I'm Senior Special Agent Johansen. Thank you for coming."

"We would have been here sooner, but the traffic outside the gates was...well, you know."

He managed a nod that was somehow both reassuring and condescending at the same time. "It's all right."

SSA Johansen was an agency man all the way. Fifty'ish, lean, with a closely-trimmed head of graying brown hair and hooded brown eyes. A pair of dark sunglasses rested on top of his head. If he had been wearing a black, conservatively cut suit, he'd have looked like a classic example of a Secret Service agent from pre-10/20. Instead, he was dressed just like the first two guys, only his clothes were navy instead of green.

Ronnie would lay money he hated the uniform. The Secret Service Agents had squawked the loudest when the newly formed NDLE—National Department of Law Enforcement—had issued one of its first national regulations: no street clothes outside of undercover operations for any branch of law enforcement. The squawking hadn't made a bit of difference since they'd no longer been able to use the argument that they needed to "blend in" to do their job protecting the president. Because the president was now surrounded by an entire squad of Marines whenever he so much as walked from his bed to his toilet. When he was in public, it was a platoon. So the S.S. had finally had to give up the dark-suit look and don uniforms just like every beat cop in the country.

"Her name was Leanne Carr," Johansen said, emotionless as he glanced down at a severed human foot. A little bit of pretty peach polish was visible through the smear of blood on the big toenail.

"That much I've heard. And that's about all."

"Construction worker found her today. Crews came in early to make up for the couple of days they missed because of the shut-down for yesterday's events and a foreman found her."

Ronnie hoped the guy had not eaten breakfast first. Considering she didn't see it anywhere on the floor, she figured he hadn't.

"She's scattered across a ten yard area in this section of the basement. Nowhere else." Frowning, he added, "At least, we don't think so. We haven't accounted for *everything* so far."

Remembering where Bailey had gone, Ronnie asked, "₁ chance of any undiscovered evidence in the room you're using as a base of operations?"

A small shake of his head told her it had been thoroughly swept. "We're set up on the main floor, two levels above here. That floor's further along, with a few offices already in use by the construction managers, project supervisors, and us. The doors were all still locked, the interiors untouched, completely clean."

All valid information. But not the information she wanted to know.

"SSA Johansen," she asked, needing to find out if her burgeoning suspicions were correct, "was I called in here because of a jurisdictional issue with the city? Because nobody's entirely clear on who has jurisdiction over the unoccupied remains of the White House? Or was it for...*another* reason?"

He didn't respond for a moment, merely assessing her with a level stare, as if sizing up her age. Her experience. Her looks. She was used to the extra scrutiny, having met a lot of law enforcement officers who figured being a pretty cop with big tits meant she didn't have a brain. So she said nothing, merely meeting his stare with a cool one of her own until he was finished doing his sexist thing.

Finally, his tone grudging, he admitted, "You're the only O.E.P.I.S. investigator in the city."

Her heart, which had gone into standby mode while she waited for his response, started beating again. A surge of adrenaline burst through her, fueling every cell in her body with anticipation and excitement. If it wasn't so damn morbid she'd want to kiss poor Leanne Carr's bloody toes.

But Ronnie kept her reaction to herself. She didn't hint by as much as a quirk of her mouth that she was thrilled to finally get to work on a real O.E.P.I.S.—or Eye-Squad, as she and her fellow trainees had begun calling it—investigation. A murder, no less.

"The initial scan of her I.D. chip flagged her as having gone through the optical implantation four months ago, which was why we immediately called you in. Our instructions were to leave the scene exactly as it was found until your arrival."

"That's why the forensics people aren't here?"

"They're waiting for you." His tone was terse.

Wonderful. Another reason for him to resent her presence.

"Let them do their jobs, Agent Johansen," she murmured.

Keeping other investigators out is not what O.E.P.I.S. is about."

No, it wasn't. Securing the evidence wasn't her job. Seeing the crime through the eyes of the witness, the perpetrator—or, in Leanne Carr's case, the victim—was.

SSA Johansen reached up and touched a button on the tiny radio attached to his collar. "Tell forensics they're clear to proceed."

He had called for them just like that, at her say-so, which startled her. Ronnie had never fully believed the assurances that the O.E.P.I.S. investigators would take the lead in any case involving one of the program participants no matter what other agencies were involved. Neither had any of the other real cops she'd trained with out in Texas.

Well, one had believed it, but he hadn't been a cop. He'd been an FBI agent, and also the cockiest, most confident son of a bitch she'd ever met. She really wished she could forget about him—Special Agent Jeremy Sykes—but somehow, she'd just been unable to do it. The man had stuck in her mind the way a splinter might stick in her finger. Both left her irritated and wishing she could get them out from under her skin.

She had to wonder if he'd worked his first O.E.P. murder investigation yet and hoped he hadn't. She'd like to beat Sykes to the punch. They'd played a game of one-upsmanship from the moment they'd met...probably because they hadn't been able to play the kind of games she suspected they both *really* wanted to play together.

Johansen might have conceded the investigation for now, but he obviously didn't like it. His mouth was pursed in a tight grimace as he continued. "The victim worked as the administrative assistant to the head of the Phoenix Group. They're the ones overseeing all aspects of the reconstruction of the Mall." He cleared his throat. "I mean...Patriot Square."

She understood his discomfort. This rah-rah-patriotism frenzy was sometimes tough to swallow. Ronnie was as patriotic as the next person, she just didn't particularly want to strip naked and clothe herself in the stars and stripes.

"So she had a sensitive position?"

He nodded once. "Pretty high clearance."

"That makes sense," she murmured. She turned to Daniels. "Every person approached and asked to participate in the second phase of testing of the Optical Evidence Program had to have a high-level security clearance."

"Yeah, I know," he said with a wry grin, silently reminding her he knew better than most. "I've always wondered how smart that was. People privy to a lot of secrets would make really tempting targets if the bad guys ever found out about this program."

Frankly, Ronnie had thought the same thing when she'd heard. "Yeah, but they wanted the testing kept hush-hush and half of those they asked turned them down."

"But half said yes," Daniels said, sounding thoughtful.

Yes, they had said yes. And that surprised her most of all.

Every person approached had been made fully aware of the risks, including the big one: The O.E.P. device was sycophantic to the optic nerve. Device and nerve were inextricably bound together—they had to be for the device to function properly. Meaning, if the camera ever had to be removed, it would be nearly impossible to do it without causing permanent damage to sensitive tissues. Blindness in one eye was a near certainty. There was a good chance of losing vision in both.

Five-thousand people had done it, anyway, lured not by their interest in the progression of science—ha—but by the staggering amount of money the U.S. government offered.

Of those who had said no, their security clearances meant they wouldn't talk about the invitation. The government hadn't wanted anybody whispering about the new technology, which sounded at best like a science fiction story and at worst like a really scary version of Big Brother.

Christ, if the civil rights guys had ranted about Americans getting simple little I.D. chips implanted in their arms, they would lose their minds over the thought of cameras being inserted into test subjects' brains.

Of course, the first set of test subjects probably wouldn't have caused too much of a fuss. Phase One, begun the year after the 2017 attack—A.D.C. in street terms—had involved a different type of lab rat. So nobody had really cared whether they could keep their mouths shut; it wasn't like there was anybody for them to tell.

Now, though, that the program was being tested on five-thousand normal, average adults out there living normal, average lives, ensuring they wouldn't talk about the tiny devices inside their heads was a pretty big necessity. Not only for security. But also because it could seriously freak the shit out of people.

"Have you worked many of these cases so far, Detective?" Johansen asked, his chin stiff, as if he found the subject distasteful.

"Several."

During her training. Not in the field. In the real world, she had worked exactly zero.

The agent's brow lifted. "I didn't know there were several cases in the metro area involving people who are part of this...experiment."

Smiling humorlessly, Ronnie admitted, "Several death-row inmates were involved with the beta testing."

That finished the man's questions and he nodded once, then shut his mouth. Funny, people always reacted one of two ways when they thought about what she did. Either being awed and asking a million morbid questions. Or deciding she was a ghoul and not wanting to know a single thing.

"Hot damn, Ron, this is it. And what a place to start. It's like winning the murder lottery."

Daniels was one of the awed ones.

"I don't suppose Leanne Carr would consider herself a jackpot," Ronnie murmured, letting her tone convey her unspoken message to her partner. Daniels was a great detective, fearless, street smart, with ingrained cop instincts that always led him to conclusions others struggled to reach. But oh, the man lacked tact.

"No. Not a jackpot," Daniels said, sounding suitably contrite. "Just another poor victim of what has to be the ungodliest spot on the face of the earth."

Amen to that.

All of them shifted their gazes down to the floor. Silence descended for a long moment. Then her partner, ever the pragmatic, cleared his throat.

"Yes?" Johansen asked.

Daniels frowned before asking the question that had been flitting around the back of Ronnie's brain for the past several minutes. The one she hadn't pulled into focus until he started speaking.

"Uh, when you say you haven't 'accounted' for everything, does that mean something's missing?" Shrugging and giving one of his disarming I'm-just-a-dumb-good-old-boy looks, Daniels added, "Because, call me crazy, but I'm looking all over this place and there's something I'm just not seein'."

A slow flush of color rose up Johansen's face, an incongruous splash of pink on the implacable agent's cheeks. He cleared his throat. Shifted foot to foot. Looked more and more uncomfortable.

Her partner, meanwhile, just crossed his arms and smiled. Ronnie knew what he was getting at before he continued. But his statement made it all the more real. All the more awful.

"Correct me if I'm wrong, Johansen, but, let me take a wild guess here," Daniels said. "One of the parts you guys haven't been able to find yet, is it by any chance the part above the shoulders?"

The agent cleared his throat. A fine line of sweat appeared just above his top lip, though the basement air was cool and moist. Nastily moist. "That is correct."

And just like that, Ronnie's worst fears, which she had been shoving away for the past ten minutes, were fully realized.

So much for her first O.E.P.I.S. case.

Because it was going to be pretty hard to evaluate the data on a microchip implanted in Leanne Carr's brain if they couldn't find her head.

Chapter 3

It was not always easy being thought of as the modern-day equivalent of the Nazi doctor Joseph Mengele. Phineas Tate had made that realization six years ago when he had won international fame—and infamy—for either being the savior of mankind, or the instrument of its inevitable destruction. Or both.

Melodrama, that's what he had always thought of the controversy. Still, sparking an international debate had been quite a feat for a seventy-year-old scientist who'd been working in relative obscurity at Virginia Tech for most of his adult life.

"And if you had known, would you have done things any differently?" he asked aloud, speaking to himself as he often did these days. After all, who better since so few understood the workings of his brain?

Would he rewrite his own past? It was something he pondered on occasion when in a contemplative mood. But not for long, because, at the end of the day, he hadn't known—*couldn't* have known—what would happen. There was therefore no gain in considering the matter.

"That dog," he whispered, shaking his head, then smoothing back the strand of silvery hair that fell forward over his brow.

It had all started so innocuously, with the dog. Just a little lost terrier one of his students had been crying over one day not long after the turn of the century. He'd asked if he could help, and had been there when she'd received a welcome call. Her beloved pet had been found and identified by a microchip imbedded in the fatty layer beneath his skin, which she'd had injected into him as a pup.

Her happiness had been something to see. He smiled, even now remembering that moment when he'd shared her joy. And suddenly, like the proverbial light going off over a cartoon figure's head, it had sparked an idea in him. Because those were the days when the news was full of the story of that poor child who had been abducted from her room while her sister slept in the next bed.

The connection had been instantaneous, and certainly not unique, since others in dawn of the bioelectronics age were already considering the same possibility. If suitable for animals, why not for people?

Some had thought he'd get the Nobel Prize when, many years later in 2016, Congress had proposed a law requiring every American citizen to be implanted with one of the microchips he had created.

Some had wanted to throw him in prison.

Phineas himself had never truly expected the measure to survive the legal challenges. Certainly some—protective parents, caretakers to the elderly, those with medical conditions—had already embraced the technology and put it to good use. Secure government installations had already been using implanted devices to insure against access by unauthorized people. In some cases they had replaced key-cards and I.D. badges, and quite successfully, too.

But despite a public weary of anonymous terrorists setting off suicide bombs in shopping malls and chemical attacks in movie theaters, mandating the imbedded identification seemed totalitarian and many had spoken out against it. Including himself.

Then came October 2017. When the world had spun in a completely different direction.

"Oh, yes," he murmured. Staring out the window of his office at the neatly trimmed lawn surrounding his brand new, state-of-the-art research facility, he rubbed his jaw. "Everything spun around that day."

And they had done it. The fools had actually made the thing into law, taking advantage of the population's numbness to get it through. They'd begun the injections within six months of the destruction of the nation's capital, when the country would still agree to just about anything if they thought it would keep the horror from being repeated.

Once the numbness had worn off, of course, the protests had started, the lawsuits had begun. Discrimination charges had abounded when lawmakers had decreed that anyone who didn't obtain—or who removed—the device would no longer qualify for social service programs. When a scandal had broken out over the sale of private medical information to pharmaceutical companies, he'd received death threats.

Oh, if he thought he had been hated before then, it was nothing compared to what the following years had brought.

But he could have changed that. Would have changed that, with his next enormous breakthrough. He had planned to offer it up as a gift to mankind. A mea culpa for his previous sins. His revolutionary optical recording device would have given him atonement. Redemption. Forgiveness.

If only it hadn't been stolen from me.

"There's been a murder."

Phineas jerked his attention away from the window, away from the past. His son, Philip, hadn't knocked on the office door, simply bursting in. His face shone with visible excitement. Over a murder.

How very odd.

"Did you hear me? We have to go now. Right now."

Phineas pursed his lips and shook his head, fussing with the handle of his desk drawer. "Blasted thing sticks. You would think with the amount of money our government spent on this building they could manage to procure for me a desk with drawers which do not stick."

His son, usually so calm and suave as he spun his financial webs, crossed the room in a few long strides that were just short of a jog. "Father, did you *hear* me? There's been a murder. We have to go." He placed his hands flat on the vast, highly-glossed surface of the mahogany desk. Phineas watched with interest as Philip's fingers spread apart, then tightened, only to started tapping an impatient staccato beat on the wood. Philip was in quite a state, indeed.

"I don't see why..."

"Because the victim is one of *ours*. One of the five-thousand." His voice almost shaking with excitement, his son added, "She was found murdered at the White House this morning."

And Phineas finally understood Philip's excitement, even if he was not able to share in it.

Well, perhaps he shared in it a little.

It appeared they were about to discover whether or not his brilliant invention, originally intended to benefit the millions of Alzheimer's victims in this country, had instead performed the function the U.S. government, and his own son, had decided it should.

Would it be able to solve a crime?

By noon, rumors of the slaughter that had taken place in the White House sub-basement had spread across the entire Patriot Square zone, flung like handfuls of sand, reaching every crevice and corner. Outside, as if they were rubberneckers at a crash scene, construction crews and authorized government employees kept showing up, trying to get the latest bit of information.

Ronnie had never fully appreciated the scope of this project until she saw just how many workers were rebuilding America's most famed monuments. "I think every carpenter, bricklayer and mason on the eastern seaboard has to be right here," she said to Daniels as the two of them stood at the corner of the site, surveying the crowd. It was about an hour after they'd arrived on scene and they were preparing to walk the perimeter.

He nodded. "No wonder the unemployment rate is so low. Wonder what'll happen now that we're supposedly at peace and assholes are gonna stop knocking down our buildings."

She had to laugh. Daniels did have a way with words. But he wasn't far off the mark.

Like the entire country, D.C. had entered an unparalleled time of economic prosperity. Sure, the gangs and drug problems still existed, as did violence and robberies. All the human cruelties continued on the way they had since time began. But, in general, people seemed satisfied. The working class was doing pretty darn well, and the rich were loving life.

Daniels seemed to be reading her thoughts. "Amazing what can happen when the U.S. decides to tell all the other countries on the planet to take a hike. Lawton's official reelection slogan might as well have been, 'Go Fuck Yourself, World.'"

Her partner was right. Pulling the country back inside its own defensive walls had, after all, been what their president had begun to do immediately after being sworn into office to replace his murdered predecessor in October of 2017. That philosophy had let him cruise back into office on his own in the next election.

After the 9/11 attacks, the U.S. had gone charging out like a wounded bear to take on its enemies. But by 2017, it had had enough. The attack on D.C. had cemented the feelings a lot of people had harbored since terrorism had become common on American soil with weekly suicide bombings and sniper attacks: It was time to walk away.

The screaming, grieving citizens had demanded that the government focus its attention, money, and military might right here on its own soil. That it stop pissing-off militants who would come here and blow up trains beneath their cities, destroy their houses of government and slaughter thousands of innocent people.

So that's what it had done. Walked away. Closed ranks. Put up fences.

So long, Europe, concentrate on your own problems for a while because we won't be around for you to blame. Africa? Hate to break it to you, but you're on your own. Abstinence makes the heart grow fonder and all that. Just kidding, we know you have that whole Aids thing going on, good luck with that! Middle East— hey, live and let live, let there be peace on earth, we'll buy your oil and stay out of your business, 'kay?

Israel? Well, uh, sorry good buddy, it's been nice knowing you.

We'll trade with you, we'll visit you, but don't ask us to get involved with your problems.

And it had worked, at least in some people's opinions. America was thriving, with no terrorist attacks in more than two years now. Of course, those same *some* people didn't give a shit that the rest of the world was going straight to hell while the land of the free and the home of the brave sat on the sidelines picking its nose.

America had become another Switzerland. It made Ronnie want to throw up. Probably not a very popular opinion these days, traitorous, some people might call it, but considering the price her family had paid on 10/20, she dared anyone to question her loyalties.

One ironic thing, though. Even with all the, "See, we were right" bull being spouted, nobody ever mentioned the idea of reverting to B.D.C. security standards. They weren't *that* stupid.

"You think Johansen's men will be able to hold all of them back?" Daniels asked, looking skeptical. A few armed Secret Service officers were aggressively blocking the entry gate, ordering the curious, shouting onlookers to stay back or risk arrest.

"An Army squad will be here soon," she replied.

If the soldiers were like the ones who had searched her earlier this morning, the construction workers would be racing back to their tractors and cement trucks any minute now.

"So I guess this team can join the other one Johansen put to work playing hide-and-seek with a head."

Ronnie, frustrated beyond belief at having her first shot at an eye-squad case literally snatched away, gritted her teeth at the reminder. She had been forcing herself to focus on the basics of a murder investigation, trusting the Senior Special Agent when he swore there was no way anyone could have left the scene with a bloody head last night after the fireworks. He seemed completely certain they would find it.

She was more skeptical. Seemed to her that if security had been lax enough to let somebody come in with weapons of torture, they wouldn't be too focused on catching somebody going out with body parts.

"Come on," she said as she headed away from the crowd at the gate, toward the east side of the construction zone. She and Daniels had begun canvassing the area while forensics did their thing in the basement. "Let's keep doing this the old-fashioned way."

"That's me, just a nice, old-fashioned kind of guy," he replied, sounding so innocent anyone who didn't know him would absolutely have bought the line.

Shaking her head and wondering how he could make her smile even on her worst days, Ronnie strode ahead of him. She found it difficult to walk these rough, patchy grounds, which had once been beautiful green lawns, and not remember what the place had been like when she'd been a kid. Living right across the Potomac in Arlington, she had come over here with her dad and brothers on Sundays to play softball on the grassy areas of the Mall. Had been enthralled by the Spirit of St. Louis in the Air & Space Museum. Had strolled into the Capitol Building and observed a session of Congress. She'd even toured the White House, for God's sake.

Now, what was left of the exhibits from the Smithsonian, after the bombings and the subsequent looting, was still under lock and key in some top-secret, protected location. Congress held session in one of those underground bunkers out west somewhere. And the president was moved from location to location, never staying in one spot for more than a few weeks at a time. Right now, he was at Camp David, surrounded by military guards with rocket-to-air missiles that would shoot anything they didn't recognize out of the sky before it got within ten miles.

Funny, really. Now that the U.S. seemed to be at peace and had removed itself as a target with its strict policy of isolationism, security was the best it had ever been. Guess that was what some people might call a day late and a dollar short. Personally, Ronnie thought a better analogy would be that it was like guarding the henhouse when the fox was wiping the fried chicken grease off his fingers with a Wet Nap.

"Is the Army going to turn over the data from the crowds coming through the checkpoints yesterday?"

Ronnie nodded at her partner. "Every person was scanned, either in the weeks leading up to the 4th, or, for the poor losers who had to stand in line an extra eight hours yesterday, on site."

"And the advance identity scans got them what, exactly?"

"Special pass straight to the metal detectors."

"How many altogether?" Daniels sounded like he didn't really want to know.

And she hated to tell him. "Attendance was capped by the government, with entry awarded by lottery in every state."

"How many?"

"A thousand per state, plus another grand for the district."

His head rolled back until he was looking straight up at the sky. "Holy shit, you're saying fifty-one thousand people were in this place yesterday?"

"Closer to fifty-five when you count the security teams, military, speakers, politicians, special guests, performers and foreign dignitaries."

"I need a drink."

"It's not even noon."

"I need a morning drink."

She understood the sentiment. Whoever the psycho was, he'd planned this very well. Because yesterday's 4th of July celebration, during which the President and a bunch of high-level celebrities had re-dedicated the newly rebuilt Washington Monument, was the first time in years any tourists had been allowed outside the viewing tube constructed above the west side of the square.

Organizers had wanted to recapture the old days when people felt safe being part of a big, public gathering in D.C. And, for the most part, they had succeeded. No, the crowd hadn't been enormous, like some from the past. There were no longer huge expanses of lawn for a million or two people to watch the proceedings on jumbo-tron screens. Still, it had been pretty impressive. The big "you didn't destroy us, we're here for good" celebration to prove America couldn't be kept down had been the largest security undertaking Ronnie had seen since 2017. Everyone had been patting themselves on the back last night at how perfectly it had gone.

Then they'd found the body parts in the basement.

Anytime before yesterday, the pool of suspects, and viable witnesses, would have been considerably smaller. Usually, only military personnel, security, and everyday workers who had gone through tons of screening were allowed inside the barricades surrounding Patriot Square. The guards were equipped to make sure no unauthorized personnel got near the White House.

But yesterday, with fifty-five thousand people milling around? *Damn.*

"Explain to me again, partner, why you and I are out here like a couple of second years trudging the perimeter? Aren't you supposed to be inside doing your 'I spy with my little eye' routine?"

A smile tugged at Ronnie's lips. Daniels. What an jerk. God, she loved him, when she didn't want to punch him. "There's nothing for me to spy on."

"What about the victim's downloads?"

"A team is en route to Miss Carr's apartment to secure her computer equipment; I'll examine it in the lab later. If she followed her training, her downloads should be easy to find. But the data dump will only include images taken with the implant through early yesterday morning at the very latest...before she came to work."

"You think you'll get anything from them?"

"They might provide something, a direction, a clue. Anyone she'd had problems with recently. But it's not going to help me at all with her actual death. The pictures of her killer are still on the chip."

"And the chip can't be accessed wirelessly once the subject is deceased."

Her partner knew the drill...he had to, being part of the program himself—a fellow implantee. Daniels' involvement had been required once she'd landed a spot on O.E.P.I.S., at least if she wanted to continue to partner with him. Which she had.

"Exactly. To prevent anyone from trying to wipe the data to cover-up the very types of crimes this thing was designed to help solve, the Eye chip dies when the subject does."

"Requiring manual removal."

"Yes." Distasteful, but necessary.

Daniels rubbed his lightly stubbled jaw, studying the vast, empty lot where the Smithsonian American History Museum used to be. "I don't suppose whoever invented the thing envisioned somebody making off with the head."

Ronnie had met the inventor of the device, Dr. Phineas Tate, during her intense O.E.P.I.S. training. She didn't think there was much the brilliant man hadn't considered. "Maybe they did, but figured it was worth the gamble. The odds were against it since so few people in the country have the chip. Nobody without high-level security clearance is supposed to even know about the program. And anyone who has it faces prosecution if they talk about it."

He continued to stare, his green eyes clear and focused. Deep in thought. "So, you thinking the obvious?"

"Of course." She'd been thinking about it all morning, and couldn't help having the same suspicion her partner obviously did.

"Whoever did this has high enough security clearance to know about the O.E.P.," Daniels said.

Ronnie nodded, taking it one dark, bitter step further. "And he took her head because he knew Leanne Carr was one of the test

Leslie Kelly

subjects."

Chapter 4

When they returned to the main entrance of the building a short time later, Ronnie noticed two men walking in a few yards ahead of them. She recognized the back of one head, that shiny, silvery-white hair was very familiar. She couldn't help smiling. Phineas Tate had been a demanding teacher, but he was also one fascinating, if peculiar, person.

"That's the chip man, himself," she told her partner, keeping her voice low.

Daniels narrowed his eyes, shading them against the high noon sun, and surveyed the men as they entered the building. "That's Tate? The man responsible for turning us all into walking bar codes? He doesn't look like Doctor Frankenstein."

"The younger one's his son. I haven't met him, but I recognize him from some magazine pictures. I think there's some story there."

"I do love a good story," he said, his eyebrows wagging.

"There was talk during our training that the senior Dr. Tate did not give the O.E.P. technology over willingly but the son strong-armed him into it."

"Nice guy."

"If this thing flies, the financial benefits could be...substantial. The father wanted his invention to be an altruistic gift. Supposedly, he was working on the eye device to help Alzheimer's patients retain their visual memories."

Rolling his eyes, Daniels asked, "Wouldn't a photo album be just as effective, and a little less invasive?"

"You know as well as I do that we're not just talking about photographs."

If they were, the device wouldn't be quite as magical. Tate had actually managed to develop a microchip that enabled the human eye to be the lens of the camera. So all the variances, the depth, the shading, the subtlety, the colors—even emotions that colored vision—would appear in images captured by the device.

It truly was brilliant.

"Yeah, I know. And I don't regret signing up, for the crime solving benefits. But it seems a little invasive for the average Joe.

Pictures on a digital frame would probably be just as valuable to somebody who has no memory of any of it, anyway."

"In theory, the camera in the optic canal would someday be linked wirelessly to a processor in the frontal cortex that would enable people to re-view the images in their mind."

"No downloading?"

"Right."

Daniels whistled, finally looking impressed. "I don't think I ever heard that part. That's some seriously science fiction sounding shit."

"He's a genius. He might have pulled it off. Besides, ten years ago, the idea of an optical camera being implanted in the brain sounded like serious science fiction, too. Movie fodder."

"Wonder how many heads he'd have to dig around in to get it to work."

Frowning, she didn't reply with her immediate thought. There would always be death row inmates who'd agree to be test mice if it got them some perks in their last months and money for their families. Human testing was just one more goody to come out of The Patriot Act. The thing seemed to bloat like a corpse rotting in the sun whenever the government wanted to do something the public wouldn't like.

"I think one of the ways they got Tate to come around was to offer him state-of-the-art support to eventually see the project through for its original purpose. But in the meantime, he's caught up in the more immediate uses of his invention."

"The spy game."

"I believe the focus is on crime solving and prevention."

"And spying."

And spying.

Once inside the building, Ronnie spotted Agent Bailey, looking a little more healthy than he had this morning. He even managed a tiny smile as he approached. "Special Agent Johansen asked me to let you know there's a status meeting going on right now in Special Agent In Charge Kilgore's office." He blanched. "I mean, sorry, in the security operations room."

Hmm. That message came through loud and clear. The lead Secret Service agent apparently didn't like his trailer and considered the sec-op room his own personal territory.

"Okay," she said.

"There are lots of high-level people showing up, wanting to know how this could have happened."

40

"Let the blame game commence," Daniels muttered.

She spared a moment to hope Daniels was wrong and the meeting would involve a reasonable group of professionals coming together to discuss strategies for solving a terrible crime.

She should have known better.

The sound of raised voices was audible even from down the hall, growing louder with every step she took toward the meeting room. More than a dozen people had gathered inside the large office, which had been nearly completed for use during construction. Unlike much of the building, with the bare concrete floors and roughly-studded walls, this one was tiled and drywalled. It also featured some state-of-the-art computer equipment and desks laden with files and paperwork.

Johansen stood practically nose-to-nose with another blue-uniformed Secret Service agent, while a female green-shirt looked on. Bailey immediately joined her. A little eavesdropping gave Ronnie the name of the other senior agent—Kilgore—and told her he was the big boss, the-buck-stops-here head of security for the White House project, the one who had his own trailer but liked this room just a little bit better. Probably because he liked claiming he had an office in the White House.

Special Agent in Charge Kilgore was the most likely one to catch the blame for this whole mess. But he obviously wasn't going to go down alone. Kilgore, a middle-aged guy whose face was about the color of a beet, was drenching his subordinates in spittle as he reamed them out. Blame game, indeed.

Elsewhere in the room, a handful of executive types in suits were asking rapid-fire questions of a guy in a hard-hat...maybe the worker who had found the victim? One man in a recognizable FBI uniform was staring intently at blueprints of the site, an Army guard right beside him.

The cacophony of noises and visible belligerence on some of the faces told her the ass-covering had already begun. Nobody was going to take responsibility for this one. A classic game of pass-the-buck was well underway. Kilgore—or his flunky, Johansen—would almost certainly shoo most of them out in a few minutes, but until he did, it seemed like the crap that was already knee-deep in this room would keep getting shoveled.

"Wake me up when it gets interesting," Daniels muttered.

"Who's going to wake me up?"

The one person she would have expected to be center-stage, exuding the air of brilliance that seemed to ooze from his pores, instead stood quietly, observing the scene from just inside the doorway.

"Detective Sloan," he said, a genuine smile softening Dr. Phineas Tate's pensive expression when he spotted her. "I was told you were here. I couldn't be more pleased that you were called in."

Nodding, Ronnie replied, "It's good to see you again, sir."

"Though, of course, not under these circumstances."

"No, of course not."

He took her hand and squeezed. "How have you been? Are you glad to finally have the chance to put all that hard work and training to use?"

"I am."

"I imagine Agent Sykes is going to be green with envy," he said, a twinkle appearing in those eyes.

Stiffening at the mention of the FBI agent who'd been both a fascinating challenge and an adversarial thorn in her side, she chewed on her tongue to keep herself from making a snarky comment.

"I can call him to come assist, if you think it necessary."

"No!" Swallowing, she forced a smile. "I mean, I'm sure he's got plenty to do in New York."

Beside her, she felt Daniels stiffen. He'd suspected from the first time Ronnie had mentioned Jeremy Sykes's name, after returning from training in Texas, that something had gone on between them. She'd never been able to explain that it wasn't what he thought. Mainly because she wasn't sure *what* on earth had happened between her and Sykes. She just knew it had left her shaken and confused. Two things she didn't like feeling.

Tate's smile faded and he shook his head. "I suppose you've heard the news? About the inability to locate the...device?" His voice had grown soft, a bit tremulous, even, which made Ronnie suspect he had seen the crime scene.

"I have."

"Appalling," he replied. "Man's inhumanity to man."

Indeed it was.

"I'd like you to meet my partner," she said. "Detective Mark Daniels, this is Dr. Phineas Tate, who created the Optic Evidence Program."

Daniels extended his hand, muttering hello and nothing more, very un-Daniels-like. Maybe he was star struck. Meeting the Einstein of the age would do that to anyone.

"And you must meet my son," Tate said, his round shoulders straightening with obvious pride. If there were problems between father and son, they apparently had not affected the elderly man's paternal feelings. "Philip, this is the D.C. police detective I told you about. One of our star trainees. Veronica Sloan."

A smooth, sophisticated-looking man with dark brown hair and intelligent blue eyes joined them. His round-jawed face was too pretty to be called handsome, but he filled out his tailored suit—which even Ronnie, a non-clothes-person, could tell was a designer one—very well. Probably about forty, he was a good four inches taller than her five-nine, and wore that confident aura of a man used to getting his way. Via his charm, or his money. He had 'playboy' written all over him.

His eyes flared as he looked her over, head to toe. Then a slow smile widened his mouth. "You didn't tell me everything, Father. I wasn't picturing your brilliant detective to be quite so attractive"

Smarmy. God, she couldn't stand smarmy men. But knowing her perceptions of the son might have been tainted by the stories of what he'd done to the father, she stuck her hand out to shake his, anyway.

Fortunately, she was saved having to make small talk by the sound of deep, ragged breathing that drew everyone's attention. One of the suit-wearing politicos, who had been standing apart from everyone else, was looking down at a table loaded with photos of the crime scene. His shoulders shook as he gradually lost the battle to disguise his audible heaves of air. Maybe he figured hauling in deep breaths would prevent him from spewing out sobs and tears.

"The victim's supervisor, Jack Williams," Philip Tate said softly, sounding appropriately sympathetic and mildly superior at the same time. As if strong emotions were anathema to him.

Well, maybe they were to rich playboys, but Ronnie had to feel for the victim's boss. If he'd cared anything about her at all, he would be devastated looking at those post-mortem pictures.

What the hell he was doing here, looking at those pictures, however, was the more pertinent issue. Right now, this room should be occupied by *only* the investigative team.

Kilgore finally finished verbally bludgeoning his subordinates, looked around, then barked an order to Johansen to get the meeting underway.

The flushed, chastened agent cleared his throat to get everyone's attention. "All right," he said, his voice raised, "we're all here now. Let's proceed with the briefing."

A quick round of introductions later and she understood why everybody and his brother had been included in what should have been a law enforcement only meeting. The reverberations from yesterday's crime were reportedly shaking the foundations of Camp David. Supposedly the president himself had demanded full participation of some of the key people involved in the Patriot Square project.

But key people like the construction foreman and lead architect? They might as well have opened the door and asked the next passing bricklayer to come on in and pour himself a cup of coffee. And the victim's own supervisor? Stupid. Even if he was the head of the whole reconstruction project, his relationship with Leanne Carr should have kept him out.

Personally, Ronnie thought if Kilgore and Johansen had any balls they would have excluded the civilians despite the wishes of the gods and generals. If the optic chip had been found and Ronnie truly had some power in this investigation, that's what she would have done. First, clear this room of all non-police personnel.

Second on her to-do list would have been getting rid of SAIC Kilgore

But it wasn't her show, not yet anyway. And Johansen now appeared reluctant to give over the investigation, as he had almost seemed ready to do this morning…probably because of his boss, who sat in a corner, arms crossed over his chest, silent and assessing like a big-ass spider watching the flies get tangled in its web.

Frankly, it made her wonder just how badly the Secret Service wanted to find the rest of the victim. For now, they seemed perfectly comfortable retaining control while bending over to take the political garbage that came with it. Which could explain why they were high-level agency guys and she would never be anything but a detective.

She wouldn't trade spots with them. Not for anything.

Gathering around a conference table quickly constructed out of a couple of sawhorses and a huge sheet of plywood, everyone quieted down, listening as Johansen ran through the pertinent facts in the case, then went around the makeshift table asking for information of all the people who were familiar with the site. She learned nothing new—no head had miraculously surfaced while she and Daniels had been outside.

Finally, Johansen looked at the chief of the forensics team, inviting him to give a report. Before the science geek could say a word, however, Ronnie had to clear her throat. She just couldn't stay quiet. Talking in generalities about site security was one thing. Specifics of the murder were quite another.

"You have something to say, Detective Sloan?" Johansen asked.

Behind him, she saw Kilgore leaning forward in his chair, as if he'd stuck his hand up Johansen's ass and was puppeting him through the conversation.

She kept her tone civil and even. "I was going to suggest that the civilians leave now."

The construction supervisor, Frank something, nodded his head and leapt to his feet, obviously thrilled to get out of here. The architect looked just as relieved.

"I believe we made it clear that we need everyone's input," Johansen said, though he didn't meet her eyes as he said it.

Okay. So Kilgore was definitely pulling his strings. Johansen wasn't happy about it, either.

"Perhaps," she said, "but considering the security clearance issues we will be discussing, don't you think it's better to close the loop?"

The security clearance issues--IE: The fact that Leanne was an O.E.P. participant. Something only a few people in this room had high enough clearance to know about.

Kilgore finally deigned to speak. "We won't be discussing any top secret issues." He hardened his gaze, staring at her in challenge. "Because there's nothing to discuss at this point."

Until the head was found. Check. She had been put firmly back in her place.

Yes, sir, that's a mighty long one you've got there, I'm sure we're all terribly impressed.

So, track two. "Sir, it's just good police work to restrict discussions about the evidence to actual investigators," she insisted, growing more frustrated at his inexplicable obstinacy. What the hell kind of law official was he? Keeping civilians—and potential witnesses—out of the case was Crime Solving 101. She had to wonder whose back he'd scratched to get to so high on the Secret Service's ladder, because it sure didn't seem like skill or intelligence had played a part.

"Look, miss," the senior agent replied, his sneer audible, "the president wants the top people on this site involved in the investigation. Those orders came right from Camp David. Are you going to question the president's orders?"

That's when she pegged him. The guy had no imagination, was a goose-stepping, completely by-the-book, couldn't-think-for-himself bureaucrat. He was apparently incapable of formulating judgments for himself.

"Are you sure he didn't mean the top law enforcement people, Agent Kilgore?" she asked, wondering if he heard the rest of the sentence, the part she didn't say: *you jackass?*

Johansen apparently heard it because she saw his head bob up and down in a tiny nod.

Kilgore opened his mouth, apparently about to release a full head of steam, when he was cut off by the only man in the room who could do it.

"I suspect that's exactly what the president meant, Detective Sloan," said Phineas Tate. "It's idiotic to think otherwise."

Kilgore blinked rapidly. His forehead furrowing, his head dropping, and his shoulders hunched, he looked like a bull lowering its head for a goring. A flush rose from his thick neck through his cheeks as he eventually realized he'd not only been contradicted, but also called an idiot.

"Shall we call the president to confirm?" Tate asked, his voice pleasant as he reached for his phone, acting like he had the commander in chief on speed dial. Ronnie had no idea if it was a bluff, but if so, it was a pretty convincing one.

Kilgore muttered something to Johansen, then threw himself back in his seat.

"Very well," said Johansen, "all those not directly involved in the investigation, thanks for your time. Please stay on site for further questioning."

The civilians got up to leave. Everyone except the guy in the expensive suit, the one who looked like he'd been trying to hold himself together by sheer force of will. The victim's supervisor, she recalled. Ronnie looked at him and lifted an eyebrow.

"I have top security clearance," he insisted, settling deeper into his chair. "I'm also the head of the Phoenix Group, and the president himself called me to ask me to help with this investigation in any way I could."

She frowned, not liking the idea, but Kilgore had apparently had enough. "Mr. Williams is staying," he barked. His tone bordering on supplicating, he added, "Sorry, Jack."

"That's fine," the executive said, offering Ronnie a weak smile. "Detective Sloan is right to err on the side of caution."

The compliment didn't improve her mood. God, this was not going well. She made a mental note to find out how well Kilgore and Williams knew each other. Given that Kilgore was the Special Agent In

Charge of the Secret Service contingent on site, and Williams was in charge of the whole damn thing, they probably interacted on a daily basis. *Cozy.*

Outvoted, outgunned, Ronnie nodded and withdrew from the skirmish, knowing she had to pick and choose her battles when it came to megalomaniacs who liked to throw their weight around.

Once the room had been emptied of half its occupants, leaving just those in law enforcement, plus Tate, his son, and the victim's boss, the chief of the electronic forensics team began to speak. "In evaluating the data from the identification implant in the victim's arm, plus preliminary findings at the scene, we are able to extrapolate a good deal of information about the crime. The victim's heart rate accelerated from its standard rate at eight minutes after two o'clock yesterday afternoon."

Shortly after two o'clock. Just when things were gearing up in a frenzy. What would have made the woman come down to the White House when one of the biggest events of the decade would soon be getting underway further up on the square? And what made her nervous—what made her heart beat faster? Had she ventured down into the basement, realized how dark it was, begun to wonder if she'd been lured there for some ruthless purpose?

"At approximately two-ten, a surge of unidentified energy reverberates through her body."

"A stun gun," Ronnie murmured.

The officious little forensics guy, who obviously liked the sound of his own voice, spared her an annoyed glance. "The clenching of her muscular tissue could indicate that type of device."

Yeah. So could sticking a metal hanger into an electrical socket, but she doubted Leanne had done that.

Zipping her lips, she nodded a conciliatory go-ahead to the expert.

"Her heart rate continues its accelerated rate for several minutes, and her blood pressure surges, then suddenly begins to drop at approximately two-twenty-five."

She's bleeding.

The cutting had begun.

"Her respirations also follow this pattern, short, quick inhalations of oxygen for several minutes, growing more shallow as time progresses."

Gasping in fear. Until her lungs had begun filling with her own blood?

"The pressure eventually slows to a level barely high enough to sustain life, then the respirations cease. The heart's final contractions occur at approximately three-twenty with all electrical impulses in the brain ending shortly thereafter."

Eighty minutes.

God in heaven. The woman had survived for nearly an hour and a half of the assault, experiencing every second of it. Initial adrenaline had given way to fear, then terror. Pain, then incoherence and finally death.

Closing her eyes briefly, Ronnie let her mind suck in the images, and her experience and imagination fill in the blanks. She could almost see the killer watching intently as he split the woman's flesh apart with his blade. Had he leaned close enough to feel her terrified breaths fall warm upon his skin? Had he delighted in breathing deeply to inhale the unmistakable scent of her blood as it gushed hot and hard out of her wounds?

Yes. Yes, she believed he had.

He would have begun slowly, wanting to savor his victim's terror as an appetizer. When he had consumed every morsel of that, he'd have started in on the main course: Her physical pain, with her continuing fear adding spice to the meal. And the post-mortem mutilation had been his dessert.

Opening her eyes, she drew in a deep breath, instinctively certain of one thing. Their suspect had not merely caused this woman's death, he'd made a banquet of it.

Everyone remained silent, absorbing the details…imagining the implications. Even the smooth, self-assured Philip Tate had grown a little pale during the report.

It was Tate senior who got back to business first. "Well, it appears in this instance that the implanted microchip was of some assistance in establishing the scene for all of us."

The forensics guy leaned forward and finally showed some genuine emotion. He sure hadn't spared any for the victim. "It's brilliant, Dr. Tate. If I may, sir, please allow me to thank you. Your invention has enabled those in my profession to leap light-years ahead in crime scene evaluation."

Tate didn't smile, didn't puff out his chest, he merely nodded once. But a brief flash in his intelligent blue eyes said he was pleased at the compliment.

He deserved it. That tiny little implant Americans had rioted against several years ago had saved a lot of lives by providing on-the-spot vitals and medical records during emergencies. It had also helped solve a lot of cases. Much as Tate's latest invention, the Optic Evidence device, would do, if this phase of the testing was a success. The inability to jump into the first genuine investigation had to be frustrating Phineas Tate as much as it was Ronnie.

"Doctor Tate, I'm wondering if there is anything else you might be able to do to help us in this investigation if the optic device is not located," one of the FBI agents said.

Funny how everyone referred to locating the device. Not Leanne Carr's head.

Glancing around the table, Ronnie noticed a confused expression on the faces of a few of the players. Bailey, the female Secret Service agent and another security dude were scrunching their brows in confusion, the addition of the "optic device" element taking them by surprise.

Kilgore, you jerk. No discussing top secret issues my ass.

"I'm afraid my expertise is scientific. I'm no criminal expert. You fine people are all far more adept at that than I." He then glanced at Ronnie. "Of course, having worked closely with Detective Sloan during her training, I can say I think that once the device *is* found, this investigation will be in excellent hands."

A flush of warmth rose in her, like she was some kid who'd been praised by the teacher in front of the class. Probably earned her a few more hate-points from Kilgore and the other higher-ups, but she couldn't deny she'd appreciated the words of support.

"Yes, but if that doesn't happen?" Kilgore pressed, apparently wanting to stage another battle in the turf war.

Tate held up a hand and shook his head, his withdrawal from the conversation almost visible, though the man never left his chair. And that was that. No more questions. No more discussion. Ronnie would really like to learn that trick.

The others around the table hesitated for one moment, then began talking, voices raising decibel by decibel as each person strove to be heard above the rest. Kilgore fumed, but Johansen did a pretty good job of keeping a calm, patient expression while the others tried to spout excuses and reasons why they were not at fault for the lapse in security on the site.

What a waste of time. It was just more of the same bureaucratic garbage that had prevented Ronnie from ever even trying to go after a higher-level job with the department.

Absolutely the only thing she found interesting was watching Dr. Phineas Tate. He sat quietly, his hands folded on the table in front of him, his eyes cast downward, lashes half-lowered. He almost looked like he was taking a nap. But she knew better. She'd spent enough time with him during her training to recognize when the man was deep in thought.

One other thing that Ronnie found worth noting was the demeanor of the victim's supervisor. Williams was obviously successful, well-dressed, well-spoken. Even handsome, in a white-bread, Ivy-league, middle-aged way. But he looked like he was trying to keep a tight reign on his emotions. During the forensic report, she'd seen his hands shake, and now, as the meeting's velocity grew, he excused himself and left the room, as if wanting to be alone before tears could course from his eyes.

Of course, anyone would feel that way about a co-worker being brutally murdered. Still, being the skeptical person she was, Ronnie had to wonder exactly what their relationship had been like. Especially since he'd been so insistent about staying in the room.

Daniels obviously noticed, too. Because while he listened just as intently, he was also busy scribbling notes onto the screen of his pocket computer then turning the thing so Ronnie could read them.

"Affair?" one of them read.

She nodded and jotted one back. "Possible. Tho he's old enuf 2b her father."

Her partner drew a large dollar sign on the screen.

Yeah. Definitely worth checking into the finances of Mr. Jack Williams, though, to be honest, he was probably attractive enough to catch the eye of a young woman Leanne's age.

If he had been having any sort of inappropriate relationship with the victim, the downloaded images from her optic chip would certainly reveal it. Ronnie hoped it wasn't the case. She truly didn't want to see pictures of the Polo-League dude doing it. Especially not through the eyes of the woman being done. Talk about voyeurism to the extreme.

Some of the death row inmates she'd trained on had liked to provide extra-special images for the investigators. Frankly, she could have gone her whole life without getting a close-up and personal view of some sick rapist and murderer jacking off. Telling herself it was all part of the job hadn't made it any less disgusting.

Williams returned to the meeting a few minutes later. The hair at his temples appeared damp, as if he'd left to splash some bracing water on his face, trying to get himself under control.

"So are we going under the assumption that this was terrorist related?" the FBI agent asked. "Because of the location, the timing, the, uh, dismembering?"

That wasn't a bad conclusion, and Ronnie imagined every one of them had at least considered it. But there was one big flaw in the theory.

Phineas Tate cleared his throat and tipped his index fingers up, tapping them together. Everyone fell silent, brought to attention as easily as if a shot had been fired. He was apparently going to mention the flaw. She'd expect nothing less.

"Your suggestions has merit," Tate said with kind, intelligent approval that probably made the agent's day. "However, there is one more piece of the puzzle regarding these events. If the person who perpetrated his atrocity did, indeed, attempt to hide the evidence of his crime by removing part of the victim's remains, we must make an obvious assumption."

The room was deadly still, quiet enough to hear the hum of the wireless fax machine silently spitting out papers on the desk and the sound of Daniels cracking his knuckles. Then Tate continued. "The perpetrator must have known Miss Carr was part of the Optic Evidence Program."

So far so good.

"And therefore must have been someone who knew her."

"Not necessarily," Ronnie murmured before she could think better of it.

Tate continued as if she hadn't spoken. "I suspect Miss Carr violated her security clearance and told someone the truth of her situation and was subsequently killed by him. The brutality hints at a personal rage, so I would assume you should be looking at an angry lover or boyfriend."

Ronnie was about to shoot holes in the theory, despite how much she admired Tate. There was another possibility—a viable one. Someone with high security clearance, or someone involved in the O.E.P. itself, could easily have known about Leanne Carr's involvement. Why that person would have killed her she couldn't say, but it was possible. And it was much too early in the game to rule anything out.

She didn't have the chance to speak. Before she could even open her mouth, Jack Williams launched back in his chair and rose to his feet. His voice shaking and his eyes bright, he exclaimed, "Leanne was a professional to her very core. A loyal, honest, hard-working young woman who would never have violated her security responsibilities. I simply will not allow you to disparage her character in such a way."

Everyone in the room fell silent, staring at the man whose face practically glowed with passionate indignation. Without another word, Williams thrust his chair out of the way and stalked out of the room, not sparing a look at any of them.

Daniels scratched something on his hand-held. "Think he doth protest too much?"

Yes, he did. Either Mr. Williams was one great, understanding and sentimental boss. Or he had a personal connection with his secretary.

Either way, when she finally began to dig through Leanne Carr's visual memories, Ronnie was going to find out.

Chapter 5

Taking the head had been a mistake. A definite misfire. *Foolish.*

It had seemed such a smart idea during the planning stages of this whole thing. And those planning stages had been so thorough, precisely timed, ingeniously designed. The location—perfect. The scheduling—impeccable. The brutality—well, disturbing. But necessary.

Everything was supposed to point to one of two things: a vicious psychopath, or a terrorist. Someone mad with rage and mental disease who had brutalized a victim as so many killers had done throughout history. Or a ruthless, driven fanatic committing the ultimate crime in order to "show" America that no matter how complacent they became, how confident they were in their security, no one was safe. No one immune. Even the president of the United States, just a few hundred yards away, could be gotten to.

Apparently the message hadn't been clear enough.

How could the authorities be so damned tunnel-visioned? The dismemberment should have been something a blind person could see. The viciousness should have indicated insanity. A headless victim should have instantly brought to mind the public executions of kidnapped foreigners in acts dating back more than a decade.

This was supposed to look like a terrorist act or, at the very least, the work of an angry, deranged, disgruntled person who'd wanted to make a brutal statement about his hatred of America.

But it sounded as though law enforcement, in their infinite wisdom, had focused on the one thing he'd hoped they wouldn't even be seriously considering yet: that the killer had known about the O.E.P. device. And therefore known the victim.

"Damn."

Leaving it would have been the wise course of action. Better to have let them find the thing and try to make something of it. They would not have succeeded. Having been so careful, so patient, so methodical…no, the authorities would have found nothing they could use to figure out who had been responsible for what had happened in the basement of the White House on Independence Day.

If there had been something, better to have taken the chance of a random, miniscule bit of information being discovered on the chip than to have the entire investigation focused on the stupid, cursed device implanted in Leanne Carr's brain. And on who might have known about it. He'd wanted to cast a wide net of suspicion. Instead, that net might have landed on a much smaller school of fish—those who knew about the O.E.P. So their suspect pool would be greatly minimized...and he would be on it.

The situation wasn't completely unsalvageable, however. Not at all. There could be a way to fix this, to redirect attention to its proper place. The authorities could be directed back toward random terrorism and violence if they believed the chip hadn't been intentionally taken. That should move the focus away from a personal connection between victim and predator.

Away from the truth.

Leanne's pretty head would simply have to be found.

Though a lot of things had changed since Ronnie had joined the D.C.P.D. nearly a decade ago, some things about police work remained the same. Witness interviews were one of them. Sure, the ultimate witness would be Leanne Carr—when the O.E.P. device was found. But in the meantime, there were, oh, about fifty-five thousand people who could have seen something important yesterday.

Needle, meet haystack.

She and Daniels were tasked with winnowing down the list and heading up that part of the investigation...probably so they'd get out of Kilgore's hair and he didn't have to be reminded that the minute the victim's head turned up, a lowly D.C. detective would be calling the shots. Ronnie didn't mind—getting away from the bigwigs and their pissing match was just fine by her.

First up on her to-interview list was Jack Williams, head of the Phoenix Group. He seemed like the person who'd been closest to the victim and she wanted to talk to him now, before he was able to learn even more inside information about the investigation. She still couldn't believe Kilgore had let him stay for the briefing.

Politely asking the man for a few minutes of his time, she wasn't at all surprised when he insisted he was too busy right now and asked that they talk later this afternoon, over at his own office. Although it was a pain in the ass, and meant she and Daniels would have to leave the site and go through security again when they returned, she wanted to play nice with this guy for now, so she and her partner agreed.

They took the intervening few hours to start talking to witnesses on-site. They certainly didn't manage to talk to fifty-five thousand people. Or even fifty-five. But they did hit about a half-dozen, which, in a case this major, wasn't too bad. And from those six—the ones who interacted most often with Leanne Carr—they'd gotten some decent information about their victim.

The young woman had been pretty, well-liked, prompt and hard-working. Though she worked at the Phoenix Group's offices a few blocks further up on Pennsylvania Avenue, she visited the site almost daily. Apparently her boss was an eyes-on kind of guy and she was his looking glass. She'd delivered messages, met with suppliers, interacted with the project managers and carried reports back and forth. A couple of the younger men commented that, though she didn't wear a ring, she must have been involved with someone, since she never responded to any of their come-ons.

Ronnie wasn't too concerned about that, knowing that if Leanne were seeing anyone, she'd find out as soon as she examined the downloads in the woman's computer—hopefully tonight. She'd gotten word that the victim's hard drive had been taken to a special lab back at the precinct, and Ronnie would be heading over later. She wouldn't be able to see Leanne's murder, and thereby identify her killer—not without that damned elusive chip in her head—but she could definitely learn more about the life Leanne had led before that final day.

Finally, as it drew closer to their appointment time with Williams, they left Patriot Square and drove the short distance down Pennsylvania Avenue. They could easily have walked it, however, swarms of people still milled about. They were even hotter and crankier than they had been this morning, and Ronnie didn't want to march through them in uniform and on a mission. Still, she was glad to see them. Obviously, if rumors of the atrocity committed in the basement of the White House had gotten out, they would have scattered in the wind by now. So somebody was doing a pretty good job of keeping a lid on the story.

At the impressively constructed Phoenix Group building, they were shown in by a quiet receptionist whose swollen face and reddened eyes said she'd heard the news about Leanne. Probably all her co-workers had by now. Ronnie only hoped they hadn't heard anything beyond, "She's dead." Hearing she'd been cut into rump-roast-sized chunks would probably have been seriously bad for morale.

"Thank you for coming down here to talk to me," Jack Williams said as they were escorted into his office, which was about the size of her entire apartment. "I realize it must have been an inconvenience."

Daniels shrugged, "Nah, not a problem. We prefer to get away from the crime scene when we're doing interviews and wanted to see the victim's work area. Plus we'll get to talk to some of her co-workers on the way out."

Hmm. Not entirely accurate—Ronnie sure would have preferred not to have to sidetrack off-site for one interview, today of all days, knowing they'd have to go back to Patriot Square to conduct many more. She'd much rather have stayed on site, so she could be nearby if and when the final part of Leanne Carr was located.

But Mark's intentional nonchalance put off a vibe and it was exactly the one that was called for in this situation. He was telling Williams that they hadn't come here at his request, that Leanne's boss did not have the upper hand in this situation. Seeing the slight narrowing of Williams's eyes, her partner's strategy had been absolutely perfect.

As so often happened, Daniels had managed to surprise her.

"Please, make yourselves comfortable." Williams waved a hand toward two chairs, standing across from his broad, immaculately clean desk. The desk's highly-glossed surface bore nothing but a single engraved pen in a stand, a blotter, and a framed photograph, turned slightly out so a smiling Jack Williams and an attractive middle-aged woman standing on the deck of a yacht could be displayed and commented on.

Ronnie did her part. "Your wife?"

He smiled fondly. "Yes. My best friend and partner. She's the one who urged me to go after this contract, even though my company was one of the newest in the running."

Obviously the Phoenix Group was now set for life with all the work going on in D.C. Ronnie had checked before coming over—Williams's company had the contracts to rebuild every federal building damaged or destroyed in the attacks.

"She will be devastated when I tell her about Leanne, who's like a daughter to both of us. She's been to our home many times, we even had hopes that she might someday date our son."

Uh huh. That's what the married-man-who's-trying-to-hide-an-affair would say. Williams might be uttering all the right words and displaying the right amount of shocked grief, but Ronnie wasn't buying it until she had definite proof of the real relationship between boss and victim.

"Can you tell us what you recall about the day of the murder? When you last spoke to Ms. Carr, where you last saw her?" Ronnie asked.

Williams nodded, his brow drawing down in a frown as he considered the questions.

"Normally, with it being a federal holiday, the offices would have been closed. However, because of the events of the day, I had my key people come in at nine a.m. All of them had special passes to attend the ceremony, but I wanted a final run-through of all the preparations and contingency plans, and I wanted everyone here to put out fires until as close to the two p.m. starting time as possible."

"Including you?" asked Daniels.

"I was here until about eleven-ten. As one of the organizers, I had to be out on the mall by noon. There are plenty of people who saw me."

Interesting that he'd offer an alibi for himself when they hadn't asked for one. Also interesting to imagine trying to round up those "people" and ask them to account for anybody in that mad crush of humanity. Sure, he'd bet any number of people had seen him…but every minute of the afternoon? Highly unlikely.

"I stopped in to say goodbye to Leanne at around eleven. I congratulated her on a job well done and told her not to stay at work so long that she missed the opening ceremonies."

"What was she doing?"

Sounding admiring, he continued, "She was in her office, handling things as she always did—with efficiency and courtesy. A transport vehicle had hit one of the concrete barrier walls by mistake that morning and she immediately got on that, arranging for its repair. When I left, I was walking by her office and heard her on the phone trying to get clearance for a mixer truck to cut down Constitution Avenue through the throngs of people." His eyes misted. "She was not the type to take no for an answer. Tenacious, stubborn, that young woman would leave no stone unturned to finish a job."

"Was Leanne dating anybody?" she asked.

Williams frowned. "To be honest, I'm not sure." He looked like there was more he could say, but wasn't sure he should.

"You know she is an implantee," Ronnie said, pushing the man a little. "We have her downloads of the days and weeks before her death. If she was involved with *anyone*, I'll find out."

She didn't threaten, didn't dangle the possibility that Williams, himself, might like to just come clean now rather than be outed by irrefutable proof. Though, if it were true, and Williams had been having an affair with his assistant, Ronnie would rather know in advance so she could prepare herself to be assaulted by the visual evidence of it.

"Well, if that's the case, you'll probably be far better than I to determine who she might have been involved with. The truth is, I think there might have been someone but she never spoke about it. I, er..."

"Yes?"

"I had the feeling it might have been someone she wasn't supposed to be seeing."

"Like, somebody who was married?" asked Daniels.

"No, I don't think she'd do that. Perhaps just someone others would consider unsuitable." The man's frown deepened and he crossed his arms protectively over his chest. "I hate having to speculate about her private life like this. Bad enough how horribly she died."

"I understand that," Ronnie said. "But it could be pertinent to our investigation."

"Well, you'll soon know better than I. As I said, she never revealed anything. She was a bit private about that sort of thing. A little old-fashioned, if you will."

Okay, Williams seemed to be sticking to his story. And considering he knew she'd find out, she began to back off on her suspicion that he was the young woman's mystery lover.

"What about family?" her partner asked.

Williams uncrossed his arms and dropped them onto his armrests, visibly relaxing a little. Ronnie made a mental note of his mood change, wondering whether his slight belligerence had been about him protecting his own reputation, or a friend's.

Shaking his head mournfully, he explained, "She was an only child, both parents are deceased. Her father was actually working at the American History Museum on *that* day."

Oh. *That* day.

Every American still talked about *that* day on at least a weekly basis. Here in D.C. the subject was virtually inescapable and there didn't seem to be one twenty-four hour period that went by when Ronnie wasn't slapped in the face—or stabbed in the heart—with it all over again.

Her father and brothers hadn't been at the Smithsonian like Leanne's late father. They hadn't even been on the Mall when the attacks started.

Her dad had been a cop, a high-level staff member working directly for the Chief of the D.C. Police Department. He'd accepted the promotion at her mother's urging—it was supposed to see him safely into his retirement with little danger and a lot of spare time. Only, neither her father nor the chief were the types to sit at headquarters and wait for reports. As word of the scope of the attacks had spread, they'd raced to the scene, anxious to help try to free the people trapped under piles of debris.

The chief had ordered her father to set up a base of operations at the Washington Monument, which appeared—at that time—to have been spared from the blasts. He did, supposedly barking orders, calling for triage, his calm, strong demeanor lending courage to all those in a panic around him.

Someone had suggested they go up inside the monument to get a clearer view of what was going on in the mall.

The explosives had been set to detonate as soon as someone stepped onto the viewing platform. Her father and four of his men had been blown out of the clear, blue sky, pieces of them raining down, falling on the statues of the soldiers at the Korean War memorial and into the reflecting pool.

The blast sent the structure tumbling down in huge chunks of concrete, and also killed seven firefighters who were using the monument as a base of operations. Among them her brother, Ethan, who'd been proud as could be at having made lieutenant at his firehouse the week before. Knowing her father, he'd wanted his youngest son safe and close by; she would bet he had called him and assigned him to the base of that monument.

Her other brother, Drew, had been employed at the Pentagon, which was, mercifully, spared that day. But Drew had been asked to attend a meeting downtown that afternoon. Not wanting to deal with traffic, he'd ridden in on a Metro train. The wrong Metro train.

It had taken weeks to dig down to the crushed hunk of metal in that underground tunnel. And months to try to sort through the bits and pieces of the hundreds of people who'd been aboard it when the tunnel imploded in on them.

Sometimes she wondered if she should have moved. A tropical island might have done the trick, might have helped soothe her spirit and heal her heart a little. Her mother would never go, however. She wanted the grief and the parades and the martyrdom. She wanted the graves at Arlington—which, as far as Ronnie could figure, probably didn't contain much more than a cup of bone or a wisp of hair that had once been part of her big, strong, funny, handsome father or brothers. Those things didn't mean anything to her--they were empty reminders, shadows of the vibrant people she'd known, of far less value than the memories that played constantly in her mind. But Ronnie couldn't abandon her mother, so she'd never moved way.

She dared anyone to start playing a my-sad-story-is-worse-than-your-sad-story game with her. To hell with anybody who said she was hard-hearted or didn't understand loss. Her heart was hard because she understood loss far too fucking well.

Unable to sit there any longer, thinking those thoughts, Ronnie got up out of the chair and began to move around. Daniels continued the interview while she prowled the office, listening attentively to every question and answer, but also examining Leanne's boss's workplace. Floor-to-ceiling bookcases filled with neatly-organized books with un-cracked spines filled one section of wall. Framed degrees, awards and commendations covered another, and below them was a huge credenza that matched the oak desk. It was covered with framed photographs—more of Williams and his wife, most often on the same yacht. A few group shots with them and their children. It appeared they had a son and a daughter, both of whom now looked to be in their twenties. It was the kind of happy display any parent would have in an office, one that told stories of special family moments, and oozed warmth and love. The picture perfect life of the perfect executive.

Huh. Why that made her a little nauseous, she couldn't say. Something about Williams just struck her the wrong way, whether he'd been banging his assistant or not.

She moved on, eyeing more photos.

"That's Leanne with me and my wife," Williams said. He'd risen from his desk and walked over to join her. "She loved coming out with us on our boat."

"Nice."

Obviously Williams pulled down big money; calling that thing a boat was like calling cancer a little infection. Boat didn't even come close to describing it, the thing had to be fifty-feet long, at least, with an enclosed cabin and a huge mast, complete with billowing sails. Williams and his wife obviously spent a lot of time on it; most of the pictures were taken on deck.

"It's a classic," he said with pride. "My grandfather built her thirty years ago and I've restored and overhauled her twice. The old man loved that beauty, I just can't let her go into retirement."

"Looks like she's far from ready for that," Ronnie replied pleasantly. Then she got back to the matter at hand. "So, Leanne liked sailing?"

"Oh, yes. After she lost her own parents, we sort of adopted her into our family." He reached out and ran the tips of his fingers over a coffee-table sized, leather-covered book, embossed with Williams's name in the front. "She had this made for me for my fiftieth birthday a few weeks ago." His voice broke a little. "She was very creative."

She reached for the book, raising a questioning brow. He hesitated a moment, as if not sure whether she was humoring him or was really interested, then nodded his assent for her to pick it up.

Okay. She *was* humoring him. Still, she made it look good, taking the book and flipping it open. She scanned the pages, seeing a lifetime of photographic images showing the progression of little Jackie Williams, drooling infant, to Mr. Williams, CEO of the Phoenix Group. Oh, and yachtsman.

"Did your wife help her?" she asked, wondering where Leanne had gotten the pictures. Hell, maybe the man wasn't full of shit and Leanne really had been as close as a daughter to them both.

"Some. I'm sure she must have given her those baby pictures. Leanne was very clever, though, she actually found some old photos I'd never even seen before by using that new Google face-search program."

"Ahh. Good for her," Ronnie said, familiar with the program. Cops had been using it for a while; the site was now popular with everyone. You simply scanned in a photograph, uploaded a .jpg of a face to the search box, and the engine would scour the Internet looking for matches. They used some high tech algorithm that matched twenty-seven points on the face or something, and usually came back with stunningly accurate results.

She'd heard there had been a few lawsuits over it. Some people hadn't liked getting busted for being at a casino when they were supposed to be home sick from work, or being with another man when they were supposed to be at the charity luncheon.

Ronnie had considered utilizing the program herself, maybe putting in her brothers' images. She'd wondered if she could find some old tidbit from their college days, stumble across a picture she'd never seen before that might trick her into thinking them alive and well out there in the world somewhere, if only for a few minutes.

She'd never done it, not sure whether it would be more painful to find nothing or to strike gold.

"So, uh, do you mind giving me a list of those employees who knew and interacted with Leanne?" Daniels asked.

Hesitating briefly, as if not sure whether to remain with Ronnie or return to Daniels, the man mumbled, "Certainly."

Leaving Ronnie standing beside the credenza with his memory book in her hands, Williams returned to his desk and retrieved a single sheet of pristine paper from a drawer. As he wrote, he blathered on about how much everyone just loved Leanne.

Ronnie feigned interest, ready to get out of here, talk to a few more people, then get back to the White House. While she waited, she absent-mindedly turned the pages of Williams's photo book, and was about to put it back on the credenza when one particular two-page spread caught her eye. Unlike the rest of the book, it was not perfectly laid out and symmetrical. In fact, it looked…choppy, or badly edited. The large page on the left contained a few pictures, including one huge group shot taken at night on a beach. Well, it contained half that shot. Considering the way other pages had been laid out, she would have expected to look on the right-hand page and see the other half of the beach photo. Instead, she saw completely different images altogether.

Interesting. Had he torn-out the other page?

Her suspicious mind immediately went to the *he's hiding something* place. An incriminating shot of Williams and Leanne on a business trip?

She shifted, making sure her back was to the man at the desk, and lifted the book a little closer, trying to commit the image to memory. It didn't take long to discount the photo-evidence-of-a-romance theory. Judging by the hair and clothes, not to mention the easily-recognizable, though much younger, Williams, the half-picture looked to have been taken way back in the eighties or nineties. No obvious reason he'd want to tear page out, unless maybe an ex-girlfriend was in the picture and the wife had gotten jealous. Or maybe Leanne wasn't as great with Photoshop as she'd thought she was.

"Well, I think we've taken up enough of your time," Daniels said.

Ronnie closed the book and set it on the credenza. "Thank you for your assistance."

"You're most welcome," Williams said as he came out from behind his desk and walked them to the door.

Daniels shook his hand. "If we need to talk to you again…"

"You may certainly call and set up an appointment if that's really necessary," the man replied, his tone losing some warmth, as if he was coming to the end of his rope when it came to being questioned.

Well, maybe he was used to that tactic working when dealing with his employees, contractors or other underlings. But it wasn't going to work with her or with Daniels. If they needed to talk to him again, they'd talk to him again. She just hoped the man hadn't put his guard totally up and wouldn't demand that talk take place at his lawyer's office. She didn't necessarily like Williams as a suspect just yet, but no way was she ready to rule anybody out.

Outside in the front lobby of the building, Daniels asked, "So, do you really wanna go interview all the vic's co-workers right now?"

Ronnie glanced at her watch. Four-ten. "No, I really want to get back over to the White House before five in case any of the people we need to talk to over there are about to leave for the day."

"I assume by 'any of the people' you're referring to just those who work on the site. 'Cause most of the people we technically need to talk to have scattered to the four corners of the globe by now. All fifty-five thousand of them."

"Don't remind me. Let's just hope Leanne's head turns up...otherwise you and I are going to be putting in for a whole lot of overtime."

Chapter 6

Returning to Patriot Square, Ronnie and Daniels picked right back up with interviews of witnesses and site workers, one after another. While Daniels was focused on specifics, facts and figures, Ronnie was already beginning to segue from D.C.P.D. detective into O.E.P.I.S. investigator. So it wasn't just the facts she was interested in.

She wanted to get to know Leanne as a person. Not just the details—the history—but how she interacted with people, her mannerisms, her personality. Strange as it sounded, part of being an O.E.P.I.S. investigator was about getting into the shoes, and the eyes, of the victim. She needed to understand what made Leanne tick. Only that way could she effectively sort through the massive data dump on the woman's hard drive, finding the details that were important and discarding those that weren't. She needed to know why Leanne's gaze might linger on a daisy but skim right over a rose, why she might pay particular attention to a newspaper but barely spare a passing glance at a magazine.

By ten p.m., she had a pretty good feel for Leanne, at least the professional side of the young woman's life. Soon she'd go into her head—right into her memories—but for now, she wanted to walk in her footsteps.

"You're sure you want to split up?" Daniels asked as they stood inside the empty room they'd been using as an interview office all evening. There was one more worker to talk to, but considering it was heading well into the night, she needed to leave him to her partner.

"I'm sure. I need to explore the crime scene—alone—before I tackle her downloads."

Daniels frowned, displeased at the plan. Not because of the rules and regs—technically speaking, they both should have gotten off-duty several hours ago and were pulling overtime right now, so the argument could be made that they weren't breaking rules by splitting up. Nor would he be worried about her physically; he knew as well as anyone that she could take care of herself. She'd saved his ass on more than one occasion and certainly knew how to take care of her own. Truth was, she suspected he had an idea of what, exactly, she was planning to do.

"You do know you're not some kind of FBI profiler, right?" he muttered, obviously not wanting to be overheard by the few witnesses and agents still milling around on this floor.

"I know."

"Don't go getting your mind all torn up."

"Considering what happened to our vic, I thought you'd be more concerned about my internal organs getting all torn up."

He snickered. "Any psycho who comes after you with a stun gun is gonna be feeling it jammed up his ass and get one hell of a shock to his prostate."

"Damn straight."

"Just...be careful," he warned her.

"I'll be fine. Back in a half-hour."

"Thirty minutes. Then I come after you."

"Okay, *Dad.*"

Daniels smiled as she turned away, but she knew if she looked over her shoulder, that smile would have faded. He was worried about her, worried about this case. One reason she'd made it into O.E.P.I.S. was because of her educational background. The O.E.P. investigators had to be part cop, part shrink. They needed to be able to think like the people they were studying. Ronnie had double-majored at Georgetown, with degrees in criminal justice and in psychology. So Daniels knew she'd be utilizing those skills and techniques while working this investigation, and he was worried about how it might affect her.

Ronnie wasn't worried. Yet. After she'd cleared one real investigation, she'd think about whether this method of truly trying to get into the victim's head was worth the psychological toll, but for right now, it seemed the wisest course of action.

Although the construction elevators were working, Ronnie headed for the nearest enclosed stairwell instead. Like a deep sea diver, she wanted time to mentally adjust to the descent, to pull her mind out of the interviews and the paperwork and put it strictly with Leanne, to almost *become* the other woman.

The place had been buzzing with people earlier; mostly investigators and witnesses, but there had also been some construction workers milling around, waiting for the go ahead to get back to work. They'd been cleared to do so in one part of the building a few hours ago, and even now, though it was fully dark outside, she heard the buzz of heavy equipment and machinery. They'd be working 24/7 to make up for the lost time this week.

That buzz began to fade as she slowly walked down the stairs toward the first basement level. The main floor had been brightly lit and populated. Her descent into the belly of the beast marked a definite change.

The heels of her boots clicked on the hard cement beneath her feet, the clicks growing louder with every step. By the time she hit bottom, she realized the clang and whirr of construction work had completely faded away. The new White House was being built to extreme specifications and would someday be about as bomb-proof as a structure could get these days. Which also made it fairly impervious to drifting noise. Of course, yesterday, it would have been louder, even down here. No matter how soundproof the building, with fifty-five-thousand people, marching bands, heavy vehicles and fireworks, noise would have sifted through the layers of concrete and insulation.

Had Leanne heard? Had she been listening to the celebration going on far above her and wondered how the world could continue going on its merry way while she was being tortured and mutilated? Ronnie paused, considering the question, thinking like the victim.

It didn't require much effort or imagination.

Yes. Of course Leanne had thought those things. Anyone would.

Ronnie blinked and tried to mentally move past what she was certain had been a real moment for the victim, and took a look around her. Not only was the basement deserted, it was a little eerie. Curling her lips, she drew in a slow, steady breath, hearing the faint brush of the air through her teeth. It was <u>that</u> silent.

Rather than proceeding down to the next level—her intended destination—she stayed on the landing, her hand on the rough-hewn handrail. The door between this stairwell and the main corridor hadn't even been installed yet, and she could see out into the vast, expansive hallway that would one day lead to dozens of offices.

Leaving the stairs, she walked into that empty cavern, peering into the long tunnel of black that stretched out on either side of her. The only soldiers battling the darkness were emergency Exit signs with arrows that appeared every twenty feet or so. The green letters cast only the tiniest pools of light, each a small oasis on the empty concrete. She counted two of them to her right, and six to her left, the furthest one out only a small dot from here. She suspected she was seeing all the way to the emergency exit at the far end, with absolutely nothing to break the monotony of nothingness, other than those tiny green pools.

Strange to imagine all the things she might *not* be seeing in those twenty-foot wide expanses of darkness between each one.

Hearing the faintest shuffle, she cocked her head and called, "Hello?"

Nothing.

"I'm Detective Veronica Sloan, DCPD. Is anyone down here?"

More silence.

Wondering if the sound she'd heard had been merely the settlement of a newly constructed wall or beam, she let her eyes continue to adjust to the absence of light, searching for a shadow or a shape that didn't belong. Though her senses weren't telling her why, her whole body was reacting to something. The hair on the back of her neck stood up, her fingers tingled. She'd risen onto her toes, as if in anticipation of a sudden, unexpected dash. From something? Toward something?

Toward. Without a doubt. Ronnie had never run away from anything in her entire life. Except, perhaps, personal relationships that threatened to get past the emotional barrier she'd set up between herself and other people.

She spotted nothing, heard nothing, not the faintest whisper of movement on the air. Apparently the creepiness of the place was playing tricks with her hearing. Finally, after a solid minute of nothingness, she went back to the stairwell and resumed her long descent to the bowels of the White House.

If the first basement level had felt terribly empty, the sub-basement would be utterly desolate. This whole area would eventually be used for storage, mailrooms, security stations and overflow office space, so it didn't rank high on the completion-list. After today's discovery, she doubted any workers were going to want to come down here for a good long time.

They certainly weren't here now.

She reached the bottom and stepped out, turning toward the left, thankful for the presence of more of those emergency exit signs. She could have flipped on some overheads—bare bulbs strung out along the ceiling—but didn't want to just yet. She wanted the atmosphere, wanted the darkness, the lack of all other sensory input, the better in which to think. She wanted the empty space and the quiet air, wanted to move through it with her senses wide open so she could pull in any impressions that might have occurred to Leanne Carr.

Knowing she couldn't go far before she'd run into the crime scene tape, she pulled a flashlight out of her belt and flipped it on. The mag cast a powerful blast of light that banished shadow. The beam landed with unrelenting harshness on the bright yellow tape, revealing the tiny evidence markers and faint spots of red on the floor where the spider-webby lines of blood had been found. The remains had been removed, of course, as had as much of the other evidence as could be gathered. But she could still see the scene in her mind, remembering with utter clarity the position of each mass of tissue, bone or sinew.

"Why did you come here, Leanne?" she whispered as she ducked under the tape. "You'd been working on this event for months, it was your baby. So why were you *here*, rather than outside enjoying the fruits of all your labor?"

During their interview with Jack Williams this afternoon, Leanne's boss had said he had no idea why she would have come to the White House, and that the last words he'd exchanged with her had been that morning, when he'd told her he'd see her at the ceremony. He'd left the Phoenix Group's office shortly after 11 a.m., fully expecting to see his assistant at the Washington Monument later in the afternoon.

The witnesses and logs said she'd arrived on the site at 1:45 p.m. yesterday, able to move through a special pre-authorized-staff-only security checkpoint fairly quickly since there was not supposed to be any work going on. She'd noted her destination as the White House, and the soldier who'd checked her in said she'd appeared preoccupied and perhaps a little annoyed.

"Of course you were," she murmured. "Because you didn't want to have to come over here, yesterday of all days."

So why had she?

Per the guard, Leanne had commented on the day's activities, quipped that there was no rest for the weary, and waved as she'd driven past the checkpoint toward State Street. From that point on, nobody else had seen her. Her electronic key-card had been used to gain entry to the building at 1:57. Not another soul was supposed to be inside at the time…so had her killer entered with her, meaning it would have to be someone she knew very well, and trusted? Or had he somehow gotten around the security and managed to keep his presence hidden from everyone? Was he some kind of damn super-spy who could have evaded detection during intense security sweeps? If she hadn't already confirmed that the old tunnel system that had been a key part of the 10/20 attacks had been demolished and closed over, she'd wonder if the killer had been utilizing them.

Leanne's internal chip said she'd been zapped with a stun-gun at about 2:10. What had happened in those intervening thirteen minutes?

Had her destination been the sub-basement all along—was that why her heart had spend up? Was she afraid?

Or had someone attacked her upstairs—chased her down into the sub-basement?

Or had he incapacitated her and then dragged her down into this dark hole so he could take his time with her?

Damn, she wished the building had been wired for its internal security system. Someday there would be cameras covering every square inch of floor space, but for now, they had nothing other than those high-security locks, agents and guards who'd been assigned to other tasks yesterday.

One thing Ronnie felt certain of: Leanne Carr hadn't randomly come here and stumbled across a psychopath. The crime had felt too deliberate and personal, the set-up was too methodical and well-timed. Someone had lured her here, like a spider catching a juicy fly, and he'd covered his tracks.

"But who?" she asked, as if some of Leanne's memories might be lingering in this stale, dank air that still smelled of blood and chemicals.

Ronnie spent the next twenty minutes circling the crime scene, moving from spot to spot, relying on her excellent memory to recall the forensic report. She considered what must have happened, minute by minute. She made a few mental notes, including pausing to wonder why the killer had stayed here, fairly close to the stairwell, rather than taking Leanne to the far end of the corridor, where it was less likely anyone would hear her screams.

"Were you *that* sure of yourself, that positive nobody would be around to hear?" she whispered, trying to imagine the killer's motivations.

Eventually, realizing she'd been gone nearly the half-hour she'd said she would be, and not wanting a worried Daniels to come down here looking for her, she cast one final look around the scene then headed for the stairwell. She continued tucking away details in her brain, each fall of her foot on a step underscoring something she wanted to consider a little more. Tonight, when she was home, lying in her bed, all these impressions would mingle and take new shape in her mind and she would see if she could come up with any new, previously unconsidered ideas. She hadn't jotted them down, not wanting even the scratch of pen on paper to interfere with the mental connection she was trying to make with Leanne. Besides, Ronnie was a visual person, she saw scenes and mentally photographed them, and would see them again and again, able to recall them with clarity long afterward. It was probably her greatest strength as an investigator.

Arriving at the main basement level, and remembering that soft, furtive sound from before, she hesitated before continuing. Something—a cop's intuition maybe?—made her step back out into the corridor. All was quiet, as before. All dark, all deserted. She cast her flashlight toward the right and saw nothing but those two eerie green pools of light on the cement. Turning to glance to her left, the same. Just those Exit lights, like before.

Or...not.

Something was different.

Her heart picked up its pace in her chest, her body reacting to the change that had occurred on this floor in the twenty minutes she'd been downstairs.

She focused and counted the Exit lights again.

"Four," she whispered.

Four lights. There were four pools of green between her and that far-away emergency exit.

A short time ago, there had been six.

Her blood surged in her veins as the implication hit her. Someone had disabled two of the lights, leaving a vast, sixty-foot swath of corridor bathed in utter blackness, as dark as the back side of the moon.

Ronnie reached for her belt, unfastened her holster and retrieved her weapon. Someone had been down here a short time ago, hiding in the shadows, remaining silent while she'd called out, waiting for her to move on. They could be here still. She shone her flashlight in that direction, craning to see. Her mag, though powerful, didn't pierce the emptiness, and mainly served to spotlight her for anyone who might be watching from down there.

She considered flipping it off right away, then thought about the layout of the sub-basement level, wondering if this floor would be laid out the same way. Her attention focused on that long corridor, she backed toward the stairwell, hoping to see a breaker box, like the one she'd noted downstairs earlier. Finding it in the beam of her flashlight, she reached for the main breaker and flipped it.

Nothing. Shit.

Beginning to feel like she had been drawn into a trap, and knowing she needed backup, she retrieved her phone to call her partner.

No signal.

Damn it. The building was probably designed that way. Future employees would likely have access to a dedicated cellular network, but right now, here in the basement, she was completely jammed.

Up another tall flight of stairs and down another corridor, her partner sat waiting for her in an interview room. But this was no typical building, it was the White House and it was huge. It would take at least several minutes to get him and bring him back here to have him help her search this floor. But if the person who'd disabled the lights was still here, those several minutes would give him time to get away. There was another, smaller set of stairs at the other end of the building, plus the construction elevators, plus the main elevator shaft, plus the emergency exit. And those were just the egresses she knew about.

There was no good, reasonable excuse for anyone to be down here, messing with the lights. So she had to consider that the person sharing this darkness with her could have something to do with Leanne's murder. She couldn't just leave and give him the chance to escape. Besides, Daniels had said he was coming after her in thirty minutes. It had been at least that, so he'd probably be showing up any time now, anyway.

Thinking of one last option, she grabbed her hand-held microcomputer, wondering if she could get online. A few taps of the screen and... *Yes!* She dashed off an email to her partner, telling him to get his ass down here ASAP. Daniels was obsessive about checking the thing and she knew he'd be here within minutes, if he wasn't already on his way. In the meantime, she'd wait, and watch, and listen, not proceeding further unless it became necessary.

She switched off her mag, then paused to let her eyes re-adjust. Stepping close to the corridor, but not into it, her Glock still at her side, she remained very still. A long moment of silence stretched before her.

It was broken by a sound as soft and small as a puppy's whimper.

She tensed, tightening her grip on her weapon, casting a quick glance up the stairs, looking for her partner. No sign of him. Hell.

Another soft, vulnerable sound came from somewhere down in that dark corridor, this time a bit louder. It sounded like...a child. A crying child.

That was impossible, there couldn't be any kids down here. But there could be somebody who was so badly injured they had strength to emit only the most pathetic cry for help.

She couldn't wait any longer. If the psycho who'd killed Leanne Carr was down here with another victim, every second counted in saving that person's life.

Stepping into the corridor, she called, "Detectives Sloan and Daniels, D.C.P.D., identify yourself!" It wouldn't hurt for the mystery man to think she already had backup.

Not expecting a response, she wasn't surprised not to receive one.

"Okay, have it your way," she mumbled.

Moving down the hallway, she hugged the inside wall, away from the tiny bit of light cast by the Exit signs. She stepped quietly, on her toes, hoping to catch the unknown party off guard. Hopefully he'd think she and her partner were playing it safe, waiting for the perp to make some kind of move, give them some indication where he was. He wouldn't expect her to be creeping toward him in the utter darkness, when he knew she had a flashlight.

She passed one green pool of light, kept walking, passed another. One more and she'd at last entered the cavern of blackness. The final sign was far in the distance. Between her and it? She had no idea.

Gauging her steps, she figured she'd just about reached the place where the first missing Exit sign would be. She looked for it, then looked down, seeing the tiniest gleam of something on the floor. *Broken plastic. He smashed them.*

Assuming her opponent had destroyed the two that would most reveal him, she had to guess he might be about halfway between her and the next missing sign. She tightened her grip on her weapon, her eyes scanning the shadows, alert to every beam, every doorway that led into every dark, unfinished room off this hall.

Then she spotted one. An open door. The only open door in sight.

She crept toward it, raising her firearm, raising the flashlight. Stepping to the threshold of what would someday be some politico's office, she paused, breathing silently, listening for any sound from within. Then, adrenaline surging, she flipped on the mag-light and barked, "Police, put your hands up."

There was no rush of movement, no opponent awaiting her in the darkness.

But that didn't mean the room was empty. She most definitely wasn't alone in it.

Leanne Carr's head sat right in the middle of the floor, staring sightlessly toward the doorway—toward Ronnie—as if she'd just been waiting for her to arrive. Her blood-matted hair was tangled around her ravaged face, her eyes open, her mouth gaping and filled with blood. She looked like a monstrous prop from a movie or a haunted house.

"Jesus."

Shuddering once with revulsion, she stepped inside, playing the flashlight's beam all over as quickly as she could to ascertain the room was empty and to avoid stepping on any evidence. There was absolutely nothing—no bloodstains, no weapons, certainly no killer. Just the gruesome remnants of a victim who had been a pretty woman thirty-six hours ago and was now a bloody ball of hair and torn-up flesh.

Well, at least she knew now what the psycho had been doing down here and why he'd chosen to work in the darkness. Why he had decided to play hide-and-seek with the head, drawing her to it with those doused lights, obviously knowing she would come investigate, she couldn't say. And their theory that he'd taken the head specifically because he knew Leanne was an implantee would have to be reexamined…at least, as long as the O.E.P. device hadn't been removed from the victim's brain through her smashed skull.

God, she hoped it was there. Not just because she longed to solve this poor woman's murder, but because she now felt personally invested. This prick had been playing games with her, taunting her, daring her to catch him. He might even have been watching her in the darkness, laughing as she moved toward him while he slipped out of her grasp.

Nailing him would be incredibly satisfying.

She was so focused on that, and on the best way to proceed with this new evidence, that she *almost* didn't hear the assailant coming at her from behind.

Something gave him away—his movement through the very air, perhaps. Every cell in her body went on high alert. Reacting instinctively, she swung around, Glock coming up.

But before she had the chance to make out any more than a figure cloaked all in black rushing into the room, she felt something smash into the side of her head.

And then she saw nothing.

Daniels glanced at the clock again. It had been thirty-two minutes since Ronnie had gone off to do her get-into-the-head-of-a-killer thing. For most people, being two minutes late for anything was no big deal. For his partner, however, it was serious. She knew he'd be worrying, watching the clock. She wouldn't keep him sweating like this intentionally.

So either something had happened to her, or she was on to something important and couldn't give up the scent. Question was, which?

He clicked his pen. Shifted some papers. Glanced at the clock.

Three minutes.

"Damn it, Ron," he muttered, knowing she would ream him if he stumbled down there and ruined some big, important moment of clarity. Also knowing there'd been a psychotic killer in this building yesterday and they had no idea who he was.

He didn't want to piss her off by being overprotective. But he'd sooner lose an arm than even think about the person who'd killed Leanne Carr getting his filthy hands on Ronnie.

Four minutes.

He grabbed his phone, thinking to text her, then remembered the signal was spotty here in the building. Reaching for his handheld, instead, to send her an email, he tapped the screen and realized the damn thing had died. He'd forgotten to put it on the charger last night and it had run out of juice. Crap.

"Oh, you're still here," a voice said.

Daniels looked toward the door, seeing Bailey stick his head into the room. The young Secret Service agent looked tired, a little sweaty. The kid's boss had been keeping him running around all day, but during every spare minute, Bailey had been hovering around them. The agent either had a serious case of hero worship for Ronnie, or he'd been assigned to babysit the unwanted D.C. cops and report back to his boss, Johansen, or his boss's boss, SAIC Kilgore, on what they were doing. Probably both. Stinking little snitch.

"Murder investigations take a little time," he finally replied.

Bailey grinned, trying to appear friendly, as if knowing he was interrupting but wanting to stick around and get more information anyway. "Everybody's got to sleep sometime, though. Are you almost finished for the day?"

"Yeah. Almost."

"Where's your partner?"

He hesitated before answering. He and Ron didn't always play by the rules and this kid's boss would probably do anything he could to mess with them. Finding out they'd split up—against regulations—could play right into his hands.

"In the can," he mumbled, rubbing his jaw and wondering how soon he could be hitting his favorite bar. Hopefully Ronnie would come walking up behind Bailey any second now, the two of them could get out of here and go back to the precinct, where she would sequester herself in a computer lab and he could call it a night.

"Huh, that's funny. I just walked past there and the janitor asked if he could lock up for the night. He didn't say anything about anybody being inside."

Bailey eyed him. Mark held his stare, silently daring the agent to make something of it. The kid looked away first.

"So are you going to leave when she gets back?"

"Yep."

"Did you have any luck today?"

Yeah, wouldn't you like to know. "We made some progress."

"Really? Like what?"

"Can't talk about it."

"Oh." Bailey hesitated, then added, "Leanne seemed like a nice woman. I hope you guys catch whoever did that to her."

"We will," Mark said, knowing his voice held absolutely no doubt. He and Ronnie were a great team on any case. With one like this, in which they were both already so invested, he knew neither of them would rest until the son of a bitch was caught.

"Good."

"Look, I'm gonna finish up this paperwork, then round up my partner so we can get outta here. I've had enough of this place for one day. I don't know how you can stand it full-time." Talk about a depressing spot to work. Having to spend five days a week locked inside the most cursed spot on earth couldn't be easy.

"Okay. Catch you later," Bailey said with a pleasant nod. Before turning away, though, he licked his lips and cast his eyes downward. "Uh, would you please tell Detective Sloan thanks from me?"

"For?"

"Just thanks. I think she'll understand."

"Gotcha."

He did get it. Ronnie had handled this guy just the right way earlier. In the process, she'd also probably made him fall a little in love with her, the way most red-blooded males did.

Something about his partner made her almost irresistible to most men. It wasn't just the looks—which were stellar—or the brains, which put him to shame. She had the most fascinating combination of strength and vulnerability. He'd never known anyone tougher or more self-confident. He'd also never known anyone as determined to not let down her guard or actually feel anything that made her uncomfortable.

He guessed that was understandable, given the way she'd lost her father and brothers in the attacks. Still, that unobtainable quality in her made her that much more of a challenge. Ronnie could make a guy feel like a totally inept screw-up, make him want to do better just to impress her, and make him almost desperate to be the one to break through her emotional barrier.

She could also make him want to dive off a cliff.

Frankly, that's how he'd been feeling more often than not lately.

"Okay, well, bye," Bailey said as he ducked out of the office.

"S'long," he replied.

Mark got back to his notes, trying to remain patient. Finally, though, unable to help it, he glanced at the clock.

Eleven minutes. *Enough.*

He got up, leaving his folders and interview notes on the table, and ambled out into the hallway. Bailey was already gone, back to the office used by Kilgore, the main Secret Service supervisor. Daniels glanced toward that door, seeing it begin to swing open. Johansen, the only one of the three S.S. stooges who actually seemed like he had a clue, was stepping out, though his head was turned toward the room as he addressed someone inside.

Hoping not to be spotted, Daniels quickly strode to the stairs, and jogged down them, skipping every other step. Though he told himself he shouldn't overreact, his inner-partner-voice kept telling him something was wrong. He'd learned to listen to that voice over the years, especially when it came to Ronnie. They might not have the personal relationship he'd once dreamed of having with her, but as partners, they were unbeatable and utterly joined.

When he reached the sub-basement, he called for her. "Ronnie? Where are you?"

No response. His concern growing, he flipped the breaker, setting the entire sub-basement ablaze, the harsh, bare bulbs spilling unforgiving light on the bloodstained floor. He could easily see in both directions and immediately knew his partner wasn't here. Weird. He hadn't passed her on the stairs, hadn't seen her on the first floor. There weren't even any roughed-out rooms on this level. There was absolutely no-place she could be that he wouldn't see her, and he didn't see squat.

His mind churning, Daniels killed the lights and trudged up the stairs. Though he couldn't imagine why she would have stopped on the basement level, he decided to check it out, and went to the breaker. Nothing happened when he flipped it.

Now general concern was becoming worry. Something was wrong. Seriously wrong.

He unsnapped his holster and removed his flashlight, very aware of the cavernous darkness. "Ronnie! Detective Sloan!"

Not a sound. Yet something made him proceed further, heading down the long, shadowy corridor, calling her name, shining his flashlight all around. His heart was pounding now, both because of the tension, but also because of his fear for her.

That wasn't a good thing; she wouldn't like him being afraid for her. But hell, he was crazy about the woman, personally and professionally. If anything happened to her, his life wouldn't be worth shit, and there was nothing he wouldn't do to keep her safe.

Beginning to wonder if he'd just somehow missed her upstairs—if she'd hit the ladies room sometime after Bailey's interaction with the janitor—he was about to turn around and go back the way he'd come. Just then, he heard a crunching sound beneath his foot.

He glanced down and saw the shards of a broken Exit sign.

"Damn it," he mumbled, his tension rising. He drew his weapon. "Ronnie, answer me."

Something made a tiny sound, a click, and he jerked his attention toward a door nearby. He ran toward it, seeing it move slightly. "Police! Get your hands up!"

Nobody rushed out, and he couldn't rush in. Because, he realized to his horror, the doorway was blocked by a limp, lifeless body.

His partner's limp, lifeless body.

The bitch had been bluffing.

She'd called out a warning to put up his hands, claiming to be speaking on behalf of herself *and* her burly partner.

But she'd been lying. Sloan had been all alone the whole time. Damn her to hell.

He should have known she was lying, since she'd been stumbling around in the darkened sub-basement by herself for twenty minutes. He *had* known, deep down, but there'd been the tiniest sliver of doubt, the possibility that her partner had met her on the landing, the lumbering ox moving quietly for a change. So, after using his little electronic toy to make a helpless sound and lure her toward him, he'd ended up abandoning his plan to grab her and take her to a private spot for a good, thorough killing.

Leanne had been easy, so trusting and weak. Sloan would have put up a fight if he hadn't gotten the drop on her. But if Daniels had come barreling down the hall after her, there would have been hell to pay. He'd have been in a fight for his life. So he'd had to play it safe.

Of course, he'd soon realized the partner hadn't been lurking in the darkness with her. In fact, Daniels had been upstairs in the interview room the whole time. By that point, though, it had been too late to go back and finish the female cop off.

"Stupid whore," he mumbled, his voice a low whisper as he watched through a window as the woman was loaded into an ambulance outside the front entrance of the White House.

He'd intended only to place Leanne's head where it could be found, and slip away without being caught. But when Detective Sloan had wandered down into the sub-basement, by herself, he'd realized he might have the chance to kill two birds with one stone. He'd decided to stick around, see if he could lure her into a trap and finish her off. Though he might not have had the time to enjoy it, to kill her the way he liked best, even a clean, quick kill would have sufficed. The main point was to snuff out her life before she got any further with her investigation. Because he'd already sensed she was a bit too clever, too observant, unlike her blustering partner.

Maybe that bash in her head had caused brain damage. Perhaps a sharp splinter of skull had smashed into her brain, destroying her memories, ruining her for good, leaving her all but dead, anyway.

He could hope, anyway.

If it hadn't, and she came through with her faculties intact, she'd be more determined than ever to find him. To get revenge.

He had to be careful. Oh, so careful. He'd always been lucky, but it had been his extreme caution that had enabled him to do what he did for so long and not get caught.

Maybe going after Sloan on the spur of the moment, without a detailed plan, had been a bad move. If she recovered, he could end up regretting that move for a very long time.

But there was no way of knowing now. He'd just have to keep his ears open, wait to find out if he'd hit her hard enough, if he'd based her skull and smashed her brains and shut her busybody mouth for good.

If not, there would be time to make new plans. And the next time, he wouldn't screw up.

Chapter 7

Trying to swim toward consciousness, through what felt like a sea of confusing, disconnected images, Ronnie flicked her eyes open. Immediately regretting that as sharp shards of light stabbed at her, she groaned and quickly shut them again.

Her head felt like it had been crushed in a vise, her brain throbbing in what felt like a too-tight skull. The slightest movement brought agony, so she remained very still, concentrating on taking slow, even breaths, trying to figure out where she was and what was happening.

"Detective Sloan? Veronica?"

Hearing the male voice, which she couldn't instantly place, although there was a familiar ring to it, Ronnie tried to focus. She swallowed, wondering why her mouth felt so dry, why her head was on the verge of exploding, and why she was lying flat on her back in a bed when the last thing she could remember was walking down the steps to the sub-basement of the White House.

"Was I attacked?" she whispered through a cottony-dry mouth.

"Yes," the man's voice said. "You're very lucky."

"I don't feel lucky," she growled. She felt like something spat out of death's mouth. Post chewing.

"It could have been worse. He might have used the other end of the two-by-four he smashed you with. That side had nails sticking out of it."

Nails. Two-by-four. Bits and pieces began coming back to her. She'd been in the basement, right? And something had happened.

"So I should be feeling grateful?"

"Just be glad he didn't stick around to finish the job."

That voice—it was so familiar. She was reacting to it, growing tense but also a little excited, feeling both dread and the tiniest bit of pleasure.

Who the hell?

Needing to know, she opened her eyes again, slowly this time, letting the light cast by the beaming overhead fluorescents drift in gently rather than assaulting her. She couldn't say she recognized the ceiling, or the fixture, but judging by the basic 12 x 12 ceiling tiles and the typical industrial lighting, she suspected she was in a hospital bed.

She shifted, feeling the uncomfortable groan of muscles resting on what felt like hard-packed straw, which further cemented the thought.

"Try not to move too much," the man said. "The doctor said you're going to have a bitch of a headache for a few days, and moving will just make it worse."

She lifted a hand to her head, feeling a lumpy bandage on the right side. Around it, her hair stuck out wildly, short and stubby. A long strand brushed the other cheek, so she must look interestingly lopsided.

Damn. Her hair stylist was gonna have a fit. And considering he lived right next door to her, he was bound to see sooner rather than later.

"How long was I out?" She thought about that short hair, hoping it was what was left after an emergency haircut, and wasn't new growth after a shave. Because that would imply she'd been out long enough for it to grow back an inch or two. "Tell me I haven't been in a coma for weeks."

He chuckled. "About eight hours."

Eight hours? Holy God.

"Technically they're calling it minor head trauma."

It didn't feel very minor. "You mean a concussion?"

"Yeah. The laceration was pretty big and they had to staple it up, so you've got a bit of a bald spot under that bandage."

Staples. Great. More metal for guards and soldiers to be suspicious about.

"The doctor will explain everything, I'm sure," said the voice, which was coming from somewhere off to her left.

The doctor. Meaning this *wasn't* the doctor.

Finally, knowing the recognition tickling the edges of her brain would drive her crazy, she carefully turned her head to the left. Her eyes still weren't working properly, and she at first saw only a tall shape, in dark clothes, standing in the corner. She had to strain to see, blinking rapidly.

As he began to come into focus, his image swimming in her mind and in her memory, she emitted a little gasp. "You!"

"Me." He sketched a small bow, then approached the bed. "How ya doin', Sloan?"

Hell. It was really him.

"You'd better not be poaching on my case, Sykes."

His mouth curved up in a half-smile, those blue eyes twinkling with secrets and merriment. She was lying here in a hospital bed, all banged up, hurting like hell, half bald, and he was smiling, handsome, perfectly dressed, and tormenting her, neither confirming nor denying that he was here to snake her out of Leanne Carr's murder investigation.

Typical Jeremy Sykes.

"You don't look like you're in any condition to stop me."

"Give me a couple of hours and I'll put you flat on your back."

He laughed softly. "Promises, promises."

She kicked herself for giving him that opening…even while knowing a part of her had done it on purpose. As always, she just didn't know how to react to the man.

They'd met in Texas, during O.E.P.I.S. training. Sykes had been the guy everybody loved but also secretly resented. It wasn't that he was hard to like, or in any way unpleasant—far from it. He was just so damned perfect. Incredibly good-looking. Friendly—he could charm anyone. Cultured—the Martha's Vineyard type. Rich—his family owned some big, global corporation. Smart—he hadn't gotten through Harvard because of his family connections but because he'd earned his way. And a good investigator—he'd been an FBI agent when chosen to join O.E.P.I.S., and had already received the highest commendation the bureau gave for bravery. He was also polite, quick-witted and reliable. All around nauseatingly perfect.

Ronnie had dubbed him Sucks the first week of training. Not just because of all of that, but also because he confused the living hell out of her. Having been raised in a house with two older brothers, and an overprotective-but-doting father, she'd been handling males since she was little. She always mentally knew where to put them, having compartments for all the relationships in her life: Family member. Perp. Victim. Friend. Partner. Boss. Lover.

Sykes hadn't fit. Not anywhere.

He'd left her confused and curious, and the tension between them had been noticed and commented on by most of their classmates. If he scored a ninety-eight percent on an exam, she worked herself to the bone to hit ninety-nine. During simulations, if he'd studied a series of O.E.P. images and found a needed piece of information in two minutes and ten seconds, she'd just *had* to find it in two-five. They'd competed on the shooting range, shot after shot, both of them leaving their classmates in the dust but neither able to ever really get the edge over the other.

There had only been one instance she could recall when they hadn't been arguing, sniping at each other or competing. It had been near the end of their training, after a grueling day of looking at the most awful images of a test subject being led to the electric chair. The man had been a convicted killer, sentenced to die by a jury of his peers, yet Ronnie had discovered an untapped well of empathy within herself as she shared his final hours of life.

The images from the O.E.P. device had almost allowed her to become him. She'd found herself mentally walking in his footsteps, as she'd been trained to do. *Her* eyes had studied a tattered, much-read Bible, lingering with obvious sorrow and fear on the 23rd psalm. *She* had been the one to take an absurd amount of time eating a final steak dinner, complete with pecan pie and whipped cream. *Ronnie's* were the feet trudging along the pitted, scarred linoleum floor that led from the cell to the death chamber.

She'd been the one who'd shed vision-blurring tears while the guards attached the straps. The one whose view had been blocked for a moment when the black hood was being put in place. The one whose very last sight on this earth had been an explosion of red as the capillaries in his eyes exploded.

The experience had disarmed her. Affected her so much she'd needed to get away from everyone and let herself deal with her surprising reaction.

Sykes had found her sitting under a tree on the grounds of the police academy where they'd trained. For the next two hours, they had shared the kind of deep, true conversation Ronnie couldn't remember sharing with anyone. He'd caught her in a moment of vulnerability, and she'd let go of her emotions, confessed her misgivings, her fears, her anxieties. As if she'd opened a door between them, Jeremy had done the same, sharing the stress he'd felt about having to fight against his wealthy parents every step of the way to follow his heart and go into law enforcement.

She told him about her brothers and father. He'd told her about his best friend from the academy, who'd been assigned to FBI headquarters…and had fallen on 10/20.

It had been an incredibly human interaction. And it had ended with an embrace, one she'd never forgotten.

There'd been nothing terribly sexual about it, even though Ronnie's heart had been pounding in her chest, her body on high alert.

The confused attraction she'd felt for him from the start had returned in full force, accompanied by a new understanding of who he really was and what really made him tick. So, yeah, she'd definitely been aware of the hardness of his chest, the broadness of his shoulders, the tender way he stroked the small of her back.

Mainly, though, what she remembered was the gentle intimacy of it. The connection of spirit. That kind of thing didn't come easily to Ronnie, and she'd never quite gotten over the fact that Jeremy Sykes, the only person she'd ever met who could intentionally get her to lose her temper—which she was half on the verge of doing right now—was the one who'd evoked such a response in her.

"What the hell are you doing here?" she asked, thrusting away the confusing memories.

He held his hands up and out, playing innocent. "Hey, don't blame me, I got dragged down from New York in the middle of the night when it became pretty obvious that you weren't going to wake up right away."

"Tell me they didn't give you my damn case."

A hesitation. Then, "They didn't give me your damn case."

She allowed herself a soft, relieved sigh.

"But, uh, they do have something else in mind. And knowing the way you feel about me, I suspect you might think it's even worse."

How could he possibly know how she felt about him when she'd never figured that out herself? She'd spent far too much time trying to understand her own mix of feelings for the man, that vacillated from reluctant admiration to attraction to dislike. Other than that one strange interlude, she was usually torn between wanting to punch his face off or to push him down and screw his brains out just to get him out of her system. Confusing didn't begin to describe it.

He approached the bed, his eyes moving constantly, assessing her, narrowing the tiniest bit as he studied her banged-up head. A muscle in his jaw flexed as he clenched his teeth, as if, beneath that breezy charm, he was furious that she'd ended up here, in this condition.

That made two of them.

"What happened, anyway?" she asked, her memories returning, but still a little fuzzy. She'd been searching the basement, had stumbled upon Leanne's head, which had been left like a gross gift in the middle of an empty room. Then…unimaginable pain.

"According to your download from this morning, an assailant came at you out of the darkness. You tried to defend yourself but he slammed you in the head. Once you were out, I got nothing but pictures of your closed eyelids."

Her jaw fell. "You looked at my downloads?"

He shrugged. "That's one reason they called me in. I extracted them wirelessly while you were under and took a peek."

That felt...intrusive. Yes, she'd known all along her job skirted the edges of decency when it came to respect for privacy, but she mostly thought about it from the perspective of investigator. Ronnie had her own code, she would never intrude where she shouldn't, or invade the most intimate moments of someone else's life without having a damn good reason. So she hadn't quite anticipated the quick jolt of violation she felt, knowing someone else had looked into *her* visual memories. It was like Sykes had opened up her mind and scooped out a piece of it.

As if reading the bit of mind he'd scooped, he insisted, "The last fifteen minutes before you lost consciousness. That's it, Veronica, I didn't look at anything else."

Fifteen minutes...still a lot of images. The O.E.P. device recorded images every single second. That was sixty per minute.

Sykes might have only gone fifteen minutes into her memories, but he'd still seen a lot. Enough to make her shift uncomfortably on the bed, thinking of all the personal stuff a person would see if they went back a full day into her mind. She only had his word that he hadn't. She made a mental note to never look at herself naked in the mirror and to shower and go to the bathroom in the darkness. And she might just have to swear off sex for good.

Hell, who was she kidding? Sex was one thing she liked enough to risk embarrassment, even if she didn't get it all that often. Huh— good thing the O.E.P. device couldn't capture what she mentally pictured, because she'd definitely imagined Jeremy Sykes without his clothes a time or two. The bastard had just snuck into her brain her somehow.

She felt heat rise in her face just thinking about some of her more lurid fantasies. Just because she'd decided to steer clear of the man didn't mean she hadn't used him to inspire a few late-night dates with her biggest, raunchiest sex toy.

He must have seen and misinterpreted the rush of color in her cheeks. "I swear, Sloan. Fifteen minutes, that's it. You don't have anything to worry about."

God, the man thought he could make her blush by looking at some personal moments from her day? Ha. She'd rather him see her wiping her ass than ever know she'd gotten herself off just by thinking about him.

"Honestly, there was nothing to see, considering you were walking around in the pitch blackness." Shaking his head, he asked, "What were you thinking, anyway? You had a flashlight, you had a partner upstairs…"

"I was thinking a flashlight would make it easier for him to draw a bead on me and going for my partner would give him a chance to get away. Plus, I wrote to Daniels and told him to come ASAP."

"He didn't get the message."

That sounded as though Daniels and Sykes had met. Talked. She wondered how that first meeting had gone down.

Not well.

"Oh," she said, realizing how lucky she'd been. "He came down looking for me after thirty minutes went by?"

"Yep. And you're very lucky he did. They're saying he probably scared off the person who attacked you."

"Maybe," she said, starting to remember more of what happened. "Or maybe the perp thought Daniels was there all along. I made it sound that way when I started down the corridor."

"Why'd you go off on your own?" he asked. He sounded a little angry, but couldn't be more angry than she was at herself.

"I heard something that sounded like a cry for help."

"There was nobody there capable of crying out. He played you."

"Yes, he did," she gritted out. *But he won't ever do it again.* "I wonder if he meant to draw me down there with that cry, thinking I was alone and he could take me out. Then, when I called out acting like Daniels was with me, he had to change his plan, not knowing if I was bluffing or not."

"Either way—whether Daniels really scared him off when he arrived, or the mention of his name intimidated the unsub—your partner saved your bacon."

Unsub. Unidentified subject. FBI speak for *We have no idea know who this monster is.*

"Not the first time." She looked around the room, wondering where Daniels was.

"He just went to call your lieutenant, who's been checking on you every hour." Sykes grinned. "Daniels didn't seem too interested in sitting here by your bedside with me."

Daniels would hate Sykes, she'd known that from the beginning.

They were everything the other wasn't—Daniels tough, shopworn, a little crass, blunt and powerful. Sykes smooth, charming, intuitive, with a way of working people to get what he wanted. While Daniels barreled through walls and didn't much care about rules, Sykes merely walked around them and found ways to get the rules changed to suit him. They couldn't possibly be more different and each of them drove her crazy, though for entirely different reasons.

"Your mother's also downstairs in the cafeteria, getting coffee. She'll be crushed she wasn't here for the big eye-opener."

"Aww, hell," she groaned, not relishing that reunion.

It wasn't that she didn't love her mother, but since Ronnie was all Christy Sloan had left, she'd become the definition of smothering parent. The horrific loss of her Dad and the boys on 10/20 had hardened Ronnie like a piece of volcanic glass, but it had smashed her mother into the softest, most vulnerable, easily-wounded creature on the planet. It took every ounce of patience Ronnie possessed to keep from crushing her with a thoughtless word, and she constantly walked on the edge of a knife between being honest with the woman and protecting her delicate feelings.

Absolutely the only thing she ever argued with her about was the job, because no matter how much her mother pleaded and begged, Ronnie wasn't giving up being a cop. Not for anything, or anyone. Not even the only family member she had left.

"She seems very worried," Sykes said, his tone gentling.

"I'm sure she is. So I guess I should get ready for another game of you're-breaking-my-heart-how-can-you-do-this-to-me?"

"Better than a game of why'd-you-go-and-get-killed-on-me," he pointed out.

A reluctant grin pulled at her mouth, but it hurt to smile so she quickly squelched it.

"You dealing okay?" he asked. He came even closer, until he stood right beside the bed. His face awash with concern, his gaze roamed over her, as if he was taking stock of every bruise, scrape and cut.

Sykes appeared torn between wanting to grab her and hug her tight or beat whoever'd done this to a bloody pulp. She couldn't say which reaction would have pleased her more. And considering they hadn't seen each other for months, she couldn't say why the realization that he felt that way hit her hard in the vicinity of her heart.

"I will be," she whispered, knowing his concern wasn't just

about her physically. He wanted to know how she was handling having been attacked by someone who was probably the person who'd brutalized Leanne Carr two days ago. Was she forever marked now, having been so close to someone that utterly evil, that black of spirit? How could she have breathed the same air of a monster and come out of it sane and whole?

Honestly, she hadn't even had time to dwell on the whole thing. Not just her injuries, but that she'd been in the same place with the same monster and could so easily have ended up like poor, pretty Leanne. When she did, she'd allow herself to have a single, nearly-hysterical moment. Then she'd stamp it down, regain control over her emotions, and get back to her job of finding the cock-sucker.

"They'll suggest you talk to someone," he said.

"A shrink?"

He nodded.

"Yeah, they probably will."

"It might not be a bad idea."

"It's never helped before."

He didn't ask why she'd seen a shrink before. He didn't have to. He knew about the demons that tormented her—she'd told him about them herself.

He reached out and gently brushed a strand of hair back off her face, tucking it behind her ear. Ronnie swallowed hard, noting the tenderness, knowing what he wasn't saying with words but still wanted to express with gestures. And she suspected he, like she, had never forgotten that afternoon in Texas, or stopped wondering what might have happened between them if they'd met under different circumstances.

"I'll be all right," she promised.

"I know you will."

He finally smiled and she managed to smile back. Something about dealing with Sykes in all his bossy-tenderness was enough to bring a smile to her face even on what had been her crappiest day of the past few years.

"I guess I'll go spread the word that you're awake."

He headed for the door, but right before he left, Ronnie remembered something he'd said a little while ago. Something about him being here, not to take over her case, but to do something she might like even less.

"Hey, Sykes, you never told me. What exactly are you doing

here? Other than going through my mental underwear drawer."

He tsked, a brow going up. "Why, Sloan, I never got near your lingerie. Are you saying I didn't go back far enough?"

Glaring, she shot back, "You go digging in my head again, you'd better hope it's because I'm dead."

His faint smile faded and his stare gained heat that she felt even from several feet away. "Let's not even joke about that."

She heard something in his voice—a note of intensity that she didn't often associate with him.

"Seeing you like that, helpless and hurt…well, I don't want to ever see that again, Sloan. Got it?"

Nodding once to acknowledge his sincerity, and that bossiness as he ordered her to never allow herself to be hurt again, she licked her lips and cleared her throat. Her heart had skipped a beat or two, and she had to keep her hand down at her side to prevent herself from reaching up to fix the mangled remains of her hair.

Damn Sykes for making her feel…cared for.

"Thanks," she whispered.

He hesitated, then murmured, "You never did meet me for that drink."

"No, I didn't."

When they'd said their goodbyes in Texas, he'd suggested they plan to get together for a drink in a few weeks to compare notes on how things were going with the O.E.P. He hadn't been proposing any kind of class reunion; she'd been the only one included in the invitation, and they'd both known it. He'd claimed they could meet on neutral territory, somewhere between New York and D.C.

If he'd given her a date and the name of a hotel before they'd left Texas, she might have considered it. A one night stand and out of her system he'd go.

But when he'd emailed her a few weeks after training to try to set it up, she'd blown him off. Not because she was a bitch. Not because she was playing hard-to-get. Not because she was disinterested.

She'd done it because she was a chickenshit. It had been hard enough to stop thinking about the man once she'd come back from Texas. Letting him back into her life—into her thoughts—was a bad idea, and she'd steered clear.

Now, though, it looked like she couldn't avoid him anymore. The decision had been taken out of her hands.

"Maybe we'll get a chance to do it soon," he said, his tone low, serious and intimate.

She met his steady stare. "Maybe."

The moment lengthened, they continued to eye each other, her with wary curiosity, him with frank interest. She sensed he had more to say, and that it probably wasn't anything she wanted to hear. Oh, she wasn't vain or stupid, she knew Jeremy Sykes wasn't pining away with love for her. He wanted her, though, of that she had no doubt. Just as much as she wanted him. But to voice that, to give life to the words and the silent longing would put her in the position of having to deal with them. And she just wasn't up to that.

Finally, he broke the silence. "I've missed you, Sloan."

She licked her lips and ignored the fluttering of her heart. "Sorry, can't say the same."

A soft laugh told her he'd seen through that lie. "You sure don't make it easy on a guy."

"Easy's over-rated." Nothing ever really came easy; Ronnie was used to working hard for everything she got. She just hadn't decided yet whether any man was worth working that hard for.

This one could be.

Maybe. But not today.

"Hey, you never actually answered my question about what you're doing here," she said, feeling foolish for even thinking that way about Sykes, given their current situation—namely, her being banged up in a hospital bed looking like somebody's yanked her half bald, and him looking as annoyingly perfect as always.

"No, I didn't," he said, his eyes twinkling, telling her he'd avoided answering on purpose.

Dread rose within her. What could possibly be worse than having this distracting man swoop in and take off with her first O.E.P.I.S. investigation?

"Oh, shit," she whispered, a possibility occurring to her. One that would, indeed, be worse.

He winked. "I think ya got it."

Steam building in her already aching head, she glared at him. "I am *not* working with you on this case. Forget it."

Okay, maybe the powers that be had covered their bases, not sure how long she'd be down, bringing in somebody else to cover for her until she got back. But, once she was well, there was absolutely no reason the two of them had to do anything together, much less work on her big case. Being thrown into Sykes's company during the nearly 24/7 frenzy of a major murder investigation would knock her for a loop she wasn't ready to handle.

He reached for the door handle, calling over his shoulder as he left.

"Hate to break it to you, Sloan, but you don't have any choice in the matter."

There had been a time when Brian Underwood had truly looked forward to his one night a week out with his buddies. Drinks and poker with his work friends had been almost a ritual, a holdover from his single days, a tradition he'd stuck to as a way to hold on to his independence, even after the allure of hanging out with the guys, getting drunk, and losing money had faded.

That had changed when he and Lindsay had started having kids. The one-night-a-week had become every other Wednesday. Even then, the gatherings hadn't necessarily been something he looked forward to anymore, but his wife insisted he go once in a while, if only so she wouldn't feel guilty about occasionally going out with her girlfriends. He always made a point of stopping at an Italian bakery and buying Lindsay her favorite dessert—fresh cannolis—as an I-love-you-thanks-for-being-a-cool-wife-and-letting-me-go-out-with-my-friends offering.

Frankly, he'd rather just stay home. That had been especially true since the baby had been born. Lindsay was with the kids all day, every day, and not only did he feel like he had to come home and do his part every night, but he also was one of those suckers who just loved babies. Especially his own babies. If things had been great when it had been just him, Lindsay, and four-year-old Michael, they had become just about perfect with the arrival of Sarah, just 3 months old and already the owner of a huge chunk of his heart.

Sitting around a smoky apartment drinking beers with a bunch of drinking, farting guys just couldn't compare.

But this week's gathering had fallen on a special day. He'd not only just scored a home run with a massive project he'd been working on for months, he'd finally gotten the promotion he'd been busting his ass for. It came with a big raise. So when his buddies insisted that he attend tonight's game at a friend's downtown apartment, wanting to share in a celebratory drink—or four—he hadn't been able to refuse.

Lindsay had been fine with it. When he'd called home to tell—or, ask—her, she'd been giddy over his good news and had said, "Yes, of course you should go. Have fun!"

"If you're sure…"

"Of course I'm sure!"

"Okay, babe. I promise I'll bring you a cannoli."

"Don't even think about it, mister," she insisted. "I'm trying to lose this rest of this baby weight. That raise of yours is going to pay for our Labor Day trip to the shore and I want to look at least somewhat decent in a bathing suit."

He laughed and insisted, "You're beautiful!" He meant that with all his heart. She was beautiful in his eyes, and always would be, whether she looked the same way she did on the day they'd met, or now when she had stretch marks, milk-filled breasts and ten extra pounds, or the way she would when they were in their nineties after a long, great life together.

"Thank you," she said. "But I'm serious. No cannoli. Promise?"

"I promise."

"Good. Now go, have fun. But behave. Remember, I know your password to your computer and can check up on you."

He had laughed at the mock-threat, a familiar one in his house. While her warning that she could check up on him was in jest, it was also possible. If she wanted to, she could check his downloads and see what he was up to every second of every minute of the day.

Sometimes he wasn't sure how he felt about that. But given the financial benefits of participating in the Optical Evidence Program, plus the boost it had given him in his civil service job, making him look like a real forward-thinking team player, he had to think he'd made the right choice. Plus, of course, he'd never do anything to betray his wife's trust. She'd claimed his heart in their sophomore year of college and he'd never even looked twice at another woman since.

Lindsay didn't have top secret clearance, as he did for his job with the Labor Department office here in Philadelphia. But his wife had been part of his decision to agree to serve as a test subject for the O.E.P. He would guess any spouse would have to, given the intimate moments that could potentially be shared via his downloads.

Lindsay never got too hung up on that, occasionally snapping off a joke when they were making love that she wanted to be sure she looked nice for the camera. That really was a joke. Although he had to retain his visual records on his own computer equipment, Brian didn't have to upload his O.E.P. data to the researchers in Washington every single day, just once a week so they could ensure everything was working correctly. For him, that was Thursday mornings. Meaning they *never* had sex the night before. His bi-weekly poker games were probably the only interesting things for anybody checking up on him to see, because Lindsay always wore a flannel nightgown, curlers and face cream to bed on Wednesdays.

Which meant he would not be getting laid tonight—not a big change, since their sex life had been sporadic since Sarah's birth. One of these days they'd get back to normal; in the meantime, he was happy to just hold his beautiful wife in his arms as she nursed their sleepy daughter.

"Okay, guys, I have to call it a night. I need to get home and get some sleep," Brian said. "I suspect Lindsay'll have me on two a.m. feeding duty as payback for staying out so late." He rose from his seat, smiling and thanking his work friends, still crowded around a card table at his buddy Dan's apartment.

"No, you can't leave yet," said Dan. "It's not even ten."

"It's after eleven," Brian said with a laugh. "I'm gonna be dead meat if I don't get home."

"Henpecked," called one of the other guys.

"And I wouldn't have it any other way." He meant that completely.

His friends refused his offer of money toward the beer and pizza, and he waved as he walked out the door of the old brownstone. Dan lived several blocks from the garage where Brian usually parked for work; they'd all walked down together after quitting time. He headed back that way, walking quickly, mentally counting the number of drinks he'd had and how long ago the last one had been. He had only had a few beers, stretched out over several hours, and didn't think he was anywhere near impaired. But he still focused on the number and the time, and how he was feeling, wanting to be certain. Not just because he'd promised Lindsay, but because he was a cautious man. His life was too good to even think about putting it at risk.

"Hey, asshole, watch where you're going!" a voice called. The shout was accompanied by a loud beep.

Brian leapt back, realizing he'd just started to cross the street against the red light. Rolling his eyes over his own stupidity, he called back, "Sorry, dude, thought it was green!"

The driver waved and Brian felt pretty sure there'd been a middle finger sticking up. You had to love the City of Brotherly Love.

Knowing there was an alley that would provide a shortcut between this street and the next, he headed for it. It was right around the corner from the little Italian bakery where he usually bought Lindsay her treats. True to his word, he hadn't done it tonight, and felt awkward going home empty-handed.

Then he thought about it. He wouldn't be going home empty-handed. He'd be going home with the promise of ninety-eight hundred more a year.

Smiling at that thought, he reached the alley and headed down it. Within a dozen steps, he was swallowed up by the darkness, the tall buildings on either side blocking much of the light from the street he'd just left, and from the one in front of him, which seemed a long way off from here. The old buildings were occupied by businesses, maybe some apartments on higher floors, but none of them with windows looking down into this trash-strewn alley.

Hmm. Maybe the shortcut hadn't been such a great idea.

Downtown Philadelphia had its rough areas and its good ones. This neighborhood was a mix, so while he didn't immediately go on high-alert, he definitely kept his eyes and ears open. He'd hate to cap off his great day by getting mugged.

Listening for anyone following him shouldn't be difficult. The night should have been louder, but the narrow alleyway had swallowed up the sound along with the light. He could barely even make out the rumble of car engines on Chestnut Street and had the strangest sense of being cut off from civilization, even though it was only by half a block. This secluded throughway must be the Bermuda Triangle of Philly, so adrift did he feel.

Suddenly, ahead of him, a shape moved in the darkness. Quick, low to the ground.

A high-pitched screech broke the night.

He leapt backward, almost tripping over his own feet, watching the inky black figure dart between two trash cans, sending the lid of one crashing down. The metal lid spun on the gravelly road, its clash and clang the only sounds breaking the silence, save the thump of Brian's suddenly raging heart.

"Damn cat," he muttered, laughing at himself. His imagination had obviously gone into high gear if a stray feline had nearly made him wet his pants. If anybody at the O.E.P. headquarters actually watched his uploads, they'd probably be laughing at him tomorrow for that overreaction.

His lips still widened in a smile, he resumed his walk, seeing the welcoming lights of the next block looming a little larger. Just beyond that intersection was the garage. He'd be home in thirty minutes, maybe even in time for the end of Sarah's eleven p.m. feeding. God, he loved holding her in his arms while he rocked her to sleep at night.

Another trash can lid clanged. "Not gonna get me this time, cat," he said with a smile as he passed the alcove from which the creature had first come.

Gravel crunched behind him. Something moved, disturbing the air. But he was slow to react; his mind seemed unwilling to scream *danger* and be called the boy who cried wolf.

"Is someone..."

Before he could finish voicing his question, a hard, metal object scraped his neck, sharp and jarring.

"What the hell?"

Stunned, Brian threw an arm up and tried to spin around. But the object came to life, sending wave after wave of electric pain shooting through him. He cried out as the muscles in his body began to quiver and to seize. He'd never known such pain, so hot and fiery, burning him from the inside-out, sending thought and comprehension away until panicked terror was all that remained. He tried to scream, but his vocal cords froze as well and his wails of pain became gurgles of agony.

Dropping to his knees in the middle of the alley, he then fell flat onto his stomach, as stiff and rigid as a board. He registered the sound of bone crunching as his face slammed into the road . Brian immediately tasted blood, plus the chalky, bony bits of his two front teeth, which now littered his tongue. He tried to breathe. With his face pressed flat on the ground, he managed only to choke on flecks of dusty gravel and dirt. Finally, with great effort, he turned his head a tiny bit and gulped some fresher air.

"Waaahh?"

He strained, trying to move again, trying to function, but could only twitch, shocked and helpless, unable to so much as lift a finger. The night was so dark. So deserted. A half a block in either direction there might be people milling about, but they were much too far away to hear his guttural, throaty groans.

The only thing he could move was his eyes. And although even thinking was difficult, his training kicked in and he did remember to try to see who it was who had attacked him.

He blinked, seeing drops of his own blood dripping down over his eyelashes, though he couldn't feel them land upon his cheeks. He saw pavement. A small, rank puddle of stagnant water. The rough brick of the nearest building.

Mostly though, he saw his own mortality.

Someone rolled him over. He stared up, through the tunnel created by the tall buildings, toward the sky far above, at the bright stars that shone over the city.

He and his little boy made wishes on those stars every night before bed.

Star light. Star bright.

Oh, God, my son, my baby girl, they need me. Please don't hurt me.

He couldn't form the words, couldn't make a sound. He could only lie there, struggling to control his terror before he choked on it.

Then he saw the figure cloaked all in black, carrying a large, sharp-bladed knife. And terror was all that remained.

Chapter 8

Ronnie checked herself out of the hospital the next day.

Everyone had argued against it—the doctors, her mother, Daniels, even her lieutenant who'd come by at lunchtime to check on her and bring some flowers from the squad. She hadn't let anybody talk her out of it, not only because it was killing her to not be working on the case, but also because staying in this miserably uncomfortable bed wasn't doing her a bit of good.

She'd finally gotten her way, promising to check-in with her regular physician to get the staples out of her head in a few days. The other concession she made was to agree not to drive anywhere—which was why Daniels was behind the wheel. Frankly, that made her even more dizzy than the concussion. There was a reason she usually drove and it had nothing to do with her being a native of D.C. and knowing the streets better than he did. He drove like a maniac, would never stop for long at an intersection if there was a way to turn on red, preferring to go blocks out of the way rather than sit still for a light.

She supposed his driving was a good analogy for his life. Impatient, quickly irritated, not content to watch and let things develop. He was utterly exhausting. But she'd given her word, so he was the one she'd asked to drive her home, rather than her mother, who would have moved in and not left for days.

The one person who hadn't been around to ask for a ride— though, of course, she'd never have asked him—was Jeremy Sykes. The FBI agent had stopped by again last night but hadn't been back since. He'd called early this morning to update her on the case, telling her Leanne's head had been removed to Phineas Tate's state-of-the-art research facility outside the city. He also admitted he was calling from Philadelphia, having caught an FBI chopper up there just after dawn, though he wouldn't say why. He merely told her he'd fill her in when he could, and promised they'd get to work together as soon as he returned.

Well, that remained to be seen. She wasn't willing to concede defeat, even though her phone calls to her O.E.P. supervisor at the National Department of Law Enforcement hadn't changed a thing. Because of the high-profile nature of this case, they wanted their two top investigators working on it *together*. He told her to suck it up, work with Sykes and like it.

Ha. Fat chance. She had a narrow window of opportunity to work without him hovering over her shoulder, speculating in her ear, when what she would want was utter silence. Damned if she wasn't going to take it.

"Keep going," she said when Daniels flipped the turn signal to head to her place.

"You need groceries?" he asked, a cautious edge in his voice, already preparing to argue against whatever she had in mind.

"I'm all right. It's time for me to get back to work."

"Ronnie, you had brain trauma."

"I'm more concerned about the trauma Max is going to do on me if he sees my hair," she said, trying to tease him out of his tense mood. Max, her next door neighbor, was also her hair stylist, and the guy was going to lose it when he saw Ronnie's new hacked-off-in-the-emergency-room look. "Come on, I can't go home until it's dark so he won't look out his window and see me."

"Scared of your hair-dresser. Pathetic."

"Yep, that's me all right." She pulled down the mirror and glanced at herself, wincing. Her dark eyes were made darker by circles of weariness and pain, though the rest of her face was pale. She had a few scratches on her right cheek either from hitting the floor or from the brush of the two-by-four against her face as her assailant pulled it away.

But the real coup de grace was the hair. It was pretty impossible.

Fortunately, a nurse had removed the big, bulky bandage this morning, covering her staples with a much smaller one that was paper thin. Thinking about it and considering the long strands falling down over her left shoulder, she fished a comb out of her pocket and carefully—oh, so carefully—parted her normally right-down-the-middle brown hair on the left. One big swooping comb-over later, and she looked only half as dreadful as before.

"Not bad," Daniels said, watching her from the driver's side. "You look like my Great Uncle Ralph. He tries to hide his bald spot just like that."

"Oldest trick in the book when you're having a bad hair day. Or a no hair day. Anyway, it'll do. Now, head up to the beltway and hit 270."

"You're supposed to go home and take it easy."

"No, I'm supposed to help solve Leanne Carr's murder." She

turned in the seat, moving carefully, still dealing with a faint headache that flared into a major one if she moved too quickly. "Plus, Sykes will be back sometime today. I want to get a leg up on him."

As she'd expected, Daniels sneered at the mention of Jeremy's name. "The great Agent Sykes. He was about what I expected."

"I told you."

"Not everything."

"What do you mean?"

Daniels hesitated, opened his mouth as if to respond, then snapped it closed. "Forget it."

She didn't prod, mainly because she feared she knew what he didn't want to say. He'd noticed the sparks between her and Sykes. Hell, everybody in the room had to have noticed when the two of them had gone after each other about the case, him insisting he was getting to work on the chip as soon as the data was made available, her threatening his life if he started without her.

Daniels, her partner, was probably the only one who'd understood the real reason for the vibes between them, though her mother probably had hopes in that direction. God knew the woman was forever trying to get her involved with some man. She'd taken a look at Sykes and lit up like the night sky on the 4th of July.

Still, she wasn't sure anybody other than Mark had correctly interpreted the scene as involving something other than dislike on Ronnie's part. She wasn't about to call it liking. But the sexual tension between her and Jeremy was thick enough to spread on toast. Maybe the fact that she and Daniels had done it once made him more attuned to her response to another man.

Another reason to despise herself for that one moment of weakness. She hated this thin veil of tension between them that had lasted almost five years. She'd hoped Mark would forget about what had happened between them, as she'd tried to. But he almost seemed to be getting worse instead of better. As if he'd understood it was just sex back then, but was now wondering if it might lead to something more.

Huh-uh. No way. Never gonna happen.

Ronnie didn't do the love thing. Oh, she loved Daniels as a partner and a friend. But romantically? Well, she had absolutely no interest in romance. She never intended to settle down, had ruled out any kind of domestic tranquility for herself when she'd seen how that had worked out for her family. Her mother would never get over the loss of her husband and children. Her brothers' widows had ostensibly

Leslie Kelly

moved on, but whenever Ronnie saw them, she noted the look of haunted sadness that had never quite left them.

Nope. Not for her. Better to be accused of caring too little than to be flattened for life because you cared too much. Going it alone was safer, smarter and the right thing for her. Besides, she and Daniels worked far too well together as partners, not as lovers. Their one sexual encounter had been born out of tragedy, not genuine passion, and would never be repeated. He was just going to have to accept that.

"So where are we going?" he finally asked, cruising past her exit.

She settled into the seat, relieved he'd changed the subject himself. "Bethesda."

"Lemme guess. Dr. Tate's version of Disneyland?"

An apt description. Ronnie had visited Tate's scientific research facility a few times and every time was left slack-jawed over some of the projects going on there. The man definitely had all the toys a geeky science nerd would ever want. Or an O.E.P.I.S. investigator.

"It seems like the logical place to go since we don't have any other real leads." Wondering if he'd learned any more about the person who'd attacked her, she asked, "Any luck with the secondary crime scene? Did you hear back from forensics this morning?"

"Yeah," he said with a sigh.

"And?"

"Nothing. No prints, no fibers, no footprints. Definitely no forgotten driver's license or confession note. Sonofabitch is like a ghost." Daniels tightened his hands on the steering wheel, gripping it like he had the assailant's neck in them. "We'll get him though; no doubt about it."

"I know."

Clearing his throat, and staring straight ahead, Daniels continued. "Hey, listen, there's something else you should know. Lieutenant Ambrose told me this morning that while you're temporarily partnering with the FBI dude, I'm supposed to team up with somebody else."

Her heart dropped; her jaw did too. "They can't break up our partnership."

He didn't look happy about it either, but had obviously accepted it. "I won't be able to help with a lot of the top secret O.E.P. stuff you two'll be doing, and they need me to run the standard D.C.P.D. side of the investigation, which you won't have time for."

Maybe not, but the idea of losing Daniels as a partner, even

100

temporarily, was enough to shock her into silence for a few minutes. They'd been together since just after she'd left the academy. He'd bitched and griped about taking on a twenty-one year old young woman and she'd jabbed right back about being stuck with an "old" geezer—the ten years he had on her seeming a lot bigger back then.

Knowing she wouldn't have Daniels by her side throughout this investigation made her feel like someone had chopped off her left arm.

"Hope Sykes is worth it," he muttered.

"He's not my partner."

"For now he is."

"Well, for now, he's not even around. So let's keep working this."

He considered, then nodded once. "Guess we can do that, at least until you're officially snatched out from under me." Then, because he was Daniels, and because he obviously wanted to smooth over the seriousness of the moment and not let on how he really felt, he wagged his eyebrows. "Although, you can crawl back under any old time."

"In your dreams, perv."

He laughed, and she joined him, but still found herself wondering how it would be to work with someone else for the first time in her career. She and Daniels were like an old married couple by this point, they thought alike, reacted alike, anticipated each other's moves.

Jeremy Sykes was an unknown quantity. Considering he already made her feel edgy—not to mention slightly inferior—she honestly didn't know what to think.

"You'll be fine," Daniels said, knowing her well enough to know what she was dwelling on. "You can hold your own with anybody, Ron, including some highbrow FBI agent."

"Thanks."

"And you know I'll be on speed-dial the minute you need backup or just somebody to bounce ideas with."

"Or a ride?"

"Yeah. That, too."

The tension lifted, they began to talk about the case, sharing some thoughts, Ronnie again apologizing for not having come and gotten him the other night before investigating those broken Exit lights. Daniels was certain he hadn't heard a soul when he'd been looking for her, which made her think he hadn't actually scared-off the guy with his presence. Probably a pretty good thing she'd called out both their names, making the perp at least consider the possibility that someone else could be coming into that room right behind her. That bluff might have saved her life.

Fortunately, they were heading opposite traffic and rush hour hadn't kicked into high gear yet. The trip might have taken hours if they'd started it at four p.m., but was only twenty minutes now at two. When they reached the Tate Scientific Research Center, Daniels insisted on pulling up in the drop-off loop out front and helping her out of the car, rather than letting her hoof it from the expansive parking garage. He made a big production of ordering her to stay put until he came around to open the door for her, and insisted on taking her arm and leading her to a bench sitting in front of a merrily gurgling fountain.

"Stay here. Just sit."

"Woof, woof."

He snorted. "I mean it, Ron, if your ass is off that seat when I get back, I'm tossing you in the car and taking you home."

"I'm not an invalid."

"All we need is for you to stand up too fast, get woozy and fall on your face. You wouldn't be much use in the case if your jaw's broken in three places."

She sat. Folding her hands on her lap, she pasted on a placid expression.

"That's better." He turned to leave.

Before he got too far, she called out, "Hey, Daniels?"

He glanced back over his shoulder, a long-suffering look on his face, as if he expected to see her turning cartwheels. When he realized she was not, his shoulders visibly relaxed. "Yeah?"

"Thanks again."

"For?"

"You know. Saving my life. Saving my jaw. The usual."

He flashed a wide grin that removed ten years and a lifetime's worth of jadedness from his ruggedly handsome face. "Maybe I shoulda let the jaw thing happen. You can't bitch at me too much if your mouth's wired shut."

"Don't count on it," she retorted. "We took that sign language class together, remember?"

He threw back his head and laughed. "Yeah, I guess you could ream me out without ever saying a word, couldn't you?"

"Bet your ass." Growing serious, she repeated the most important part of the conversation. "Seriously. Thank you."

He shrugged. "Don't mention it, partner."

He got into the car and drove around the long, sweeping driveway, heading for the nearest parking garage. Ronnie stared after the car, thinking again how lucky she was that she'd drawn him for a partner. If he hadn't found her in the basement the other night, she could have bled to death. He'd apparently picked her up and carried her through the darkness, upstairs, bellowing for help, and had refused to be kept out of the ambulance that had taken her to GWU Hospital. He'd hovered as much as her mother at her bedside, and while she knew he'd been angry at himself for being out of the room when she'd regained consciousness—leaving Sykes there to be the one she saw first—he'd managed to hide it pretty well.

Though they'd promised each other never to keep count, she knew this latest incident now put him one up on her in the saving-the-life-of-your-partner routine. She'd hauled his ashes out of the fire twice. The White House attack had made the third time her partner had done the same for her.

She owed him. Big time. Not for the first time, she wished she knew what, exactly, he wanted from her. Then again, fearing that he wanted something she was unable to give, perhaps it was just as well.

Never the most patient woman, she shifted on the uncomfortable stone seat, peering through the trees toward the parking deck, watching for Daniels. She did not, however, try to get up for a better look. Claiming she was fine was all well and good. Standing up and proving she *wasn't* would be a sucker's move.

"Well, hello there Detective Sloan. I'm surprised to see you—and very glad you're all right. You don't look much the worse for wear."

"Mr. Tate," she said, eyeing Phineas Tate's son, Philip, who'd just emerged from the building, a golf bag slung over his shoulder. Accompanying him was another man, about the same age, blond, also carrying a golf bag. He looked just as wealthy, jaded and lazy as Phineas's son.

Tate was dressed in lightweight pants and a light colored shirt, his hair artfully messed, his glasses designer, his smile plastic. She wished she could like the man, especially because she so liked the father. But there just wasn't much to like, as far as she could see.

"A little hot for golf, isn't it?"

"I like to get nine holes in a few afternoons a week. Do you play?"

"No."

"Too bad." Then he pushed his sunglasses up onto the top of

his head, stepping over to eye her closely. "You really were hurt, weren't you?" he murmured, as if just noticing her gauntness and the crazy-ass hair-style. And the fact that she was just sitting outside the building as if she'd lost the use of her legs. He glanced back at his golfing companion. "Detective Sloan was injured on the job. She's quite the hero on the D.C. police force."

The other man murmured something appropriate, still looking bored.

Ronnie shrugged. "I'll be fine."

"Terrible things happening," Philip said, shaking his head and frowning. "Awful things."

But apparently not awful enough to interfere with a golf game. Check.

"Listen, I've been meaning to call you," he said. "I want you to know I am at your complete disposal. If you need me to run interference, or even serve as an *interpreter*, don't hesitate to ask." His words were accompanied by a hint of laughter.

"Interpreter?"

"My father and Dr. Cavanaugh are wonderful, brilliant people, but they're, well, I suppose you'd call them eggheads. They tend to talk above everyone else and it can sometimes be hard to pin them down. They talk in big pictures, in concepts. I know as a police officer you're probably more interested in detail and fact."

"Yes," she admitted, not liking to agree with the younger Tate, because of her loyalty to his father and her belief that the son was being slightly critical. That said, she knew Philip was right. Phineas Tate was a big picture person who sometimes seemed as though he lived in a very different world. They didn't speak the same language.

"We're going to miss our tee-time, Phil," the man's companion said, impatience seeping into his voice.

"Here," Philip said, ignoring his friend. He dug into his pocket and pulled out what looked like a solid gold business card case. Flipping it open, he retrieved a pristine linen card and handed it to her. "My work, home and cell numbers." His lips curled up a little in the corners. "Call me any time, day or night."

She supposed that charm—and his looks and money—got him lots and lots of phone calls from just about any person he gave his card to. But she doubted he usually gave it to people like *her*. No, she definitely suspected his tastes ran in other directions.

Ronnie carelessly shoved it into her pocket. "Will do."

He hesitated, as if waiting for her to say more, then finally added, "And if I think of anything I'll call you as well."

"Feel free. I can usually be reached at the precinct."

His soft laugh said he'd gotten the message: She wasn't handing over her private numbers.

"That's all right, Detective Sloan, I know how to get you."

That's what you think, McSleazy.

He wasn't getting her at all. Frankly, though, she suspected she was beginning to get him. The flirty-playboy thing was a little obvious and a bit overdone. She'd begun to suspect she knew why.

"Phil?" his friend prodded.

"Just a minute, I'm not finished. Look, why don't you go start up the car and get the a.c. running?" he asked, tossing his keys to his blond friend.

The other man caught them, offered Ronnie a tight smile, then sauntered off toward the deck.

"I suppose you heard they have successfully extracted the device from the first victim?" Philip said when they were alone.

She nodded, immediately wishing she'd just mumbled a response. Jerking her head, especially out in the sunlight, was not doing her any good.

"I have been told that the device was a bit damaged."

She sucked in a breath. "Is it salvageable?"

"Oh, I have no doubt of that. My father's protégé, Dr. Cavanaugh, has been hard at work on it since yesterday. If anyone can retrieve the data stored within, she can."

The chip being damaged and unusable was something she hadn't even considered. That would suck beyond all rational possibility.

"Wait a minute," she said, something just occurring to her. His words hadn't quite penetrated her groggy, pain-filled brain at first, but now something he'd said really stuck out. "You said they extracted the device from the *first* victim."

"That's right."

"Meaning…"

"Yeah, Sloan. Meaning exactly what you think it means."

Damn. It was Sykes. She didn't have to risk an aneurysm by swinging around to double-check that, she felt the man's presence as he moved into place right behind the bench, dropping his hand onto it, near her shoulder. Not quite touching, but close enough that his fingertips brushed the cloth of her blouse.

He'd obviously come from inside the building; she'd had no idea he was here. He must have finished with his mysterious out-of-town business. Too bad Philadelphia was only forty-five minutes away by helicopter and he'd gotten back fast enough to intercept her before she'd had at least a little time to work on Leanne's chip.

Thrusting aside all that, she asked the obvious. "Are you saying there's been another murder?"

Sykes stepped into place beside the bench, his tall form thankfully blocking the sun from her aching eyes, at least for a moment. Of course, sitting there looking up at him wasn't much better for her head, and might have made it spin a little faster.

"Yes. That's why I was gone. Another O.E.P. test subject was murdered last night in Philadelphia. The methods used by the killer were familiar—disturbingly so. It looks like the cases have to be connected. There are just too many commonalities for it to be a coincidence."

Well, that was a new wrinkle. Ronnie had felt pretty sure that Leanne's murder had been a personal one, that she'd been killed by someone who knew her and wanted to make her suffer. But if another victim had turned up in another city, they'd have to reconsider the theory.

'I'll let you two get to work," said Philip Tate, nodding pleasantly as he pushed his sunglasses back into place. "I'm sure I'll see you later— I'll pop into the lab when I get back to check on how you're getting along."

The guy acted like he was their boss or something. Ronnie managed to grit her teeth and smile faintly, again wondering about the mysteries of the gene pool that would give Phineas Tate a son like this one.

Once they were alone, Sykes murmured, "So, you heard I was going to be back and came up to meet me, huh?" His voice held not the faintest hint of irony. But she knew him well enough to know it was there.

"I had no idea where you went and wasn't going to wait around for you."

"Like I didn't wait around for you yesterday?"

Hearing an almost offended note in his voice, she peered at him, trying to remember exactly what he'd said yesterday, about what he was doing and where he was going. "You mean you *did?*"

"Of course I did," he snapped. "I told you I wasn't snaking your case. We were asked to work on this together. Once you woke up and I confirmed you'd be fine and able to get back to work soon, I put off going either to your precinct to examine the vic's downloads, or here to check out the chip." He dropped onto the bench beside her, sitting close enough for their legs to brush. He invaded her personal space, not threatening, but intimate. As if knowing she was still a little unsteady and woozy, he put a hand on her arm, just above the elbow, holding her firmly but not tightly. "What's it gonna take to get you to trust me?"

Hell, he'd have been better off asking what it would take to get her to sleep with him. That she was already considering. Trust wasn't even on the radar. It was a much harder thing for Ronnie to give up than a piece of ass.

"I'm working on it."

"I guess that's the best I can hope for."

"Yeah, it probably is. I have to work with you. That doesn't mean I have to like you."

"You mean you don't?" His lips quirked.

"No, I don't," she snapped, angry at him for taunting her into saying it when they both knew it was a lie.

"You keep telling yourself that, Sloan."

She would. Day and night until Sykes skipped on back up to New York where he belonged and she could work on forgetting him all over again.

He tilted his head, scrunching his brow as if trying to recall something important. "I'm curious, did you ever watch those old Charlie Brown cartoons when you were a kid?"

That question came totally out of left field. She slowly nodded. "Uh...I think so. The Christmas one, maybe."

"Okay."

She waited. He offered no further explanation. Finally, she snapped, "Well? What about them?"

"Oh, nothing, really. I was just thinking of how much you remind me of the character Lucy."

Ronnie thought about it, trying to remember the cartoon. It had been years since she'd seen the old holiday special, and for the life of her she couldn't figure out what he was talking about.

Except, she suddenly remembered what the character looked like. Indignant, she glared at him. "Was that a hair crack? I haven't exactly had time to get it taken care of, you know."

He snickered. "Not even close. I was thinking more along the lines of the way Lucy was always so rotten to Charlie Brown."

"Awww, did I hurt your feelings Charlie?"

He ignored her. "And it was obvious to everyone that she was so abrasive and mean to him because she had such a thing for him."

She could only gawk at him. "That's some ego, Sykes."

He turned to face her on the bench, draping one arm across the back of it, so close to her shoulders she almost felt the weight of it. "When are you gonna admit you've been thinking about me almost nonstop for the past few months?"

She grunted. "When are *you* gonna admit that not every woman's dying to have you?"

"Not every woman," he said. He didn't say anything else. He didn't have to. The words he didn't say hung there loud and clear between them in the silence. *Just you.*

She met his stare, held it, forced herself to remain completely noncommittal. She didn't blink, she barely breathed, utterly determined to brazen-out the moment and not let him know she'd heard those words he didn't say.

Finally, seeing the twinkle in his eyes as he realized she was, essentially, trying to engage him in a staring contest in some effort at domination, she grumbled, "Oh, shut up."

That made him laugh out loud. Damn, he even had a sexy laugh—throaty and warm.

"So are you ever going to fill me in on this second murder?" she asked, shifting a little further away on the bench.

"You told me to shut up."

"Did I ever tell you what we used to call you out in Texas?" she snarled.

"You didn't have to. I heard all about you dubbing me Sucks."

Breezy as always. The jerk. "Look, Sykes, I don't do *banter*. Would you just tell me about the case?"

He nodded. "Sure, let's go inside out of this heat."

"I'm waiting for my partner."

He stiffened, staying right where he was. "Oh."

"I've already heard the good news about our partnership," she said, sounding droll, figuring he was worried about how she'd react to having her partner yanked away from her and this case.

"I had nothing to do with it, Veronica, I swear."

"As if I really thought you could pull those strings to get him reassigned," she said with a disbelieving grunt. "I understand the reasoning behind it. But Daniels doesn't deserve to be totally shut out.

He's an outstanding detective and we can use his help."

"Agreed. So let's let him do what he does best while we handle the O.E.P. device evaluations."

Surprised he'd agreed so readily, she couldn't help eying him suspiciously. Sykes was being very nice—very agreeable. She didn't entirely trust that. She'd seen the man work his charm on people, usually getting whatever he wanted out of them, and couldn't be entirely sure he wasn't setting her up for something. "What do you want in return?"

"Jesus, woman, you really have a suspicious mind," he said, sounding half-rueful and half-offended.

"Where you're concerned, I do. I haven't forgotten the way you manipulated your way right into the lead position of every damned training exercise in Texas."

"You just haven't learned the art of playing nice yet. Didn't your mother ever tell you it's easier to catch flies with honey than with vinegar?"

"Sure. And I asked her why on earth anybody would want to catch flies when it's so much easier to just swat them," she retorted.

Laughter escaped his lips, deep and masculine, and despite herself, she found herself warming to the sound.

"Oh. *You're* here."

She flinched, hearing her partner's voice. Daniels had finally returned from parking the car and he looked none too happy to see Sykes sitting with Ronnie, his arm draped across the back of the bench, nearly touching her shoulders.

"Glad you could join us, Snoopy," Sykes muttered.

Her partner puffed out his chest. Sykes, if anything, sunk a little more comfortably onto the bench beside her.

God, she didn't need this macho boy garbage. She wasn't the damn cheerleader torn between the football player and the motorcycle riding stoner. Right now, they were both getting on her nerves tremendously.

"Let's go," she snapped, immediately rising to her feet.

She wished she hadn't. Her equilibrium was off and she swayed. Sykes launched up beside her, putting a hand in the small of her back to steady her. "Easy Sloan."

"I'm fine," she insisted.

"Do you think we should get her a wheelchair?" Daniels asked, his animosity disappearing as real concern took over.

"No way are you putting me in a wheelchair," she said, not even wanting to consider the possibility of the two of them joining forces against her. "I just stood up too fast. I'm fine. Now let's go inside and get to work."

Not sparing either of them another word or glance, she shook off Sykes's hand, pushed past Daniels, and walked steadily into the building, using every ounce of will she had to avoid letting them know that her entire world was spinning just a tiny bit off its axis.

Chapter 9

Although the Tate Scientific Research Center was a secure site, where experiments of a top secret nature were performed, security wasn't too bad. It only took a few minutes to go through the metal detectors, explain a few resulting beeps, show her I.D., tell who she was and why she was here, then she was through.

Sykes and Daniels were still jumping through the hoops, at two different ends of the security checkpoint, as if they couldn't even stand to be in the same line together. She'd have thought it would be an easy matter for Sykes to come back in, since he'd obviously been here a while, but they made him go through the whole procedure again.

For the first time since she'd found out, she decided it was probably a good thing Daniels had been temporarily reassigned while she worked with Sykes on this case. Cops were used to having one partner. They trained that way, to work as a pair, to think as a pair. Throwing a third person in the mix was a professional triangle she didn't want to tackle.

As far as a personal one? Well, that she didn't even want to consider in the realm of possibility. Daniels was her partner, friend, and surrogate big brother, sometimes seeming like a pseudo replacement for the two she'd lost. Sykes was a cocky competitor who attracted her and confused her too much for her own good. So both of them were best steered-clear of.

Steering clear, of course, was impossible. She needed them both. While she was less than 100% well, she couldn't possibly rely on her senses and judgment alone to examine the data from the murder victims' downloads or O.E.M. chips. Sykes had to be involved. Yes, she'd rather just keep working with Daniels, but he wasn't trained the way Jeremy was. So if she wanted to be involved with this case, it didn't seem like she had any other choice. She *had* to work with Sykes.

Still, she mentally reaffirmed her decision to call on Daniels whenever she could, both because it was the right thing to do, and because she knew she could count on him. This case might be important to the O.E.P., but it was also important to the D.C.P.D. And while computer imaging and high-tech video capture might help, nothing beat good old-fashioned detective work, and Mark Daniels was the best detective she knew.

Not waiting for them, she walked toward the reception desk, a broad expanse of black marble which extended across the entire width of the lobby. Several uniformed workers stood behind it—security guys and administrative types—and they all smiled pleasantly as she approached. She hadn't even reached it, though, before she heard someone calling her name.

"Detective Sloan!"

All those people behind the reception desk snapped to attention, their vague smiles becoming wide, their obsequiousness undeniable. The boss had arrived, stepping out of a nearby elevator as if he were Jesus coming down from heaven in a boxcar.

"You poor dear, I heard about what happened, what on earth are you doing here, child?"

Phineas Tate, looking like a skinny, overprotective grandfather, hurried to her side.

"I'm fine, sir, thank you."

He shook his head, tutted and clucked over her, insisting on pulling her hair out of the way so he could see her wound. He poked and prodded, clucking a little. Christ, she felt like she had when she was a kid and her mom would spit on a napkin to clean her face.

"I still can't believe you're here when you should be home in bed."

"I really am okay. We have a case to solve, Dr. Tate, and it would take a lot more than a whack on the head to keep me from solving it."

"Well said," he told her with an approving nod. When Sykes and Daniels joined them, he greeted them both by name.

"Good to see you, sir," said Sykes, extending his hand. "I've just come from Detective Sloan's precinct and have the files from the victim's data dump."

Ronnie cast him a suspicious look.

"I said I haven't examined them," he insisted. "They refused to send them electronically since they're evidence, so I stopped by and picked them up to bring here, figuring this is where you'd come first."

She could probably have accessed the files remotely, though it might not have been technically above-board. And Sykes was all about being above-board...at least, so she assumed. She guessed she would find out for sure in the coming days.

"And you, Detective Daniels," said Tate, "has any of this excitement caused you to have any second thoughts regarding your involvement in this…experiment?"

"You mean, as a detective?"

"No." Tate lowered his voice, though no one was nearby and all of Tate's staff were busy trying to look occupied. "I mean as an implantee."

Daniels shook his head once. "Not a bit. In fact, after Ronnie was attacked the other night, I sent over my own downloads in case the device caught anything my eyes missed."

"I know. Thank you for that. We did have an in-house person look at them and he found nothing." Tsking, Tate turned to lead them toward the bank of elevators. "Do you have any other leads?"

Daniels shook his head, taking up the rear as they entered a huge, mirrored elevator. "Like I told Ronnie, our friend's a damn ghost. I don't know how he's getting around without being seen."

"I can't stop thinking about those old tunnels," Ronnie murmured. "They were supposed to be completely demolished during reconstruction. But you know, it's always possible there could still be access to one. There've been stories about secret tunnels involving the White House and the Metro system going back to the Truman era, maybe they overlooked something. "

Her partner nodded. "Right there with ya. I've requested another meeting with Jack Williams, of the Phoenix Group, of course he hasn't called me back. I also have a call in to the lead architect in charge of the White House and he's even harder to reach. But I'll keep pushing until I've got everything they have on the project."

"Are they stalling?" Tate sounded shocked.

She found that refreshing, that someone could still be surprised about the ass-covering that went on in a situation like this one. Tate obviously lived in his lab and didn't know a whole lot about how the real world worked.

Daniels merely smirked. "Like an old gas-guzzler on the freeway."

"That's shameful," Tate said.

"Maybe they didn't overlook anything," Ronnie mused. "Just because they *said* the tunnels would be destroyed—because that's the way the public demanded it—doesn't mean it's what actually happened. They could have secretly rebuilt one or more of them."

The government was all about secrets these days. She could definitely see that happening. The country didn't want the reminder of how vulnerable they'd been; but since the president would never actually live in the White House, mightn't the CIA, the Secret Service, or somebody have fought to preserve the historically significant pre-10/20/17 tunnels? Not just for security, but perhaps as some weird, twisted kind of memorial to be used sometime in the future.

She could almost see it as a tourist attraction. *Here, ladies and gentleman, was where a team of terrorists detonated the first high-tech device; the one that turned the Oval Office into a round pile of cement and rebar, burying President Turner and three members of his cabinet.*

Yeah. That'd bring in the lookie-loos.

"That would certainly explain how a head could have remained out of sight for twenty-four hours," Sykes speculated. "And how our unsub could be getting in and out without anybody knowing about it."

Daniels for once seemed to agree with Sykes. "I've pulled maps of the old tunnel system—it woulda been easy for somebody to get out and blend with the crowd pretty quickly on the 4th."

"Perhaps I can assist you," said Tate. "If the lead architect is not being forthcoming, I can put in a call to the president. I imagine he would know the truth of the matter and order the full details of the reconstruction be made available."

Daniels, eyes wide and more than a little impressed, slowly nodded. "Uh, yeah, if you could do that, I'd appreciate it."

"Let's go up to my office and I'll call right now."

When they reached the private floor on which Tate's offices and personal labs were located, they all followed the scientist out of the elevator. Just as she'd been the first time she'd come here, she found herself a little turned-off by the obvious grandeur and opulence of the place. Though a high-tech scientific facility, the center boasted some incredible décor that seemed like it would be more appropriate for a gallery or a five-star hotel.

She spotted several pieces of artwork, including a few paintings that looked like genuine Monets—stuff people might have actually gotten to see at the National Gallery in the old days. The carpeting beneath her feet was thick enough to sleep on and the entire exterior of the building was glassed so walking down the hallway toward Tate's office felt like being inside a fishbowl big enough to be seen from space.

There was tasteful, and then there was overdone. This place went a tiny step beyond overdone, venturing into pretentious territory, and she strongly suspected Philip Tate had been the one responsible. Phineas just didn't seem like the type who'd give a damn what hung on the walls as long as he had the best electron microscope in the world.

Inside Tate's office, Ronnie stood in a comfortable seating area, eschewing the plush leather couch. She felt a little too much like a guest and what she wanted was to forget about all the trappings and get into the lab. Still, this side trip would serve one purpose. Neither she nor Daniels had said anything out loud, but they both knew that Sykes's presence here meant there really was no legitimate excuse for him to stay, other than to serve as her chauffeur. And she could just as easily call for someone from the precinct to come up and get her. Or, hell, cab it. So Tate helping her partner get an entrée to do more detective work would be an excellent note upon which they could split up for now.

She, Sykes and Daniels all watched, ears open and mouths closed, as Tate sat behind his desk and reached for the handset of his video phone. He pushed a button.

Twenty seconds later, a face appeared on the monitor.

Holy shit. The guy really *did* have the president of the United States on speed dial. That was him, wearing a T-shirt and a golf cap, having a video conference with Dr. Tate. Bizarre-o.

Their discussion was brief, but cordial. Though she couldn't hear everything the president was saying from across the room, it was easy enough to make out Dr. Tate's side of the conversation. He explained the situation, answered a few of the president's questions, then nodded and hung up.

He laced his fingers together on top of his desk and smiled at Daniels. "You can proceed directly to the Phoenix Group's offices at your earliest convenience, Detective. The president will make sure that Jack Williams is available to you, and will instruct Williams to bring in any other project supervisors or architects you wish to consult."

Daniels walked over and extended his hand to the scientist. "Thank you very much, sir, you've saved me a lot of legwork."

The older man shrugged off the thanks. "Partly selfish of me. I want this project to succeed, of course, and will not stand for obfuscation or territorialism blocking this investigation."

"It won't," Daniels promised. Then he returned to face Ronnie. "I'll keep you posted on how it goes."

"You gonna be able to play nice without me around to referee?"

He snorted. "Since when do you play nice?"

"Good point."

"Call me when you're ready to leave and I'll swing back up and get you home."

"That's not necessary," Sykes said, "I'll take her."

"I brought her up here," Daniels said, his face reddening a little bit.

"Look, I'm not anybody's prom date," she snapped. "I'll get a damn cab."

"I'd be happy to have my personal driver on standby to take Detective Sloan wherever she wishes to go," said Tate, his tone holding the tiniest bit of reproof.

Ronnie thanked the man, shot her partner a last quelling look as he headed for the door, then said, "Okay, where do we work?"

"Let's go to the lab and meet Eileen," said Tate. "She's expecting you and has a work area all set up for you."

Falling into step on either side of the old man, Ronnie and Sykes pressed him for the latest information on the program. Though this was the first real case either of them had worked, there were plenty of other investigators in other major metropolitan cities, so theirs could hardly be the first one altogether. Hearing that theirs were the first test subjects who'd been murdered wasn't a huge surprise. So far, the only other cases being worked around the country had included robberies, petty crimes and domestic abuse. A few test subjects had died, but of natural causes, not murder.

"So it appears you two are the only ones working an active murder case," Tate concluded.

Which just turned up the heat on the stove on which they sat. The pot was already simmering, the longer it took to solve this thing the closer they'd get to boiling over.

"Lucky us," she mumbled.

"Now," said Tate as they reached the elevators and he punched the call button, "tell me about this second victim, Agent Sykes. I have been given only the sketchiest of details."

"Ditto," said Ronnie.

Sykes began to rattle off the facts. "Brian Underwood. Male, age thirty-four, Caucasian. He worked for the Department of Labor in the Office of Public Affairs in Philly. Had an excellent performance record and had just received a promotion."

"Personal life?" asked Ronnie.

"Reportedly a very happy marriage with two young kids and a house in the burbs. Bank accounts all look normal—no red flags.

Friends all say he was the nicest guy in the world and didn't have a single known enemy."

"Huh," Ronnie said, not quite trusting that. Everybody always said the deceased was the greatest guy in the world at first, while the shock of a murder was still on them. Later, when the numbness wore off and it didn't seem quite so disrespectful to dish about the dead, his friends and co-workers would spill their guts. They'd find out the dude had a skeleton or two in his closet, of that she had no doubt.

The elevator arrived and they boarded it, heading for a higher floor on which this highly-regarded Dr. Cavanaugh worked. Another employee was already aboard and immediately launched into a conversation with Dr. Tate, who answered his questions with patience and intelligence.

Now feeling more than a little tired and still ever-so-slightly dizzy, Ronnie edged close to the side wall of the mirrored elevator. Trying to be surreptitious, she leaned her shoulder against it, thankful for the support.

Of course, Sykes noticed. The damn man noticed everything. A concerned frown creased his brow. His voice lowered, he asked, "Are you all right?"

"I'm fine."

"If you're not up to it, I don't mind starting this on my own. I'm assuming by your occasional grimaces that you have a headache the size of Mount Rainier, and by the way you've been swaying when you walk that you feel a little bit off-balance."

"I said I'm fine," she snapped, jerking herself upright. And instantly regretting it when the elevator started to spin.

He immediately moved closer, sliding an arm around her waist to steady her. Part of her wanted to slap his hand away, another sincerely appreciated the support. The most traitorous part of her liked his nearness a little too much.

"You're not totally fine, Veronica," he murmured, gentle concern lacing his voice.

It got to her, that gentleness, that worry, when accusation might not have. The brush of his fingertips on the small of her back distracted her, as did the warmth of his exhalations as he leaned close to speak softly, as if he'd already realized that to argue with her was one sure way to make her push herself even harder.

"Please don't overdo it. If you need to take the rest of today off in order to be up for working tomorrow, then do it. Because as much as

I'd like to see you go home and stay in bed for an entire week, I need you too much."

Those words landed in her brain in a mixed jumble. Him needing her, being in bed for a week. Whoa. That caused a seriously dangerous juxtaposition of images.

"I promise not to solve these murders without you. Or at least to pretend you were indispensable to my investigation," he said, obviously trying to tease her into a better humor.

"Cocky jerk."

"Stubborn female."

She had been accused of being stubborn on occasion but she certainly didn't like to think that one personality trait defined her. Though determined, she wasn't stupid.

Sykes had a point—she wouldn't be any use to anybody if she pushed herself too hard and sidelined herself for a week. So she forced herself to calmly evaluate the situation and consider the options. She straightened her back, lifted her shoulders, flexed her fingers, shifted her hips, turned her head, gauging how every movement affected her.

Wince, wince, wince, wince, cringe.

Wincing was no big deal. Cringing she could survive.

She could do this. Her head might feel like she'd out-drunk an entire football team last night, but otherwise, she was fine. A cold glass of water and a comfortable chair would do her wonders.

"You're right, I'm not feeling great."

Jeremy reached out to punch a button on the elevator, but she grabbed his hand and stopped him.

"That said, I'm not at death's door, either. I do not intend to push myself back into a hospital bed. So once we get to our work space, I promise I'll sit down and take it easy. Just get me there, okay?"

"Do you promise you'll let me know if it gets to be too much?"

"I do. And thanks for your concern."

"Hey, we're partners now, at least for a little while."

That felt so strange, like she was a wife cheating on her husband, that she didn't reply. Fortunately, she didn't have to. The fourth occupant of the elevator got off, leaving just her, Sykes and Tate again.

Sykes stepped away from her, turning his body a little, to face the elderly doctor, but keeping his hand pressed very lightly against her spine. Just that tiny hint of support gave her everything she needed right now.

"I apologize for the interruption," Tate said.

"Not a problem." Sykes returned to their previous conversation. "Now, back to our Philadelphia victim?"

"Yes, please."

"Apparently Underwood and some friends went to a co-workers apartment after work to play cards and celebrate his promotion. He left at a little after eleven, alone."

"May I ask the, er, means of death?" Tate murmured.

"He was decapitated. Most of his body was found on the ground in a back alley."

Though she suspected she knew what he meant, Ronnie couldn't help asking, "Most?"

"The head was sitting on top of a garbage can behind an Italian bakery with a rotten cannoli stuffed in its mouth."

"Such an exhibitionist," she muttered.

Having had her own run-in with a disembodied head, she could imagine how the person who'd found that one had reacted. Hopefully he or she didn't have a concussion to show for their gruesome interaction.

"The owner came in at five this morning to get the day's baking started and found Underwood staring at her from the trash pile. She flipped out, ran right out to the nearest city street for help and got hit by a garbage truck."

Ronnie slowly shook her head. Okay, so there were worse things than a concussion. Garbage truck trumped two-by-four any day.

Sykes added, "They think she's going to make it."

With lots of scars and horrible memories, undoubtedly. She had to wonder if their killer had been hoping that would be the case. Obviously he got off on displaying his kills in shocking ways, liking the pageantry and drama of it. Leanne had been scattered all over a basement, and her head disposed of on another floor altogether. This Philadelphia victim had been dumped like…well, like garbage. It was simply twisted.

They reached the twenty-second floor. Dr. Tate gestured toward the door as it opened.

Stepping out, Ronnie said, "So there's a lot of showmanship."

"Very much so," Sykes said, following her out.

"Can you do any FBI woo-woo profiler magic to help us out with this guy?"

"You know as well as I do that I'm not a profiler. But, off the top of my head, I'd say he's smart—though probably not as smart as he thinks he is. He wants to be recognized, there's definitely an element of 'look at me!' to these murders, not only because he likes the attention, but it's as if he's saying, 'I know you can't catch me.'"

"That's what he thinks."

"That ego is probably what will trip him up."

"Fascinating," said Dr. Tate, who'd been listening silently to the conversation. "I suppose I never really considered the perpetrator to be anything other than a madman."

"Oh, he's nuts all right," said Ronnie, not doubting it. "This isn't a run-of-the-mill killer who's killing to accomplish a specific purpose. He's getting off on it."

"Horrible," the old man said, shaking his head delicately, as if his sensibilities were truly offended by the whole thing. She supposed his reserved, secluded, scientific mind didn't usually have to think about things like that.

They turned a corner and headed down a long hallway lined with closed laboratory doors on either side. Occasionally one opened and a white-coated technician or researcher scurried out, only to stop and suck up to the boss before moving on. The building seemed to go on forever, she honestly couldn't imagine how much the government had invested in it. Of course, given the miraculous things coming out of it—and out of the head of Dr. Tate—she suspected they were getting their money's worth.

Sykes cleared his throat. "Once the I.D. chip identified Brian Underwood as an O.E.P. participant, I guess they got in touch with you, Dr. Tate?"

"Indeed."

"Then I got called in and went up to nose around. The M.E.'s doing an autopsy this afternoon and said he'd call me with the results. I figured once I had his chip and most recent downloads—which I do—there wasn't much else I could do there and came back here to get to work on them." Though his lips didn't twitch, a small twinkle appeared in his blue eyes as he added, "I didn't want Detective Sloan to think I wasn't just as anxious to get started working with her as she is with me."

If a nice, genteel old man hadn't been with them, she might have snapped back a nice, genteel *fuck you*. But probably not. She and Sykes had formed some kind of truce. She wouldn't go nose-to-nose with him again until she felt a whole lot better.

They had apparently reached their destination at last, because Tate stopped in front of a locked door with a high-tech identification panel on one side. He held his arm under a bar code reader, which I.D.'d his chip, then went a step further and put his hand on a palm-reader, which further confirmed his identification, and the lock automatically clicked open.

"High-tech security," Sykes said.

Tate nodded, pushed a few buttons and said, "Might as well get you two cleared through so you can access the building by yourselves. I know you might need to work odd hours when there aren't always people around."

He gestured toward the panel and nodded at Ronnie.

"Just my palm?"

"Yes. I've already entered your chip information—actually, my assistant did that before you got here. That will get you inside the building. But in order to get into Dr. Cavanaugh's labs, you must take this further step."

Wondering if they were figuring out how to spin straw into gold behind this door, considering they acted like they were guarding Fort Knox, Ronnie did as he asked and pressed her palm against the screen. It flashed twice, a red button lit up, then it turned green and beeped.

"All done," Tate said. "Now, Agent Sykes?"

Sykes did the same thing. Afterward, gave her a thumbs up, grinning, as if to silently congratulate them both on having made it into the super-exclusive smart guy's club.

They stepped through the door, but rather than proceeding down yet another corridor, Tate hesitated. "It appears, Detective Sloan, that I might owe you an apology."

"What for?"

"In the briefing the other day, I believe I—what is the expression, steamrolled?—over your suggestion that the killer could have something to do with the project itself."

Oh, yeah. He had.

"I was convinced the first victim had violated her security clearance. But this new crime obviously changes things."

It certainly did. Because with the proximity, the histories of the victims, the lack of any connection between them other than the O.E.P., the brutality, and the head-games—emphasis on head—it seemed their murder cases had to be connected. Which made it far more likely that someone with access to the files of the entire program had to be involved. Otherwise, how could anybody know about them both?

A little excited at this admission, Ronnie asked, "So how much does that help us? I mean, how many people could there be who'd have that kind of information?" They could have narrowed down their list of potential suspects to a handful of people, which would make things a whole lot simpler.

"Well, between my staff, government folks, those involved in the training, the medical and technical professionals dealing with each individual involved...perhaps a few hundred."

Hundreds. Crap. Still, it was better than the entire populations of Washington or Philadelphia.

"I wish it were that small a suspect pool," said Sykes, sighing.

She tensed, realizing Sykes was about to make the prospects a little dimmer.

"We have to consider the possibility that the program files have been compromised. Our killer might not have come by his knowledge of the O.E.P. legitimately. Hackers could have gotten into the records."

"Oh, I shouldn't think that possible," said Tate, though he sounded a little doubtful.

"Considering how much of a target you had on your back after the I.D. chip program was implemented a few years ago, I'm sure there are people out there trying to break into your systems or maybe even offering money to your employees to give them data."

The old man sputtered, but he couldn't deny it.

Speaking kindly, Sykes continued. "Some anti-medical-technology terrorists might now be staging a new, more violent kind of protest against your inventions."

Ronnie hated to admit it, but that idea made a lot of sense. Tate had been vilified by a lot of people because of the chip implantation law. He had enemies all over the place.

So their suspect pool might be a whole lot bigger than the populations of Washington and Philadelphia combined. In fact, the killer—or killers—could be just about anyone in the entire country.

When they were introduced to Dr. Eileen Cavanaugh, Ronnie immediately began forming impressions of the other woman, who looked to be in her mid-thirties. Her handshake was firm, and she seemed friendly enough, insisting that they call her Eileen since they were going to be working in close proximity for a while.

That should make Sykes happy, because the woman was drop-dead gorgeous. Wearing glasses that gave her a brainy-sexy-teacher look, and a lab coat that did nothing to hide her ample curves, the blonde looked more like a stripper dressed up in costume than an actual scientist. If Daniels were here, he'd probably be tripping over his own drooling tongue right now. Sykes was always a little more circumspect and even he took a second look.

The other thing she noticed—the woman appeared insanely devoted to her boss. In fact, from the moment Dr. Tate led Ronnie and Sykes into the secure area, Dr. Cavanaugh had hovered over the old man, fussing over him like she was his daughter or his nurse. She'd smoothed his jacket, straightened his tie, asked if he'd eaten a good, healthy lunch. Noting Dr. Tate's long-suffering expression, Ronnie had the feeling he was well used to his protégé's overprotectiveness.

"Well, I assume you've heard that the Carr device was damaged?" the woman asked once she'd gotten Dr. Tate comfortably situated in a chair.

"We've heard," Ronnie said. "Have you had any luck recovering anything?"

"Just about. There are a few patches of data I couldn't reconstruct, though they were from earlier in the day, not the attack itself." The woman made a face. "Which was terribly gruesome."

"No kidding."

"Obviously the attack occurred in an area that was quite dark, so the images aren't the best. I've done what I could to brighten them. I think you'll be pleased." She turned toward Sykes, and her voice might have warmed up the tiniest bit. Her gaze definitely took a quick trip over his tall, broad form. "I hear you have something for me?"

Yeah, and she looked as though she'd like to get something from Sykes all right. Ronnie's jaw tightened the tiniest bit. To give him credit, he didn't respond to or even acknowledge the flirtatious gambit.

"I do." He lifted his briefcase, setting it on a high metal table. Opening it, he retrieved a small plastic sample case, in a sealed evidence bag. "The M.E. in Philadelphia didn't like having to just sign this over to me. He was territorial, and, I suspect, more than a little fascinated."

"I'm sure he was," she replied.

But probably not fascinated enough to risk prison by tampering with the device, or making any illegal backups of its content. The moment the murder victim's I.D. chip was scanned, an urgent notice would have come up to contact Dr. Tate's office and not proceed with any further examination. The M.E. would have been told exactly how to retrieve the device, and who to give it to. Beyond that, he'd be left wondering what the hell he'd just been a part of, even as he was warned under threat of prosecution against ever speaking about it to anyone.

Cloak and dagger stuff, these scientific experiments.

Sykes showed Ronnie a micro-drive. "Here are Ms. Carr's backups, everything until early on the morning of her death. Your lieutenant says he hopes I'm showing you this at the hospital because if you really went through with your threat to check-out early, he's going to be very unhappy."

Ronnie eyed the drive, noting that he wasn't handing it over, and grunted. "He's never happy."

Sykes held up another small drive. "I also have Underwood's. Now we just need somewhere to look at them."

"I've set up a workspace for you both back here. All the files from the Carr chip are already loaded on your system, Detective Sloan," Eileen said, turning to lead them into a small room nearby. Inside were two work-stations, set up back-to-back. Both had what looked like state-of-the-art computer systems. She recognized the on-screen logo that would launch the O.E.P.I.S. program, her mind already clicking as she recalled all she'd learned during training.

Remembering something else they'd learned about in training, Ronnie immediately looked up at the ceiling, intensely curious. Spying two small, camera-like devices, she sucked in a surprised breath. Directly beneath them, on the floor, were two flat, three-by-three white squares, that looked almost like floor mats. Each one had a line of tiny, blue lights around its entire edge.

And each probably cost the lifetime salary of an average cop to create.

"You did it," she whispered, a little stunned, not believing they'd have taken the technology quite so far, quite so soon. It had sounded so science fiction'y when they'd been told about it in Texas, and she'd figured the final product would be years away from completion.

"Yes, we've finished it," Dr. Cavanaugh said, obviously proud.

Tate clarified. "It's still in the testing phase. We thought we'd see how well it works for our top two O.E.P. investigators."

"Cool," said Jeremy, sounding like an excited kid.

She didn't echo the word, but she definitely shared the sentiment.

When they'd been in Texas, and had discussed how to best experience the O.E.P. memories of a subject, they'd been told that Dr. Tate's labs were working on a new projection system for use exclusively with this project. Images that appeared one way on a small computer screen could be interpreted quite differently when life-size. They'd learned in training that when trying to walk through someone else's visual memories, it was best to do it as literally as possible—almost to the point of really *walking* through.

This new system would allow them to do exactly that.

Rather than flashing the images on a standard monitor, or even on a large wall screen, a state-of-the-art projector suspended from the ceiling would cast down a chip's images to a receiving pad on the floor. Together, the projector and the pad were designed to build a three dimensional pictorial experience.

It could be viewed from outside.

Or experienced from inside.

If she stepped on that pad, she would be inside the picture. The outside world would disappear, the projection would surround her, a 360 degree panorama with the computer system using the data from all the O.E.P. chip images to fill in entire vistas.

She would be completely inside the chip implantees visual memories.

Inside murder victim Leanne Carr's death.

She swallowed hard, thinking about that. She wasn't sure she would be up to walking in the woman's footsteps for those final minutes of her life. It had sounded brilliant in theory, but in practice—having pieced together what that horrific experience had been like for the young woman—it seemed a whole lot more awful.

"You don't have to utilize all aspects of the program," Dr. Tate said. He eyed her kindly, as if realizing exactly what she was thinking. "Beholding the deeply fleshed-out images from a few feet away should still be every bit as effective."

Dr. Cavanaugh scrunched her brow in confusion. "But what's the point of that? We have the capability, why not dive in and experience it all the way it's meant to be experienced."

Sykes stepped closer to Ronnie, dropping a hand onto her shoulder as he answered. "Stepping on that thing to pretend you're on the slopes at Aspen or that you're hang-gliding above the Grand Canyon is one thing. Given what happened to our victims, I'm sure you can understand our reluctance."

Whether he truly was reluctant, or just backing her play, she didn't know. Either way, she appreciated it. And Sykes was right. This new invention would probably be a huge financial success when they went public with it and offered it as a video gaming option. But there were some things that would be incredibly hard to experience in such a lifelike fashion. Death, among them.

"Oh, of course," said Dr. Cavanaugh, her face reddening.

"Use it as much or as little as you like," said Tate. "If it's too intense, you can always go back to the traditional monitors."

She doubted she'd have to go that far, and figured she had the stamina to stand a few feet away from that high-tech floor mat and watch the rapid progression of images before her, in 3-D, seeing them just the way Leanne Carr had, though not exactly being inside them.

Or, okay, maybe she'd be sitting. She wouldn't forget her deal with Sykes.

Dr. Cavanaugh quickly ran over some operating instructions, which seemed simple enough. Everything was controlled by each work station and they could segue back and forth between the projection system and the screen at the flick of a button.

"Thank you," said Sykes once the scientist had finished explaining. "I think we're probably ready."

"Excellent," said Tate. "Dr. Cavanaugh will get to work on the Philadelphia chip while you two get started. If there's anything you need, one of her staff members will be happy to assist you."

His young protégé holding Dr. Tate's arm, as if he were the one who'd recently been whacked in the head with a club, the two scientists left the room, leaving her alone with Jeremy Sykes. And with the pictures of Leanne Carr's final moments on this earth.

She just needed to decide: Was she going to view them?

Or live them?

Chapter 10

As soon as they were alone, Sykes turned around, went back out into the hallway, to a water cooler right outside the door. He yanked a paper cup from it, filled it up and returned with it. Pressing it into her hands, he then pulled a chair into place behind her and gently pushed her into it.

"Better?"

She sipped the icy water and relaxed into the chair. "Better," she said. "I don't feel quite as much like throwing up or falling over anymore."

"I'd like to think I make you weak in the knees, Sloan, but I doubt it's *all* due to me."

"Gee, how modest of you."

"That's me, I'm a humble guy."

She snorted.

"Well, I'm at least a guy who knows the difference between a woman with a concussion and one who's attracted to me."

Hmm. Was there a difference? It bore considering.

"Because, while your mad crush on me could explain the weak legs, no way do I make you want to throw up

"Mad crush? What, are we in high school?" she said with a definite eye-roll. The man was too damned cocky to be believed. "That's some ego you've got. Get me that trash can, I think I *am* gonna be sick now."

"Be sick later," he said, pushing her chair toward her work station so she could see the files already listed on the screen. "Now we have work to do."

He was right. They did have work to do. And while she'd let the potential of Tate's new imaging system distract her for a moment, just seeing the long list of time-stamped images from Leanne Carr's O.E.P. chip made her want to dive right in.

So she dove. Her fingers flying on the keyboard, she began pulling up files, unable to resist the urge to do what she was not supposed to do—go right for the time of death. Yes, she'd been trained to be methodical and precise, to establish a baseline of a subject's interactions, to start at the beginning of every day. But this was a murder. If Leanne had gotten a clear look at her attacker's face, this whole thing could be solved within the next couple of minutes.

She doubted she'd be that lucky. Were they dealing with a terrorist or crazy psycho killer who did not know Leanne was an O.E.P. test subject, he wouldn't have thought to conceal his face from his own victim. But with the second killing, it looked very likely that he did know.

Likely, but not absolutely certain. Hell, perhaps Sykes was right and it was somebody who'd hacked into some of Tate's files. Maybe he had no idea what the O.E.P. really was and wouldn't even realize he was being recorded. It was worth a shot, anyway.

She cast a quick peek over her shoulder at Jeremy and realized Mr. Perfect was scrolling down his own screen at a rapid fire pace. He didn't have the final day's images from his victim—he'd just given that tiny chip to Dr. Cavanaugh—but he had the man's downloads from probably a couple of weeks preceding his murder. Sykes was scanning through them, obviously ruling out entire days' worth of memories, his frustration probably mounting as he waited for Dr. Cavanaugh to give him the files from the victim's last day.

In just a brief glance, Ronnie saw the same faces of two adorable children—one just an infant—and her heart clenched. Brian Underwood was a man who had loved his children; that was evident in every tender stroke of his gaze upon their sweet little faces.

Who had Leanne Carr loved?

Ronnie's suspicions still raised by the woman's boss, she couldn't help being curious about Leanne's earlier downloads, which would reveal so much about her life in the days leading up to her death. Even if she found the face of the killer in Leanne's final visual memories, Ronnie would still likely have to go back to the days, weeks, possibly months preceding it in order to try to find a motive, or discover how the victim's path had first crossed her killer's.

There was much to do. But starting at the end was a lure that proved utterly irresistible.

"You're skipping most of the day and going straight to her last minutes, right?" Jeremy asked, not even looking back at her. As if he had eyes in the back of his head.

"You read my mind."

He spun around in his chair. "Hey, you're an open book."

God, she hoped not. "You think it's a bad idea?"

"Hell, no, I'd be doing the same thing. Getting inside the victim's head and figuring out who they were and why they might have been targeted is all well and good but nothing would beat a high-res jpeg of the face of the sick bastard who killed them."

She breathed a sigh of relief, glad Sykes was willing to skirt the rules this time.

"So, do you want to share?" he asked. "Let me take a peek too?"

"I'll scratch your back if you scratch mine." Before he could make some flirtatious remark in response, she put a hand up, palm out. "I mean, I show you mine now, you show me yours later."

Shit. From the frying pan into the fire. *Why* did Jeremy Sykes turn her into an idiot? The men she regularly chewed up for lunch and spat out for dinner would be laughing their heads off to see her almost subconsciously playing sexy word games, with which she was completely unfamiliar. Ronnie had always been the blunt, get-to-the-point type. If she wanted sex with someone, she simply told them, made sure there were no pesky diseases involved, and let the chips—and pants—fall where they may. But with Sykes, she found herself dancing around this sky-high *thing* between them, as nervous as a virgin at a frat party. It was stupid. And it pissed her off.

"I'll hold you to that," Sykes said with a chuckle. That dimple in his cheek flashed, but to give him credit, he didn't go any further. Thank goodness. "Yours first. Later, we'll do mine, then run them on a split screen and see if we notice any similarities."

"Good plan. Do you think the last ten minutes will be enough?" she asked.

"I read the autopsy report. You really think she still had her eyes open eighty minutes in?"

"She could have died with them open. A picture of the bastard's face might have been captured as she drew her last breath."

"It's worth a shot—we can always back up."

Okay. Ten minutes it was. Ten minutes of hell, she had no doubt.

Ronnie tensed, unable to control the tiniest hint of unease. If watching the final hours of a death row inmate had been difficult, how would it be with a murder victim, a nice, pretty young woman whose biggest crime might have been having a secret boyfriend? Not just that, they'd be watching them life-size, in all their three-dimensional evil.

Sight was such a personal, intimate thing. Part of the brilliance of Dr. Tate's chip was that it almost seemed able to convey the emotional response of the implantee, to make his or her feelings come alive for whoever saw the pictures later. The panicked shifting of attention back-and-forth between objects heightened tension and built fear. A long, covetous stare so easily displayed want or desire. A tender gaze on a beloved face was soft and unmistakable. Tears not only blurred the vision but evoked such regret, such sadness, it was enough to make her eyes sting.

There was no way to remain impersonal in this job. No way to view these as crime scene photos, taken hours later after the heat of the crime had cooled and the victim's soul, if there was such a thing, had long since departed. There would be no CSI crew, no rookies putting up yellow tape, no witnesses clamoring to tell the tale, no jaded cops cracking jokes while secretly feeling queasy. This was just victim and predator.

And Ronnie and Sykes. They would be *in* this—in Leanne's head, in Leanne's murder—the moment they started to watch, whether they stepped onto that mat or not. It was the ultimate voyeurism, the mind rape of a dead woman.

It's also your job and it's the best chance for justice that woman's got. So stop the mental hand-wringing and get to it.

She set up the projector, remembering Dr. Cavanaugh's instructions.

"We're not going inside this first time, right?" Sykes confirmed.

"I don't think so."

"Yeah. I think it would take a lot of mental preparation for that."

"Or a lot of alcohol."

She scrolled to the last ten minutes of Leanne Carr's life, highlighted the entire list of images—six-hundred of them—drew them into a slideshow and set the speed on its slowest setting. For now, she wanted to see each picture individually, to note and interpret each impression. Later, she'd speed things up and watch the events closer to real-time. Obviously, people didn't go through their lives capturing visual images only every second. The human brain processed what the eye saw much faster than that. The average movie, for instance, displayed roughly twenty-four frames per second. So seeing the quickest possible progression of a series of still images recorded from someone's eyes made the experience seem more lifelike—and less like a series of drawings in one of those old-fashioned cartoon flip-books.

For right now, though, the one-by-one approach would be best for noting specific clues. It would also be easier on her, would allow her to build one small wall of separation between herself and the victim, to remind her brain that these were pictures of something that had happened in the past, not something she was truly experiencing right now.

She needed to dip her toe into this icy cold pool of death, not dive into the deep end.

Ronnie grabbed the remote control, then swiveled her chair, too filled with tension to even regret having moved fast enough to jiggle her aching head. Sykes did the same thing, scooting his chair closer to hers until they sat side by side. Ronnie looked at him, silently asking a question, and he nodded that he was ready.

She clicked the *Start* button and the lights in the room immediately went down, the better to see the projected images before them. A pause as tense expectation filled the air, and her heart began to beat in time with each screen change.

The movie of Leanne's mind began.

Dark. So dark. Eyes closed? No. Open. Just dark. Cave-like. Claustrophobic. Terrifying.

Lids half closed.

Blink.

Open.

Images take shape. Glint of green. Exit sign nearby. The only light. It's enough.

Shadows. Stillness. Nothing moves. Alone. Abandoned.

On the ground. On her back. Looking up. Rough ceiling. Bare bulb. Unlit. Wires. Pipes. Sprinkler head. Entrance to stairs. Escape? Impossible. Empty. No help coming.

Picture's blurry. Tear-filled. Red. Blood?

Darkness. Darkness. Darkness. Eyes closed. Darkness. Darkness. Darkness. Darkness.

Eyes open. New image. Head turned. Concrete block. The wall. Pale. Chalky surface. Eerie. Ghostlike. Rough.

Spots on it. Blood. Her blood. Leanne's blood. So much blood. Turn away. Look away. Don't look. Blink. Don't look. Blink. Can't stop. Must look. Must understand?

Eyes close.

Darkness. Darkness. Darkness. Darkness.

Open. Light. Exit sign. Focus on it. Light in the dark. A glimmer of hope.

No. No hope. No exit. No escape. No rescue. No chance.

Eye movement slow. Lethargic. Death is near.

Head turns. Slow motion. Inch by inch. Hurts to move. So much pain.

Back to ceiling. Spot on ceiling. Water stain on ceiling. Why water stain on ceiling? Her blood on ceiling?

Eyes close. Darkness. Darkness. Darkness. Darkness. Darkness.

Eyes open. Hand lifted off floor. Staring at hand. Twitching finger. One twitching finger. Others gone. Bloody stumps. Just…gone.

Finger pointing. Pointing. Hand raised. Pointing. At what? Staring. What is it?

Tools. Left behind. Construction tools. Workers tools. Heavy equipment. Circular saw. Jackhammer. Lathe. Use them? Did he use them? Cut her with them? Tools of torture? No. They're not bloody. So why the pointing? Takes effort to point. Such effort. Such pain. Still pointing. Why? Why? Blood dripping. Bloody stumps. Why?

Gaze jerks. Frantic looks. Back. Forth. Back. Forth. Stairs. Ceiling. Is he coming back? Where was he? Is this the end? Will he finish it now?

Darkness. Darkness. Darkness. Hide in the darkness. Squeeze eyes shut. Don't look. Don't see. Don't let it be true. Darkness. Darkness. Darkness.

Eyes open. Slowly. Reluctantly.

Have to look. Have to see. Have to study. Have to leave a clue.

Stairs. Ceiling. Light. Light. Bright. Oh, God, bright light. Blinding.

On his head. Why does his head glow? A helmet. Miner's helmet. Bright flashlight. Whiting out the world..

Eyes narrow. Close. Darkness. Darkness. Darkness. Darkness. Darkness.

Sliver of light. Trying to see. Trying to peek. Must see. Capture his image. Capture his face. Name her killer.

Squinting. Down low. The floor. Away from the light. Protect eyes from the light. Study the feet. Look at the shoes. Dark shoes. Black shoes. Old shoes. Scuffed shoes. Maybe boots? Can't tell. Covered by pants. Dark pants. Black pants. Blood-spattered pants. Long. Hang over shoes.

Eyes shift. Up the legs. Thick legs. Long. Man's legs. Powerful legs. Blood-spattered legs.

Higher. Black shirt. Long. Hangs over pants. Loose. Nondescript. Blends in. Dark in the darkness. Black in the blackness.

Hands. Such powerful hands. Black gloves. Leather. Soft. Wet. Dripping wet. Dripping red. Blood droplets falling.

Her blood. Life falling away. Drop by drop.

Higher. Look higher. The face. The face. The face.

The light! Oh, God the light. Hurts..

Eyes close. Light still stabs. Flashing. Flashbulbs? Camera? Pain. Pain. Terror. Pain.

Open again. He's kneeling. Face invisible. That damn light!

But hands. Hands are visible. Hands are holding something.

A saw. God help me, a saw. He's going to use a saw.

Going to cut and saw and split and tear and gash and rupture and gouge and rip and rend and hurt and hurt and hurt and hurt and hurt.

Tears. Blood. Head moving. Back. And forth. And back. And forth.

No. No. No. Please, no. No. Please. Please.

God. Help me. Let me die. Let it end. Please.

Eyes close.

Darkness. Darkness. Darkness. Darkness. Darkness. Darkness. Darkness. Darkness.

Nothing but darkness.

The eyes never reopen.

The system knowing the show was over, the room lights came back up as soon as the last 3-D image disappeared from the projection pad.

For a long time after the slideshow ended, Ronnie just sat in the chair, inhaling—slowly. Exhaling—slowly. Reminding her heart to beat. Telling her lungs to send oxygen out to all the cells of her body. Ordering her tear ducts to hold tight. Trying to remind herself that she was alive, that the terror wasn't hers, that the thoughts hadn't been hers, the fear, the pain, the anguish, the sadness, the nightmare hadn't been hers.

But oh, God, had it felt like she'd owned it. She had lost herself in those images, had imagined thoughts and feelings and pleas, not sure if she was making them up in her head, empathizing or somehow channeling things Leanne had really thought and felt and said.

Those fingers. That bloody hand. The agony, the effort it must have taken to hold it up.

She couldn't conceive of it. Couldn't even imagine what other parts of Leanne Carr had already been brutally cut off before that point. Had her feet been gone yet? Her ears? Her breasts?

How could any human being do that to another person—hurt them so much—yet not finish it and bring on the blessed relief of death? As she'd suspected when she'd first heard the forensics report, this sick monster had made a banquet off Leanne's death. He'd savored every last bite of it. He had to have, otherwise there was absolutely no reason to keep her alive for so long.

Sykes was also silent, sitting rigidly in his chair, a muscle flexing in his jaw as he did the same thing she was trying to do: deal with what they'd seen. When she cast a quick peek at him, she noted his lips moving, as if he were mumbling something under his breath. Leaning a bit closer, she heard him reciting numbers. Counting backward, from twenty-nine, to twenty-eight, and on down.

He continued until he reached zero. Then, and only then, did he speak.

"Looks like he was working alone. At least at the end."

Realizing he'd counted back from one hundred in order to bring his emotions under control, she reminded herself to try that trick sometime. He seemed calm, reasonable, even if that tone did contrast sharply with the luminous glint in his blue eyes that made her suspect they'd grown wet during the slideshow.

"He's also big," Sykes added. "Without much background to gauge against, I'd still guess his shoes were at least a size twelve."

She'd caught that, too. "There was one screen where you could see his shoe in relation to the circle of green light cast by the Exit sign. I'm sure we can get Dr. Cavanaugh or one of her people to give us a size on that and we can come up with a pretty close estimate."

"Excellent."

Silence again. Considering, absorbing, thinking.

Packaging. She, at least, was packaging her emotions, parceling out the anger and the grief and putting them into separate compartments in her mind, keeping only the analytical skill and the cop intuition at the forefront.

"The miner's helmet," he said, "was unexpected."

"Very."

Disguising himself all in black had been a good start in obscuring his identity for the camera, but blinding his victim—and the O.E.P. device—with painfully bright light had been a master stroke. He'd been practically invisible behind that light once he'd appeared on the screen.

"That's not the type of thing you'd have lying around in your car. He planned carefully and brought that with him."

"Our job just got a lot harder, didn't it?" she asked. "There's no way he didn't know about the device. I mean, it seemed pretty likely before, but that pretty well confirms it."

"I'm afraid so." Jeremy crossed his arms over his chest. "We're going to have to go back."

"I know."

She didn't swivel her chair and reach for the keyboard, needing just one minute more.

Sykes didn't ask her if she was okay, and she appreciated that. Because only someone without an ounce of humanity would be able to describe themselves as okay after what they'd just seen. She wouldn't be okay for quite a while. But she didn't have to be okay to do her job. She just needed to be vigilant. And observant. And strong.

Finally, when she'd prepared herself as much as she could, she turned her chair and began to build a new slideshow. "I guess we should go all the way back to the beginning."

"Of the day? Or from her arrival at the White House."

"Let's take it from her arrival at work that morning. Something drove her out to Patriot Square. Maybe we'll get lucky and see what made her do it."

And if not, maybe they'd at least be able to see who she'd bumped into when she got there, perhaps catch a glimpse of whoever it was who'd hit her with that stun gun. Ronnie didn't imagine the suspect hadn't caught her by surprise, in an attempt to conceal his identity—he'd certainly taken pains to do so later. But everybody made mistakes. It would just take one slip-up, one reflection in a window, one glimpse of a profile, or a sleeve of a suit or a uniform. Anything.

They began again. This time, Ronnie set the speed a little faster, but clutched the remote controller tightly in her hand so she could pause the sequence if they noted anything important. With several hours worth of images to get through, they didn't need to focus on every individual one, especially those from first thing in the morning.

The room darkened.

Leanne's work day rose out of the floor like a misty memory. Ghosts and wisps of the past gained shape and took form.

And they were right there with her.

Things went fine initially, but at about 9:48 a.m., when Leanne was at her desk, working at the Phoenix Group office, the images blacked out.

Jeremy muttered a curse. "Dr. Cavanaugh said there were spots she was unable to recover."

God, did she hope they didn't lose the conversation, message or phone call that had driven Leanne to her death. No, she didn't expect that they'd be lucky enough to see the name or phone number in a caller

I.D. box from a pivotal call, or see her directed to go out to the site by her boss or someone else she worked with, but it was at least possible.

She fast-forwarded. The scene picked up again about six minutes later. A bathroom shot. Awkward, embarrassing. So intrusive. She sped up. Sykes didn't say a word.

Back in the office. Ten minutes later. Leanne at her desk.

Their victim spends the next half-hour working. They see her hands on her keyboard, typing like a madwoman, jotting notes, answering phones, having conversations with smiling co-workers who pop their heads in her doorway. Busy day, busy woman. Energetic, happy woman from the vibe of these shots.

"They were all excited about the celebration," Ronnie mused.

"I'm sure they were. They'd been working on it a long time."

Eleven a.m. Leanne's boss enters, just as he'd said during the interview. They speak briefly, he smiles broadly. Williams reaches out and puts a hand on her shoulder, his expression earnest. He looks like he is congratulating her. Thanking her. Giving her all the strokes and kudos a good boss would give an excellent employee. There is certainly nothing intimate about the exchange.

"Damn," she muttered. "I'd kind of liked him for this."

"That's Williams? Head of the Phoenix Group?"

"Yes. You haven't met him yet?"

"No, but I read the FBI file on him when I first flew down the other day."

"The FBI has a file on him?"

He raised a brow. "You really think somebody who got the contract to rebuild the White House isn't going to draw some attention?"

"Oh. And he seems on the up and up?"

"Looked that way. Rich, spoiled ex-Senator's son from Florida. His granddaddy founded a multi-national corporation that makes super-exclusive yachts."

That explained a lot.

"He used family money to start his own global construction business. Married more money. Became a big success and then landed this job, supposedly because of his retired daddy's connections in Washington."

"Not exactly the type to slaughter his secretary in the basement of the White House."

"Not on paper, anyway."

She sighed and turned her attention back to the screen.

More chatting. More writing. Printing something out. Leanne ate a yogurt and a banana, eating with one hand while busy continuing to work with the other. A woman Ronnie recognized as a receptionist from her visit to the office the other day popped in. Smiled. Spoke. Waved goodbye.

It was after one now. Time was growing short. *Something* had to happen soon.

Another black-out. This one lasted about six minutes.

When the pictures resume, they show Leanne primping in a hand-mirror, staring at herself as she fixes her makeup, plucking a stray hair, pursing her lips.

"Wonder who she's expecting," Sykes said.

"Or where she's off to."

The smiling victim rubbed lipstick off her teeth. Fluffed her hair.

"Did we miss it?" Ronnie asked, wondering if during that blackout there had been a call from Leanne's mystery-man. Had he asked her to come meet him for some kind of assignation at the White House? Of course, that would mean he had a high security clearance since nobody should have been there at that point.

Unless he'd been using those phantom tunnels.

"I don't know. Maybe she's just getting ready to go to the celebration."

Ronnie checked the time stamp. 12:55. "Maybe. But it's still a little early. Her boss told Daniels he expected her around 1:45."

Not *too* early for her to have left for the big event, but Leanne seemed like the type who would have stayed in the office until the last possible moment, holding down the fort, ready to douse any potential fires. But why else would she be primping if not to leave for the celebration? Could someone be coming up to visit her? Maybe bring her lunch?

Leanne did not get up and leave. Instead, once she'd finished fixing her face, she got back to work, typing up an email. Ronnie was able to pause the screen and read it. Nothing important.

Another blackout began. "Damn it," she muttered.

This one was the longest yet—almost ten minutes.

"Don't panic," Sloan said.

She sipped her water. Not panicking. Well, not too much.

The images returned. No big change. Still busy-work, glances at the wall clock as if Leanne were measuring how long she had until she needed to leave. Or until someone came to see her?

Within a couple of frames, she realized Leanne's phone must have rung.

She reaches for it. It's the one on her desk, a typical hand-set, with no caller I.D. display.

Ronnie paused the slideshow anyway, whispering, "Who's on the phone, girlfriend?"

"You think this is it?"

"It could be."

Slow motion imaging. Leanne answering the phone. The image tilts slightly—she's tucked the receiver into the crook of her neck. She's staring at her desk. Leanne grabbing a pen. Doodling on a pad. Swirls, infinity signs. A heart.

"Huh," muttered Sykes, obviously noticing as well.

It was all easy, smooth. Until it wasn't. Then something happened. The conversation turned, a demand was made? A threat?

Leanne begins gripping the pen tightly. Her knuckles whiten with the effort. The pen's tip digs into the paper, gouging it. The fingers of her other hand clench into a fist on the desk. The phone slams down.

"Yeah. I think this is it. The people who saw her outside the White House said she seemed annoyed. Whoever just called her said something that made her think she had to go over there and she is not happy about it."

"The tone definitely shifted," he agreed. "She'd been having a great day, until that call."

Ronnie grabbed her handheld and dashed a note to Daniels, asking him to check with the Phoenix Group switchboard and find out who had called Leanne's office at approximately 1:19 p.m. on the 4th. God, did she hope he could find out.

Back to the images. Another few minutes of Leanne putting her things away, tidying her desk—quickly. There was a quick sequence of odd head movements. She scanned the office, one side, then a wide, sweeping plane toward the other. Then she did it again.

She's shaking her head. Angry or disgusted.

Oh, yes. That was it. That phone call had changed her mood and driven her away from her desk, and she hadn't expected to come back that day.

When Leanne grabs her purse and leaves her office, yanking the door shut and smashing a key into the lock, it becomes obvious she's begun her unwanted mission.

They continue to watch. They see her avoid the pedestrian traffic below by taking a high tunnel-bridge through three office buildings. All owned by Phoenix, Ronnie assumed; she hadn't even realized it when she'd driven past them.

At the last building, she rides an elevator all the way down to a garage. Though she's close enough to walk, she heads for her car, through an abandoned lot—filled with cars, but utterly devoid of people—never once even looking around to double-check security. As if she's so accustomed to this that she doesn't even consider the possibility that she could ever be in danger.

She gets into her postage-stamp sized vehicle and exits the garage, driving a few blocks through massive crowds to a marked employees checkpoint. It is not the one Ronnie had used to access the White House, but a smaller, though just as heavily guarded, one.

Leanne parks, gets out, jogs over. The guards apparently know and trust her far more than they did a lowly uniformed D.C. cop, because they relax as she approaches. The soldier who searches her is smiling at first, but his smile fades. Apparently Leanne isn't her chatty self—more evidence of her mood—and he lets her pass through pretty quickly.

So far, everything matches all the evidence they have gathered, from time stamps to witness statements. They're getting to the critical point.

Leanne parks in a deserted, graveled construction parking lot on what will one day again be the White House lawn. She makes her way to the building, rushing, staring at the ground, occasionally shaking her head in annoyance. She reaches the highly secure entrance, punches in some numbers and presses her upper arm against a screen. The scanner read her implanted I.D. chip and the door clicks open.

Ronnie leaned forward in her seat, realizing that, beside her, Sykes was, too.

It's after two. Inside, Leanne doesn't hesitate, she walks quickly down the main floor corridor, heading for... "The stairs. She went down by herself," Ronnie mused.

"All the way?"

They watched. The victim paused at the landing only long enough to flip a breaker—turning on the lights that wouldn't work for Ronnie the other night. Then she continued down.

"Yes, all the way."

At the bottom, Leanne turns on the lights, walks out into the

139

center of the corridor, and stops. She looks one way, then the other. There is nothing to see, nothing but the construction tools left behind by the workers who've been locked out on this day. She's entirely alone.

She checks her watch.

Suddenly, the lights go out.

Blackness. This must be where her heart-rate sped up. She's got to be nervous now, even if she hasn't realized she's in danger. What's she thinking—power surge? Faulty wiring?

But she keeps her cool. Pulling her phone out of her purse, she turns it on, holding it up so the lit screen provides illumination.

Then it happens.

One second she's looking at the stairs, toward which she has turned. The next she's staring at the ceiling, her eyes having jerked hard, rolling up into their sockets.

It is 2:09. He'd just hit her with the stun gun or some other debilitating device that sent her electrical impulses into a frenzy and put her right down on the floor.

"He killed the lights, snuck up on her and stunned her from behind. She never even heard him coming," Sykes said.

Yes, that's exactly what he did. He'd hugged the shadows, stayed out of her line of sight. They didn't see the tiniest glimpse of him. Ronnie even scrolled back to see if there might be the faintest reflection in the phone screen, but was disappointed.

She watched the slideshow, staring at the roughed-in ceiling of the sub-basement for several frames. Leanne was down, immobile. But the picture changed the tiniest bit every second, as if she'd been jerking uncontrollably.

Finally, after a solid minute of it, Ronnie paused the image. She got out of her chair and went into the hallway to the water cooler, refilling her paper cup. Draining it in a few gulps, she bent and filled it again, needing not only the icy chill of reality but also the brief break from what they were doing.

Because they hadn't found anything to help them in the prequel to the attack.

That meant they had to slog forward.

They'd seen the horrible last ten minutes of Leanne's life when she'd been a mutilated wreck.

Now they had to watch every brutal thing that had been done to her in the sixty minutes leading up to it.

Chapter 11

Jeremy Sykes wasn't a sexist.

In the six years he'd been with the FBI, he'd never treated a female colleague any differently than a male one. Respect, cooperation and courtesy were standard, no matter who he was dealing with. He would sooner have slit his wrists than make any woman he worked with think he didn't believe her capable of doing her job, merely because of her sex.

But now…this…Jesus Christ.

He was having a hard time holding himself together. Because a part of him—a big part—wanted to pick-up Detective Veronica Sloan out of her chair, carry her out of this stuffy little computer lab, and take her home to bed.

Well, he'd wanted to take her home to bed for a long time. Since the first time they'd met. But today's impulse had absolutely nothing to do with wanting to have sex with her. Right now, he simply wanted to hide her away, to put her in a comfortable, secure place, pull the covers up to her chin, and urge her to rest and recover. He didn't want her to spend one more minute thinking about the gruesome, horrible things that had been done to an innocent woman named Leanne Carr. And oh, God, did he not want her to see them.

He'd never seen anything like it.

He never wanted to again.

He definitely never wanted to sit there while someone else— someone who'd recently been attacked by this same sick psychopath and was still weak and in pain from that attack—had to watch it as well.

"Stop. We can stop now," he muttered through a dry mouth. They were sixty-eight minutes into the attack. Leanne was already on the ground, already alone, and had been for several minutes, her attacker having disappeared somewhere. They knew how this story ended and how the rest of this scene played out. The monster with the black shoes and the black pants and the miner's light on his helmet would be back in two minutes to finish the job.

"I can't," she said, sounding as though she was biting the words out from between teeth that had been glued together.

141

He reached for the remote, which she held in a death grip. She jerked her hand away, not looking at him, not taking her eyes off the three-dimensional projection. "Don't," she snapped.

"Please, Veronica....Ronnie."

"We owe...her...this," she insisted, the words coming out almost as tiny exclamations. Or sobs. "She endured it. We have to watch every single second because we owe it to her to do everything we can to catch him."

All right. Maybe someone did. But did it really have to be her? Did Ronnie, so bruised and battered and weary after her own brush with this psychotic animal, really have to be slapped in the face with what might have happened to her had she not been smart enough to pretend her partner was with her during the search of that basement?

The possibilities of what could have happened made him shudder.

No, Ronnie wasn't an innocent young administrative assistant. She was hard and tough and strong. He'd seen her kick-box the shit out of every opponent stupid enough to take her on in the ring during their weeks in Texas, and he knew she could handle a weapon better than any other professional he knew—save himself. But she'd still taken a two-by-four to the head. Had still been knocked to unconsciousness. She would have been utterly helpless if that monster had decided to play his sick games with her the way he had with Leanne.

Thinking about it—letting his mind go there—he found himself gripping the armrests of his chair so hard one of them snapped off in his hand. The crack of it startled Ronnie and she flinched, jerking her attention off the projection and toward him.

He stared at her, knowing his face had to be revealing exactly what he'd been thinking, imagining, feeling. But he didn't look away, not ashamed of it, not embarrassed by it.

He cared about her. He didn't know her well enough to make that claim, certainly had no right to make any kinds of demands on her. He'd never even kissed the woman.

But he cared about her enough that he wanted to go out, find the man who'd hurt her and rip him apart with his bare hands.

"Okay," she eventually said, not even looking back at the images, which would soon descend into the blackness of Leanne's final minutes. "I guess there's nothing else to see."

"I've seen enough to last me my entire lifetime," he snapped.

There was only one thing he was grateful for: That Leanne Carr had drifted in and out of consciousness throughout the attack. She'd seen—watched—some of what had been done to her. But other things had, mercifully, remained out of her vision. So while they'd borne witness to the aftereffects, they hadn't had to sit through every slice of the blade.

Ronnie flicked a switch on the remote and shut down the slideshow. The final, dark image disappeared in a snap, and the lights went up, that innocent white square on the floor bearing no evidence of the horrors that had been visited upon it during the last hour.

"Nothing," she whispered. "He left us absolutely nothing."

"We know what he was wearing. We will know his shoe size. We can probably figure out how big his hands were, too, and I am certain we'll get his height off one of the shadows."

The prick hadn't worn his lighted helmet the whole time. There were several moments when he'd put it down on the floor, and the light it cast had sent his shadow tumbling behind him into the darkness of the basement. He'd lay money Dr. Tate and his people would be able to use that.

Unfortunately, even when he wasn't wearing the helmet, the unsub had been very careful to conceal himself, his bloody, gloved hands constantly checking to ensure his hood remained in place. Jeremy had absolutely no doubt—none—that the unsub had known about the optical chip and had taken every precaution to hide his identity. Not only with his obscuring clothes, but also with the simple black hood he wore over his head. Why would a killer do that if he was sure the only witness would soon be dead?

If he had any deep-set remorse, or felt any guilt about what he was feeling, he might have wanted to hide his face from his own victim. But there'd been absolutely no sign of remorse. He'd relished his crime, enjoyed every second of it. No inner ghost of shame would have made him hide his identity from Leanne. He'd have wanted her to know who he was, knowing that would fuel her terror. No, he hadn't been hiding from his victim, he'd been hiding from the spy buried inside her head.

"Tell me it was enough. Tell me it was worth it," she pleaded, sounding weak and unsure, as unlike her as he'd ever heard.

He couldn't tell her that right away. He honestly wasn't sure anything would be worth what they'd gone through, unless it was the chance to see this monster fry in the electric chair for what he'd done. But with the clues so minor, honestly, he didn't know.

Finally, though, knowing what she needed to hear, he replied,

"Yeah. It was worth it. It'll help us nail him, Ronnie."

Her ragged, audible breaths began to even out. "Good."

He waited, letting her gather her thoughts, trying to regain control over his own.

Ronnie cracked her knuckles, one after the other, as if needing to do something with her hands. Beating somebody was out of the question right now, so she apparently settled for abusing her own fingers. "I have to admit I'm having my first doubts about this program. I don't know many people we trained with who'd be able to sit through that."

He'd thought the same thing. "Same here. And as for stepping inside that house of horrors and living it up close and personal? Forget it."

She nodded her agreement.

"Fortunately, I don't think many will have to," he added. "There are only five-thousand test subjects nationwide, all healthy, young adults. All highly screened, with background checks and security clearances, so they're not out there doing drugs or engaging in risky behavior."

"Except when they're being hacked to death."

"I wasn't finished," he said, giving her a reproving glance. "Once we catch this guy, and stop these murders, things should go back to normal. Statistically, those five-thousand shouldn't be dying anytime soon. The program will be able to focus on them as witnesses to robberies or potential terrorist acts."

"Or state secrets. We both know the government wants its spies to be implanted next."

"Sitting through a straight month of boring political speeches at functions all over the world would be better than another hour of that," he said with a nod toward the empty projection space.

"Yeah. It would." She ran a weary hand over her face, then said, "Okay, let's go over what we know."

She'd put away the horror. He did the same. Time to get back to work, to be investigators rather than merely witnesses.

They began to compare notes on what they'd seen, both of them careful to avoid talking about the atrocities in anything but the most clinical terms. If they went down that road, if they let the emotion back in, it would swamp their little boat of calm and he just couldn't allow her to sink. Not on his watch.

He'd seen Veronica Sloan vulnerable before—though never as vulnerable as she was right now—but he'd never seen her weak. So he wasn't surprised that she was able to push past everything she'd been feeling and focus on just the case for the next two hours. They made notes, made plans, made calls, identified specific images, batted ideas. But eventually, her weariness couldn't be kept at bay.

"Sykes…Jeremy…would you please get me some more water?"

He immediately did as she'd asked. Ronnie wasn't the type to ask for anything and he had to assume she was completely worn out, not just mentally, but physically.

He came back and handed her the cup, seeing the way her hand shook as she lifted it. She dipped her fingers in it and lifted the cold droplets to her face, smoothing them on her temple. The headache must have returned with a vengeance.

"Do you have any pain medicine?"

"I can't take anything except over-the-counter. They said they couldn't give me anything stronger because of the concussion." She reached into her pocket and withdrew a small, sample-sized packet of Ibuprofen. When she tried to tear it open with her teeth, she couldn't manage it.

His heart twisting, he pulled it away from her and opened it himself. Then he lifted the small pills to her mouth. She didn't even argue. She merely parted her lips and accepted them gratefully.

That was when he decided she'd had enough. They were done for today. Ronnie might kick up a fuss and argue about it, but she was going home to get comfortable and put this day behind her, whether she liked it or not.

He told her. And she kicked up a fuss and argued. In the end, though, probably because she was a professional and was smart enough to know the difference between being brave and being stubborn, she finally agreed. "Dr. Tate offered to have his car…"

"I'm taking you home," he insisted.

"You don't have to do that."

"Look, it's on my way. My hotel's down in the city."

"How do you know it's on the way? You don't know where I live."

"Sure I do. I'm an FBI agent."

To his surprise, that actually startled a rusty laugh out of her mouth. She lifted her hand to her head and winced, as if laughing hurt her, but the amusement in her eyes went a long way toward convincing him she was going to be okay.

"Creepy stalker dude," she mumbled.

"Hard-headed cop chick."

"What a pair we are."

Oh, they could be. Someday, he suspected, they *would* be. But not today.

"You're going to go home, go to bed, and not think about this case at all until tomorrow morning, all right?"

"You're pretty good, Sykes, but you can't keep me from thinking all night long."

He suspected he could. He definitely suspected he could come up with ways to occupy her for an entire night so thinking about a murder case would be the very last thing she'd want to do. He couldn't do it now, though, not when she was injured and emotionally cracked.

When she was well and healthy, and this case was over, he was going to finally do something about this strange relationship they had, namely climbing over the protective, aloof wall she kept erected around herself. But that was for later, when life could again resemble normal. In this room, in the shadow of that projection unit, with the agonized screams his brain had inserted as a soundtrack to the slideshow, normalcy seemed like a forgotten dream.

"I might not be able to, but I bet I bet your mother could," he threatened.

She groaned, obviously knowing the threat wasn't serious, but lightly slapping his arm anyway. "Don't you dare call my mother."

"I think she liked me," he said, wagging his brows, knowing he sounded smug.

"She likes anyone she thinks might slow me down and make me push out a few grandbabies for her."

Her face reddened and she lifted a hand to her temple again, though this time, he suspected it was to block her embarrassed eyes from his sight. She hadn't meant to say that. Ronnie had a habit of forgetting to be careful around him sometimes and he knew it drove her nuts.

"You'd think she'd have figured out by now that I am *not* mother material," she snapped, sounding angry at herself.

"I don't know," he mused, "I can see you raising a couple of bad-ass rugrats who regularly get kicked out of school for beating-up bullies who pick on other kids on the playground."

Her hand remained by her face, shielding her expression, but there was no disguising the raw tone in her voice as she replied, "Never. Not *ever*."

He didn't say something light and teasing, like, *maybe you just haven't met the right man.* She sounded like her mind was absolutely made up, her decision set in stone. Knowing her the way he did, he figured there had to be a reason for it.

Turned out, there was.

"Did you know I was assigned to help with the recovery effort at Air & Space?"

He suspected he knew where this was going. "No."

"Daniels and I both worked at the site for six days after it was deemed cleared of explosive devices. Then we were moved over to the staging area where the forensics guys tried to piece together whatever remains they'd managed to find." She dropped her hand and turned in her chair to face him. Her dark, haunted eyes told him the rest even before her words did. "10/20 was on a Friday, you remember that, right?"

"Of course."

"Popular day for school field trips, Fridays. And Air and Space was the most popular Smithsonian destination for kids."

Oh Jesus.

"You know, seeing a parent howling with grief while they hold a bloody shoe that they last saw when they tied it onto their six-year-old's foot kinda cures you of any thought you might ever have had of traveling down the happy-family-road."

He reached out and took her hand in his. She didn't pull away, didn't make a snarky comment. She just let him lace his fingers in hers and hold tight for a long, commiserating moment.

"You were already in New York, right?" she whispered, obviously remembering from their conversation in Texas.

"Yes. I'd left D.C. seven months before."

Though they'd talked about it some, they hadn't had the full conversation. The one Americans almost always had when the subject turned to that day.

Where were you when on it happened? Do you remember how you found out? Did you know anyone who died? Do you remember the shock of hearing President Turner didn't make it? Wasn't it a blessing to find out the first lady and her young children had left the White House the night before for an impromptu weekend getaway? Did you watch the coverage of the funerals? What about the trials? Did you agree with the public hangings? Do you think they'll ever catch the rest of the conspirators?

Five years later and the questions and answers were always the same. The grief still hadn't left the country's consciousness and, like survivors of a war who fell into telling old stories whenever they came together, so, too, did just about every American. Especially those in law enforcement. The post mortem would continue for decades, he imagined, until the last American alive on that day passed out of this world.

"But you came back."

"Of course. I was temporarily reassigned, stayed for three months working on the investigation." Those were days he didn't like to think about. Trying to focus on solving the brutal crimes—so many of them, so many suspects, so brilliantly conceived yet so utterly evil and malicious. Having lost his closest friend and several colleagues, he'd sometimes wondered how he could get through another day of it.

Knowing what he knew about Ronnie—about the even more devastating losses she'd experienced, he found himself asking, "Didn't you take any time off? *After*?"

"No."

No. That was all. No further explanation.

He understood. Continuing to work, driving forward and catching the terrorists who'd slipped through the nets was all any cop or agent had been able to think about. It went above grief to a pure, basic need for vengeance.

He wondered if she'd felt she'd gotten hers.

He wondered if she'd realized yet that it didn't matter a damn and certainly didn't assuage the pain.

"Enough of this," she said, putting her hands on the arms of her chair. "Let's get out of here before things get maudlin."

"Okay. As long as you promise to let this go for tonight, go home and recuperate."

"I'll go home and I promise I won't do a thing more until I'm feeling better," she said.

He looked for a hedge in there, for something that said she was covering her bases or making a fingers-crossed-behind-her-back promise, but could find nothing.

"Guess we should go tell Dr. Cavanaugh we're leaving," he said.

"If you don't mind, I think I'll just wait here while you find her and let her know." Her words were almost sighed. She leaned back in her chair and her eyes drifted closed, those thick, inky black lashes falling onto her pale cheeks. She looked ready to drop.

"I'll be back soon." Then, because he simply had to, he reached out and carefully smoothed her hair back off her cheek, fingering the silkiness of it, wondering how she'd managed to hide the fact that a huge hunk of it was missing.

She mumbled something, as if she'd already fallen into a light sleep, and he left the room, cursing their unsub again for making Veronica Sloan too weak to even slap his hand away and pretend she didn't need anyone at all.

Ronnie waited until Jeremy's footsteps faded away down the hall, then she opened her eyes, spun around toward her work station and grabbed a microdrive.

While she thought about what she needed to do, she told herself she hadn't lied. She'd promised she wouldn't think about the case until she was feeling better. But she already knew she'd be feeling better in a few hours, after the medicine kicked in and she was at home in comfortable sweats and fuzzy slippers.

So she might as well make sure she had something to do for the rest of the night.

She moved quickly. Not only did she not want Sykes to know she intended to work all night if she had to, she also worried that he might bring Dr. Cavanaugh back with him. While Phineas Tate and his staff seemed perfectly fine about her and Jeremy working on the files and chips of their victims here in their secure facility, she wasn't sure how they'd feel about her taking the info off-site.

Especially info they hadn't technically offered.

Something one of them had said earlier today had stuck in her mind, but she hadn't really thought much about it until a couple of hours ago. It was when Ronnie had been talking about the number of deaths they might expect to see among O.E.P. participants. As Jeremy had pointed out, the test subjects been carefully screened. They were young, healthy, with no risk factors, so there shouldn't be a lot of deaths.

And yet, hadn't Dr. Tate mentioned that some of them had recently died? He'd insisted of natural causes, but something in her couldn't help wondering about that. If the implantees had all been chosen specifically for their good health and safe profiles, how likely was it that some would already have died? Maybe the doctor thought the deaths had been natural—but, in truth, couldn't they have been early victims of this same monster, who'd escalated to a more blatant form of murder with his most recent attacks?

She needed to know. But she certainly didn't want to accuse Dr.

Tate of being wrong, or covering anything up. So she decided to just do a little digging herself.

The first thing she needed was a list of all implantees. Fortunately, a guy Ronnie had dated throughout her freshman year of college had worked at an Apple store and considered himself a master at online vigilante justice. So she knew her way around a hack.

Interestingly, after they'd parted ways, that guy had invented some social media site for people who had no lives to meet and interact with the cyber avatars of other people who had no lives. Everybody lied and invented these amazing stories about how fabulous they were, how handsome, how rich, how successful. They all lived happily in fantasyland—fully *knowing* none of it was true—that only their avatars had those lives, not their real-life counterparts. They went to school, paid their bills, got married, bought homes, raised kids…all without ever actually laying eyes on any other living person behind the other avatars. But nobody cared. As long as their little cyber people were happy and rich, they didn't mind that in the real world they remained sad, boring and lonely. It blew her mind, but everybody seemed to be doing it nowadays, loving their Cybertopia lives more than their real ones.

Of course, her ex had made a freaking fortune on the thing and was now some long-fingernailed recluse living in southern California.

Sending him a silent thank-you for being a good teacher, if not a good lover—or a faithful one—she snuck her way into the Tate Scientific network and searched for the O.E.P. files. There was a lot of security when it came to specifics about the chip, but she wasn't interested in that, anyway. All she needed was a list of names.

It took a little digging, and every minute she dug was another she feared would bring the click of Sykes's footsteps in the hallway. But finally, she found it.

"Yes!"

She quickly copied the files onto the microdrive. Then she considered what else she might want. Knowing she wouldn't be able to sit through Leanne's murder again, she didn't even think about taking the data from the chip. The backups from Leanne's home computer were another matter, however. Sykes had brought those up from her own precinct, and she had every right to take them. But she suspected he'd be looking for them the moment he got back, if for nothing else than to make sure she didn't do exactly what she intended to do tonight.

To play it safe, she copied all the files over onto the micro-drive, and had just popped it out of the system when she heard Sykes and

Cavanaugh speaking just down the hall.

"Detective Sloan," said the pretty doctor as they entered the room, "I hear you've had about enough for the day."

"I think so."

The other woman came over, crouched down in front of the chair, and peered into Ronnie's eyes. "How bad is the headache?"

"Low and dull."

"Your pupils look all right. Any numbness or weakness?"

"No."

"Nausea or vomiting?"

"Neither. Honestly, I'm just weary. It's been a long couple of days."

The other woman straightened, then looked at Sykes. "You should be fine taking her home."

Good grief, he'd asked the woman to do an examination?

"She offered to check on your progress since you left the hospital against doctor's advice," he insisted, as if reading her mind, something he was pretty good at.

"Yes, I did," Dr. Cavanaugh said. "Now, go home and get some rest. I'm sure you'll be feeling much better tomorrow."

"I'll hold you to that," Ronnie said as she rose from her chair a little more slowly than technically necessary. No point in having Sykes wonder if she'd had nefarious reasons for sending him out of here.

"Let me grab my things," he said, gathering his documents and files and slipping them into his briefcase. As she'd anticipated, he also went to her work station and ejected the disc containing Leanne's history. He didn't look twice at her, obviously having fully bought the idea that she was far too tired and achy to even think about doing any work at home tonight.

Which just showed he wasn't quite as observant a law enforcement official as he was presumed to be.

Chapter 12

After going home—courtesy of a quiet car ride with Sykes, during which she'd pretended to doze off, just so she wouldn't have to talk to him while trapped in a small, confined space where every breath tasted like man—Ronnie took a lukewarm shower. It was too damned hot out for a steamy one, and the coolness felt great on her skin. So great that after getting into comfortable, loose-fitting clothes, she laid down on her bed with a cool cloth on her face. She didn't sleep, but just relaxed and willed her blood to stop thumping in her temples. Doing some meditation exercises she usually sneered at, she found herself slowly drifting into a peaceful doze and the headache finally released its tenacious grip.

Feeling better, she got up and picked up the phone, knowing her mom would be showing up at the door if she didn't hear from Ronnie soon. Their conversation was tense—Christy started down the, "Why don't you quit that dangerous job?" road and Ronnie cutting her off. The most she could do was offer to be careful, which wasn't enough, had never been enough, would never be enough.

By eight-thirty that night, she was ready to get back to work. Grabbing a frozen meal, she ate at her dining room table while she scanned through the entire list of O.E.P. test subjects and managed to find the names of those who had died—aside from this week's victims.

There were six. All had been in their thirties or forties and had died within the past two months. All, according to the notation in their files, had died of "natural causes" which weren't identified in the files.

Huh. That didn't sound right to her. Six formerly health, young adults dying of natural causes in the past eight weeks? Okay, maybe statistically it was possible—she had no idea what the normal death-rate in that age bracket was, or what was defined as "natural" causes. For all she knew, getting hit by a bus might be called "natural" by some people. But it still sounded funny to her. Especially because other people in that same control group—the O.E.P. implantees—were currently being bumped off in gruesome ways.

Of course there was one other difference between these six and her first murder victim: They were all male. According to the records she'd swiped from the Tate network, every woman in the study was still alive. Obviously they hadn't gotten around to updating Leanne Carr's record yet.

Though she knew there were other things to do—like looking at Leanne's backups—she just couldn't shake the feeling that those six deaths meant something. She still hated the idea of pressing Dr. Tate for information about them, but definitely wanted more information.

Glancing at the clock, she thought about what Philip Tate had said that afternoon: *Call any time, day or night*. And he'd promised he spoke her language and could help her in ways his father and Dr. Cavanaugh could not.

She definitely didn't want to encourage the guy or make him think she was at all interested in him personally, but her curiosity was killing her. She couldn't move on to other things until she found out more. So, before she could think better of it, she retrieved his business card from the pocket of her pants in the bedroom and dialed his cell number.

"Detective Sloan!" he answered, sounding delighted to hear her voice at nine o'clock at night.

"Hi there, Mr. Tate, I'm so sorry to bother you this late."

"Please, call me Philip," he insisted. "And it's no bother at all. I was just sitting out on my patio grilling a steak for dinner and having a glass of 2015 Chateau Margaux."

"Late dinner," she replied, not recognizing the name of the wine. She was more of a beer girl, herself.

"No rest for the wicked, I'm afraid. I was at work until an hour ago."

Unable to resist the opening, she asked, "What, exactly is it that you do for Tate Scientific?"

He laughed, as if used to the question. "Not the science'y stuff, that's for sure."

Right. No Science'y stuff for the golfing playboy.

"I'm strictly management. I oversee contracts, supply orders, HR, insurance issues, government communication. I let the eggheads do their thing and make sure they have the equipment and contracts to play and experiment."

Okay, she could see a need for that. She somehow suspected his father wouldn't be much good in that regard. Tate senior seemed like the type who'd forget to put his shoes on in the morning if he were anxious to get to work on an exciting new experiment at the lab.

"Want to come over and share my steak and drink my wine?"

She forced a casual laugh. "Thanks, but I'm sitting here in my pj's with a cold cloth on my head."

"Maybe another time."

"Mmm."

"Now to what do I owe the pleasure of this call?"

Being careful to avoid admitting where she'd gotten the information, she said, "I was actually wondering about the deaths of the O.E.P. participants..."

He cut in. "Well, you know more about those than I do."

"No, I'm not talking about the two murders. I mean the other six."

Silence. A long silence. Then, finally he replied, "I'm sorry, Detective Sloan, I'm afraid you've caught me at a disadvantage. I don't know what you're talking about."

Interesting how the flirtatious bluster had bled out of his tone. He sounded wary, hesitant.

"You're saying you don't know anything about the fact that six men implanted with the O.E.P. device have died of supposedly natural causes in the past two months?"

Another pregnant pause. He cleared his throat.

"Mr. Tate?"

"This is embarrassing, Detective Sloan, but the truth is, I don't pay a whole lot of attention to the technical side of these experiments. I watch the money and the orders and the deadlines and leave the rest of it to my father and his team."

"So if there are sudden deaths in the middle of an experiment, you don't even *hear* about it?"

"What are you getting at, Detective Sloan?" he asked, his mood and tone definitely cooler.

"I'm just trying to do my job, sir," she insisted, keeping calm and collected, not wanting to escalate this into an argument. The last thing she needed was for junior to go running to daddy and mess up Ronnie's great relationship with Phineas Tate. "I heard there were some deaths, wanted to make absolutely sure those other men couldn't have been murdered by our suspect, perhaps in a way to make it look like they'd died of natural causes."

"Well, I'm afraid I can't help you," he insisted. "And frankly, I'm questioning your information. Where did you hear about these so-called deaths?"

Whoops. Time to end this call.

"Listen, forget I bothered you, okay? I'm sure it's not connected, believe me, I just want to cover all the bases trying to find this guy."

"I'm sure you do," he said, his tone regaining the tiniest modicum of warmth. "I do hope you find him soon and don't get distracted by any wild goose chases. Frankly, Detective, I think you should double-check your sources, because you're obviously getting some skewed information."

She thanked him, apologized again for disturbing him and ended the call. But after she hung up, she couldn't help sitting there, thinking about his words and his attitude.

Tate had definitely gotten chilly when she'd mentioned those other deaths. Whether it was because he truly didn't know about them and was embarrassed at being caught so out of the loop, or because he did know about them and was angry *she* knew, she couldn't say. Whichever the case, she wasn't put off, no matter what she'd told him. If anything, her instincts were pinging even harder than before.

She wanted to find out about those deaths. And she'd find out, one way or another. Somebody out there knew how those men had died, and even if she had to get on the Internet and track down their obituaries, then contact the funeral homes herself, she'd do it.

But she couldn't do it tonight. In fact, there was nothing else she could do regarding those mysterious O.E.P. deaths right now. It would have to wait for morning.

She still wasn't tired, though, and had plenty more work to do. Starting by going back to the beginning—to Leanne Carr's visual memories.

"Okay, Leanne," she said as she pulled up the other set of files she'd back up onto the micro-drive today, "let's see what your life's been like lately."

She wouldn't even think about watching Leanne's murder again. Frankly, she didn't think she'd ever be able to sit through that nightmare one more time, unless she was strapped down and forced to, and she most definitely wouldn't do it alone in her own living room. This was her place of peace and security—she wouldn't consider violating it by allowing the specter of such horror within its walls.

But Leanne's backups from the weeks preceding her death shouldn't contain anything other than normal day-to-day stuff. With, she hoped, a few out-of-the-ordinary moments that might explain how the young woman had drawn the eye of a psychopath.

Finishing her dinner, she cleaned off the table and went into the living room of her small apartment. Ronnie didn't own a television. Some people still did, her mother among them, but most now just watched stuff online. Not being very interested in any regular programming, she probably could have just caught up with the few shows she watched on the tiny screen of her pocket-sized unit. But there was one show she liked to see as close to real size as possible.

It was cheesy, it was dated, it was stupid and had been on forever…but she really loved *So You Think You Can Dance*. She was a sucker for people who could move gracefully. Mainly because she, herself, couldn't dance her way out of a lie much less across a stage.

Right now, she was glad she'd splurged on the huge monitor, which she quickly connected to her handheld. Because it would allow her to sprawl on the couch and watch Leanne's life unfold on the big screen in front of her. It wouldn't be anywhere near the experience she'd had at Tate's lab, with that intense projection system, but it should suffice for this kind of work.

Opening the files she'd copied from the micro-disc, she searched for the back-ups from Leanne's O.E.P. device. The I.T. guys at the precinct had dumped Leanne's entire hard drive onto the disk, and she had to scan through page after page of files to find them.

As she scrolled down, one file name caught her eye. It was one of many, going by in a blur, but for some reason it just popped out at her, demanding attention. It read: WilliamsBDay.

Hmm. She wondered if the file had something to do with the memory book Leanne had made for her boss. The one with the possibly missing page.

Because she was the suspicious type, Ronne couldn't resist the urge to check. She double clicked on the folder name, bringing up the next menu, and found a long list of jpeg images. And, one document called Membook.

She clicked on that, bringing the mock-up of the book up on the large screen. She recognized it immediately, seeing the same cover photo and text layout that she'd seen the other day in Williams's office. She clicked through the pages, yawning as she scrolled through the obligatory baby pictures and second birthday pony ride shots, looking for the page that had drawn her attention the other day—the one with half a beach scene.

She reached the middle of the book and saw the image she'd been seeking. Changing the viewing dimensions so she could see a two-page layout, she immediately realized that yes, a page was missing out of Williams's book. In the original design, there had been a full, large picture stretching across both the left and right pages of the book. She recognized the left half. The right side she'd never seen before.

She studied it, wondering what made it so special. There was nothing suspicious in it, nothing that hinted at scandal or mystery. Just a large group of teens and young adults standing around a bonfire on a beach. Young adults, guys and girls, maybe twenty in all, they looked happy, drunk and excited. Some of them had probably wandered off down the beach, some may have puked in the surf, some had likely fallen asleep near the fire. It was exactly like a million other spring break photos out there on the world wide web.

So what had made Williams tear it out?

"Maybe he didn't, idiot, maybe the printer messed it up," she mumbled, realizing she was creating a mystery that might not be mysterious at all.

Or maybe Leanne changed her mind and had a new version printed. Maybe she'd only included half the picture because it was the half that included her boss—Jack Williams—who stood almost directly in the middle, close to the seam. He was standing between two girls, a redhead and a blond, one of whom was on the left side of the photo, the other on the mysterious right.

"Hmm. Wife on one side, ex-girlfriend on the other?" she whispered, thinking she recognized the blond.

Stop wasting time, a little voice in her head said.

She realized she'd been stalling, trying to put off the moment when she would find the correct backup files and have to begin the arduous task of watching Leanne's final days. To think she'd been excited about it a few days ago. Now, having witnessed the woman's horrible death, she'd been putting off getting sucked any further into her life. It was like watching the end of a sad movie first. Going back and watching the happy parts made it twice as depressing.

But it was her job. Glancing at the clock, she realized she'd wasted ten minutes on this meaningless search. Angry at herself, she backed up through the files and folders and returned to the main directory. She had enough to do trying to go through Leanne's visuals, she didn't have time to speculate on her boss's old secrets.

Not sure how far back to start, she decided on one week. If Leanne had been stalked before her murder, chances were her killer had crossed her path shortly before her death. He'd have wanted to keep an eye on her, figure out her routines, make sure he could lure her to the spot he'd chosen for her execution.

She queued up the images—thousands and thousands of them—and set the speed as fast as it would go. Images would fly by; she wouldn't be able to see them all. But she should be able to get the gist of what was happening in each "scene" of Leanne's life. Being able to fast-forward through the times when the woman had been alone, or sleeping, she could then slow down when the victim had been interacting with other people.

She took a deep breath, settled into the couch, and began, determined to get through this with her emotions intact.

But, after a half hour, she realized the strongest emotion she was feeling was boredom. This was going to be one hell of a tedious job. Seeing the minutiae of another person's life when they were doing something exciting was one thing. Watching them pluck their eyebrows, wash their face, brush their teeth, drive their car, sit at their desk, answer phones, take messages, type memos and eat yogurt was about as boring as it got.

She was in for a long few days if something in this case didn't break soon.

About to pause the show so she could go in and pop herself some popcorn, she flinched when she heard a sharp knock on her front door. Glancing at the clock and seeing it was ten-forty, she slowly rose from the couch and crept across the living room.

She'd already talked on the phone to her hairdresser-neighbor, Max, who had gasped when she'd told him about her hair, and knew he was going to be out late tonight. Her mother lived way down in Virginia and their phone conversation earlier hadn't ended on a note that would inspire a cozy, friendly pop-by. So who would be visiting her this late, she didn't know.

A hint of tension crawled through her. She'd been so focused on solving these murders, she hadn't really had time to evaluate how she felt about her own attack the other night. Or the fact that her attacker—a psychotic killer—might have come within seconds of brutally killing her as well.

Now that all came flooding in. So she moved silently across the carpet to the table in the foyer, where she always placed her service weapon when she got home. She unholstered it, dropped it to her side and went to the door.

Another knock.

"Who is it?" she barked, wishing she had insisted the landlord install a peephole.

"Hey, Ron, it's me. Let me in."

"Daniels," she whispered, immediately re-engaging the safety on her 9mm. She unlocked the dead-bolt and twisted the knob to let him in. "What are you doing here?"

He eyed her, his lips twitching when he saw the ragged T-shirt, sweatpants and fluffy slippers. The twitching stopped when he noticed the Glock in her hand. "Atta girl. Safety first."

"Bullet in your partner second? You should've called ahead."

"I've got news," he said, pushing past her and entering the apartment. Going right for her kitchen, he opened the refrigerator and scrounged around in it. "Seriously? No beer?"

"Nope, sorry."

"You don't even keep some hidden away for guests?"

"Is that what you are? I thought you were home invader the way you burst in here."

"You'da shot my ass if I were." He grabbed a bottle of juice, then reached for a closed storage container and flipped the lid open, sniffing the contents. "I'm starving!"

"It's fine," she explained, wondering when he had last eaten a decent meal. He was more the out-of-a-box-or-a-bag type. Ronnie, while not very domestic, did like to eat healthily and had stir-fried the chicken and veggies he was holding just a couple of days ago.

He tossed the container in the microwave, punched a button, then turned to face her.

"So, what is it?" she asked, knowing something big must have brought him over here tonight.

He grinned. "The tunnels."

"Yes! I knew it!"

"The president apparently didn't even know and man is he pissed."

She had to hear this. Dropping onto a kitchen chair, she said, "Tell me everything."

"I met with Williams, who's a little less grief-stricken today."

She rolled her eyes.

"And with his lead architect, dude named Frank. He was at the briefing the other day."

She remembered him. He'd stood up and bolted from the room as soon as the civilians were told they could leave.

"While we're sitting there, a call comes in from Kilgore."

She also remembered him, the officious head of the Secret Service continent assigned to the White House. "So how is Mr. Happy?"

"Not so happy. In fact, he was on a tear, talking so loud I could hear him through the extension. It seems Dr. Tate's questions this afternoon got the president a little curious. He made some phone calls, including to the head of the CIA and the Secret Service, and found out that, despite the wishes of every person in the country, somebody made the decision that there should still be emergency tunnels under the White House."

"Oh, yeah, sure. Of course they did. 'Cause they worked so well the last time."

He snickered. "Apparently it was a 'need-to-know' situation and somebody had decided the president didn't 'need to know.'"

"And neither did the cops investigating a brutal murder, right?"

"Exactly. Oh, by the way, it's still top secret and if you tell anyone they'll throw you in a windowless cell and never let you see the light of day again."

"Got it," she said, getting up to grab a glass. She filled it with ice and then with milk, ignoring her partner's moue of disgust. Whether he was more grossed out by the milk, or by the ice, she couldn't say. Daniels usually didn't even bother to ice his bourbon.

After he'd retrieved his dinner from the microwave, Ronnie gestured toward the drawer containing the forks. "So, did you get a guided tour?"

"Courtesy of Mr. Phoenix Group and Mr. Secret Service themselves. They swear it's the only one. It's accessed by a secret door behind the wall of breakers at the base of the stairs in the sub-basement."

She nodded. "That's why he stayed close to the stairs to work on Leanne. If he'd heard anything he would have gone right for the tunnel."

"Yep. It goes about a half a mile and comes out—get this—in the basement of a maintenance building near the Washington Monument!"

Of course it did. Right where throngs of people would have been on Independence Day. So many thousands that nobody would have noticed one individual person's movements. It explained why they hadn't found any hint of someone gaining access through the White House's electronic security system. And how their ghost had gotten in and out again despite the presence of police, military, guards and witnesses when he was returning Leanne Carr's head.

Speaking of… "Do you think he had the head stashed in there the whole time it was missing?"

"Hell, yes. No doubt about it—we found a pool of blood and a plastic tarp it was sitting on. And that wasn't all."

Her blood coursed more quickly through her veins. "What else did you find?"

He stirred the food, lifted a big forkful to his mouth and chowed down, talking while he chewed. "The mother lode."

Her heart rolled over. "Weapons?"

"A knife. Black clothes. Blood smears. Forensics took everything back to the lab—maybe we'll get lucky with a spare fiber or print. Hopefully this guy didn't think we'd find his hiding place so quickly."

She wasn't very hopeful. Their suspect wasn't stupid. He had to know others were aware of the existence of the tunnel, even if the cops and investigators weren't. Sooner or later, he'd have to assume somebody in the know would have checked it out. So she doubted he'd left behind anything incriminating. Still, maybe they'd get super lucky.

"Can't help thinking about what might have happened if he'd managed to drag you into that tunnel before I got downstairs the other night."

Ronnie had been intentionally avoiding those thoughts, not wanting to imagine what the killer could have done with an unconscious victim, some weapons, some time and a half-mile length of tunnel.

A lot. A whole hell of a lot.

She swallowed, pushing a flash of mental images away, and said, "But that didn't happen. So, did you find anything else?"

Scrunching his brow in confusion, Mark added, "Actually, yeah. There was a hard-hat with a light on the front of it."

She sunk down into a chair. "That's definitely his." She quickly told him about what she and Sykes had seen on Leanne's O.E.P. files, explaining how the suspect had used the miner's light to blind his victim and her implanted camera.

"So," Daniels said as he finished eating, "this guy knew about the O.E.P., he knew Leanne had an implant, he knew about the tunnel, and he knew how to get in and out of it without being seen."

They fell silent, digesting all that. It had seemed clear from the beginning that they were dealing not with a random terrorist, but with somebody who'd specifically gone after Leanne Carr.

This new information took things a step further.

This didn't sound like someone who'd followed her, found out where she worked and figured out a way to get her there to kill her. For the perp to know this much detail, have such insider knowledge, he *had* to be someone who was very familiar with the site. Familiar enough to know about a tunnel so secret that even the president of the United States hadn't known of its existence.

"So who knew all those things?" she murmured. "And of the people who did, who would want Leanne Car dead?"

"I'll have a list by tomorrow."

"Excellent."

She hoped it was a short one. A very short one. Already, she populated it with an obvious name—Jack Williams. She made a mental note to check on where Leanne's boss had been the other day during the time of her attack, and the next night, when Brian Underwood was murdered in Philadelphia. She also resolved to make a few phone calls and find out what she could about Kilgore. He was Secret Service and had a high level security clearance, but he was also an asshole. Assholes didn't necessarily equal murderers, but her instinctive dislike and distrust of the man made her want to know at least a little more about him.

She had no idea whether Bailey or Johansen knew. It seemed doubtful, but if they'd been working on the site for months, it was at least possible. And certainly the lead architect and his key people would be aware, as well as the construction workers who'd rebuilt it.

Shit. Maybe the list wouldn't be that short.

"Now, tell me what else you found out from your eye-spy routine today," he said. Then he tilted his head from side to side, cracking his neck, and pulled off his uniform jacket. "Wait, never mind. First, I gotta take a leak."

He had been here a few times and knew where the bathroom was, so he didn't wait for her to give him permission. He merely left the kitchen, walking through the dining area into the living room. And there, apparently, he stopped.

She heard his low whistle, and wondered what had caught his attention.

"Holy shit, Ron, if I'd known you were having a porn party, I woulda brought my collection of Big Tits In Tube Tops blue-rays."

Confused, she walked out to join him and realized he was looking at the oversized computer monitor sitting on the living room table. She'd been watching Leanne's backups when he'd knocked, and had been so startled she hadn't even paused the slideshow. During the

162

last several minutes while they'd talked, Leanne's memories had continued to play out on the screen.

And oh, God, were they hot.

"That's our victim," she whispered, seeing Leanne's peach-tinted fingernails scraping the bare chest of a naked man, whom she was studying with obvious lust and desire. She was in no way paying attention to his face, instead focused entirely from the neck down. As they watched, she tangled her fingers in his wiry hair and moved down to lick his nipples, kissing her way down his midriff, his abs...lower.

"Whoa," Daniels barked when it became pretty obvious they were about to see a birds-eye view of a guy getting blown.

Ronnie hurried over to the couch, grabbed her hand-held and paused the show. Seeing where the picture had stopped, she rethought that strategy—*hmm, not circumcised*—and stopped the thing altogether.

"So, should I pop the popcorn?" Mark asked.

"I was just about to," she admitted. "But I think I've lost my appetite."

Many parts of this job pressed her squick button. Seeing a woman having hot sex up against a wall in a dimly-lit room within a few days of her brutal murder smashed that sucker flat.

"It's pretty nasty, partner, but we need to find out who Mr. Big Dick is," Daniels murmured, knowing her well enough to know she dreaded going back and watching the whole scene.

But he was right, they did need to find out, and they wouldn't be able to i.d. him by the erect penis they'd both so unfortunately gotten to see, up-close and personal.

"I know." She threw herself back on the couch, feeling her headache start to come back.

"Want me to watch it for you?" he asked, his tone not holding the slightest hint of salaciousness. He wasn't offering because he wanted to get any kind of voyeuristic thrill, he was doing it because he knew she didn't want to.

"No, I need to do it," she said with a resigned sigh. "But thanks."

As uncomfortable as it might be to watch something like this in front of someone else, she knew Daniels would provide a great backup set of eyes and a needed second perspective. Besides, watching it tonight, with him, seemed less troubling than the possibility of sitting through it tomorrow, with Sykes. *That* she couldn't even stand to think about.

"Can you stay and help me slog through it? I've got a week's worth of images here and I guess I should find out not only who this guy is but just how often this kind of thing was going on."

"You sure?" he asked, his tone a little gruff, like he was suddenly embarrassed by the idea.

"I'm sure."

"Okay. Give me a minute," he said, heading toward the bathroom like he came here every day of the week.

Funny how comfortable he was—how comfortable they were around each other. Maybe that's why she didn't feel any sexual vibe between them, the way he apparently still did. He was just Daniels— eating like a slob, bitching about needing a beer, stopping to take a piss. Just her partner. Not somebody she thought about in a sexual way.

Even so, sitting here with him, watching somebody else have sex, was going to be anything but fun. Yet it had to be done. Though she knew she couldn't have a drink after the recent head injury, she strongly wished she could go to the pantry, pull out a bottle of scotch and take a shot.

"Okay," Daniels said as he returned and plopped down on the couch beside her. He had pulled a note pad out of his pocket and flipped it open. "In case I need to make an emergency sketch of that guy's cock and balls."

She snickered in spite of herself. "You jackass." Then her laughter faded and she cued up the files. She'd scrolled back to what looked like an image of Leanne walking down a lit corridor, fully clothed, and re-started the program there.

"Hey, that's the White House!" Daniels said, leaning forward and dropping his elbows onto his knees.

"Yes, it is," she agreed, recognizing the hallway dissecting the main floor.

Leanne was alone, glancing down at a file folder tucked into her arm, jotting a note on the exterior of it with a pencil.

Suddenly, the image went dark. But not because the lights had gone off—she could actually see tiny slits of brightness shining between…

"Are those somebody's fingers?" Daniels asked.

"I think so," she said, putting the image together in her mind. Somebody had clapped their hands over Leanne's eyes. She didn't appear to struggle—her own hands didn't come up and pull at the ones blocking her vision. Had her lover grabbed her for a quick assignation?

The timing certainly fit—they were only a couple of minutes away from the blow-job scene.

The hands over the eyes moved away and Leanne was again looking down the hallway. She was also moving again, but the perspective was odd. Things in front of her were getting smaller—farther away—rather than bigger and closer.

"She's walking backward," Daniels said.

"Yes. Like she's being tugged away by the guy who grabbed her."

Tugged away playfully, sexually...by someone who'd played these games with her before.

Perhaps he had his arm around her waist and was whispering in her ear. They had no way of knowing. She only knew that Leanne didn't seem to be at all worried or trying to get away. She was voluntarily taking those steps.

Suddenly Leanne begins to move her head, so she can look down. A man's hand is visible on her breast. An arm is looped around her waist. Still no struggle going on. She's liking this, letting it happen. The hand is cupping her, claiming her, pinching her nipple through her thin blouse.

"Wait, stop!" Daniels snapped.

Ronnie did so, immediately.

"Back up a couple of frames."

She again did as he asked, not sure what had caught his attention. She stared at the screen intently, going back frame by frame, watching Leanne's head move back up in tiny jerks. She saw the same deserted hallway, the plain-tiled floor, the bare white walls that would one day be elegantly decorated and trimmed with elaborate paintings and artwork.

And then she saw something else.

"Who's that?" she whispered, realizing this was what must have drawn Mark's keen eye. She had obviously blinked because the image was well in the background and didn't appear for long.

"I don't know," he replied, moving close to the monitor so he could study the man, who was visible in the shadow of a nearly closed doorway up the hall. He was facing the camera—facing Leanne and her mystery man—but Ronnie didn't think they'd even noticed him. He appeared in a couple of frames—there for two or three seconds and then gone. In those seconds, his shadowy, indistinct image had been caught by the O.E.P. device, but not seen by the people upon whom he was spying.

Interesting.

She moved forward again, to the frames immediately after he'd disappeared inside that room, and noticed the door had been left open a few inches.

"He's still there spying," Daniels said, "you can't see him but you can practically feel him."

"Definitely."

But who? What kind of person would see two people behaving in an extremely inappropriate manner—in the frigging White House—and, instead of confronting them about their behavior, would merely step back and spy on them?

Creepy to the nth degree.

"Can you keep going backward, so we can maybe see the name or room number on that door?"

She did so, sending Leanne back in time, and further up the hallway, to the moment right before her mystery man had put his hands over her eyes. Their victim never got close enough to the door in question for them to read any identifying signs, but it didn't matter. Ronnie suddenly realized right where it was. She and Daniels had been in it two days ago.

"That door leads into the operations office where we held our meeting," she said, knowing she was right. "I remember it being the last door before that alcove you can see a little further down the hall."

"You're right." Daniels crossed his arms over his chest. "Lots of people in and out of that office every day, I would assume."

"Hey, you know what they say about the word assume making an ass out of you and me," she mused, remembering everything she'd learned the other day. "From what I can recall, it sounded like SAIC Kilgore had pretty well claimed that room for his own office. I don't think he liked being out in his trailer, he wanted to be able to tell people he had an office in the White House."

"So, the head of the on-site Secret Service unit is a Peeping Tom?"

"I don't think that bothers me as much as the fact that he didn't put a stop to something that was so inappropriate," she said.

"Not to mention he didn't tell us one damn thing about this incident. There's no way he wouldn't remember, this was only, what, a week ago this past Tuesday?"

She checked the timestamp on the file. "Yes." Just seven days before Leanne's death. So why hadn't Kilgore said anything?

"What kind of law enforcement officer doesn't mention that a murder victim was having a secret affair with someone on the job?"

"A shitty one," she replied. "Or one who didn't want to mention it because it might reveal some secret of his own."

"Like?"

"I dunno. Maybe he did something about that knowledge. Maybe he used it to try to put the moves on Leanne?"

"Ick."

God, did she hope Leanne hadn't kept Kilgore quiet by giving him some of what she'd given to the mysterious man from the closet. That was one sex scene she definitely didn't want to sit through. "I guess it's possible it wasn't Kilgore," she admitted, "but I'm definitely going to have to ask him about it."

"Oh, goody. He liked you, I could tell."

She snorted. "Okay, *you* ask him about it."

"I can hardly wait." He kicked his long legs out in front of him, crossing them at the ankles. "I think we can get back to our porn star wannabe now."

She noted the time and the image number. Then, keeping the speed slow, she started the slideshow again. They watched the hands covering Leanne's eyes, watched the backwards steps.

Suddenly, they're back into a cluttered storage room. Leanne is pushing the door shut. She twists the lock on the knob—there was no coercion here. Her hand rises and she flips off the light switch. Darkness. She turns around to face a shadowy man-shape who is utterly undistinguishable.

"Damn it," Ronnie whispered.

"Chill. It gets brighter, you know it does.

Yes, she knew…she'd gotten a much better look at this stranger's junk than she'd ever want to. She only hoped the lighting improved before things progressed to the drop-to-your-knees stage. She'd really prefer to see his face and identify the man before she had to take another gander at his genitals.

The couple on the screen shifts. Leanne turns, walking deeper into the room, close to an uncurtained window. She glances back, looking at her own hand, which is twined with a masculine one. She tugs him with her, away from the door, into a private corner of the small room, pushing some boxes out of the way.

The window is now easily visible. It is night out. *Why is she working so late?* But there is light coming from somewhere—enough of it to brighten the corner of the room. Perhaps construction lighting, used to aid night-shift workers on this project, which had been worked 24/7 in recent days?

Leanne reaches the back corner. Stops. Turns around and stares at the shadowy man moving toward her. She's looking at his body, staring with lustful intent at the tented crotch of his pants. She watches him move his hands to the top of his shirt and begin to slide the buttons free.

He comes closer. She lifts her hands to help him. Her pale fingers are stark against the…the…*green* shirt. It's a green shirt. A dark green shirt.

Recognition began to tingle in the back of Ronnie's mind. Her suspicion grows, though she has trouble believing it at first.

The shirt is undone, tugged up out of the pants. Leanne moves in to kiss his throat, her focus on the cords of muscle in his neck. Then on his jaw—smooth, hairless. Then his cheek—youthful looking. Then his nose—straight, small.

Then his lips, parted for a kiss.

The couple looks at one another and he shifts a little, as if wanting to better see her face. In that moment, he moves right into the light coming from the window, which shines like a spotlight on his features.

Ronnie's suspicions are confirmed; she knows him immediately. But the shock makes it hard to believe for a second.

"Him?" Daniels barked in disbelief. "That was the dude she was going down on? That punk's hung like a race-horse?"

"Yeah," she muttered, not as stunned that Leanne had chosen this particular man for her lover, or even as surprised as Daniels was by the man's endowment. Frankly, she found it far more shocking to think about how he had behaved on Wednesday.

How could he have stood there, in clear sight of his lover's mangled remains, giving Ronnie her first run-down of the crime scene they'd been called out to investigate?

Because their victim's mystery lover was the man who'd led Ronnie to Leanne Carr's torture chamber. It was Secret Service Special Agent Bailey.

Chapter 13

As Dr. Eileen Cavanaugh had predicted, Ronnie woke up the next morning feeling a lot better. She wouldn't describe herself as completely back to normal, but her headache had finally gone away and she was no longer woozy or off-balance. The staples in her scalp were the tiniest bit itchy, which she took as a good sign.

Quickly showering, she got dressed for work and headed into the kitchen. Rather than grabbing a quick bite and heading right out the door, as she would on most Fridays, she made herself a big breakfast. She was starving, having eaten next to nothing in the hospital and only grabbing a frozen dinner last night. So she scrambled some eggs, fried some bacon, made fresh coffee and squeezed orange juice.

She made enough for two. Not because she had company—Daniels certainly hadn't spent the night. He'd left at around one a.m., after they'd gone through more of Leanne's data dump, in which they'd found another X-rated encounter between the murder victim and Agent Bailey.

No, it wasn't him she expected to share her breakfast with. She had already told Daniels she'd be in a little late, and glanced at the clock while she ate, waiting for the pounding that would almost certainly be sounding on her door at any time.

It came at 7:50.

"Girl, I know you're in there, open up and let me see how bad it is."

Biting her lip, knowing Max was going to lose his shit when he saw her, she went to the door and opened it. "Good morning."

"Ack!"

He burst in, a flurry of hands and motion, immediately pushing her into a kitchen chair so he could examine the damage.

Max, who was utterly gorgeous, charming, had great taste and worked as a hair-dresser, should, by all rights, be gay. Instead, he was the most hetero guy she knew. He was worse than Daniels when it came to women and his apartment door should revolve for ease of entrance and exit. His picture could be posted online to illustrate the term man-whore, and he loved to chortle about his sexual exploits whenever they had a movie night or got together to have a few beers.

Fortunately, he wasn't attracted to her. He liked her—loved her, he often said—but when it came to sex, he was strictly into the girlish, weak and helpless type. Which so didn't describe Ronnie.

That was a good thing. She liked him, a lot, but wouldn't let him touch her with his cootie-covered self on a dare. That thing between his legs had been in more woman than Tampax and she'd often warned him it was going to catch some nasty disease some day.

"Okay, we can fix this," he said.

"Eat something first," she said, gesturing toward the big breakfast.

He sat down and ate, but she knew his attention was still on her head. He kept getting up between bites, walking behind her chair, pulling what was left of her hair, twisting it and muttering.

After he'd eaten, he reached for his big satchel, in which he'd carried over shears, combs and a drape, which he proceeded to slide over her shoulders. "I think this could end up being the greatest thing that could have happened to you. You know I've been dying to get a little creative on your boring head. Wish you'd let me add a splash of color, too. Blue streaks would be awesome with this jet black tone."

"Forget it. Just do something simple," she insisted with a sigh. "I don't want to mess with it any more than I have to."

That's why she'd always kept her hair long. Yanking it into a ponytail, or a bun, which she always wore to work, was simple and quick, just the way she liked it.

Max didn't make any promises, and immediately got to work with the comb and the shears. He was careful around her injury, but otherwise pretty ruthless when it came to yanking her head this way and that. "How'd it happen, anyway?"

She'd told him on the phone that she'd been hurt on the job, she hadn't given him any details. Nor could she. That didn't, however, mean she couldn't tell him the truth.

"Got whacked in the side of the head with a two-by-four."

He rolled his eyes. "Okay, *don't* tell me."

She chuckled. Hey, she'd tried, anyway.

As he worked, Max started telling her about his latest conquest, a girl he'd met at the supermarket. Ronnie barely listened, her thoughts going back to somebody else's romantic exploits. Namely Leanne Carr's. She just couldn't stop thinking about the erotic relationship the woman had been having with the oh-so-young-and-innocent-looking Agent

Bailey. He of the nine-inch schlong.

Okay, so maybe *that's* why the relationship had continued.

Still, it was beyond frustrating to realize Bailey had been having sex with the victim and had been privy to every single bit of the investigation into her murder. She was, of course, incredibly suspicious of him, although she didn't immediately like him as the killer. No, he hadn't told anyone that he and Leanne were having sex. And yes, he'd stood right there by Leanne's dismembered corpse and lied to Ronnie's face about how well he had known the woman. But there was one thing that just didn't fit. The killer had acted like he'd known about the O.E.P. device. And Bailey, she felt pretty sure, didn't know about it.

First, there had been his confusion during the briefing. Then, of course, was the fact that he'd hidden their personal relationship. If he knew Leanne was an implantee, he'd have to have realized the authorities would have very blatant proof of their sexual relationship just as soon as they examined the downloads. Bailey could have made things a little less humiliating—and suspicious—for himself if he'd just come clean about it up front. Admitting the affair, he could have said they'd kept it secret because they'd hooked up on the job, and thrown himself on the investigators' mercy.

He hadn't done that. Instead, he'd lied, as if truly believing he wouldn't get caught.So it was really doubtful he'd known about the device.

Meaning it was really doubtful he was the murderer.

Doubtful. Not impossible. He could just be very clever and manipulative.

"So, that guy I saw leaving late last night..." Max said, interrupting her thoughts.

"My partner."

"Daniels, right?" Max said. *Snip snip.* "Is he the type you like— big, brawny, crude?"

"He's the type I like for a partner," she drawled back, knowing where Max was going. Just because he didn't want to have sex with her himself didn't mean he wasn't constantly trying to push her to get laid by somebody else.

"Such a waste," he informed her, tsking. "You're too young to live like a nun, Ronnie. Your vagina's gonna grow adhesions and close up one of these days."

"And you're too smart to live like a porn star. Your dick's going to either fall off from some venereal disease or get chopped off by some woman you did wrong."

He laughed. "Okay, okay, I'll mind my own business."

"Thank you."

"So, you working on that White House murder?" he asked, changing the subject.

Ronnie stiffened. She hadn't paid any attention to the news since she got out of the hospital and had no idea how much information had been leaked. "Yeah. What have you heard?"

"Just that some woman was killed there the other day."

Whew.

"Plus a lot of nonsense that she was all chopped up and shit. Nobody really believes that."

Double whew. "Good."

"How's the old place look?" he asked, sounding more interested in the construction project than in the case.

"Surprisingly far along," she admitted, thinking about the hours she'd spent in the most famous house in the world. "It's a lot better on the inside than the out. It was kind of strange walking down the corridors, going right into the Oval Office, imagining what it looked like five years ago. They're rebuilding everything exactly as it was back then."

Complete with one stupid tunnel the public isn't supposed to know about.

His hands stopped moving. She didn't have to look up to see he'd paused to reflect…to almost offer up a moment of silence, the way most everyone did when it came to that subject.

On a day when so many had died and an entire section of one of the greatest cities in the world had been wiped off the map, the assassination of the president sometimes almost got overlooked. President Turner's death would always just be part of the awfulness of 10/20/17, not a monumental minute in history in and of itself, the way JFK's or Lincoln's murders had been. Probably because killing the president had merely been a little side bonus for the terrorists. They were happy it had happened, but the point hadn't been to try to destabilize the government by wiping out any key players. Rather they'd just wanted the whole country so terrified they'd make a tectonic shift in political direction.

And oh, had they gotten what they'd wished for.

"One of my clients went to the dedication ceremony on Tuesday," Max admitted, his tone suitably subdued. "She said it was like the old days—King's speech or Obama's inauguration."

"Minus about nine-hundred-thousand people, maybe."

"Yeah. But I guess the way everyone was kept in close, with

nobody sprawling all the way up both sides of the old reflecting pool, it seemed more crowded."

She considered asking Max if his client had happened to notice anybody splattered with blood or carrying a head cruising around the place, but figured that was probably a long shot.

"I wouldn't have gone even if I'd won one of the lottery tickets," he said as he snipped and tweaked. "I don't care if that whole place was covered with cameras, I wouldn't be in a big crowd in D.C. on a bet."

Cameras. Covered with cameras.

It had been, of course. There had been news cameras and security cameras on the Army vehicles. Ronnie knew one of the other detectives had been assigned the task of going through them, looking for any activity near the White House. Now that she knew there was a tunnel that ended up near the Washington Monument, she made a mental note to have him tighten the scope of his search.

She also started thinking about something else. Each state had given out tickets by way of a lottery. Only a thousand per state.

It's a long shot. A really long shot.

Still, it was at least possible that one of those fifty-five thousand people at the event was an implantee. What if someone attending the Independence Day event had an O.E.P. device in his or her head? And what if they'd been anywhere near the maintenance building where that tunnel ended up?

Her heart beat a little faster. Long shot. But not impossible.

"Thanks, Max," she said.

"For what?"

"You just gave me an idea."

"Well, don't thank me for that, honey. Thank me for *this.*"

He retrieved a large hand-mirror from his bag and held it in front of her so she could see the results of his labors. Ronnie stared for a minute, stunned into silence. Her jaw fell open; she could see the reflection of her own fillings, and quickly snapped it shut.

"Wow," she said, shocked at how quickly he'd made a real hairstyle out of a hacked-up mess.

She'd kept her hair long out of laziness, assuming that, if she ever did get it styled, cut or layered, she'd have to deal with curling and blow-drying and all that nonsense for which she just didn't have the time. But Max had done some serious magic with nothing but some scissors, hair gel and his own hands.

Her hair was short, but not at all boyish. It was still feminine, just very modern, sleek. Though short on the sides—especially where it had already been chopped off, Max had left her some length that he'd swept forward over her brow in jagged bangs. It was sexy, attention-getting and, she had to admit, pretty damned hot. She liked it. A lot.

"That looks amazing," she said, meaning it. "Thank you so much."

"Any time girlfriend. If I'd known it would just take a two-by-four upside your head to let me give you a fabulous look, I'd have hit you myself long ago."

"Spoken like a true friend," she said, laughing as she stood up and brushed the hair off her uniform.

Promising him a home-cooked meal and a bottle of tequila in the future as payment, she said goodbye and walked him to the door. The attack the other night had been painful and dangerous, but she had to admit, something good had come out of it. For a moment, at least, she'd been able to laugh with a friend. She greatly feared she wouldn't be doing much more laughing until after this horrible case was solved.

Though Daniels had offered to pick her up for work that day, Ronnie had insisted on getting a patrol car to swing by and get her. Daniels lived in the opposite direction, and she hadn't known how long it would take to make something decent out of the mess on her head. It was a testament to Max's skill that, not only did she get to the precinct by nine, but she also got a lot of looks and catcalls when she walked through the squad. Including from Jeremy Sykes.

She'd asked him to meet her and Daniels here so he could be present when they talked to Agent Bailey. Daniels had contacted the Secret Service agent this morning, told him they had a few questions and asked him to come in to the precinct. He should be arriving shortly.

When she arrived at her desk, she found Sykes sitting on a corner of it, looking every bit the cool, calm Fed and not a frenzied, overworked, perpetually irritated city cop like everybody else in the building.

"Nice," he said, eyeing her closely and nodding his approval. A gleam appeared in his blue eyes, and she warmed beneath it, in spite of herself.

"What's nice?" asked Daniels, looking confused.

"Forget it," she replied with a laugh, knowing her brothers would have been exactly the same way.

"Got the background check on Bailey," he said.

Sykes appeared confused. "Guess that's part of what we need to talk about?"

"Yeah, it is." She cast a quick look at her partner, who shook his head, telling her he hadn't yet revealed anything about what they'd learned the night before. Wanting to get out of the loud bull pen, so they could actually hear each other during their conversation, not to mention avoid being overheard when she talked about watching somebody else's uber-personal "sex tape," she said, "Let's go grab some coffee."

"Be right there," said Daniels. "I want to read this over before our friend shows up."

"Okay, come to the back when you're done."

She led Sykes to the break room, which was fortunately empty. To her surprise, the hardest part about filling him in on the latest twists in the investigation wasn't admitting she'd sat with her partner and watched their victim having wild sex a few days before her death. It was telling him how she'd gotten Leanne Carr's data dump.

She'd sort of hoped he would forget that part—and her promise not to do any work the night before. But not Jeremy Sykes. As soon as she finished telling him everything she'd learned—from Daniels's discovery of the tunnel, to Leanne and Bailey's graphic sexual encounters—they'd found two so far, and she wasn't finished going through the downloads—he went right for the part she'd hoped he would forget about.

"How'd you get the files?"

Daniels had come into the room, but he remained quiet, watching her, waiting for her to answer.

"I had every right to access them," she finally said. "You brought them for me, remember?"

"I know that. But how did you get them? I still have the micro-drive I brought up to Tate's lab."

She busied herself pouring another cup of stale coffee into a cracked mug and mumbled, "I burned a copy when you went to find Dr. Cavanaugh."

To her surprise, Sykes merely barked a deep laugh. "You coulda just taken the original drive. I brought it for you, ya know."

Maybe. But he'd only shown it to her; he hadn't exactly handed it over.

"I figured you'd harass me for wanting to work last night."

"You mean you seriously thought I believed that, 'I'm much too weary to do any more work today,' crap? Jeez, Veronica, how big an idiot do you take me for?"

Her jaw dropping, she snapped, "Well then why'd you make such a big deal about insisting I promise not to think about the case?"

"Because I figured that would at least get you to put it out of your mind for a couple of hours. I knew you'd *try* to keep your promise. But you're too good a cop to spend a whole night ignoring a murder investigation."

Her hand tightened around the mug; she was both glad he knew her well enough to understand how she worked, and annoyed that she'd gone to such lengths to get the data. Here she'd jumped through hoops, thinking she'd been so clever, and he'd been ahead of her every step of the way. And once again, he'd managed to surprise her. She had recently begun to wonder if her assessment of Sykes—made on the first day of training in Texas—was totally accurate. Had she put him in a round hole, when he was actually a square peg?

"So, anything *else* you want to tell me before we dive in?" he asked, raising a brow, as if he already knew she had something else to confess.

She caught her lip between her teeth, wondering what he'd figured out. She hadn't yet revealed what she'd learned about those six dead O.E.P. test subjects, but there was no way he could know she'd acquired that data, too. Wanting to get them both caught up on everything before Bailey arrived, she told them what she'd learned.

"Wait, you're telling me you actually hacked into Tate Scientific's files and stole a proprietary list of patients involved in a medical trial?" Surprisingly, that indignant question came from Daniels, not Sykes. "Shit, Ron, what were you thinking?"

"I was thinking," she explained, "that maybe there are more than two victims out there. That maybe those other six men somehow tie-in to our case."

Sykes, who'd listened quietly during her explanation, reached into his pocket, pulled out a small, folded sheet of paper, and slowly unfolded it. He lowered it to the break-room table, pushing it toward her with the tips of his fingers. She glanced down and saw six names. Six familiar names.

"Damn."

"What can I say? Smart minds."

"How'd you get them?"

"I hacked into the Tate network when we first started working, before we watched the Carr files."

176

Her eyes rounding into saucer shape, she exclaimed, "That's so *non*-Sykes of you!"

"Maybe you don't know me as well as you think you do."

No, maybe she didn't. *Square peg. Round hole.*

"How long did it take you to get them?" she asked.

"Six minutes." His brow rose in challenge. "You?"

She smirked. "Four."

"I had to do it while you were still in the room," he pointed out.

"I had to do it after I'd also had to copy your microdrive."

"Okay, okay, you win this round," he said with a helpless laugh.

"Amateurs," Daniels said with a scowl. "You're pretty proud of yourselves, regular little hackers, huh?"

"Oh yes," Sykes replied.

"You're as bad as she is."

Sykes leaned against the wall, his arms crossed, studying Daniels. "Funny, you don't strike me as somebody who always plays the rules."

While Sykes usually did. Which made this conversation all the more surprising.

"I'm not," Daniels replied. "But *she* usually does, and considering one of us needs to keep our nose clean, I kinda count on her to do it. We don't both need to land on the D.C.P.D. shit list."

Ronnie was barely listening to her partner's complaint, still too stunned to realize that Sykes had also been stepping out of bounds, following interesting little twists and turns in the case. Here she thought she'd been the only one with that suspicious mind, the only one who'd heard about some other implantees dying of natural causes and leapt to some pretty startling conclusions.

Sykes had not only thought it, he'd beat her to the punch in starting to investigate.

Somehow, though, despite always being in competition with the man, she found herself exhilarated by that realization, rather than annoyed by it. She was actually smiling by the time Daniels finished chewing her out for being reckless.

"All right, all right, I can see you're happy with yourself," he muttered, throwing himself into a chair. "But next time you decide to go all bad cop, do me a favor and make sure *this* guy,"—he jerked a thumb toward Sykes—"hasn't already done it for you."

"Okay, you're right," she said, suitably chastened. Because Daniels had a point. If she and Sykes weren't always so busy competing, and trying to one-up each other, they could have doubled their efforts and halved their risks.

Appearing glad she'd at least acknowledged his annoyance, Daniels barked, "Well? What'd you find out? 'Cause we all know you did something with this list."

Glad he'd finished scolding, she told him what she'd learned from Philip Tate, and went on to admit her plan to call every coroner or hospital associated with the six deaths if she had to.

"Let me do it for Chrissake," snapped Daniels, snagging the sheet of paper off the table. "You two aren't any good at this sneaky shit. You probably left all kinds of electronic evidence on their network."

She doubted that, but was so grateful that her partner was taking over this one part of the investigation, she couldn't argue the point,

"Daniels? Sloan? Your witness is here," said a uniformed patrolman who'd stuck his head into the room. "I put him in interview room three. He looked a little nervous."

"I'll bet," she said, knowing Bailey had to have been waiting for them to find out about his relationship with Leanne. The fact that he hadn't volunteered the information didn't say much for his intelligence, especially if he knew Leanne was involved with the O.E.P.

He didn't.

The three of them started toward the door, then all paused. They hadn't worked out who would be doing the questioning, or which of them would be in the room. Technically, Sykes was a guest here. But he was also a key part of this investigation. She honestly wasn't sure whether he should be in there or not.

"I'll wait in the observation room," he said, making the decision.

"Okay, that might be best. Bailey doesn't know you," said Ronnie. "He might be less likely to talk in front of somebody he hasn't met."

Daniels frowned, as if he wasn't sure he agreed with the strategy. "He also might be less likely to talk about the sexual aspects of the relationship in front of you, Ronnie."

She bristled. "That's ridiculous."

"I know it is," her partner said, holding his hands up defensively. "But the thing is, Bailey was skittish and embarrassed around you from the start. When you finally threw him a bone, he acted like a kid with a crush. I don't think I ever told you that a few minutes before I found you in the basement the other night, Bailey specifically asked me to 'thank you' and said you'd understand why."

178

She had no freaking idea why, but nodded for Daniels to go ahead.

"If he's aware of the existence of the O.E.P. device, and realizes you actually saw him doing the victim, he's gonna be a mess."

"I'm not entirely sure he is aware of it," she admitted.

Sykes eyed her in surprise. "But the killer had to know. Not only was it pretty damned obvious because of the way he disguised himself, with the clothes, the hood and that crazy miner's light, but the Philadelphia murder cinches it."

"I know. Honestly, I hope I'm wrong, and that Special Agent Bailey was aware of Leanne's participation in the program, because it would make him a much more viable suspect. The truth is, though, I haven't seen any indication that he was. He doesn't seem like a good enough actor to have faked his confusion at the first briefing, when the O.E.P. issue came up."

"I guess that explains his I'm-gonna-puke expression when we first showed up, too," Daniels said, speaking slowly as he thought back to the other morning, which seemed like it had taken place ages ago. "I figured it was just the gruesomeness of the scene, but apparently he was reacting to something a lot more personal."

"Maybe he kept the relationship secret because he knew that if anybody found out, he might be looked at for the murder," she said.

She assumed that's why he had kept quiet, though how he could have stood there with those body parts and not gone slightly mad, she didn't know. He must have one heck of a strong self-preservation instinct.

Daniels lifted a hand to his face and rubbed at his eyes, which didn't even look the tiniest bit bloodshot this morning. He might not have stopped at a bar to tie one on after leaving her place last night, which made for a nice change. "You know what else, he was there when somebody mentioned Leanne's backups being taken in for you to examine, Ron. He'd had sex with her twice in the last week…"

"At least twice," she interjected.

"Right. Meaning, if he were aware of the scope of the program, he had to know what you'd see."

Sykes nodded, obviously understanding where they were going. "He's in law enforcement, he would understand that things would go a lot better for him if he came clean about their sexual relationship before you found out about it."

"Exactly," she said. "He could have put his own spin on it, made himself appear he was being totally up-front and honest, and come off looking a lot less suspicious."

They all fell silent for a long moment, considering. Then Daniels muttered, "Shit. You might be right. That punk-ass kid might not even have a clue we saw him doing the nasty with our murder victim a few days before her death."

"Meaning he's probably not the murderer," Sykes said.

She knew neither of them were ready to rule Bailey out completely, and neither was she, but the basic facts definitely took the wind out of their sails. Still, just because they had doubts about his guilt regarding Leanne's murder, SA Bailey still had a lot to answer for. He'd lied to them, led them in the wrong direction. He could have admitted his relationship with her, perhaps helped them with the investigation, but he'd wasted their time instead.

That pissed her off, to be honest. She probably ought to get a cold drink and take a few seconds to calm down before she confronted the guy.

Daniels cleared his throat. "Don't kill me, partner, but even if the kid doesn't know about the program, it still might not be a great idea for you to be in the interview room."

She gaped.

Sykes held a hand up, cutting off her argument. "Sorry, Veronica, I'm with Daniels on this one. If Bailey knows about the implant and knows you saw him, he's going to be embarrassed. If he doesn't know about the implant, doesn't know you saw him, he's going to stick to his story in order to save face with you. Either way, your presence could be a detriment."

She choked back a growl of frustration. Because they were right, and she knew they were right. Shaking her head, she waved them toward the door. "Go on. I'll watch from the observation room." Then, because she knew them well enough to know this temporary truce as they united against her wouldn't last for long, she admonished them both. "Play nice. If he senses any kind of dissention between you two, he'll do what he can to exploit it."

Her partner and the FBI agent stared at each other for a long moment. Then Sykes nodded and Daniels shrugged. That was about as close to a declaration of friendship as they'd ever be likely to express. But beggars couldn't be choosers. She'd take what she could get.

Chapter 14

Skirting the interview room where their witness sat, cooling his heels, Ronnie headed for the room next door. It was small, bare, with just a table and chair and one broad window that overlooked the room next door. The glass would allow Ronnie to see what was happening, and an intercom would enable hear to hear. Bailey was in law enforcement, so he would know someone was observing from the other side. Hell, anybody who'd ever seen a cop show on TV would know that. Hopefully, he wouldn't realize it was her and decide to be uncooperative.

Things started out well. Daniels took the lead, Sykes content to stand quietly in the corner, his arms crossed over his chest, leaning against the wall. He appeared almost disinterested, but she saw the keenly focused expression on his face and knew the pose was a deliberate one. They wanted Bailey to let his guard down.

Daniels led the young Special Agent through a series of basic questions—stuff they'd already covered in interviews with others out at the Patriot Square site. Then, just as the agent settled back into his chair, looking a little relaxed, as if he'd expected far worse, her partner hit him with the big one.

"So, Special Agent Bailey, we've been led to believe you might have had a closer relationship with the victim than you've said."

The man shot straight up in his chair. "What? That's crazy. Who told you that?"

Daniels, who'd been sitting across from the man, scooted his chair forward, making it squeak on the dingy tile. Bailey flinched, his tension visibly increasing with every second.

Daniels merely smiled. "Is it true?"

"That's nuts," he snapped. Again, not answering the question. "I'm a married man and I love my wife. I would never cheat on her."

Uh, right. Just like he'd never mislead investigators trying to solve a murder.

Ronnie had been in on enough interviews to know how easily some people lied. Bailey was trying not to. As if hedging, throwing out indignant replies and skirting around the issue were going to get Daniels to back off, without Bailey ever having to actually say the words, "No, it's not true."

He obviously didn't know her partner. Or Sykes, who walked over and sat on the edge of the table, looking down at the agent. "Detective Daniels never said anything about you cheating on your wife. He asked if you were closer to the victim than you'd led us to believe. Why would you immediately assume he was talking about a sexual affair?"

Bailey sputtered, looking back and forth between them. "But, he said...I thought he meant..."

Sykes sighed. "Okay, well, since you put it out there, did your wife know you were having sex with Leanne Carr?"

Bailey's eyes bugged out and his face went bright red. "I resent that accusation!"

"Resent it all you want. You still did it," Sykes replied, completely unflappable. "Come on, Bailey, we know all about it."

"How? That's impossible." He crossed his arms over his chest, huddling in his chair. Mumbling like a little kid accused of breaking the cookie jar, he added, "Nobody can prove something that didn't happen."

Sykes and Daniels exchanged a glance, then both looked toward the two-way mirror, toward her. She knew what they were thinking. Bailey sure wasn't acting like he knew there could be any kind of photographic evidence.

He didn't know about the O.E.P. He had no idea Leanne had a camera in her brain.

Daniels tapped his fingers on the table. "So, you're saying that wasn't you who, last Tuesday evening, snuck up behind her, put your hands over her eyes, and tugged her back with you into a storage room, where she proceeded to..."

"Oh, my God! How do you know that?" Bailey looked completely shocked. Though because he'd been caught out having sex with a woman who was later murdered, or because he'd cheated on his wife, she couldn't say.

"We just know. Now, how long was it going on?"

Bailey hesitated, his eyes shifting back and forth, between Daniels and Sykes, and then at the mirror. It was like he was looking right at her.

"Is *she* in there?"

Daniels tilted his head in confusion. "She?"

"Sloan. Detective Sloan. Is she watching this?"

Sykes provided a smooth reply. "You do remember that Detective Sloan was attacked in the basement of the White House the other night, and was badly injured, don't you?"

Bailey sighed in relief, and Ronnie almost laughed. Two could play at that not-actually-lying game.

"Is she okay?" the young man asked.

"She will be," said Daniels, sounding both sad and angry. "I'm gonna get the person who did that to her and make him wish he was never born."

The color fell out of Bailey's face. "You're not saying you think I had anything to do with that. I was in your office, talking to you when it happened."

"You could have hit her, then come up to see where I was and establish an alibi."

"But I didn't. I would never have done that, I couldn't hurt a woman!"

"No, you just cheat on them," said Sykes.

Bailey glared up at him. "You don't understand."

"Infidelity? Oh, I understand that, it's not terribly complicated."

His eyes growing luminous, Bailey buried his face in his hands. A small sob emerged from him and Ronnie had to wonder whether he was crying for his wife, for Leanne, or for himself for getting busted.

"You're not going to have to tell Tanya, my wife, are you?"

Okay. Himself. Little slimeball.

"She'd never understand."

"Wives usually don't," Daniels said, sounding disgusted.

"It's just, we went to high school together, I'd never had a chance to, I dunno, sow my wild oats or anything. I don't want to upset her or have her think it meant anything."

Ronnie was suddenly glad for the mirror that made it impossible for him to see her rolling her eyes in disgust.

"Leanne didn't know I was married at first," he admitted. "I never wore my ring at work."

"When did it start?" Sykes asked, still sitting above Bailey on the table, like a quiet father figure to whom the man could safely confess. Meanwhile, Daniels resembled the angry older brother who might beat the shit out of him at any moment.

They did this good-cop/bad-cop thing pretty well. Better than she and Daniels usually did, considering they both typically fought over who was bad-cop and neither could pull off a convincing *good* one.

"We started messing around about a month and a half ago. Just flirting at first, then one day it went a little farther and next thing you know we're making it on the floor of the Oval Office."

Bailey sounded almost pleased with himself for that. *Punk.*

"Ever 'make it' on the floor of the sub-basement?" Daniels asked, ice in his voice.

Bailey finally remembered who he'd been proud about having sex with, and blanched. He swallowed visibly, his throat fluttering. "I didn't know it was her at first. Not until after they found her chip and got her identity. I went into the bathroom and puked until I thought I'd pass out."

"You seemed to have pulled yourself together by the time my partner and I got there," Daniels said.

"I guess. But believe me, I went home that night, locked myself in the bathroom and cried like a baby. I told Tanya I was sick." He shook his head, actually appearing distressed now. "Look, I didn't love Leanne, but I liked her and we had fun together. What happened to her was brutal, man. Nobody deserves to die like that, and I hope you catch the bastard who did it and fry him."

Was this guy really so clueless that he had no idea he was a suspect? He was focused on not letting his wife found out about an affair; so far it didn't appear to have occurred to him that they might like him for the murder.

So they *didn't* like him for the murder, but he couldn't know that.

"Agent Bailey, can you account for your whereabouts throughout the afternoon of the 4th?" asked Sykes.

Bailey's hands fisted and he drew them into his stomach. "You don't think…you can't…"

Daniels leaned across the table, glaring at the man. "Just answer the question, Bailey."

"I was on duty the entire time," Bailey insisted. "I signed in at the security trailer at 9 a.m., and was assigned to different duties throughout the day. I wasn't out of sight of somebody I work with for more than a ten minutes that whole afternoon!"

Sykes pulled a notebook out of his pocket and dropped it onto the table. "Give us the name of every person you interacted with and everywhere you were from 2:00 p.m. until 4:00p.m."

Bailey nodded quickly, grabbed the pen and pad and began

writing. As he did so, he continued to mumble excuses for the affair, and to explain why he hadn't told them about it. "If I'd thought I could help with the investigation, I would totally have told you. But the truth is, I hadn't even seen Leanne for two days before she died. I knew absolutely nothing."

"You still didn't think it mattered?" Daniels slammed a hand flat down on the table, making the suspect flinch. "Come on, Bailey, you're supposed to be in law enforcement. You know there's no such thing as an unimportant detail in a murder investigation!"

Tears rose to the young man's eyes. "I know. I'm sorry. I was…ashamed."

Good. He should be.

"Plus, it would have made me look really bad. Kilgore's a stick-in-the-mud. If he'd found out, he probably would have fired me, even after Leanne died."

Kilgore *had* known, at least if they were right about him being the person caught so briefly on the O.E.P. chip watching Bailey and Leanne. If he were really such a stick-in-the-mud, why hadn't he done anything about it? She'd have thought he would have confronted the young lovers and warned them to stop their behavior.

Maybe he did. But maybe it wasn't Bailey he confronted.

Hmm. She had to wonder if Kilgore had sought-out Leanne, and made a mental note to look for him in the rest of the downloaded files.

Bailey babbled on. "If I lost my job, Tanya would want to know why. I mean, what would I say to her? I couldn't tell her I was messing around."

"Start thinking, dude. If you're a murder suspect, she's gonna find out," Daniels snarled.

"But you can't suspect me! I didn't do it, check these names, these people will tell you I couldn't possibly have done that. It would have been physically impossible for me to be in two places at once."

Sykes took the pad, glanced it over, folded it closed and put it back in his pocket. Rising from the table, he walked over toward the mirror, looking through it as if he could see her, though she knew he could not. He winked. Then turned around.

"So, Bailey, now that we know you were a lot friendlier with Ms. Carr than you've let on, why don't we start from the beginning. You tell us every single thing you know about her…and then we'll decide whether or not we believe you."

Leslie Kelly

Although Ronnie very much wanted to confront Special Agent in Charge Kilgore with her suspicion that he'd been the one spying on the sexual encounter between Bailey and Leanne Carr, she knew she needed more evidence. She and Daniels had gotten through a few days of Leanne's backups at her apartment last night, mostly by fast-forwarding through anything that looked unimportant and only watching physical interactions with other people. So far, she hadn't found anything else involving Kilgore, but she wasn't finished looking yet.

Sykes had some looking of his own to do. Dr. Cavanaugh had finished working on Brian Underwood's chip. Plus, he'd barely made a dent in that man's backups from his home computer. So after they'd finished with the Bailey interrogation—all of them agreeing it was doubtful he was their man—Ronnie agreed to ride with Sykes up to Bethesda, to Phineas Tate's research facility. Daniels had planned to go back to talk to the lead architect, Frank, as well as Williams and Kilgore, to try to find out more about that tunnel and who could have known about it. He also promised to try to find out what he could about the six dead O.E.P. test subjects.

Upon arriving at Dr. Tate's building, they were greeted by Dr. Cavanaugh, who showed them to the same lab they'd used yesterday. Ronnie hadn't been able to help holding her breath, wondering if the woman would comment about some unusual activity on these work stations yesterday—when somebody had been poking around the Tate network—but she said nothing of the sort. Apparently, she and Sykes were better hackers than Daniels gave them credit for.

Or maybe the pretty scientist was just distracted. As she had yesterday, Cavanaugh paid more attention to Sykes than she did to Ronnie, which was fine by her. Let him be the charming FBI agent who everybody liked, she was content being the hard-ass bitch who didn't make friends but sure got results.

"So, we going to start with Underwood's death?" Sykes asked as soon as they were alone.

She hated the prospect of it, after what they'd witnessed in this room yesterday, but knew it had to be done. "Okay."

He hesitated. "You're sure?"

"We made a deal. You watched mine, I'll watch yours."

"I really wish we were talking about something else here," he said, mild and rueful.

She managed a very faint smile, then put away all light thoughts and prepared herself for what was to come.

He set up the slideshow. "Ten minutes again? Witnesses claim he left his friend's apartment only ten minutes before his implanted chip says he died."

"That's a relief." Just ten minutes. She could stand ten minutes. *Ten awful minutes.*

Because it was, of course, awful. The only positive was that it didn't come anywhere close to the level of horrific violence of Leanne Carr's death. Probably because the killer had known he had an entire building and hours of time to spend with Leanne, while Underwood's murder had taken place in a back alley in the middle of downtown Philadelphia before midnight. The suspect could have been interrupted at any time, so he had acted quickly.

The imaging of the projection equipment was so incredibly powerful, Ronnie could almost swear she heard the crunch of her own footsteps on the gravel as she walked through that alley. She could practically smell the reek of the garbage can, almost reach out and grab the cat that had leapt into Underwood's path, startling him into a sudden stop.

She could almost feel the exact moment when the attack had occurred.

After having stunned the young father, the black-cloaked assailant had pulled out a large knife and slit Underwood's throat. Ronnie and had watched the blade descend, watched the brutally sharp tip draw close to Brian's face before moving down beneath his chin. Then the knife had flicked sharply. The images had begun to fade, gradually winking out. Brian Underwood had been dead—his O.E.P. device going inactive and shutting down—within a few minutes of the initial attack, once the electric impulses in his brain had ceased.

That had been a blessing. Whatever mutilation had been visited upon the corpse, the beheading, for instance, had all taken place post mortem. As ridiculous as it was to think any murder victim could be considered lucky, when they compared the Philadelphia murder to the one in Washington, they had to think Underwood had definitely had the better end.

"Not much help, was it?" Sykes asked, rubbing a weary hand over his rugged jaw as the lights came back up and the machine shut back down.

"The cloak is new," she pointed out. Leanne's killer had worn a long black shirt and black pants. By the time he got to Underwood, he'd added a long, totally concealing cloak that covered him from shoulder to foot. Perhaps it was because he knew there was a greater risk of exposure. Who knew what he'd had on beneath it? If he'd had to make a quick getaway, he could have whipped the cloak off and been wearing a brightly-colored uniform underneath it.

"Yeah. Interesting fabric, too. Shiny. It caught the light."

She'd noticed that, too. When she'd first seen the cloak, she'd had a quick flash of intuition. "It almost reminded me of a Halloween costume."

"Me too. I also got one glimpse of his shoes. I never saw them against anything else to try to gauge their size, but I did notice they were black and shiny, not scuffed up like the other night."

"A killer who shines his shoes between attacks?"

"Maybe he had to clean off the blood."

They looked at each other, obviously both thinking about that, all the tiny pieces of the puzzle swirling around, trying to fit themselves against those they'd collected from Leanne's murder scene. They didn't quite line up. Not yet. But they would someday, of that she had no doubt.

She glanced at the notes she'd jotted down during the slideshow. "And of course, there's the knife."

"Right."

They had managed to still a frame in which they could make out the tiny etching on the murder weapon. Blowing it up to a hundred times its size, they'd been able to get the brand name, and would check it later.

That was all. A cape, a shined shoe, and a knife with a name even Ronnie had heard of that was sold on probably a thousand different websites.

Brian Underwood's O.E.P. chip hadn't helped identify his killer any more than Leanne Carr's had hers.

"So, I guess we go back to the data dumps," he said.

"Guess so."

He ran a hand through his hair, making it stick up, giving him a boyish look. "I'm already exhausted thinking of how many times that man looked at his kids."

She heard the emotion in his voice and understood it. She'd barely glanced at Ryan Underwood's backups yesterday and had been greatly affected by the depth of his emotion for his children. Before she could think better of it, she reached out and put a hand on Sykes's arm.

"Just take it slow and if you ever want to switch, I can take over for a while."

He nodded, not cracking any kind of joke, not saying anything about the fact that the downloads she would be examining would at least have some hot sex in them. There was nothing funny about this, nothing to ease the ugliness of it, which was far greater, she believed, than either of them had anticipated when they'd been in training.

She didn't regret having agreed to be part of this program. She loved the concept of it. It was the actual execution that sometimes gave her pause. Because while she'd always had a great deal of sympathy for victims of violent crime, she had never even imagined what it would be like to walk in their footsteps while those crimes were being committed.

"Thanks," he replied.

They turned their chairs away from one another and got busy on their individual work stations. Whenever either of them needed to examine something in more detail, they utilized the 3-D projector. Each stopped what they were doing to help the other when necessary.

She just wished it hadn't been totally necessary for Sykes to turn around and watch with her while Leanne and Bailey went at it again on the Saturday before the young woman's death. Apparently Special Agent Bailey's wife thought he worked on the weekend, but this interlude had taken place at a seedy hotel. Once again, the sex had been raunchy and a little rough, which both of them seemed to like. *God, I don't want to be thinking about what kind of sex someone I saw chopped into tiny pieces liked!*

Fortunately, unlike her partner had the night before, Sykes didn't make a single inappropriate comment. He merely watched, took some notes, and had her rewind at one point when a car cut Leanne off as she drove out of the hotel parking lot. When the scene had transferred into something more normal—Leanne grocery shopping, then going home, feeding her fish, making dinner—he'd mumbled something about how awkward their job could be—uh, *yeah*—then had turned around and calmly gone back to work.

By the time Ronnie got through the all the visuals from Leanne's weekend—leaving just one day of the final week of the woman's life to view—her eyes were blurry and dry. She glanced at the clock, saw it was nearly seven, and pushed her chair back from the work station.

"You ready to wrap it up?" Sykes asked, turning around to eye her from the other side of the small room.

"Yes. You?"

"I think so. When Underwood wasn't sleeping, he was either

working, or looking at his wife and kids. I got through most of the week already."

Her heart twisted as she thought of those fatherless children. She had to wonder if Tate or the government would give the man's widow back any of his downloads. When those babies grew up, it might be very special for them to see themselves through their father's eyes. They could experience the tender emotions that had flowed off him, shining and vibrant. Those messages of love from a now-dead man, a father they probably wouldn't even remember, would be very special. She made a mental note to talk to Tate about it, and to offer to pick out some lovely moments she'd seen whenever she'd looked over Sykes's shoulder or up on the wall screen.

"I don't think I can look at another minute of mine right now," she muttered, trying to smother a yawn but not succeeding. "I only have one day left. If I don't find anything on that, I'm going to have to go further back in her data dump. Damn, I was hoping to find something in those last seven days."

There were many more weeks on the woman's hard drive. She only hoped they could solve this case before she had to go through all those images that stretched back months, to when Leanne was first implanted with the O.E.P. chip.

"*Hoping* to find something? What are you talking about? You found a *lot* more than I did."

She cocked a brow. "Was that a crack about the size of Bailey's johnson?"

He let out a loud laugh and the tension in the room, which had built hour after hour throughout the day, eased up. They both needed the mental time-out, and she didn't regret making the joke.

"Wow, you're easily impressed," he told her, his eyes twinkling with wicked merriment.

"Yeah, in your dreams," she grunted. Because if Sykes had more in his pants than Bailey did, the man would be in L.A. making porn movies.

Ugh. Porn movies. She *so* wasn't in the mood to see any more of the Leanne and Bailey show.

"I think I'll take the data home and watch the last day at my place."

He lifted a micro disc. "Need this?"

Grinning, she replied, "Nah, I've got it covered."

He grinned back, obviously thinking about her machinations of the previous evening, when she'd stolen data he'd been fully prepared to hand over to her.

"I'll do the same thing. Not like there's much else to do in my hotel room."

Ronnie swallowed, licked her lips and turned away from him, not wanting to think about what Sykes might do to keep himself busy in his hotel room. As she turned and began to shut down her computer, she thought she heard him chuckle, as though he knew exactly why she'd so quickly ended the conversation and turned her back on him.

"Oh, you're both still here," a voice said.

Ronnie looked toward the doorway as Philip Tate entered. The executive was dressed in a pristine, charcoal-grey suit that showed off his tall form and gave his dark green eyes a smoky look. Apparently Friday's weren't a regular golf day.

"We were just about to call it quits for the night," said Sykes.

"Yes, yes, of course," the other man replied, sounding a little distracted.

He crossed his arms, leaned against the doorjamb, then straightened again. "Have you had a productive day?"

"Oh, definitely," Sykes replied with an easy smile. But he didn't go into any detail. Tate and his son might be giving them the use of the lab space, and might have provided the O.E.P. chip, but this was still a murder investigation. And Philip Tate knew about as much about that as he did about his father's experiments. IE: Nada.

"Good for you," Tate said, smiling. "Glad to hear you've gotten some use out of one of the old man's brainchildren."

Tate's smile looked forced. He wasn't as smooth and self-assured as usual, and obviously had something on his mind. She wondered if he just didn't want to say it in front of Sykes.

A possibility popped into her head: the six "natural causes" victims. Perhaps Tate had some information on them and didn't want to get into it with anyone but Ronnie.

"You know," she said to the man, wanting to get him alone so he'd drop his guard and reveal what he knew, "I really could use a steak and a glass of wine after a long day's work."

Tate's eyes widened in surprise. "I'd be happy to feed you," he insisted with a genuine-looking smile.

Sykes, however, wasn't smiling. His mouth pulled down into a deep frown and his brow furrowed as he stared at her. Hard. He obviously knew her well enough to know she wasn't going to encourage or flirt with somebody involved in a murder case. It probably took him less than ten seconds to recognize her motives. And he wasn't happy about them.

"We can stop and get you something on the way back to your place," he insisted as he rose from his chair. He grabbed his suit coat and slung it over his arm. Sykes had unbuttoned his cuffs and rolled up his sleeves, revealing the flexing, muscular forearms, which flexed even more as he fisted both his hands. He was obviously tense and worried.

"Don't be silly, I can see Detective Sloan home." Philip said. "I wanted to talk to her anyway. We can get to know each other a little better over a quiet dinner."

"Detective Sloan had a concussion a few days ago. She shouldn't be drinking any wine."

He sounded like her father. But the look on his face was much more like angry, slightly jealous lover.

He's not your lover. He's not jealous. He doesn't give a damn about you beyond wanting your help to solve this case and possibly wanting to get into your pants.

"I'll be sure she drinks nothing stronger than juice and I'll get her to her door safe and sound," Philip said, reaching out and offering Ronnie his arm.

She wasn't used to that kind of chivalry, but figured she'd play along for now. Besides, she had been dealing with a head injury. Having sat in that chair for hours while she looked at Leanne's downloads, she was feeling a little bit less than steady on her feet.

"Fine," Sykes said. His eyes piercing hers with a silent warning, he added, "I'll call you later tonight. Or you call me. After you get your…steak. If I don't answer, don't hang up. It sometimes takes *six* rings for me to get to the phone."

She nodded once. Sykes had made it clear that he knew she was after information, not a steak dinner. That emphasis on *six* was a direct reference to the six dead O.E.P. test subjects. He knew she wasn't really going out with Tate because she had any interest in him but because of the case and wanted her to know he knew.

He said nothing else. The silence told her he was supporting her, though the stiffness of his jaw and tight set of his lips meant it was only reluctantly. She knew he'd be waiting for that phone call. If he didn't get it, he'd probably show up at Tate's house. God, with her luck, he'd bring Daniels. Her own private belligerent, competitive asshole cavalry.

"Goodnight, Sykes," she said. "I'll talk to you later."

"Yes. You definitely will."

She turned to leave the room with the man in whom she had absolutely no interest, leaving behind the one she couldn't get out of her mind.

"Veronica?"

She glanced back over her shoulder.

"Make sure you chew your steak thoroughly," Sykes said. "You don't want to choke on it."

Chuckling inwardly, she snapped off a cocky salute, and walked out on Philip Tate's arm.

Of all the changes in his life over the past fifteen months, the one Eddie Girardo just couldn't get used to was eating by himself.

He'd been married for eighteen years. Eighteen years of waking up to breakfasts Allie would make for him and the kids before they all left for school or work. Eighteen years of dinners he'd help prepare, either chopping up vegetables for a salad or grilling hot dogs in the back yard of their Richmond home in the summer. Growing up in a big Italian household, he'd learned to help in the kitchen at a young age and often challenged his ex-wife to cook-offs, which the kids would have to judge. Eddie Junior usually voted for his dad's cooking, since they were the only members of the penis club—a joke they'd shared, given the fact that it was two of them against Allie and three girls.

It had been a perfect eighteen years of family meals.

But now his wife was eating another man's hot dog.

His daughters had been bribed out of their father's affections by their stepdaddy's credit cards.

His own son had allowed the lure of vacations in the islands and tickets to the Super Bowl to replace any thoughts of his old man.

They'd abandoned him. And it was when he forced himself to sit in silence at the big, empty kitchen table that he missed them the most.

He reached for his bottle of Jim Beam, which seldom left his side these days. When he was at home, he carried it around with him, the bottle dangling morosely from listless fingers. At work, it was often stashed in his briefcase or his desk, or sometimes in a small flask in his pocket.

He and Jim were old friends. In fact, he'd say Jimmy-boy was the most faithful friend he had. They'd met during Eddie's college years and had been practically inseparable since, even though others had tried to tear them apart. They'd gone through good times and bad together—the bad coming mostly when Eddie tried to kick Jim out of his life. Usually at his wife's insistence.

But he'd never left his friend behind for long, always crawling back to the bottle when things got tough. Jim had taken the sting off the disappointment he'd felt over the years when his job had gone nowhere, when the bills had piled up, when his wife had been a cunt and his daughters little bitches and his son a long-haired punk. Jim had always been there.

Now that he and Jim were the only ones at the table, though, he couldn't help thinking back to those days before Allie had walked out on him, claiming she couldn't be with a man too weak to give up something that was killing him. Ha. That had been the excuse, but he didn't believe it. She'd hooked up with that rich asshole she was now married too pretty damn fast. She'd probably been cheating on him all along.

Before that, though, when his son was a toddler and the girls were still in pigtails, sitting around the dinner table with his family had been the best part of each and every day. The girls would giggle and pretend to eat their peas. Eddie would beg his dad to take him out and push him on the swing after dinner. Allie would smile at him from across the table, silently affirming with him that life was so very good.

And it had been.

Right up until that bitch had walked out and taken their kids with her, leaving him this chair, this table, and his old buddy Jim.

"Screw her, right my friend?" he mumbled, lifting the bottle to his mouth and taking a deep swig. He was thirsty, having just arrived home from work, dealing with the stress of being a government accountant. A desk jockey, a numbers cruncher, he would never go any higher than he was right now, and the weight of that bitter disappointment sometimes crushed him when he added it to all the other woes of his life.

He stared down at the plate in front of them. It contained a slice of pizza—hard after being reheated in the microwave—and some canned peas. He couldn't say why the two belonged together, but he'd eat them all the same. He just always had a pantry full of canned peas, stocking up whenever he went to the grocery store, and he always reached for those cans when making himself something to eat.

'Cause Daddy eats the peas.

He'd always let the girls pretend to sneak their own onto his plate, as if he and Allie didn't see them do it every time. Once little Eddie had gotten big enough, they'd thought they could get him to help out, too, as if the boys in the family would automatically do the nasty stuff like eating peas. Their little brother had disabused them of that notion, and had quickly become adept at shuffling-off his own unwanted vegetables until the pile on Eddie's plate looked like it would reach as high as his chin.

He would make a big production about how he couldn't understand how that pile just seemed to keep getting bigger, and how lucky it was that he liked peas. The girls would argue that they weren't really peas, they were cranberries, or small cherries, giggling as always over the fact that he was color-blind. He'd shovel them on down, pretend to be outraged that he'd been fed peas instead of berries, and they would howl with laughter.

"Daddy always eats the peas," he muttered, scooping up a forkful of the things and shoving them into his mouth.

They tasted lousy—tinny, smooshy. They were also a little salty, though whether that was from processing or because he'd been crying onto his plate again, he honestly couldn't say.

All his food tasted salty lately. Salty and bitter.

He dropped his fork onto the table, wincing at the clatter. His head hurt. It always hurt these days, the silence in the once laughter-filled air making his temples throb. Reaching for the bottle, he brought it to his mouth and gulped greedily, needing something familiar, something loved.

Warmth in the mouth, heat in the throat, fire in the gut. Every sensation welcomed and familiar.

Unlike this stupid table.

Tempted to grab his fork and smash the tines into the smooth wood, which Allie used to so lovingly polish every week, he hesitated when he felt a rush of warmth against his back. Richmond had been in the grip of a heat wave since late June, like the rest of the mid-Atlantic region, so the air conditioning was always running. He always kept it set on a nearly frigid temperature, figuring if she wasn't here to bitch about the electric bills, he might as well enjoy himself.

So where had that warmth come from?

He wondered if somehow the French doors that led from the dining room out onto the patio had drifted open. That seemed impossible, of course. He rarely went into the back yard anymore, not able to stand seeing the old swingset with its now creaky, rusty chains. He couldn't even remember the last time he'd opened the heavy privacy blinds that hung over that door, much less unlocked it.

Pushing back from the table so he could go check, he hesitated when he heard the familiar squeak of a floorboard in the hallway.

"Allie?" he called, the word leaving his lips before his brain had even formulated it. "Little Eddie?"

He spun around toward the hallway, excitement building in him, even as the Jim Beam swooshed with the peas and pizza in his stomach, threatening to come back up.

That was okay. If he got sick, Allie would help him. One of the girls would get a cold cloth for his head. Another would run for the mop.

"Girls?"

The interior of the house was shadowy; the only things moving other than himself were the dust motes swimming in the stale air. Though it was barely seven p.m., the interior was quite dark. He usually kept the curtains closed, wanting his privacy, just in case anybody should come by. He had a lot of privacy anyway, of course, since the house was in the country in a sparsely populated area. The kids had loved that when they were little and had enjoyed running around in the woods, but had complained incessantly about it as teenagers. Occasionally, delivery people would come by, or a hiker from the nearby state park would tromp through the yard, taking a shortcut between the campground and a nearby lake.

Now, though, there was no-one here. He was entirely alone, and had been, every single day for a very long time.

"Except for you, friend," he said, lifting the bottle again.

He tilted his head back, and the bottle up, and began to swallow, and gulp, and drain every drop. The liquor hit his system hard, making the ceiling above him look like it was spinning. He wondered if it would spin for the Dr. Frankensteins at the lab who looked at the images from the crazy camera in his head. Or would they just see the ceiling, white, with the crown molding Allie had insisted on, all normal. Normal—and pulling away.

He was falling. Flat onto his back. He hit the wooden floor with a thud, knocking the wind out of himself and banging his head but good. He'd leaned back so far his feet had slipped out from under him and like some kind of old, useless drunk, he'd fallen on his ass.

Eddie didn't know whether to laugh or cry.

Then he saw something that gave him a third option.

A black-cloaked figure stood above him, shapeless, mysterious, blending in with the shadows in the hall. In each hand, he held sharp objects, wicked and gleaming, meant for something deadly and violent.

Eddie tried to scream.

Tried. But failed.

Chapter 15

Although Philip Tate made it very clear he wanted to take her back to his home to cook for her himself, Ronnie made it equally clear that a steak restaurant would do her just fine. Then he tried to choose the place. Still in uniform, with had no intention of going home to change into something more suitable for the kind of swanky joints he probably frequented, she insisted on a chain restaurant near her home. He literally winced when he saw the big, brightly-lit, mooing cow on the sign out front.

"Believe me, this wasn't what I had in mind when I extended the invitation," he said as they followed a waitress, winding around a sea of crowded tables.

"Don't let the ambiance—or lack thereof—fool you. The food's great."

They reached the table and he held out a chair for her. "I think the company is more important than the menu," he said, that charming, flirtatious tone saying he fully expected her to simper or blush or some girly bullshit like that.

Ronnie didn't simper. She didn't blush. And she was never girly.

So as soon as the man took his seat opposite her, she cut to the chase and brought up the subject he'd obviously been avoiding since the moment they'd parted ways with Sykes back in the parking lot of the research facility.

"Why did you really seek me out tonight, Mr. Tate? Do you have some information to share with me?"

He flinched, obviously not used to the direct approach. "Philip, please."

"Okay, Philip. Why are we here?"

"Because you dragged me to this place."

"I meant, why did you ask me out."

"Can't I just have been interested in getting to know you better?"

"Come on, we both know I'm not your type."

His expression grew wary. "How do you know my type?"

"I met your type, remember? Your golfing buddy?"

If he'd had a drink in his hand, he probably would have spilled it all over himself. She couldn't help thinking that if he was that far in the closet, the man had more serious problems than being spoiled.

"I...how..."

"Seriously? You talk a good game, but it's pretty obvious."

He appeared stunned. "You're incredibly observant," he muttered. "I mean, almost nobody knows."

"Let me guess, your father wouldn't approve?"

"He's very...sheltered. And old-fashioned."

Considering gay marriage was pretty commonplace everywhere in the country nowadays, she had to imagine Phineas Tate's sensibilities leaned toward the Victorian. Still, he seemed like a loving parent. She wondered if his son was doing him a disservice by assuming he knew how his father would react.

"It's just easier this way, to, you know, play the role."

"Of slimy playboy?"

Philip shrugged, looking both sheepish and a little apologetic. When he wasn't being flirtatious and smarmy, she found him a bit more likable. Too bad Philip played his role well enough to prevent people from getting to know the real him. She suspected he might be a halfway decent guy beneath the shell.

"So, tell me why you wanted to talk to me."

He began to speak, then paused as a waitress came to take their order. When he looked at a loss to interpret the menu, Ronnie ordered for both of them. "Two Big Bertha Specials. Show mine the front of the grill to make it break out in a sweat, then slap it on a plate. His..."

"Uh, rare also?" he said, looking as though he didn't know whether to laugh or sneak out.

"Gotcha hon," the waitress said, snapping her gum before sauntering away.

"Now," she said the moment they were alone again. "Tell me. Is this about the deaths I asked you about? Of the program participants?"

Tate reached for his water glass, eyed it as if to make sure it wasn't contaminated, then sipped from it. Swallowing, he mumbled, "You were right."

"I know. There have been six deaths, haven't there?"

"Yes. Six. From all over the country." He clenched his hands on the table top, lacing his fingers together. "I had no idea, truly."

"How did they die?"

199

"I don't know. The notations on their files say 'of natural causes' but when I try to go deeper into their records, I can't find anything. I guess when they died they were just eliminated from the program and their files locked up."

"Mr. Tate—Philip—is there any way you can look into this for me, try to find out what you can about how they died? It just doesn't make sense that six healthy, young adults who are all connected to this program would die so soon after implantation. It's possible our suspect had something to do with those deaths, that he made them look like something other than murder."

Philip nodded slowly. "I'll try, but only on one condition."

She tensed. "What's that?"

"Please don't say anything to my father about this."

"Surely he already knows these men have died."

"I mean, about your suspicions that they might have died because of their involvement with the program." Tate's shoulders slumped, he suddenly looked weary and a little sad. "He's a noble man, Detective Sloan. He had dreams of saving people's memories, preserving their dignity."

Dreams that had been yanked away because his son had pushed him to go for the fast buck. Not that she was about to say that. She suspected the younger Tate's guilt already ate at him.

"It's bothering him terribly to think Ms. Carr and Mr. Underwood were targeted because they'd agreed to test the implants. If he finds out there may have been several more victims, it could crush him."

Funny, that didn't sound like a man concerned about his business or his bottom line. He sounded genuinely concerned about his elderly father.

Her estimation of Philip Tate going up another notch, she nodded her agreement. "I'll do what I…"

The rest of her words were cut off by the loud jangle of her phone. She usually turned it off when dining out, but considering she was working a case, hadn't done so tonight.

"I'm sorry," she told him, glancing at the screen. "It's Special Agent Sykes."

"Boyfriend's checking up on you, is he?" Tate said, teasing her like they were old friends.

She frowned. "He's not…look, let me go take this in the vestibule. I hate people who talk on phones in restaurants."

He nodded and said, "I'll try not to eat your Big Bertha while you're gone."

Walking away from the tables, she connected the call and lifted the phone to her ear. "Jeez, Sykes, I haven't even had my salad yet."

"Ronnie, I need you."

Her heart flipped. "What is it?"

"There's been another murder."

Oh, hell.

"I just got a call from one of Dr. Tate's people. Richmond Police contacted them to tell them a Virginia man was found dead in his home."

"Was he a..."

"Yes. His data chip i.d.'d him as an O.E.P. participant." Sykes paused, then added, "He'd been decapitated."

God. Another one. That made the third murder this week; there had been one every other day. This killer was ruthless and relentless, like nothing she'd ever experienced in her career. From D.C. to Philadelphia to Richmond. He had a nice little killing field going on, with plenty of potential victims. After all, those three cities had a lot of high-level government workers and contractors with top secret clearances that would have made them ripe for the program. She didn't know how many of the five-thousand test subjects lived in this geographical region, but she'd suspect it was a large percentage.

D.C. was a perfect location, an easy ninety minute drive south to Richmond. An hour in the opposite direction to Baltimore, another hour to Wilmington. Forty-five minutes further to Philadelphia. Then straight up to New York City. The I-95 corridor was like a death route for anybody targeting victims in the biggest metropolitan centers on the eastern seaboard.

"Sloan? I assume you want to come down to Richmond with me?"

"Absolutely," she told him. Remembering how he often traveled, though, she added, "But I *really* don't like helicopters. It's not far—can we drive it?"

"That's fine. I'll pick you up at your place in a half-hour."

During the drive down from D.C., Ronnie learned all she could about the new murder from Sykes. He, meanwhile, pressed her for information about her abbreviated dinner with Philip Tate. She kept telling herself it was just because he wanted to know what she'd learned about the case. But something about his stiff jaw, highlighted by the low lighting of the dashboard and the passing headlights of oncoming cars, made her question that.

So, after she'd told him what Tate had revealed about the six deaths, she added one more thing. "He's in the closet, by the way. But keep that under wraps."

Sykes took his eyes off the road to gape at her. "*What?*"

"You heard me."

"But, he was practically all over you," he snapped, acting like he didn't believe it.

"Guess he was on the prowl for a new beard. Seriously, he's so used to hiding who he really is, I'm not sure even he knows what he wants. But it's definitely not anything with a vagina."

A horn blared and Sykes jerked the wheel to straighten out the slightly-drifting car.

"Would you please pay attention to the road now and drop this gotta-protect-Ronnie's-virtue act? Because, believe me, I can look out for myself."

A laugh burst from his mouth, but he kept his eyes front. "Protecting your virtue? That's what you thought I was doing?"

"Something like that."

"Bullshit. It wasn't your virtue I was worried about, it was my own sanity."

Not understanding, she merely tilted her head in confusion.

"The dude's rich, good-looking and a player."

He might be those things, but he couldn't hold a candle to the man sitting next to her. Not that she was about tell him that.

"I was jealous as hell."

That word, jealous, bounced around in her head, stunning her with its bluntness and simplicity. That was as close to a confession of his true feelings for her that Sykes had ever uttered. To be honest, she wasn't sure how she felt about it. Except a little dazed.

"Jealous?"

"He's used to getting what he wants, when he wants it."

"Well, he doesn't want me, and he never will," she mumbled, still not sure how to react. Knowing Sykes wanted to screw her was one thing. Jealousy added an emotional component to the whole thing, one she was nowhere near ready to deal with.

"I know, I know, the bad-ass Veronica Sloan doesn't want to with stuff like men who are interested in more than a quick lay."

She desperately needed to steer this conversation back onto safer territory, even if she had to play shallow to do it. "You mean it'd be quick? Aww, Sykes, you break my heart."

He didn't even crack a smile, not the least bit distracted. "You're going to have to deal with this sooner or later."

Playing shallow hadn't worked. So she stuck with playing dumb. "With what?"

"With what you feel about me."

Closing her eyes and trying to remember how to breathe, she replied, "What is it you think I feel about you, Sykes?"

A tiny smile appeared. "You want me. But you don't want to want me."

Well, he'd nailed that one right on the head.

He wasn't finished though. His smile faded as he went on. "You think being in an actual relationship will make you weak, so you don't want to lower your guard and let me—or anyone—get close. You're also worried about getting your mother's happily-ever-after hopes up, afraid of looking weak, concerned about giving up control, utterly terrified about being hurt or experiencing tragic loss again. You're even bothered about how it will affect your relationship with Daniels."

She couldn't speak. It was as if Sykes had slipped inside her head, evaluated all the confusing thoughts and feelings she'd been having for the past few months, and summed them up into a few short sentences.

"Am I getting warm?"

"You're on fire, you jerk," she admitted, hearing her own voice crack as she let him get one step closer to knowing her—really knowing her, the way nobody else did.

"Don't panic, Veronica," he ordered, reaching over and squeezing her hand. "I can be patient."

She remained stiff, not squeezing back, but not pulling away either.

To her shock, he didn't merely entwine their fingers, or offer her a reassuring pat. Instead, he actually lifted her hand. In the confining shadows of the car, she could barely make out his expression as he brought her fingers to his lips and pressed a soft kiss there.

Oh, hell. She was doomed.

That soft, quiet touch screamed his intentions louder than if he'd held a bullhorn. The gentle, easy brush of his lips on her knuckles had been as natural for him as breathing, as if he was already her lover, already knew how to touch her, how to please her, how to *calm* her.

Nobody else did that. But, she'd realized in recent days, Sykes could. As easily as he could make her fume, he could deflate her anger and give her a sense of peace, a certainty that everything would be all right.

He wasn't demanding anything, merely underscoring his words, putting an exclamation point on his claim that he knew her. Really knew her…and wanted her just the same.

Which was not only surprising, but utterly terrifying.

But you don't know everything, mister.

He couldn't possibly know what she really wanted or what she intended to do about it. How could he when she didn't know that herself?

She pulled her away from him, dropping her hand onto her lap and clenching the other one. "I should call Daniels, let him know what's going on," she said, knowing she sounded cold and terse. It was all she could manage right now. He'd given her too much to think about; she needed to retreat and regroup.

His deep sigh expressed his disappointment in her, but she didn't let that change her mind. She wasn't ready to have this conversation. Maybe she never would be. So much for thinking she could just have sex with the man and get him out of her system. She greatly feared that doing what she'd wanted to for months—going to bed with him—would merely cement his position in the forefront of her life. And her heart.

Forcing away all of those thoughts, she pulled out her phone and dialed Daniels's number. She'd been out of touch with him all afternoon, and wanted to see what he'd found out. When they'd parted ways at the precinct earlier, after the Bailey interrogation, he'd had a long To-Do list. She was anxious to see what had been done.

"Hey, partner, you heading home for the night?" he asked as soon as he answered.

She quickly explained the situation, telling him she was in the car with Sykes, heading south. She only hoped her voice hadn't changed, that she didn't reveal that Jeremy had just rocked her world.

"Oh," he said, the tone growing frosty. "That sounds fun."

"If walking in on another scene like the one at the White House can be called fun? Sure, yeah, I'll go with fun."

He had to have heard the bite of anger in her voice. "Sorry. When'd the guy buy it?"

"Sometime around 7:30 this evening. Just a couple of hours ago."

"Well at least you'll be on scene pretty quickly. How did everything else go today?"

She went over what she'd done at the Tate lab, basically telling him she'd learned nothing and had been forced to endure yet another episode of the Leanne and Bailey horny-hour.

"Tell me true," he said, laughter in his voice, "did you have a hard time keeping your eyes above his belt when you were watching the interview today?"

"You're such a twelve-year-old boy."

"You didn't answer my question."

"I'm taking the fifth." Because, to be honest, she had dropped her gaze once or twice, wondering where on earth that skinny, gawky kid hid *that*. "Now, tell me what you've been up to. How are things going with the rookie?"

"I ditched him," Daniels said, unrepentant. "He was slowing me down, asking a million questions, so I put him in the research lab pulling up old case files I have no interest in."

"Rule-breaker.'"

"Takes one to know one, Ms. Hacker."

"Speaking of which, anything on that list of names?"

"Yeah, I got some info back on two of the O.E.P. dudes who died recently."

"The natural causes deaths?"

An inelegant snort told her that was a stretch. His words confirmed it. "If you call one of 'em blowing his own head off after he'd killed his wife, and another leaping off a moving high speed train 'natural causes,' then I guess you could say that."

She gasped. Beside her, Sykes glanced over, raising a curious brow. She covered the mouthpiece of the phone and muttered, "Natural causes, my ass."

"Murder?"

"Sounds like suicide, but you never know. Maybe they were just made to look that way." She returned her attention to Daniels. "How'd you get the info?"

"The Internet is a wondrous thing, my friend."

Oh. Right. A basic web search. Yeah, that'd work.

"Sorry, I just didn't have time to do it," she said, feeling bad for having dumped the task on him when the answers had been found so easily. Well, at least regarding two of them.

"I'm not done yet. I've printed off everything I've found on those guys, but I haven't even really started digging into the rest. But believe me, I will."

"What about the list of the people who knew about the tunnels? Did you ever get it?"

He cracked his gum into the phone. "Yep. Actually, I just left the White House. I've been over there for the past four or five hours. Got the list from Jack Williams, then talked to everybody on-site whose name was on it. After that, SSA Johansen went with me to poke around and see if we could dig up anything else."

"And?"

He hesitated, as if he wasn't sure whether to say anything or not.

"What'd you find?"

"Might be nothing," he admitted. "Could have been something left behind by one of the construction workers."

Her curiosity rising, she said, "So what was it?"

"Just a little key. It's an unusual shape, I'm not really sure what it might fit."

Her heart began to beat faster. "Safety deposit box? A storage unit?"

"I don't think so."

"Any prints?"

"I bagged it and will definitely find out."

"Sounds good," she said.

"Hey," Sykes said, interrupting the conversation, "we're low on gas. Think I'll pull off. You hungry?"

"Considering you cost me a half-pound of meat, yeah, I'd say I am," she replied. Right after she'd heard from Sykes about the Richmond case, she'd bailed out on her dinner with Philip Tate. He had insisted on driving her home and hadn't looked too heartbroken to leave the restaurant without eating the dinner they'd ordered.

Through the phone, she heard Daniels grunt. "Sounds like you're busy. We'll touch base later."

The remark Sykes had made about her concerns regarding her partner, and how their relationship might be affected if she got involved with someone, reverberated in her ears. Jeez, dealing with these two was like walking a tightrope. Never having engaged emotionally with many men, she'd never had to deal with trying to balance someone's feelings with her own desires.

This—whatever *this* between her and Sykes ended up being—wouldn't be easy.

"Okay," she said, watching as Sykes flipped on the turn signal and moved into the exit lane. "Turn right," she told him, spying the sign of her favorite fast food joint.

"Yes, ma'am," Sykes tossed off with a laugh.

Daniels grunted again, obviously displeased at having half her attention.

"I gotta go," he said.

"All right. Thanks for your help today."

"Help?" He sounded prickly, offended. "I'm doing my job, in case you forgot about it. I'm not an errand boy working for you and your FBI friend."

"I know that," she said, wishing she'd chosen her words better. "I meant thank you for checking out those names I snagged off Tate's computer. I know you don't approve of how I got them."

"Doesn't matter whether I approve or not, Ron," he said, sounding a little appeased. "The fact is, something is up with that. I'll bet my manga porn collection that I'm gonna find out the other four dead guys all bought it in very unnatural ways too."

She wasn't going to take that bet. Not only because she had absolutely no interest in cartoon characters having sex, but because she strongly believed her partner was right.

Disconnecting the call, she fell silent while Sykes pumped gas into the tank. She mumbled what she wanted when he pulled up to the drive-thru window of the fast food place, but remained pretty quiet for the rest of the drive down to Richmond, trying to figure out what she thought of all the things Sykes had said. And the things Daniels had not.

She didn't necessarily feel like part of any kind of triangle, since she knew that, deep down, Daniels loved her the way she did him—as a partner, a close friend, almost a sibling. But that didn't mean she didn't feel guilty as hell that her partner was feeling a little shoved aside by somebody Ronnie had the hots for.

The hots? Get real. You know it's more than that.

Maybe. But she didn't want to think about that.

She turned up the radio to fill the silence and they finished the drive without speaking. It took longer than she and Sykes had expected—over two hours. The victim, Eddie Girardo, lived south of the city in a rural area near a state park, close to the North Carolina state line. She had sensed Sykes's impatience as they'd sped down I-95, his hands gripping the steering wheel of the unmarked, FBI sedan, and had half-wished she had just agreed to take a chopper down, despite how queasy they made her.

Finally, though, they arrived, spying the flashing lights of a half-dozen police and rescue vehicles that lit up the night on this dark, country road. The location had probably made it easier for the killer to take out his victim on a pretty summer evening, before it was even dark yet. Sykes had been told that Girardo's data chip indicated he'd died at around seven-forty p.m. It hadn't even been dark out yet and the murderer had been brazen enough to strike.

They walked into the house, learning that the victim's remains had not yet been removed. Fortunately, though, this case wasn't nearly as brutal as Leanne Carr's murder.

Eddie Girardo had been a middle-aged, divorced father of four. His wife had remarried and moved with her kids to another part of the state, and, judging by the empty liquor bottles in the recycling bin, and the spilled alcohol on the floor near the corpse, his closest companions had been liquid rather than solid.

Early reports said he was a loner, had few friends, and didn't go anywhere except to his job at the Richmond federal building and back home. If it hadn't been for a hiker spotting the back door swinging in the breeze, and a spot of blood on the hand-railing on the porch, they probably wouldn't have found the man for days. Instead, he'd been discovered less than an hour after his murder.

"So, you gonna explain to me why I had to stand here with my thumb up my ass, waiting for you two to show up, rather than actually doing my job and getting this poor son of a bitch out of here and into a body bag? Or two?" asked the lead detective, who'd greeted them at the door, briefed them and led them inside the house.

Ronnie visibly bristled at the man's tone, so Sykes stepped in to answer the question, courteous and professional as always. "I apologize, Detective Baranski. There's not a whole lot I can tell you, except that this man's murder is connected to an investigation of two other murders in the D.C. and Philadelphia areas."

"That why the FBI's involved?" he asked. "Because it's a multi-state thing?"

"Something like that," said Sykes.

They stopped in the doorway that led from the foyer to a small hallway. Here, judging by the large pool of blood in the center of the floor, was where Mr. Girardo had fallen, and where part of him remained. The biggest part.

Shuddering, Ronnie glanced toward the kitchen, which lay at the other end of the hallway. Even from here, she could see the open freezer door, marked by evidence flags and tape.

The man's head was inside, on the top shelf, placed between a container of ice cream and loaf of bread. Right in front of his mouth, pointing toward his lips, was a hot dog in a bun. It had been carefully placed there to look like the disembodied head was about to chow down.

Ronnie bit back a grunt of disgust. "Looks like our boy's playing games with food again."

Sykes nodded his agreement, adding, "I wonder if anything's stuffed in his mouth."

Not walking down through the hall, where the murder had taken place, Sykes instead cut through the nearby dining room to get to the kitchen. Ronnie followed, watching as Sykes walked over to examine the freezer more closely. He leaned in, eye level with the late Mr. Girardo's head, and snapped on a pair of latex gloves. Moving carefully, trying not to disturb anything, he pushed the victim's lips apart and looked inside the dark, cavernous mouth.

A tiny, green object fell out, rolling off the edge of the freezer and landing on the floor. Sykes flinched, jerking back and looking down at the thing, which had landed next to his foot.

"It looks like a pea," he said.

"Do you think there's some kind of message in that?"

"No clue." He gestured for a forensics technician to come over and bag the pea. "I'm sure a shrink would have a field day. Underwood with the cannoli, this guy with a hot dog pointing right at him and a pea between his lips?"

"Weird. But I would imagine it means *something*."

While the technician gathered the tiny bit of evidence, Detective Baranski came into the kitchen to watch. "Go ahead and bag the head so we can put it with the rest of the body," he told the technician.

"We don't mean to rush you," Sykes said, still playing nice. "We can wait a little while if you're not ready to bag him yet."

"Wait for what?" the detective asked, his eyes narrowing. Judging by the way he held himself—the hunched shoulders, the clenched arms—he was prepared for a fight, and had come in here looking for it.

"For you to finish whatever you need to do here before we leave with the head," Sykes said pleasantly.

She was reminded of that flies/honey/vinegar thing and found herself wishing for a flyswatter. She suspected they were going to need it.

The detective's face flamed and a vein popped in his forehead. "You're not taking this guy anywhere."

"Perhaps you don't understand, detective," said Sykes, still somehow keeping his cool, though his tone displayed the barest hint of steel. "We are authorized to completely take over this crime scene and remove anything we want."

"Oh yeah? And are you authorized to take the shit-storm that'll pour down on my head if I let you do it, and thereby ruin the case against the crazy nutjob who did this?"

"Detective…"

"Don't even try talking me into it," the barrel-chested man insisted, his brows drawn together in a violent frown. "You're not taking it 'til the M.E. examines it and signs off, which won't be until morning."

"We can't wait that long!" snapped Sykes, a little of that famous cool drifting away.

"Tough. I'm the one whose ass will be on the line if this gets FUBAR. I'm the one who'll have to go into a courtroom where some slick, high-priced lawyer will rip me a new one for releasing this guy's head to two people who aren't even in my jurisdiction, just because some damn chip in the vic's arm says I'm supposed to."

Sykes was rapidly becoming furious, she could see the bunching of his muscular shoulders under his suit jacket. "You're obstructing justice."

"So get me fired. Tomorrow. After I make sure I've covered my ass and made sure this investigation went strictly by the book."

Knowing Sykes was building a nice, full head of steam, which might be interesting to see explode—another time, when the situation wasn't quite so critical—Ronnie stepped in to diffuse the situation. She grabbed Sykes's arm. "Look, forget it. We can wait until morning. I'm sure Detective Baranski will contact the M.E. and ask him to come in early so we can take possession and get back to D.C."

She cast a demanding glance at the Baranski, who opened his mouth as if to bluster. But when he saw the warning shake of her head and the narrowing of her eyes, not to mention the way she was gripping Sykes's arm in her hands, her nails digging into him to keep him from losing his cool the way he *never* lost his cool, he nodded once. "Yeah.

Sure. That's exactly what I'll do."

He'd saved face, which, she suspected, was the whole point of this ridiculous exercise.

"Damn it, Veronica..."

"Cool it, Sykes," she insisted, not letting him go. She lowered her voice a little, watching as Baranski left the room. "We don't need to escalate this. We've done a pretty good job of keeping a lid on the press. So far nobody's connecting the cases and there hasn't been any detailed coverage of the level of violence. But if this cop gets belligerent and starts screaming about the feds stomping on his case, the press will pick up on it and there goes our media blackout."

He blew out a harsh breath and thrust a hand into his hair, then finally nodded that he'd gotten himself under control. Sykes looked tired, and she wondered how much of his anger and frustration were caused by the fact that he'd been working almost nonstop for several days. At least she'd had her own place and bed to go home to at night. He'd been living out of a hotel.

Which reminded her.... "I guess we should find a place to stay down here. It's almost midnight. It doesn't make any sense to drive back up to D.C. tonight, and then come back down in the morning."

"There's a decent place out by the interstate," said the technician who'd just come back into the kitchen. He carried a body bag sized for a small person, or a child.

She supposed they didn't typically carry head-sized ones.

"Thanks," Ronnie said, grabbing her phone. "I'll call and get us a couple of rooms while you finish getting whatever information we'll need from here," she told Sykes.

"Why don't I make the call?" he said, the words sounding like they came from between clenched teeth. "I probably shouldn't be in the same room with that asshole right now."

"Why, Sykes, are you saying I get to play nice cop? Start spreading the sugar instead of the vinegar?"

A tiny smile made his lips curl up. "Think you can handle it?"

"You'd be surprised by what I can handle," she said, wagging her brows, glad she'd been able to lighten his mood, at least a little bit. Then, before he could respond, she left the kitchen and went looking for Baranski.

Chapter 16

Ronnie spent the next hour gathering all the information she could about the case, knowing she would be able to gain a lot more once they retrieved the O.E.P. device from the victim's head. The Richmond detective loosened up a little, though he didn't go so far as to apologize for being a dick. Still, he was cooperative, answering any of her questions, offering to find answers to the ones he didn't know. Sykes stuck close to the forensics guys, who were friendlier and more helpful, as if realizing there was a lot more going on here than a typical murder case. For the FBI to have an out-of-state agent here within a couple of hours of the discovery of the body, they knew something big was going down.

Finally, after the remains were taken away, and all the evidence marked, photographed and bagged, the local guys called it a night, meaning they could, too. Good thing. It was after one a.m. and she was beyond tired.

"Come on, let's get out of here," Sykes said, taking her arm and leading her out the back door as the last two cops finished packing up their stuff. "The hotel's ten minutes away. Think you can stand sleeping in your clothes, or do we need to try to find a 24-hour Wal Mart?"

They probably could—the behemoth chain appeared to have stores in every town in America nowadays.

"That's not where we're staying, is it?" she asked, suddenly remembering the store chain had recently expanded into the hotel business. Wal Mart Villas were designed for shoppers who wanted to spend the whole weekend on a destination shopping trip where they could save money by spending every penny they had.

"No. But I'm sure we can find one, if you need to."

Ronnie didn't really want to waste time shopping for something to wear to bed when she usually slept naked anyway. "I'm good. Let's just go."

They arrived at the hotel a short time later. It wasn't a standard roadside dive, where you could drive right up to the door of your room. Ronnie had stayed in her fair share of those over the years. Instead, they had to go inside and take the elevator up to their rooms, which were side-by-side, on the fifth floor.

When they reached her door, Sykes unlocked it and pushed it open for her. She stepped inside, leaving him in the hallway, but before he moved on to his own room, he held up his briefcase, which he'd hauled in from the car. "Hold up a sec."

He reached into it and withdrew a small, travel-sized tube of toothpaste.

Her eyes widened and she thought she'd never seen anything so wonderful. "*Seriously?*"

"Yep. You'll have to use your finger, though. I only have one toothbrush—I'd offer to share but I wouldn't want you to get all trippy about it and think it meant we were going steady or something."

She couldn't help it; she fisted a hand and punched him lightly in the upper arm. "Jerk." Then she grabbed the toothpaste. "But a well-prepared jerk, so I forgive you. Got anything else in that magic bag?"

"Uh huh. I always keep a few things in here, just in case I have to take an out of town trip."

"You don't happen to have a spare T-shirt and a pair of women's underwear in there, do ya?"

A wicked grin appeared on that tired, handsome face. "I've got a T-shirt, but I'm wearing it right at this moment."

She shivered lightly, imagining how that shirt would feel, all warm from his body, soft and sexy and broken in by that muscular form. And how it would smell—sultry and musky and sweaty. Man-smell was one of her favorite things in the world, and she imagined she would be enveloped in it if she pried that shirt off him.

Swallowing, knowing she was playing with fire, she murmured, "Please don't tell me you're wearing the ladies underwear too."

He laughed softly. "'Fraid not."

"And you don't have a spare pair in your magic bag?"

He swallowed, then rubbed a hand against his lightly grizzled jaw. She could hear the raspy sound from a few feet away, and every feminine inch of her reacted to it. She doubted he had a razor in that briefcase, although it was possible.

She hoped he didn't. Ronnie liked the five o'clock shadow that spotlighted the strength of his jaw. She liked thinking about that roughness brushing against her skin.

"Funny, I took you for somebody who wouldn't bother wearing anything to bed," he finally said, his voice a purr.

Their eyes met, their stares locking. They'd both been playing word games, both ratcheting up the tension over the past few moments, when they'd been standing a few feet away from a large, hotel room bed, far from home, away from everyone who knew them and everyone else involved in this case.

They might both swear it hadn't been intentional, but, deep down, she suspected they'd both gone there on purpose.

"So, Sloan, you gonna invite me in?"

And there it was. The moment that had been building between them for months, since the first time they'd met in Texas, when she'd seen him, assessed him, judged him as a gorgeous asshole who she wanted with a desire that bordered on desperation.

She licked her lips. "Can we separate this out from the things you said in the car?"

He could have lied. Could have made promises he didn't intend to keep. But that wasn't Sykes.

He slowly shook his head. "No. We can't."

The blunt honesty, combined with the look of hunger on his face, melted her resistance, making him that much more attractive. She knew all the reasons she shouldn't invite him in, should say goodnight and shut the door.

There was also one good reason to invite him in: Because it was inevitable. They were inevitable. They had been since the day they'd met.

Time to make a decision, to do it or rue it. Suddenly, Ronnie was sure of only one thing. She wasn't going to rue it. Not ever.

"Yeah. Come in Sykes," she ordered, stepping back and pulling the door open.

He did. She pushed the door shut behind him. Flicked the lock.

A heartbeat. Then they were in each other's arms.

Their first kiss was hot and hungry. He tasted just as she'd thought he would—minty and spicy, hot and delicious. He devoured her, his tongue plunging against hers, and she twisted in his arms, turning her head, wanting him even deeper.

She pushed off his jacket. He tugged her blouse free from her pants.

They edged sideways to the bed, exchanging kiss after kiss. When they bumped into it, they didn't fall to its plush surface right away, still focused on getting out of all the damn clothes that were separating them.

Something ripped. A button flew. Groans and sighs grew louder as did the sound of every gasping breath they exchanged.

Finally, his pants hit the floor, tangling with hers, and she was able to savor his strong, powerful body pressed against her from shoulder to knee. She cried out at the feel of his erection, thick, hard and heavy against her groin. Needing to see him, she fell back onto the bed, looking up at him as he crawled over her.

"Holy shit," she whispered, her mouth going dry and her whole body shaking in anticipation. "Now I really am impressed."

His eyes glittered in the low lighting of the room and he studied every inch of her as he covered her with his body. "I've been impressed with you since that first day in Texas, on the shooting range, when you told me I was a fucking show-off when I proved I could shoot .14 splits."

"Gee, you're such a romantic," she said with a laugh, loving the blunt way they talked to each other. She'd always loved that their connection, while hot and physical, was also based on how alike they were. He spoke her language, if a little more elegantly, and she appreciated the way they communicated.

Especially now.

"You want me to tell you how beautiful you are, Veronica?" he asked, kissing her throat, tasting his way down to the nape of her neck. "Because you are. You're the most beautiful woman I've ever seen. I've wanted you so much that when you refused to meet up with me after our training was over, I was ready to put in for a transfer to D.C. just on the off-chance I might bump into you."

She closed her eyes, tilting her head back, loving the feel of his mouth on her. He used it everywhere, kissing his way down to her breasts, sucking her nipples until she was squirming beneath him. When he went lower, to taste the rest of her, she went a little crazy and dug her nails into his shoulder as she rolled back and forth on the bed.

She was whimpering with need by the time he moved back up and thrust into her in one hard, violent stroke. She buried her face in his chest to control her cries, and thrust up to meet him, their hips pounding together in heat, in need, in passion.

It was crazy-good. Also just crazy.

She knew they shouldn't be doing this, that she shouldn't have let anything happen to them. But damned if she could make herself regret it. Because while Jeremy was driving into her, forging a connection between them that she sensed would never be completely broken, she couldn't remember a single reason they shouldn't be together.

Although the day had started out well, and he was pleased with the information he'd uncovered, Daniels had been restless ever since he'd talked to Ronnie, who'd been on her way to Richmond with the Superman disguised as an FBI agent. He knew they would be there on business. Knew it was the case—another horrible murder—drawing them out of town together.

That didn't mean he liked it. And telling himself they were just working didn't put an end to the twisting in his gut or the faint nausea that stayed with him after he hung up the phone.

She wanted the guy. Wanted him bad. He'd known Ronnie for a lot of years, and he knew when she was hot for somebody.

Watching her with him had been brutal over the last couple of days. Because he'd known, from the minute he'd met Sykes at the hospital, that the two of them were going to end up together. Maybe not forever, maybe not even for the long term, but for at least a little while, Ronnie was going to be his.

Perhaps that was why he'd detoured after the phone call, heading not for the precinct, as he'd told her he was, but for a friendly bar he liked to frequent when he felt like slumming it and getting a little rowdy. The place, Rusty's, wasn't so-named because the owner had red hair or a dumb nickname. It was called that because the building looked on the verge of being condemned. The metal shutters and window casings were speckled with rust, the wood floor pitted and scarred, the tables sticky and wobbly. And the booze was strong and cheap.

He hadn't been drunk for a few days, and he'd definitely been missing it. Tonight, when Ronnie was in Richmond, possibly overcoming her last mental hurdle about letting something happen between her and Sucks, had sounded like a damn good time to break his dry spell.

He'd arrived at the place at a little before ten, taken a stool at the end of the bar, and ordered straight bourbon. A few regulars had greeted him, asking him where he'd been.

None of the patrons in here knew he was a cop, and he wanted to keep it that way. People tended to be on their guard when they were aware they were in the presence of an armed officer of the law. Preferring to keep the liquor and the conversation flowing easily, he generally stayed out of the occasional fights and turned a blind eye to some of the negotiations for illicit sex that went on at the back tables.

216

Fortunately, he didn't have to ignore any drug deals. The owner of Rusty's might be a roughneck, but his own kid had gotten addicted to Pure V and ended up in the morgue, so he had a zero tolerance policy for any of that crap.

After downing one glass of straight bourbon, Daniels had switched to beer. He had to drive home tonight and wasn't about to risk a DUI. Even though he hadn't gotten wasted, he did get a nice little buzz on, at least for a while. It dulled his frustration about Ronnie and Sykes. Eased the pain of it, too.

Folks around him were in a pretty good mood, despite the heat and the rumors about the White House murder, and he'd even managed to have a few friendly conversations. But now, after several hours in the loud bar, his alcohol-high had worn off, and his curiosity over everything he'd learned today had come back with a vengeance. Still trying to work out the mystery of the six deaths Ronnie had uncovered, he pulled the Internet printouts out of his pocket and looked them over. The reports were pretty blunt, straightforward, and if these guys hadn't been connected by the O.E.P. device in their heads, he would just have assumed they were two more overstressed dudes who'd gone off their rockers and taken the violent way out.

"Hey, pal, it's Friday night, work week's over!" said a young stranger down the bar. He grinned and held up a glass.

"Actually, it's Saturday morning," Daniels replied with a smile. "But you're right. Don't need to be working on this here."

He folded the pages and stuck them back in his pocket. It was time to get out of here. His mind was now back where it belonged—on the case—and he knew he'd wasted enough hours worrying about what might or might not be happening between his partner and Mr. Fantastic. He glanced at his watch. It was twenty-five after 1:00, a little more than a half-hour before closing time. He wanted to be back in the squad at 7:00 a.m., five and a half hours from now. Time to go.

Needing to make a pit-stop before he hit the road, he headed for the can. When he came back, he saw a full stein of his favorite tapped beverage sitting on the bar in front of his vacant stool. "What's this?"

The harried bartender waved a hand toward the crowd. "Some dude bought it for you. Said you needed to loosen up."

Probably the guy who'd told him to stop working. Daniels looked around to thank him, but didn't see him. "Guess a few sips for the road won't hurt," he said, lifting the glass and gulping a deep mouthful. "Tell him I said thanks," he said as he lowered the mug to the counter.

He reached into his pocket to settle his tab for the earlier drinks. Feeling the slickness of plastic, he suddenly remembered the small baggie in which he'd dropped the key he'd found in the tunnel at the White House. He'd sealed it inside, not knowing if it was evidence or just a random piece of junk lost by some construction worker. Either way, though, he should have taken it straight in and had it processed.

Damn, he was a screw-up. He should never have allowed that phone call from Ronnie to make him forget he was a cop on a case, first and foremost.

But that was done. He was finished with the feeling-sorry-for-himself thing. Ronnie might not care about him the way he wanted her to, but she was still his partner and his best friend. The last thing he wanted to do was screw that up by acting like some stupid, melancholy teenager who couldn't get the girl he wanted.

Dropping money on the bar, he headed out the door. Rusty's was located in southeast D.C., near Anacostia, which had tried to gentrify itself in the last decade, but failed pretty spectacularly. So Daniels was always watchful when walking the streets, even though he was armed and probably more dangerous than any punk kid who'd dare try to jack him.

Tonight, though, he was having a hard time staying watchful. In fact, as he left Rusty's and started down the street toward his car, which was parked in a lot around the corner, he couldn't help wondering why the sidewalk felt like it was in motion. It seemed to be rolling under his feet, and at one point, he staggered so hard he ended up against the side of an abandoned brick building.

"What the hell?" he mumbled, mad at himself for having drunk some of that last beer. That'd been stupid and it had obviously affected him, maybe because he'd had so little sleep and hadn't been drinking all week. It looked like he was going to have to sleep off the effects in his car before heading home. He only hoped he beat Ronnie in to the precinct tomorrow as he really didn't want her to see him looking as hung over as he suspected he was going to be.

Though Rusty's had been crowded when he left, the street surrounding it was deserted. The residents lived a little closer to the river, homes and condo buildings huddled around a waterfront project that was supposed to restore the neighborhood but hadn't done a very good job of it. Other than the ancient St. Elizabeth's hospital, there were no big businesses within ten blocks of here and the small ones were mom and pop operations that were open only during daylight hours and barred their windows at night. The two nearest ones—a deli and a pawn shop, had been closed for hours. And every other building was abandoned, graffiti-covered and boarded up.

Urban blight, they name is Anacostia.

Blinking as the dim streetlight in front of him looked like it split in half and replicated itself, Daniels put a hand out. He wasn't entirely sure he trusted his eyes right now, inclined to believe he ought to feel his way down the street. He honestly couldn't believe how quickly the buzz had crept on him, considering he'd been feeling completely sober a half-hour ago.

He also wasn't sure he could trust his ears, because he suddenly thought he heard the faintest whimper. He stopped in his tracks, cocking his head, listening.

He heard a car horn, the sound of breaking glass, the rumble of a garbage truck on the next block.

And one thing more.

"Please help me."

He shook his head, trying to focus, still not sure he could believe what his ears were telling him Because that faint plea had sounded like it had come from a kid. God knew there should be no kids on this block alone at this time of night. Or any time of night.

A whimper followed the cry. Then a louder one.

"Kid?" he barked, knowing now that he was hearing *something*. Though he was slow to react, and a little off-balance, he didn't even think about ignoring the cry. Somebody was in trouble. A little one who'd wandered away from home? Maybe been snatched by a neighborhood perv?

He turned toward a nearby abandoned building, certain the noise had come from within. When he heard a tinkle of broken glass, he went to the door and pushed it. It swung open easily, the lock long since broken. The place had probably been used as a flophouse or a drug hangout. It was definitely not where any child belonged.

"Kid, are you lost?" he called, blinking again as he tried to adjust to the low lighting in the building. The boards over some of the front windows had been dinged-up and broken over the years, and some light seeped in from the streetlights. Just enough for him to make out the empty room in which he stood.

The place had apparently once been a shop of some kind, because the front door had opened into a large, single room, with a long, rotting-counter on one wall and sagging shelves on another. In the center of the floor were piles of trash, debris, a torn, filthy mattress and a toilet tank. No kid.

He pulled out his flashlight, fumbling it in his thick fingers, which seemed none too steady. Deciding then and there that he'd never drink again so long as he was able to save the poor little one who was obviously in serious trouble, he closed his eyes tightly, focusing, then opened them again and flipped on the light. It cast a hard beam across the piles of junk, and also revealed a swinging door, dangling by one weary hinge, that led from this front area into what had probably once been a stockroom.

Another whimper.

His instincts warned him to be cautious, to proceed slowly, but his need to do something proactive drowned them out. If he'd had his service weapon on his hip, he would have at least unsnapped the holster by now. Unfortunately, he'd locked the 9mm in a gun case in his trunk when he'd gone off-duty. Right now, he only had the small backup piece at his ankle, and he wasn't going to pull it out until he'd assessed the situation. Given the way his head was spinning, the darkness, and the proximity of a young child, he might accidentally shoot the very person he was trying to protect.

"Please...."

Hearing that helpless cry, he strode toward the back room, but again, feeling the ground sway a little beneath his feet, pushed too hard and stumbled over the toilet tank. He mumbled a curse, but managed to stay on his feet. The flashlight, however, hit the floor with a thunk.

He had just bent over to grab it when he heard the creak of a floorboard. Still confused—far more confused than he should be after one shot and three beers spread out over several hours, he suddenly realized—he looked between his own legs and saw a dark shoe move into place behind him. It was certainly not child's size.

His reactions were slow, dulled from the alcohol, but Daniels still came up fighting. He swung around, throwing the weight of his entire body at the dark figure and was satisfied to hear the assailant's oomph as he tackled him to the floor.

"Son of a bitch," he snarled, thinking at first he'd caught some druggie who'd been about to rob him.

Then he noticed the black clothes. The black hood over the head. The gloved hands holding a state-of-the-art, police and military issue stun gun.

His blood chilled. This wasn't a random mugging. He'd been lured here, just as Ronnie had been lured by this psychotic prick last week at the White House. There probably wasn't even a real kid anywhere in the vicinity. The cries for help had likely been recorded, a speaker placed in the back room to draw him ever deeper into the darkness.

He was about to fight for his life, and he knew it.

The attacker rolled away, launching to his feet. Daniels followed, staggering, his head now spinning and waves of nausea rolling up from his clenching gut.

"You…the bar…you drugged me," he mumbled, everything becoming clear even though his brain was still muddled and his reflexes totally screwed up.

"Just lie down, Detective Daniels," the cloaked man said, his voice a low whisper, sibilant and laced with evil. "Lie down and go to sleep."

"Fuck you," he snapped, springing forward. He swung his arms like a bear, not knowing exactly where to grab, but certain that one of the three black-draped figures in front of his stupefied eyes had to be the real assailant.

The man ducked away from him, spinning just out of reach so that only Daniels's fingers brushed his black cloak. The world grew a little more wobbly, the floor seeming to sway beneath his feet. He was having the hardest time keeping his balance and his whole body began to shake.

"Give up."

"Not a chance." He lunged again. This time, his shoulder hit the perp square in the middle, sending him stumbling against the front wall, which groaned and creaked.

"Stubborn bastard!" the psycho snarled.

He lifted the stun gun. Daniels spun around, kicking out with his leg. He'd never been as good at kick-boxing as his partner, but he could definitely connect with somebody's arm if it was holding a weapon aimed in his direction.

Crunch. Boot met wrist. The thing went flying.

Now his opponent got worried. He began to scoot backward, edging along the wall toward the door.

"Not…so…fast," Daniels growled, finding it hard to catch his breath.

Whatever the perp had slipped into his drink—that last beer

purchased for him by a mysterious benefactor—it was getting down to business now. If he'd consumed the whole thing he probably would have been unconscious five minutes ago. As it was, he had to struggle to resist the urge to sit down and take a nap. Only extreme willpower kept him upright.

"I don't have time for this," the man snapped. He stopped retreating and pulled out a semi-automatic, which he'd probably hoped to avoid using because of the noise it would make. "Where is it? Give it to me."

Daniels attention was focused on the weapon. But not so focused that he didn't realize his assailant had dropped the thick whisper and spoken in his true voice. A voice that rang remarkably familiar.

He knew this guy. Knew the killer. But his fuzzy brain wasn't letting him associate the voice with the person.

"What did you do with it, is it in your car? I know you came straight here and didn't take it to your precinct."

The key. He was talking about that key Daniels had found in the tunnel. The tiny, innocuous-looking object obviously had meant something. It was a clue that would reveal this bastard's identity, not just to him, but to Ronnie.

She would see the key, sooner or later. He'd made damn sure of that by looking at the thing at least five different ways since the moment he'd spotted it, stuck beneath the edge of a baseboard in a dark corner of the tunnel. Oh, yes, she'd see it.

As long as this cocksucker didn't take his head and hide the evidence locked away in the device in Mark's brain.

"Screw you," Daniels muttered, smiling a little as he realized this psychotic monster would soon be caught. Whether Daniels was alive to see it, though, remained in question.

From outside, there came a loud shout. Somebody at Rusty's, calling goodnight, no doubt.

"Don't make a sound or I'll blow the head off anybody who comes in here to help you," his attacker snarled, his panic rising, becoming louder than his words. "I mean it!"

Mark believed it. This killer had murdered many people, he wouldn't stop at one more.

He bent over, dropping his hands onto his knees, knowing his opponent expected him to lose consciousness. But he wasn't quite there yet. Oh, no. He was far too interesting in seeing if he could slide his hands down his legs until they reached his ankles. He was going for the holster attached just above his right foot. His backup piece was his last chance to disarm this guy before anybody got hurt—including himself.

The drugs pounded at him from within. He swayed and pitched forward. He lunged, trying to stop himself from falling, but was unable to do it. Finding himself on the ground, he rolled across the floor, trying to make himself a small target.

Even from a few feet away, he could see the way his attacker smiled beneath the hood. *Think you can wait me out, huh? Expecting me to pass out?*

Maybe the bastard hadn't stuck around inside to make sure Daniels finished that entire, drugged drink, and didn't realize his intended victim wasn't quite as out of it as he was supposed to be. He was waiting for the perfect moment to bring out the knife so he could do his thing in silence, without the sound of a gunshot to draw any unwanted attention.

Desperate, Mark bit his lip, drawing blood, needing the pain to focus. Salty fluid dripped down his throat. He spat it out, bending over at the middle as if sick.

It gave him the chance he needed to grab his small backup piece off his ankle.

He brought it up. His assailant's eyes widened in shock. He raised his gun as well.

Two shots rang out. *Boom! Boom!* Flashes of light, acrid chemical smell. And pain. Oh, Christ was there pain. It bloomed in his chest, small and warm at first, then exploding outward with incredible fire. It scorched him, branding him with awful sensation.

He'd been hit. Couldn't draw breath. The lung, maybe?

He fell back, blinking, trying to focus as the man drew closer, fearing he'd missed him. There'd been too many figures in black for him to aim properly; he was seeing not everything in triplicate and couldn't imagine how heavily dosed that drink had been.

Mark didn't for a minute think the sounds of those gunshots would draw help. In this neighborhood, they'd send people scurrying for cover and it would probably be an hour before any cop came out here to investigate. He was finished. Done for.

"Where is it?"

He slowly shook his head, not willing to speak, even if he'd been able.

The killer dropped to his knees beside him, patting him down, from his shoulders to his waist. Slipping a gloved hand into his pocket, he pulled out the small plastic bag and nodded in satisfaction.

"Thank you very much, Detective Daniels," he said as he brought his weapon up again. "You've been most helpful."

That was when it hit him. He put the voice with the face, and understood now. He knew who it was, knew who'd attacked him, knew who'd killed Leanne and had attacked Ronnie.

Bastard. You evil, sick bastard.

With the recognition came another kind of understanding. He considered the timing—tonight's death all the way down in Richmond. The other clues that didn't quite gel.

And he understood why the puzzle pieces hadn't exactly fit.

The gun came up. Daniels rolled onto his right side, hoping he appeared unable to bear to look at it, that he didn't want to watch death rushing toward him. He counted on the monster's malicious streak to draw things out, to want to build Daniels's fear.

To give him a few precious seconds.

In those seconds, he planned to take the last chance he would have to send the last message he'd ever send.

He slid his left hand up across the floor, painfully, willing his killer not to pull the trigger too soon. When his fingers were within sight, lying limply in front of him, he focused on them, trying to remember the classes, the shapes, the motions. The letters.

It had been a few years since he and Ronnie had taken that sign language class, all detectives being required to do it. He only hoped he remembered correctly.

The first three came to mind immediately. He formed the shapes as quickly as he could.

An R. An O. An N.

Got your attention now, don't I, sweetheart?

He was growing weaker by the second, losing so much blood he could actually smell it now.

He stretched his fingers, trying to loosen them, thinking about the next letter he needed to form. He could picture it in his mind and tried to recreate it with his hand, losing sensation and feeling, not even sure he was making any sense at all.

But he kept trying. He signed a letter. Then another.

"What are you doing? Stop that!"

A click. Nothing. The gun had jammed. The figure in black cursed, trying to fix it, preparing for the kill shot, and when he heard the magazine slam back into place, he knew his time was up.

There was not a second to spare, no time to spell out a name. He had one more chance, one last opportunity to send a final message that Ronnie would hopefully see and interpret.

He knew what it had to be.

Gathering his will, he jerked both the index and middle fingers of his left hand straight out, staring at the V shape they made with every ounce of strength he had left.

Suddenly, hideous pain. Horrible, awful, brutal pain. And blood, spewing red, gushing, covering everything.

He howled, shocked and horrified, realizing that while Mark had been waiting for the bullet, the fiend had used his knife.

Daniels had done the best he could, and he hoped to God his partner would understand his message. There was nothing more he could do, no further message he could send.

Because he no longer had a hand.

Chapter 17

Falling asleep in Jeremy Sykes's arms had definitely been the highlight of Ronnie's week. Month. Year. Whatever. After the intense sex, they'd collapsed together, sharing the bed as easily as if they'd shared it all their lives. She woke up knowing her life had irrevocably changed.

Then the phone rang.

Still groggy, lying next to Sykes's naked body in the pre-dawn light, she got up and grabbed her pants, which were still on the floor where she'd tossed them. She dug for her phone, answering it on the fifth ring.

"Detective Sloan," she barked, recognizing the phone number from her precinct back in D.C.

"Veronica? It's Ambrose."

Her lieutenant. Why he'd be calling her at 5:45 a.m., she had no idea. "Yes, sir?"

"Where are you?"

"I'm at a hotel just south of Richmond, sir." She quickly explained what had happened last night—coming down here, having to wait until morning for the latest murder victim's remains to be released into their custody. She spoke clearly and succinctly, sensing Ambrose was tense and anxious about something. "I should be back up to the city by no later than noon."

"Get here sooner."

She froze, her grip tightening on the phone. "What is it?"

"I'm sorry as hell to tell you this, Sloan..."

Her stomach heaved. She threw a hand over her mouth, wanting instead to throw it over her ears so she didn't have to hear what she suspected her boss was about to say. Because it was going to be bad. Life-changingly bad.

"It's Daniels."

"Oh, God," she moaned.

Behind her, Sykes awoke. Obviously hearing the strain in her voice, he leapt out of the bed and came to her side.

"What happened?" she asked. "Is he all right?"

"He was attacked in a vacant building on the south side late last night."

She closed her eyes, drew in a breath. Pushed it out. Drew in another. "Is he alive?"

"Yeah."

Another slow exhalation. Then she asked the question she knew she had to ask. "For how long?"

Ambrose didn't sugar-coat it. "It could be any time. Doctors are working frantically, but they just don't know."

She stared at Sykes, saw him already grabbing his clothes, yanking them on, ready to leave the very second she hung up the phone and got dressed.

"I'm on my way.

Although Ronnie had insisted she could fly back to D.C. by herself in the FBI helicopter he procured for the trip, Jeremy wasn't about to let her go it alone. As he drove her to the nearest airport, where the chopper would meet them, he called Detective Baranski. Perhaps it was hearing that Ronnie's partner—a fellow cop—had been shot that took the lead out of the other man's ass and the bitchiness out of his mood. He put up no argument when Jeremy told him he'd arranged for the latest victim's head to be transferred into the custody of an agent out of the Richmond field office. It would be driven up to Tate's lab in Bethesda later today. Baranski also extended his sincerest condolences.

God, did he hope they wouldn't be necessary, that Daniels would pull through.

Once they were in the air, he tried to get Ronnie to eat and drink something. She hadn't had a thing since their stop at the fast food place last night, and he doubted she'd be making time for any meals anytime soon. So he pushed a bottle of juice and a breakfast burrito he'd purchased out of a machine into her hands and ordered her to eat.

She sucked down the juice but ignored the food. "What if he dies on the table?" she muttered.

"He won't."

"I wasn't there for him. He's my partner and I wasn't there."

He'd heard the refrain several times in the hour since they'd gotten the call. "Ronnie, don't do this to yourself."

"I could have stopped it."

"Ambrose said he'd been at a bar in a really bad neighborhood," he insisted. "He was in the wrong place, at the wrong time.

She finally looked at him, giving him her full attention, those big brown eyes wet and anguished. "You really think that? You seriously believe this wasn't connected to our case, that Daniels got taken down, shot and hacked up by some random drugged-out street punk?"

"I don't know," he admitted.

That was the truth. He didn't know what to believe. He only had what her lieutenant had told her to go on. Well, that and the call he'd made to the hospital to find out Daniels's condition.

Critical. In surgery, slim chance of survival.

He'd never really gotten friendly with the other man, mainly because Daniels had been belligerent toward him from the moment they'd met—like a third-grader who didn't want the new kid in school to play with his favorite little girl at recess. Still, Sykes had respected him. Not just for his loyalty as a partner, but for his determined professionalism and his abilities as a cop. He'd been highly impressed during yesterday's interview of Agent Bailey, and thought that if they'd met under different circumstances—and weren't both crazy about the same woman—he and Daniels could have gotten along very well.

Absolutely the last thing he wanted was for the other man to die. The death of any law enforcement officer was bad enough. But for Ronnie, who'd already suffered so many horrible losses in her life, it would be almost insurmountable.

"Why would he do it?" she mumbled, sweeping a frustrated hand through her short hair, a tangle of spikes and swirls this morning since she hadn't even brushed it after leaping out of bed to answer that early phone call. "He was on the hunt, he'd stumbled onto something with those deaths. Why would he go out and tie on one last night?"

Sykes could guess, but he didn't wait to verbalize it.

Daniels was no fool. The man had to have seen the tension that had been building between him and Ronnie from the minute Jeremy had hit town. Knowing they were going to another city last night, and could very well end up being gone overnight, he had to have been imagining the worst.

It might have been the worst thing Daniels could have imagined, but it was among the best things that had ever happened to Jeremy. He had been attracted to Ronnie from the very first—drawn by her sexiness, impressed by her strength, wowed by her intelligence, blown-away by her determination. Going to bed with her had been all he'd ʻnught about for a long time, and it had been better than his wildest fantasies. Last night had been the culmination of every sexual desire he'd felt in his entire adult life.

This morning, she looked at him like she'd rip his hand off if he dared to touch her.

It didn't take a shrink to figure out why. The guilt was eating at her. Guilt that she'd been in Jeremy's arms, in his bed, having incredible sex, when her partner was being brutalized.

Hell, Daniels wasn't even his partner and Jeremy felt guilty as hell, too.

They didn't talk much during the ride. Her concern for Daniels kept her from thinking about her fear of helicopters, and she even managed to pick at her food. There would be no stopping once they touched down; she would be on the go, doing whatever it took to ensure her partner's survival from that point on.

There would definitely be no post mortem of what had happened between them in that hotel room. That conversation had been indefinitely postponed. Honestly, right now, given the way she drew away from him if he got within a few inches of her, he had to wonder if they'd ever have it.

Or if last night would ever be repeated.

Another reason to pray to whoever was listening that Daniels survived. Because if her partner died, Jeremy knew Ronnie would forever associate the night she'd decided to take him into her bed with when she hadn't been there for her best friend and partner.

When they got to Reagan National Airport, a patrolman was waiting to pick them up and take them to the hospital. Ronnie plied him with questions on sight, but he was able to offer no new information. Daniels was still in surgery, no news was good news, blah blah blah.

They rode in silence to Washington Hospital Center, and Ronnie was out of the car the minute they pulled up outside. Sykes thanked the young cop who'd chauffeured them and went in after her. She'd practically started running once she got within sight of the critical care wing, and he quickened his pace to follow, seeing her bound up to an older, uniformed cop and start plying him with questions.

"Lieutenant, please, don't sugar-coat it," she was saying as he joined them. "Not for me. Not about my partner."

The grey-haired, kindly-looking man nodded, his sympathetic frown not disguising the firmness of his conviction as he said, "I think he's gonna make it."

She sagged in relief. "Really? He's out of surgery?"

"No, the doctor said it'll probably be hours yet. But come on, Sloan, you really think a couple of bullets are going to kill the most stubborn man either of us have ever known?"

"A couple of bullets and a hacked-off hand could do the trick," she snapped, visibly deflating. She wasn't in the mood to accept faith in place of medical certainty. "I can't imagine how much blood he must have lost before somebody found him."

The hand had surprised him, to be honest. Jeremy could see a violent gang banger shooting Daniels during a robbery. He could also see their psychotic killer bringing out a knife and cutting off a body part. But the two together just didn't mix.

What the hell had Daniels gotten himself into last night?

"The doctors said they'll try to reattach the hand. If that doesn't work, I hear they're doing great things with prosthetics."

"If he lives long enough," she said, her pessimism not swept away by her boss's words.

"The first thing they gotta do," Ambrose admitted, "is stabilize him and repair the damage from the bullets. The first one tore through his left lung. The second, apparently fired after Daniels was already on the floor, really tore up his intestines."

Ronnie rubbed at her eyes, as if pushing any possible tears back in their ducts. When she'd pulled herself together, she reopened them and nodded for her boss to continue.

He did, explaining some more medical stuff that Jeremy didn't totally understand. It was enough to hear that another cop's internal organs had been turned into origami by a psychopath's bullets and that his hand had been lopped off for good measure. Beyond that, all he needed to hear was that Daniels would pull through.

Nobody could say that yet, though.

"It's just lucky there was an ex-Marine in that bar Daniels had just left. Everybody else ignored the sound of gunshots, but he wouldn't do it," explained Ambrose. "Took him a little while to get anybody else to agree to help him search after they heard the first two shots. Once the third one happened, though, nobody could pretend it had been a car backfiring. He pretty much guilted everybody in the place into going out and finding out what the hell was going on."

"Thank God," she whispered. "I wonder if they scared off the assailant."

"I bet they did," said the older man. "He didn't have a chance to finish the job and ran away before he could do any more damage."

"What he did was quite enough," Ronnie mumbled. "Has Mark's chip been evaluated?"

"Yes. The E.M.T.'s got that data in the ambulance."

Jeremy was glad to hear it. At least the chips were good for more than determining if somebody was old enough to buy cigarettes. All ambulances had been equipped with scanners to gather information about patients from those pesky little implants in their arms. It was one good thing that had come out of that program—lives had been saved because medical workers had known instantly about allergies and other medical conditions.

"They're saying Daniels drank beer and bourbon."

Hell.

"But his blood alcohol wasn't over the legal limit." Ambrose let out a deep, disappointed sigh. "They also found Pure V in his blood."

"That's utter bullshit," Ronnie snapped. "I *know* Daniels. He has never once used drugs in the decade since we met. No way would he start tripping in the middle of a murder investigation."

"I know, I know," her boss said, holding his hands up, palms out to cut off her defensive tirade. "The people at the bar swear he just had a few drinks, nothing else."

"So somebody slipped it to him?"

"Sounds that way. The bartender says he remembers somebody buying Daniels a round but can't remember who it was."

More likely the bartender had a record and didn't want to get too involved, lest the police look into his own background a little too closely.

"Listen, Sloan, you should also know, somebody from Phineas Tate's group was over here several hours ago, looking to access...well, you know."

Sykes listened a little more closely. The images on Daniels's O.E.P. device would be the best clue they had to catch his assailant, at least until the injured cop got out of surgery and woke up. "Did they get them?" he asked.

"Yes. They made it here just before he went into surgery and downloaded them wirelessly."

That download would hopefully answer all their questions, and put them on the path to finding the man who'd done this. If it had been a random mugging, no way would the perp have known to cover his face. If it had been the White House killer...things might be a little tougher. But the bastard had to make a mistake sooner or later. Jeremy had no doubt Daniels would have put up a fight, and yanking that hood off might very well have been where he'd started.

"Listen," he said, "why don't I go over to Tate's lab and start working on the images, try to find out who the hell did this. The sooner the better, right? There's nothing I can do here, anyway."

Lieutenant Ambrose began to nod, but before he could say anything, Ronnie cut him off. "I'm coming with you."

"You don't have to do that." Jeremy moved closer and lowered his voice. "You should stay here, be here when he comes out of surgery."

"Waiting here while they try to patch him up isn't going to do Daniels one bit of good. You know what will? Going there, getting into his downloads and finding out who did this to him, so that when he wakes up, we can tell him we've got the sonofabitch in custody."

"But it doesn't have to be you who does it. I can evaluate them," he said, hating the thought of her tormenting herself even more by seeing exactly what had happened to someone she cared so much about.

"No." She shook her head forbiddingly. "Daniels is *my* partner. If anybody's going to share that awful experience with him, it's going to be me."

He knew what she was picturing, what she imagined would happen. Ronnie's guilt was making her desperate to pick up the cross and bear it for a while. She needed to do something to share the pain of what had happened to Daniels. And there was one surefire way for her to do it.

She was going to go to that lab, step on that little white mat and put herself directly inside of her partner's awful, painful memories.

Although she wanted to go straight to the lab and get to work, losing herself in the effort and killing time while she waited for word on Daniels, Ronnie asked Sykes to swing by her place first. It was eleven a.m., she was wearing the uniform she'd first put on twenty-seven hours ago, hadn't brought a brush near her head in just as long and felt disgusting and wrung out.

Sykes agreed, and they headed to her apartment, riding in another FBI vehicle that someone from headquarters brought over for him. When he told her his hotel wasn't far away, and that he wanted to go there and clean up, too, and would return in a half-hour, Ronnie nodded, glad for the separation. It would give her time to pull herself together. Having been with Sykes all night and all morning, including during these awful hours when she'd been torn up with worry over Daniels, had made it tough for her to think clearly.

She wasn't stupid. She knew the guilt she was feeling was a little illogical. Daniels was a grown-up, he'd made a bad choice and oh, had he ever paid for it. Whatever Ronnie might or might not have been doing at the time, and whether her decisions might have played a part in establishing her partner's mood, wasn't the point. The only person who was really to blame was the killer who'd attacked him.

She knew all that. Logically. Rationally.

But logic and reason in her head were fighting a war with grief and despondency in her heart. And they were losing. Grief and despondency had gripped her hard, slapping a thick layer of *it's-your-fault* over every one of her thoughts.

Trying to focus only on what had to be done, she took a quick shower, got herself back into some kind of decent condition, ate a peanut butter sandwich and headed outside to wait for Sykes precisely twenty-seven minutes after he'd dropped her off. He got there ninety seconds later, she hopped in the car and they took off.

"Any updates?" he asked.

"Not a word."

That was the end of conversation for the remainder of the ride to Bethesda.

Since it was a Saturday, the Tate Scientific facility was fairly deserted when they arrived. There were a few cars in the parking deck, including one or two in the reserved spaces closest to the entrance, but it looked like all the everyday workers were at home for the weekend.

Reaching the front entrance and finding it locked, they both passed their upper right arms below a wall-mounted scanner. The doors clicked open and they entered. Tate had been true to his word, having provided them after-hour access.

Perhaps because the building was locked down, there were no security officers at the gates. She supposed the fortress served as its own security on weekends. Not for the first time, she couldn't help wondering what other kinds of experiments were going on here. It seemed like the government had spent a king's ransom on the place; she couldn't see them doing it only for the Optical Evidence Program, no matter how promising it looked.

"Eerie," said Sykes.

"Very," she agreed.

The lobby was cavernous, the silence deafening. Their footsteps clicked across the tile floor as they headed for the elevator. Though she imagined Phineas Tate, or Dr. Cavanaugh, might be working today, she didn't suggest they stop in their offices to say hello. She was too numb, too shattered inside to even think about making small-talk. Or, God forbid, hearing any messages of condolence about her partner.

They finally arrived at their assigned lab. When she walked through the door, Ronnie saw a sticky-note attached to the monitor of her work station.

"Detective Sloan—we were so sorry to hear about the attack on your partner. His most recent files have been downloaded on both systems for the use of you and Special Agent Sykes. Good luck. E. Cavanaugh."

Ronnie balled up the note and pitched it on the counter, then took a seat in front of the work station. Sykes moved his chair over to sit beside her. When she reached for the mouse to scan for Daniels's backups, he put a hand over hers.

"Are you sure you're up for this?"

That was a stupid question. Of course she was sure.

She hated the very thought of it, dreaded it and wanted to lash out at the world for making it necessary, but yes. She was sure.

"I'll be fine," she insisted.

"Are you going to…"

"Yes. And don't try to stop me. If it were you in that hospital, I'd do the same thing, and if it were me, I know you would, too. Whatever it takes, Jeremy. That's what we do to solve this from here on out. *Whatever it takes.*"

He was silent for a moment, but didn't argue. Instead, he turned his chair around and moved to his own work station. "I'll watch it on the monitor while you're inside."

"That's fine. I won't want to stop once I start, so if I call something out, make a note of it, would you?"

"Of course."

She started the program, located the backups marked *Daniels* and considered them.

"How far back are you going?" Sykes asked.

Ten minutes certainly hadn't been enough with either Carr or Underwood. But this hadn't been a torture session, or a mutilation. She knew her partner well enough to know it wouldn't have been easy to ᵗke him by surprise, so she wanted to see exactly what he'd seen in the ᵗral minutes leading up to the attack.

"What was it Ambrose said right before we left?" she asked, not having been paying close enough attention as her lieutenant walked them out of the hospital. "About what the E.M.T.'s discovered about the timeline?"

"That the readings of Pure V in his system meant he'd ingested it less than a half-hour before he was first injured."

Right. Ambrose had also told them witnesses said Daniels had left the bar at around 1:30 a.m. What happened in the several minutes after that, she didn't know. But she did know that at about 1:45, he'd been shot, at least that's when his blood pressure had started to drop. It had plummeted sharply again a few minutes later, apparently when his hand had been lopped off. By that point, he was so near death, they hadn't been able to determine when the second shot had been fired. The fact that the prick had shot him while he was already down on the floor, bloody, helpless and in agony, enraged her.

"I want to know how he got hold of that drug." It had probably been in the drink the anonymous person had bought him. She only hoped Daniels had found and thanked the guy face-to-face. "Let's see if Daniels spotted the person who bought him that drink. Thirty minutes."

Sykes looked over his shoulder, his mouth pulled tight. "That's a lot."

"I'll be fine. From the sound of it, he was sitting in a bar for much of that time."

Doing what? Nursing a few beers and talking with some buddies? Thinking about the case? Unwinding after a long day?

Or had he been feeling rejected by his partner, who seemed to have moved on to someone else, professionally and personally?

She killed those thoughts, knowing she—and Daniels—couldn't afford them right now.

Taking in a deep breath, then slowly releasing it, she turned on the projection system. Picking up the remote controller, Ronnie rose from her chair and walked over to one of those innocuous-looking white floor mats and stepped onto it.

"Ready?" Sykes asked.

"Yeah."

"Remember…I'm right here."

She nodded, then, before she could change her mind, hit the button to start the projector, setting it to pause on the first image until she was ready to proceed.

The lights fell. Beneath her feet, laser lights began to rise, filling in the space all around her. One second, she was standing inside a small, windowless computer lab. The next, she was sitting at a bar, looking at a rough-looking guy with wiry grey hair who held a shaker in one hand and a shot glass in another. The guy's mouth was half-open, his eyes half-closed, Daniels O.E.P. device catching him mid-blink.

She resisted the urge to reach out and grab the bar, her equilibrium doing crazy things as the world changed so drastically around her. This wasn't like looking at a life sized picture, the room had depth and texture. She turned her head to one side, then to the other, moving very slowly. The picture didn't move with her—that blinking bartender didn't travel around her entire field of vision. Instead, what she saw changed by tiny inches and degrees. She was seeing a full panorama of the room, knowing she was moving out of Daniels's current perspective—facing the bartender—and into the world the computer had built around her. It was utilizing all the rest of the images captured in his device prior to this one, particular moment.

It was breathtaking. Shocking. A little terrifying.

Sliding her feet a bit further apart, she braced herself like a captain on a rolling ship. Taking slow, even breaths, she reminded herself that this was just like a movie, not real life, although it felt every bit as realistic as the room she'd just left behind.

As ready as she would ever be, she pressed the *play* button to begin the slideshow. She'd set it at faster than one image per second, wanting to speed through the minutes and lose herself in them the way Daniels would have.

The bartender finished blinking, closed his mouth, shook the shaker, filled the shot glass, called to someone over his shoulder, all in a flash.

There were no sound effects, obviously, but at first Ronnie would swear she could hear the tinkle of glassware, the raucous laughter of a drunken woman whose reflection she could see in the mirror behind the bar. With every deep inhalation, she could almost catch the odor of yeasty beer, pungent liquor and sweaty bodies. Those bodies seemed to fill the room, it was a crowded Friday night. They were all around her, far too many of them to fit on a three-by-three mat. The depth perception of this thing was absolutely remarkable.

She—*Daniels*—sits the end of the bar. Beside him is a weary-looking old man who keeps tapping his fingers on his glass—tap, tap, ·p. The sound catches Daniels's attention; he looks over a few times.

man looks up. Their eyes meet. He mutters something—an

apology?—and stops tapping.

Daniels doesn't have a drink in front of him. Nor even an empty glass.

He looks down, reaches into his pocket and pulls out a sheathe of papers. Unfolding it, he places them on the bar.

Printouts. Articles. Stories about the two suicide cases he'd told her about earlier in the day.

He's not wallowing, he's working. Oh, thank God.

Ronnie read along with him, making a mental note to get copies of them for further perusal later. Someone must have said something, because Mark looks up, turns his head. A young man—cute, a little glassy-eyed and tipsy—is smiling from a few seats away. He says something, lifts his glass. Daniels nods. Then he reaches down and folds up the papers again, putting them away.

Were you the stranger who bought him the drink?

The guy looked innocent enough, and she'd certainly never seen him before, but she wasn't about to rule anybody out.

After another couple of minutes of sitting there watching the people around him get more drunk, Daniels glances at his watch. 1:25 a.m. She knows he will be leaving in about five minutes.

He rises from his stool. Her perspective shifts a little, goes higher, and then they're moving. It is the strangest sensation to be moving forward through a crowded room while still having her feet planted firmly beneath her. One thing she notices—he doesn't seem unsteady. His vision is clear, his steps certain. He doesn't seem at all intoxicated and certainly isn't stoned.

Daniels walks toward the back of the bar—smiling faces offer greetings or hand-waves; he is known here. Liked.

He's heading for the men's room. She doesn't speed through the scene, or close her eyes. Things like privacy or embarrassment have no place in this exercise. This is her partner and every move he makes, every person he sees, could be important.

When he goes back to the bar, there is a full beer sitting on it, right in front of where he'd been sitting. Ronnie sucks in a breath. Somewhere, in another universe, Sykes whispers, "Bingo," but she ignores him.

Don't drink it. Please don't.

He speaks to the bartender, who shrugs in disinterest. Daniels looks around the place, doesn't make eye contact with anyone. Then he breaks the rule every teenage girl learns before going to her first party:

Don't trust an unattended drink.

He picks up the mug. Sips. Gulps, really. But not the entire glass. He downs perhaps a third of it, then lowers it back to the bar. He has another brief conversation with the bartender. Then he looks down as he reaches into his pocket. Ronnie sees a corner of something plastic—a small package? An evidence baggie perhaps? But he shoves it back down and pulls out some cash instead. He drops it on the bar and walks out.

When he hits the street, she begins to notice the change in his vision. Everything is the slightest bit blurry around the edges. The outdoor scene looks a little off-kilter, like he's got his head tilted. And he wobbles a bit, reaching out a hand to touch the exterior wall of the building as he begins to walk away from the bar.

The drug is kicking in. She couldn't even imagine how much Pure V must have been in that glass for a third of it to have hit him so hard. Whoever the attacker was, he'd probably gotten lucky that Daniels had not consumed more, and that he'd left when he did. If he'd downed that whole glass, he would have ended up passed out on the floor.

That interested her and she made another mental note. This killer obviously wasn't very good about gauging dosage. So maybe this drugging attempt was his first time. She didn't wonder why he'd done it—Daniels was no petite woman like Leanne Carr, or a skinny, young father like Ryan Underwood, or a tired, middle-aged accountant like Girardo. Taking him head-on would have been stupid and the perp obviously knew that.

When she realized Mark had stopped walking and was turning to look at a ramshackle, abandoned building, she shook her head, reminding herself to focus. Something had drawn his attention. A noise? A cry for help? She remembered the trick her attacker had played on her, that sound in the darkness that had drawn her into his trap. Had her partner succumbed to the same kind of lure…did this mean he was, indeed, attacked by the same person?

Daniels goes in. The room is even darker—filthy, shadowed, desolate. It is like being in another world, the lights and people of the bar a distant memory.

Ronnie's pulse pounded and her tension rose. She knew what was coming. Knew it was about to happen.

It does. Daniels trips and she sees with him that someone is behind him. Before his gaze even travels up, Ronnie recognizes the scuffed, black shoes.

They were worn by the same man who'd killed Leanne Carr.

"Oh, God," she breathes, hardly even aware she'd spoken.

Daniels comes up fighting and swings around. In a normal state of mind, he would be more than match for the coward dressed all in black, but he's been weakened.

She wants to cheer when he kicks the stun gun out of the killer's hand, but begins to shiver when Daniels bends over as if he's about to fall.

He's reaching for his ankle. His backup piece. *Do it! Go for it!*

She feels like she is watching an action flick, and the hero is about to turn things around and win the day in the final reel. But she knows how this movie ends and tears form as the two men face each other, weapons drawn, and exchange shots.

Daniels misses his; the O.E.P. device captured the tiniest splintering of wood as the bullet exploded through a flimsy window covering just over the killer's right shoulder.

His opponent doesn't miss.

Ronnie is suddenly flying through the air, backward, landing hard on her back and looking up at the ceiling. She feels no differently, and yet pain explodes deep within her as she imagines what her partner is feeling.

Oh, God, oh, God, please let it be over.

But it can't be over yet. She can't stop now, even though she knows there is worse to come. Not now when she's so close.

Her dear friend rolls onto his side. He's…he's bringing his left hand up, staring at it intently. So steadily. She doesn't think he's incoherent, as his movements seem deliberate. She becomes more sure of it when his fingers begin to move, jerkily, but intentionally.

It takes her a second to process, but when she does, when the truth hits her, she almost staggers off the mat.

"Oh, Jesus," she whispers. Tears fill her eyes as she watches Mark form the letters R-O-N with his fingers.

A message. He sent her a final message. In what might have been his last coherent minute on this earth, her partner was reaching out to her one last time.

She blinked away her tears, desperate to understand what he was trying to tell her.

His hands spasm, his fingers jerk. While she knew he wasn't there, that this wasn't happening right now, she couldn't help but lift her own hand. She reached out to him, wanting to clasp those fingers and tell him he didn't have to try anymore, that he'd be all right and she would take it from here.

He forms a fist, clenches it, and his pinky pops straight up.

"Is that..."

"Sign language," she snapped at Sykes. "Write down the letters. The first three were RON. That's an I."

The hand shakes, the pinky drops. The fist unclenches.

His fingers straighten. Then the thumb drops. He shifts his hand to reveal a perfect L.

Ronnie barked out the letter, focused only on catching each nuance of the message, not on trying to put them together yet.

He holds that for a few beats.

"Come on, you can do it," she whispered.

The fingers fall. His hand is flat on the floor now, as if he doesn't have the strength to keep it up. Then, with a sudden surge of motion, he lifts his arm again, makes a fist, and deliberately jabs his middle and index finger straight out.

"A V!" she called.

Daniels stares at his hand. And stares.

Suddenly there's a flash of light on something reflective. The very next image is splattered red. Blood, spurting, gushing, exploding from his open wrist.

"Oh, Jesus, Mark!" she cried, knowing exactly what had happened.

He beholds his brutalized arm, sees his hand is gone, then everything goes black.

Chapter 18

Jeremy stopped watching before the screen even went black.

Seeing what had happened to Mark Daniels on a twenty-inch monitor was one thing. He couldn't imagine being an actual part of the visual memories. Drs. Tate and Cavanaugh might have thought they were inventing something magnificent for humanity, but as far as he was concerned, their little magic box was a torture chamber. Seeing through the misty shadows of the projection when Ronnie's hand went up, as if she could clasp her partner's, he'd wanted to smash the damn projector so it couldn't wound her any more.

Instead, he'd pushed back from his workstation and gone to her side, knowing it was almost over, knowing she would need him when it ended.

The very second the images went black, he grabbed her and pulled her off the mat, holding her in his arms as she groaned and flailed in his arms.

"It's okay, Ronnie. It's me, it's Sykes. You're fine, you're back."

She stopped struggling and sagged against him. He felt the heaves in her chest as she gasped for breath and tried to bring herself back under control. He could do nothing but offer her silent support, stroking her back, whispering words of comfort into her hair. He knew nothing would ever erase the mental images she'd just willingly experienced, but he wanted to at least make sure she knew she wasn't alone.

After a long minute, she began to pull away. He let her go, taking a small step back, but keeping one hand on her arm, wanting to maintain human contact whether she wanted it or not.

"I'm fine," she insisted.

"I don't see how you could be."

She fell silent again, not trying to pretend all was well. Another minute ticked by. At last she said, "Okay. Not fine. But I'm better."

That was as much as he could hope for right now.

"Did you take notes?"

Yeah, he'd taken notes. He'd written down every letter. But oh,

God, did he not want to tell her what they were or what he suspected they meant. "Yes."

She snagged her bottom lip between her teeth and raised her damp, anguished eyes. "He was talking to me at the end. Sending me a message."

Oh, he most definitely had been.

"I know," he told her. He didn't elaborate, hoping she would change the subject, talk about the people in the bar, the papers Daniels had studied, the drink he'd so rashly consumed. Anything except the meaning of those last, desperate words.

She pulled away from him, walking over to his work station, grabbing the pad of paper he'd been scribbling on. Hell.

"Ron," she said, reading the first line. "I got that much. Jesus, how did he have the presence of mind to do that, to spell out my name, knowing I'd see this?"

"I guess he had something pretty important to say," he replied, his tone subdued, sad.

"So what was it?" she said, a puzzled frown on her weary face. "I, L, and V, those were the letters I called out?"

"Yeah," he mumbled.

"It looked like there were some others he was trying to make in there, but I honestly couldn't tell what they were. Sometimes his hand just seemed to be clenched in a fist, others his fingers just sagged."

He kept his response low, gentle, waiting for her to stumble about the realization he had already reached. "I noticed."

She raked a hand through her short hair, sending it up into wild spikes. "I don't understand," she snapped, studying the page. "I can't think of a single word that has the letters 'LV' right in a row."

She was getting it now.

Jeremy stepped over, putting a hand on her shoulder, squeezing gently.

"What?" she asked, wary, a little defensive. "What aren't you saying?"

"Think about it, Veronica."

Her eyes narrowed as she thought, but no light bulb of realization changed her expression.

"Start from the beginning. 'Ron, I…'"

"L something v?"

Her mouth fell open in shock, her eyes growing saucer-sized as possibility struck her.

"No. No way."

"You know how he felt—feels about you."

She spun away from him. "That's bullshit."

"He's in love with you, it's written all over his face every time he looks at you."

"Shut up, Sykes," she snarled. "You don't know what you're talking about. You don't know him like I do. There is no way in hell you're ever going to convince me that Mark Daniels spent the last, precious seconds of his life doing something as sappy as telling me he loves me."

He knew she didn't want to believe it. If he were in her position, he wouldn't want to believe it either. The guilt was already pressing down on her, adding that burden might crush her completely. But he didn't see any other explanations.

"I have to get out of here," she whispered. She crossed her arms around her middle. "I want to go back to the hospital."

"Okay. I'll take you."

She opened her mouth as if to argue—obviously, she didn't even want to be in a car with him right now, feeling furious and betrayed by what he'd said, but she had no other choice.

"I'm taking his backups," she said, challenging him to argue.

"That's a good idea," he murmured. "I'm sure there are moments from earlier in the day that could be important."

She went to her work station and began backing up the files. "Yes, of course there are."

Their ride back to the hospital was silent and icy cold. Sykes would be hard pressed to admit that he and Ronnie had spent the previous night together; right now, she looked like she wanted to slap him across the face.

He didn't push it. She'd come to accept it sooner or later.

But as they reached the hospital and she hopped out of the car, he couldn't help wondering if that last, desperate message from Daniels had done more than convey his true feelings. Jeremy greatly feared it had also spelled doom for his own relationship with Ronnie.

Because, live or die, Daniels last, Herculean effort was going to stay with her for the rest of her life. And Jeremy honestly didn't know if she was ever going to allow herself to get over it.

"I love you?" she mumbled, rolling her eyes as she stalked across the hospital waiting room. Back and forth she went, practically wearing a path in the tile. "No way. You didn't. You wouldn't!"

Would he?

She just couldn't make the picture come together in her mind. Okay, she could see why Sykes would leap to that conclusion. He didn't know Daniels the way she did. He hadn't been there through some of the incredibly rough, dangerous situations they'd shared, when Mark's abrasiveness and toughness were the only things that had gotten them through.

She'd believe her rough-and-ready partner had wasted his last moments saying *I love you* the day she started to again believe in the Easter Bunny.

No, not again. She'd never believed in that big, stupid rabbit. And she would never believe this.

"Anything new?" she asked as a nurse marched by the room, pausing to glance in and stare at her, probably because word of her stalking and muttering had spread around the unit.

"No, he's still in surgery," the woman said.

Ronnie was alone in the waiting room, her lieutenant having gone back to the precinct an hour ago. Other cops came in and out, though none were here now. Daniels's family—a mother, a brother, an ex-wife, some cousins—lived on the west coast and would arrive late tonight. Sykes hadn't offered to stay, wanting to keep working the case, which probably just as well. So it was just her. And with each hour that passed, she vacillated between relief that Daniels wasn't dead yet and dread because he'd been on an operating table for more than ten hours and how could anybody survive that much damage?

"Can I get you anything? Is the coffee holding out?"

She glanced at the industrial-sized pot, which she'd sucked down to the dregs. "I've probably had enough."

"Okay then," the woman said. Then, looking back and forth to make sure she wasn't being overheard, she added, "I heard a couple of the nurses saying things were going well, and that he was one heck of a tough man."

She smiled and nodded. "That he is."

Too tough to spell out freaking I-love-you!

Nope. She just didn't believe it.

Knowing she needed to get busy doing something or go crazy, she finally remembered the files she'd copied before leaving the research facility. Her handheld wouldn't be great for viewing the images on, but it was the best she could do here. Besides, she was wasting time when she could be trying to catch whoever had attacked Daniels.

Sitting in a back corner, where nobody could walk in and look over her shoulder at the tiny screen, she plugged in the micro-drive and pulled up Daniels's downloads. She wasn't going anywhere near his last half-hour. But there had been a lot of other things going on yesterday. He'd mentioned them on the phone last night and she wanted to get a little better handle on some of the things he'd told her.

She ignored much of the morning. She'd been at the precinct for the Bailey interview, and knew Daniels had spent the early afternoon on the Internet looking for info on those six dead O.E.P. implantees. She intended to do the same thing, and read the articles he found, but for now, she was more interested in the time he'd spent at the White House. He had specifically mentioned finding something in the mysterious tunnel.

"A key," she murmured. "A strange, little key."

When she'd called him at around 9:30 p.m., he'd said he had just left the White House, where he had explored the tunnel. So she started there.

She went back to the 8:30 mark and opened the file. Seeing that Daniels was already in what looked like it could be the tunnel in question, she backed up several minutes. When she reached the sub-basement, she stopped reversing and went forward again.

Daniels wasn't alone. SSA Johansen was with him, and the two of them were opening a secret door behind that breaker panel at the base of the stairs. Ronnie hadn't been back over there since hearing about the thing, so she hadn't had a chance to see it in person. It was, she had to admit, pretty impressive. So well hidden, she never would have known to look for it.

"Okay, so about that key...."

She slowed things down, watching for several long, slow minutes as Daniels and Johansen explored. The tunnel was well lit, but she noticed her partner still had his flashlight on and was using it to spy in corners, crevices and anywhere else that wasn't easily visible with the naked eye.

About ten minutes after they'd started exploring, Johansen said something that stopped Daniels in his tracks. He turned around, shining the beam of his light toward a baseboard that hadn't been sealed around the bottom. Johansen obviously had a very good eye, because Ronnie doubted she would have seen the small, flat black metallic object stuck halfway beneath the baseboard.

Daniels went over, bent down and examined it, without touching. Then, realizing it might be important, he pulled out a rubber glove, put it on and gently tried to pry the key out. It took a little bit of twisting, but he popped the thing free and lifted it up for a better look.

Ronnie paused the screen, staring at the key. It was, as Daniels had said, small and unusual looking. Black, a rounded top, little thumb-nubs, then a stubby cut end. It definitely didn't look like a key to a car, a house or a safety deposit box.

She thought hard-motorcycle? Storage unit? Nothing rang a bell.

Zooming the image in as tightly it would go, she magnified the key to a huge size. That's when she saw the number. Engraved into the key, just above the first cut, was the number 76 in a circle. She grabbed her small note pad, flipped it open and made a quick drawing. Hopefully some expert would be able to tell her more about it.

Continuing on with the downloads, she went all the way through the tunnel hunt, noting the alcoves, the twists and turns. She also noted—through Daniels, who also noted—that it was well equipped for an emergency. There were medical kits mounted on the walls every thirty feet or so, with symbols for defibrillators. There were also fire extinguishers, panic buttons, even mounted, glass-front boxes with what looked like night vision goggles inside, perhaps in the event of a blackout. What a hideous place to be stuck if the lights went out!

Eventually, Daniels and Johansen reached the other end of the tunnel, came out in the maintenance shed near the Washington Monument, then turned around and went back the way they'd come. There was nothing more to see and she skimmed a lot of their return. She didn't slow things down again until Daniels got in his car, at a little after nine.

"That's all, folks," she mumbled, knowing there wasn't much more to see. She'd called him not long after this, and knew he'd gone to the bar right afterward.

Frustrated, she decided to find out what she could about that little mystery key.

Going online, she did a quick search for the words key, 76. She got a ton of hits for musical instruments—keyboards—and sighed in frustration. Trying several variations, she finally thought about what the key might fit. It looked like it was for some type of engine, so she tried that.

This time, she actually had some luck. A page full of images of keys appeared on the small screen. She scrolled down, and finally saw one that looked exactly like the one Daniels had found in the White House tunnel. Clicking the link, she was taken to a page about...

"Boat motors," she whispered.

The key was apparently very old, hard to find and had been used for watercraft with an Evinrude or Johnson Outboard motor.

Wheels started to turn in her brain, clicking away as she tried to fit the pieces together.

Not just a key, a boat key. Not just a boat key, an old boat key, the kind that might be used on an old, classic yacht.

Her heart was beating fast now. Very fast. Suddenly wondering what had been done with the key, she picked up the phone and called her lieutenant. When he answered, she didn't even say hello, barking, "What happened to Daniels's personal belongings? Did the E.M.T.'s take it off him? Are they here at the hospital?"

Her boss didn't question her sharp tone, he knew her well enough to know when she was on to something important. "His clothes, possessions, everything he had on him was bagged in the emergency room and is now here, in my custody."

"Was there a key? A small, black key, with the number 76 stamped on it? Daniels would have bagged it."

"No."

The doubled heartbeat now went into triple overtime. "You're sure?"

"I'm positive, Sloan, there was no bagged key. The only unusual thing he had on him was a sheath of papers with printouts about some suicides. Otherwise, just his wallet, badge, keys—his personal ones—the usual." Someone in the background called for him and he barked an impatient reply. Then he got back to her. "What have you got?"

"Not sure yet," she said, meaning it. "Right now, it's just a suspicion, I need a little time."

"Call me as soon as you have something and don't do anything without backup," he ordered.

Agreeing, she ended the call and continued to think.

The key/yacht connection had instantly made her think of Leanne Carr's boss, Jack Williams. She'd liked the man for the crime from the start, mainly because she'd considered him the perfect person to lure the woman to the White House on Independence Day, and because of how closely he'd stuck to the investigation. The only thing she had no clue about was a motive.

Then she remembered the memory book. And that torn-out

photo.

She glanced at the clock, hating to leave when Daniels might get out of surgery at any time. Finally, though, driven by a compulsion to follow this new clue to the end, she left the hospital, getting a cab to take her home.

Once at home, she stripped out of her sticky clothes and got comfortable, knowing she might have a lot of looking to do. Then she went to the table and retrieved the micro-disk with Leanne's files. She plugged it into her handheld, hooked that up to the huge monitor, and plopped onto the couch. She didn't go looking at the memories from Leanne's O.E.P. chip. Instead, she scrolled through those other documents retrieved from her hard drive. To the one called Membook.

Opening it, Ronnie went right to the large, group shot on the beach—the one half missing from the final book. Remembering what Williams had said about how his assistant had gotten some of the pictures, she did the same thing. The new Google face-and-featured search wasn't perfect, and you could get a lot of false positive results. But the one in the book *had* been Williams—she knew that much—and she had the feeling Leanne had found it online. Because if Williams wanted to keep the picture a secret, he certainly wouldn't have left it around the house for his wife to find.

Using the software to capture the faces of all the people on the right side of the photo—the side torn from the book—she started a wide search, looking for any matches. Because there were so many at once, she had no problem finding the same photograph, which had been posted on somebody's Facebook page at least ten years ago.

"The Internet never forgets," she muttered as she studied the shot. Now came the hard part. "Who here did you not want to be associated with?" she whispered.

She was going to have to single out every face on that side and see what she could find about each one.

Because she had noticed right away that the person closest to Williams on the torn-out side was a pretty young woman, she started with her. Cropping her face, she enlarged it as much as she could, then added it to her search parameters and began again. She bit her fingernail as the program began to load hits on the screen.

There were lots of hits. Her eye was drawn to the very first one, a newspaper photo. Newspaper meant newsworthy.

She clicked on the link and was taken to the source photo, posted with an article from the Miami Herald dated April 13, 1991. The minute she read the first paragraph, everything began to fall into place. The timing, the lure, the violence, the crime.

The memory book.

Going back to the search results and clicking several more links, reading all the follow-up articles, she became even more certain. She understood. At last, she understood.

Though she thought about calling her lieutenant, Ronnie knew he'd want to take time putting together a team to evaluate her findings. She didn't need a team. She just needed one sharp, brilliant mind. So she picked up the phone and called Sykes. She didn't tell him anything over the phone, instead asking him to come over.

He was there in under ten minutes.

"It's Williams," she said the moment she swung open her front door. "Jack Williams killed Leanne Carr."

He didn't ask stupid questions or question her certainty. He merely stalked in and said, "Explain."

She did, telling him about the key, about the memory book, the photo and the search. She pulled up the images as she spoke, proving her case clearly and concisely.

"That girl's face shows up in dozens of newspaper articles because she was brutally murdered in April of 1991. She was a college student from Wisconsin, visiting Florida for spring break. She was cut to pieces, her body dumped on the beach. It was one of the most violent murders Miami ever saw."

He seeing it exactly the way she did. "M.O. sure sounds similar."

"Doesn't it? One of the articles said that somebody close to the case hinted that police were suspicious of someone, but they couldn't find any definite proof of a connection between him and the victim. It also implied this person had powerful connections and they couldn't act without more evidence."

"Williams."

"Right. His father was a senator, remember? They would have lawyered him up so fast and threatened so many lawsuits, the cops would never have moved on him without a rock-solid case and sure wouldn't have released his name to the press."

"Think this beach photo would have given them the proof they needed?"

"Absolutely. It would have at least shown a connection between Williams and the victim."

"Jesus. Can you imagine what he thought when he opened that

birthday gift and saw that picture staring up at him?"

"He must have panicked. Until that moment, he probably thought he'd gotten away with this decades ago."

But there was no statute of limitations on murder. He'd have to know that.

"Tearing the page out wasn't enough," Sykes said. "He had to make sure Leanne hadn't stumbled over anything else about this young woman."

Her bitterness creeping into her voice, she replied, "Yes, and I think he figured he might as well have some fun while he was taking care of his problem."

They were both silent for a little while. Thinking about that. About a nice young woman, well-liked by everyone, including her boss and his family, being lured by him to her horrible, brutal death. Had she known? Had she figured out who he was?

Considering just how evil this crime—and the one in 1991—had been, she had to assume he would have wanted her to know. He'd been careful not to let himself be seen by that camera in her head, which, of course, he had known about, but he would have done something to clue her off. Because that's just how evil worked.

"There's one thing that doesn't fit, though," Sykes mused. "Well, two things, actually."

She was way ahead of him. "Ryan Underwood and Eddie Girardo.

"Right."

"I know. It stumped me too. Then I started thinking about that case several years ago, when a guy who wanted to kill his wife went to a store near his house and put poisoned capsules in packages of over-the-counter pain medication. He bought one, his wife died, as did a couple of innocent people who'd bought the other bottles. Everybody thought she was the victim of a random killer."

"I remember. So you think Williams killed two other implantees when he realized everybody was focusing on the fact that Leanne was part of the O.E.P. experiment? He wanted to make it look like it was connected to the program, not the person?"

"Philadelphia and Richmond are pretty close to D.C.," she said with a shrug.

"How would he find out their status as implantees?"

"I don't know," she admitted. "But he's got a lot of money and a t of connections. I imagine he could pay for any information he wanted. Frankly, it's the best I've got. We won't know for sure until we question him."

At that, Sykes let out a rude noise.

"What?"

"You really think we're going to get anywhere near him with this? We're going to have to walk on eggshells with this guy. We can't just call him in for questioning like Bailey."

She hated to admit it, but she knew he was right. They would have to be extremely careful and they needed more evidence than they had now to even try to talk her boss into having Williams brought in.

"If only we had that stupid key," she muttered. "I'll bet it had his fingerprint on it."

The key's presence in the tunnel might not have been damning, but it did help add to the pile of circumstantial evidence that might have brought the man down.

"Think that's why he attacked Daniels? So he could get it back?"

"Yes, I do."

Sykes frowned. "So how'd he know Daniels had it? He wasn't with him in the tunnel."

"Definitely not." She snapped her fingers. "But Johansen was! What if he told him? He might have mentioned it to Williams, might be able to make some kind of connection between them."

"We need to talk to Johansen."

She was already on her feet, not even wasting the time it would take to get into her uniform. Fuck regulations. She'd tear the White House apart in jeans and a T-shirt if it meant catching the man who'd attacked her partner.

Sykes was right behind her as they walked out the door. When they reached the parking lot, he headed for his FBI vehicle and she went to her car.

"Wait..."

"I'm driving," she snapped. "My head's fine and I really need to grip something in my fists and choke the shit out of it."

He held up his hands. "Okay, just don't mistake my throat for the steering wheel."

"Not a chance. But believe me, if I had a shot at Williams, he'd have a really tough time ever swallowing again."

Chapter 19

Because of the shut-downs on the site last week, Ronnie knew crews were working around-the-clock at the White House, which meant the Secret Service would have to have a presence. She hoped to find Johansen on site, but if he wasn't, they could at least find out how to reach him from somebody else in the office.

First, of course, they had to go through security. Jesus, if she'd thought it had been bad during the morning after a murder, it was ridiculous on a Saturday night. That could be because more drunks were out and about, protestors and the like, but it could also be because she pulled up to the security gate a little too fast.

"Get out of the vehicle!" a voice shouted. Meanwhile, six body-armor wearing soldiers leveled their weapons at the windshield of the car and three more came running from further down along the fence-line.

"Whoops," she mumbled, wishing she'd taken the time to get her uniform back out. It wouldn't have gotten them past this checkpoint but it might have made it slightly less probably that they were gonna get shot.

"Please don't get me shot tonight," Sykes said, groaning.

She opened the door, putting her hands on her head as she stepped out. "Sorry!" she called. Then, hoping to speed things up, she added, "I'm Detective Veronica Sloan, D.C.P.D., that's Special Agent Sykes. We're investigating a murder."

"Shut the hell up," the glaring, stone-jawed soldier replied.

Sykes apparently didn't like that. "Watch your mouth, soldier."

Ten pair of eyes, armed to the teeth, swung in his direction.

He didn't back down. "I understand protocol, I know you're doing a tough job, but there was time when the armed forces actually treated people with respect. There was also such a thing as professional cooperation between the military, cops and the FBI."

The aggressive one took a step forward, murder in his eyes, then a voice barked, "Stand down."

A sergeant, who'd been hidden in the shadows behind a nearby truck, apparently smoking a cigarette, which clung to his bottom lip, emerged. He walked straight over to Sykes, his bushy brow pulled down into a frown. When he got close, he didn't snap at him, he instead stuck his hand out. "Howya doin' Lieutenant?"

Ronnie's mouth fell open. Sykes was ex-military? She would never have guessed that. Not in a million years. He was so...educated, and squeaky-clean. It boggled the mind.

Sykes grinned. "Just fine, Sarge. It's good to see you. Didn't know you'd pulled White House duty."

"Shit duty is what it is." He waved a few of his other troops over. "Go ahead and scan them...with *respect*."

The first soldier, who'd been so aggressive, backed up, trudging, as if knowing he was going to get reamed out shortly.

The screening was over in under three minutes. The fastest she'd ever experienced. During that time, she eavesdropped a little on Sykes's conversation with the sergeant, who'd apparently served with him in Iran before he'd left the military and joined the FBI.

Was she ever going to really know this man? Or would there always be new facets, layers to discover? She hadn't had time to dwell on it—on them—for obvious reasons. But for just one second, she allowed a hint of sadness, near pain, to stab her dead center.

Things would have been tough to work out between her and Sykes before Daniels had been attacked. Now she honestly didn't imagine how they ever could.

That would have been painful to realize yesterday. After last night, what they'd shared in that Richmond hotel room? It was, quite frankly, devastating.

Okay, pull a Scarlett O'Hara and think about that tomorrow, she told herself.

Thanking the sergeant, they headed through the gate toward the White House. Coming up on it at night was a different experience. During the daytime it looked like a monstrous beast. In the dark, with the spaced spotlights shining only on certain areas of it, there were glimmers of the building it had once been...and would be again. She could almost see the graceful columns and stately grounds, both of which were a long way off. Still, for the first time since coming back here last week, she was reminded of the warm, patriotic way this place used to make her feel, before the world had exploded into blood and fire in 2017.

Maybe it could happen again. Maybe she and everyone else in the country would feel it again. She certainly hoped so, anyway.

Reaching the nearest construction crew, they flashed their

identification, asked which of the Secret Service agents were on site and were informed Johansen and Kilgore were both here. After being admitted to the building, they went inside and headed for the security office.

"We're looking for SSA Johansen," said Ronnie as they entered the room, surprising Kilgore at his desk.

The SAIC flinched, shoving what looked like a magazine he'd been reading down onto his lap and crumpling it in his fists. "Ever hear of knocking?"

She cast a pointed look at the sign on the door, clearly marked as the security center. "Oh, sorry, I didn't realize this your *private* office."

Beside her, she heard Sykes quietly tsk. *Honey and vinegar, Sloan.*

"What do you want him for?" Kilgore asked.

She carefully explained about wanting to ask what had been found during the search of the tunnel last night, revealing as little as possible. Kilgore, who had to have heard about Daniels, didn't even ask his condition. The ass.

"Last I saw SSA Johansen was about twenty minutes ago," he said, leaning back in his chair and crossing his arms over his chest. "He got a call, then said he was going to walk around. He mentioned needing to check-out something in the sub-basement."

"Does he usually do that? Go walking around checking windows and doors like a rent-a-cop?"

The SAIC sneered. "No. We're not security guards, you know."

No, they weren't. And a routine sweep seemed very much beneath the pompous Secret Service agent and his team. Very curious.

They turned to leave, but before they did, something occurred to Ronnie and she had to turn around. "Question for you, Kilgore."

His jaw stiffened at the disrespectful tone.

"Whyd'ja spy on Bailey and Leanne Carr doing it and never put a stop to it?"

The belligerent man's eyes almost popped out of his head. She noted that he immediately reached for whatever magazine he'd been reading when they walked in and pushed it down onto the floor below his desk, as if that would shield it better from their view. Unfortunately for him, all it did was make it easier to see beneath the desk. She caught a glimpse of a graphic image of a couple involved in a sex act, and immediately grasped it.

"Friggin' pervert," she muttered as she turned and walked out of the office.

He sputtered something behind her, but she didn't even acknowledge it. She had absolutely no use for the man and if and when this awful case ever ended, she would file a complaint against him.

"Sure hope you don't ever get White House detail under that guy," Sykes said, his tone low and reproving.

"He's a creep."

"Definitely. But not necessarily the kind of guy you want to call a pervert to his face."

"I call them as I see them," she snapped as they reached the stairwell.

They jogged down, taking the stairs a few at a time. About halfway down, she suddenly got a chill, remembering the last time she'd come down here. Thankfully, this time, she had backup.

When they reached the bottom level, she saw all the lights were on. Stepping out into the corridor, near the area where Leanne's remains had been scattered, she called, "Johansen? SSA Johansen?"

Nothing. Not a sound, not a whisper, not a movement.

"Strange," Sykes said. "You'd think he would have killed the lights when he was finished.

Yes, she would have thought that. But another thought occurred to her. She approached the breaker panel, lifting a hand to the mass of switches.

"What are you doing?"

She thought about it, pictured what Johansen had done last night, when he'd been down here with Daniels, and pulled what she thought was the correct sequence of levers.

A click and the entire wall behind the panel popped out an inch.

"Holy shit, the mystery tunnel?"

"Uh huh." She stepped inside. As soon as her feet crossed the threshold, the lights came on, washing in a wave down the long corridor, which sloped down slightly as it led away from the White House in the direction of the Washington Monument.

Sykes followed. "Think he's in here?" He raised his voice and called for the agent, but they heard nothing in response.

Ronnie was about to suggest they go upstairs and search the basement—her second least favorite level in this building—when she spotted something on the floor a few feet away. It looked like a scrap of fabric. Small and ragged, the green square appeared to have been torn off someone's clothing. Or someone's green uniform.

Right beside it was a tiny red spot. Liquid. Shiny.

Blood.

"Sykes," she said, nodding toward it.

He was already unsnapping his holster, way ahead of her. His voice a thick whisper, he said, "I'll take point."

She nodded, retrieving her weapon as well, holding it down at her side.

They edged down into the tunnel, walking quietly. Although they could see a good distance in front of them, because of the powerful overhead lights, the hallway made a sharp turn about ten yards ahead, and they could make out nothing beyond it.

Every so often, they would catch sight of another tiny, red spot. Eventually, they got a little bigger, going from a pinpoint to the size of a dime, then a nickel.

Whoever was bleeding was in trouble. He'd staggered down this hallway—been pushed, or ordered at gunpoint—getting worse with every step he took.

They hugged the inside wall, edging toward that unknown turn in their path. Ronnie thought hard about Daniels's download, remembering that the next section of the tunnel went for about five yards, before turning sharply again, this time to the left.

Just about to whisper that to Sykes, she froze when every light in the place cut out.

Blackness descended. Her pulse fluttering wildly, Ronnie fought to control her reaction. Instinct was trying to take over, trying to remind her of what had happened the last time she was trapped down her in the dark with a madman.

It's not the same. He won't catch you off guard.

Plus, this time, she wasn't alone.

Sykes moved closer in the darkness, until his warm breaths fell onto the side of her face. "Emergency lights will come on," he said, his voice as light and soft as a butterfly's wing.

She waited. Her pounding heart kept the time.

Nothing happened. No emergency lights. She imagined their opponent, who was in charge of rebuilding this entire place, knew his way around an emergency power generator.

Finally, realizing they weren't going to come on, Sykes asked, "Flashlight?"

She again cursed herself for not taking the time to change into her uniform, on which she'd clipped a nice, sturdy little mag the other day after her dark-adventures in the White House. "No."

"I left my damn phone charging in the car. Yours?"

She groaned softly. "You're not going to believe it, but I raced out of my place without it."

A phone screen might not have done much good, but anything was better than this inky world in which they'd been thrown.

"I believe it," he said. "Because, sometimes, if it weren't for bad luck, you'd have no luck at all, Veronica Sloan."

"Tell me about it." She just hoped her partner had luck enough to make it through the night. And that she and Sykes had enough to get them out of this hellhole.

"Back? Or forward?" Sykes asked.

She thought about it. They were at about the halfway point, if her memory was correct. Going back in the blackness through which they'd already come seemed moderately better than going forward into the unknown. But it didn't mean they wouldn't be walking into a trap, no matter which way they went. Williams could have been hiding somewhere in the basement when they went into the tunnel and followed them in. Or he could be ahead of them with Johansen's body.

Damn it, think, think.

Suddenly, an option popped into her head. She remembered everything Daniels had noticed and thought frantically, trying to figure just how many steps they'd come. They'd been looking forward, focusing on finding Johansen, or Williams, and she hadn't paid any attention to all those emergency supplies left like bread crumbs for missing children along the trail.

But it couldn't be far. There had been more medical kits, yes, but there had to be at least one of the boxes she was looking for between here and the entrance.

"I've got an idea," she whispered, gripping his arm. Holding on, she pulled him to the other side of the tunnel. She put her free hand up on the wall, a little above her head, and began walking back towards the White House, feeling every inch of the way. Her eyes hadn't adjusted the tiniest bit. They were moving through blackness, it was as dark as a sensory deprivation chamber, and she had to rely only on touch. It was dizzying, frightening being totally blind, especially knowing they were not alone and were, most likely, being stalked by a predator.

Come on, come on, where are you?

Her hand hit the corner of a box that protruded out from the wall. She let go of Sykes, reached up and felt its outline, picturing what Daniels had seen. This one felt smaller, with a hard, metal front and a solid latch on the top. *Medical kit.*

Not what she needed.

She grabbed him again, kept going. Three steps. Five. Ten. *Hell, is it higher? Lower? Am I on the wrong damn side?*

Finally, her hand brushed something else. She sucked in a breath, released Sykes again, felt along the front, noting slick glass.

Yes. This might be it.

Her fingers worked the bottom latch and she rolled the door up. So far so good. She patted along the inside of the cabinet, praying she didn't feel a fire extinguisher or a defibrillator.

"Bingo," she whispered with a relieved sigh when her hands came in contact with what felt like a pair of binoculars.

"What?"

"Sight!"

She reached in, grabbing the night vision goggles. Though these were a different model than she'd ever trained on, she knew enough to get them strapped onto her head. She felt for the switch, found it, flicked it. A faint buzzing sound began, nearly inaudible, and suddenly a shadowy green world opened up all around her.

Smiling in relief, she started to tell Sykes what she'd found. But as soon as she turned toward him, she gasped in horror. Because emerging from the darkness, right behind Jeremy, was a large, black-cloaked figure wearing night vision goggles of his own.

It was Jack Williams.

Sykes was between her and the assailant, blind to his presence.

"Down!" she barked, swinging her weapon up instinctively. Sykes didn't react at first, having no idea a killer stood three steps behind him. Ronnie tried to shove him out of the way, since he was blocking her shot. Before she could do it, though, Sykes shuddered. She felt a jolt as electricity zipped through his body, leaping into hers, shocking her so hard she stumbled back and dropped her Glock.

Sykes dropped like a stone to the floor, immobilized and defenseless.

She dropped, too, picking her legs up and landing on top of him just as Williams turned toward her and fired his gun. The noise inside this enclosed chamber was deafening, wall-rattling, and her ears rung.

"Bitch!" he screamed.

He'd obviously crept up with the stun gun, hoping to incapacitate one of them before having to give away his presence by firing a shot. And it would have worked, if Ronnie hadn't found those night vision goggles and been prepared for the assault.

Now he wasn't launching a surprise attack, and he wasn't fighting someone who was totally blind. She wasn't sweet, innocent Leanne Carr. She hadn't been jumped in an alley, shot with a stun gun, incapacitated by a club to the head. She wasn't her poor partner who'd been drugged.

She was tough. She was strong. And she absofuckinglutely furious.

She didn't even waste time trying to find her weapon. She merely reacted, stayed alive, knowing she had to in order to keep Jeremy alive. He wouldn't be able to defend himself; she was the only chance he had.

And damned if she was going to lose him, not now that she'd finally realized how very much she cared about him.

She instinctively rolled away just as Williams fired again. The smell of gunpowder choked her and she wasn't hearing much. She could actually feel warm fluid running out of her ears and suspected her eardrums had ruptured. But that was okay. She still had the goggles. She could see that dark form in the eerie greenness. As long as she could see him, she could beat him.

She didn't hesitate afterward the echo of that last shot ended. She launched off the floor, throwing herself at him. He let out a hard oomph, staggering backward. Ronnie flung her arm out and swatted the gun out of his right hand, then spun around and kicked the stun gun out of his left. He lifted his fists to fight her.

"Bring it on, you piece of shit," she snarled.

She drew on every moment of training she'd ever had, punching him in the throat, throwing all her weight into the blow. She felt his windpipe crunch, heard the choking cough as he tried to breathe. But he didn't go down, he continued to fight, hitting her in the midriff, then landing a stinging punch against the wounded side of her head.

That just pissed her off even more. She threw a punishing right in the area of his kidney, backed up and kicked him in the gut so that he flew back against the wall. He slid down it, but as his ass hit the floor, he reached down and drew a long, wickedly-sharp looking knife out of his boot.

"You like cutting up innocent girls?" she yelled, having to raise her voice to hear it. "You pathetic freak, why didn't you just take a knife and slice your own throat?"

He roared, came at her from below. She leapt back, stumbled over Sykes's prone form and lost her balance. Falling flat on her back, she felt the breath leave her lungs in a hot, painful gush. She looked up to see Williams crawling closer, the knife gripped in his fist.

Something bumped her arm. She felt the faintest brush of fingertips on her hand, then a hard, blunt object pressed her palm.

Sykes. Handing over his own weapon.

She grabbed it, wrapped her palm around the grip and swung it straight up just as Williams launched toward her, wildly thrusting his knife in front of him.

She squeezed the trigger.

Direct hit.

The bullet smashed into the right eye piece of the night vision goggles, through his eyeball and into Jack Williams's brain. Glass flew, sparks erupted, and he flew back against the wall, sliding down it to a heap on the floor, leaving a trail of blood, skull and matter to mark his descent.

His reign of terror was over. That offered a hint of satisfaction, but she wasn't going to celebrate until she found out whether Williams had killed her partner.

Ronnie gave herself a minute—one—to mentally deal with what had just happened. She lay on the floor, gasping, Sykes sprawled beside her. His fingertips brushed her arm and his Glock was on her stomach, her hand still wrapped tightly around its grip.

Knowing Johansen was still out there, and could be injured, though, she forced herself to move. Her head ached, her ears were ringing uncontrollably and she thought she might have a couple of broken ribs where Williams had landed a powerful blow.

She got up. "I'll be back," she promised Sykes, whose eyes were opened, but who was unable to speak. "Gotta find Johansen. Get some help."

He blinked a few times, those incredible blue eyes swimming not with pain but with gratitude. They'd come through this. Despite everything, they were going to be okay. Both of them.

She thought of Daniels and clarified that thought.

All of them. Please God.

Stopping by Williams's body, she touched his throat and confirmed there was no pulse. Patting him down, she quickly found a phone in his pocket and pulled it out. She wasn't exactly surprised to see there were no service bars down here—she hadn't really expected them to be. *No luck but bad luck, right?*

Well, no. She wasn't ever going to think that again, not after how incredibly lucky she and Sykes had just been against a murderous psycho.

Ronnie stumbled up the tunnel, heading toward the Washington Monument. Turning a sharp corner not far from where the lights had gone out, she spied a crumpled heap on the floor ahead. She raced to Johansen, finding him alive, but badly wounded. She utilized one of those emergency medical kits on the wall to staunch the flow of blood from the stab wound in his chest. He was going to die without proper care, and she couldn't get him out of here by herself. She forced herself to leave the unconscious man, heading down the tunnel, running as fast as she could, praying the goggles didn't give out before she got to the end, not supposing the screen of Williams's phone would have enough juice to help much.

At last, the exit. She slammed into the metal emergency bar, and burst into a small room. Spying a set of stairs, she hurried up them, then kicked open a locked door. The moment she was outside, she lifted the unfamiliar phone and dialed 911.

While the phone rang, she drew in several deep, desperate breaths, shaking, adrenaline still coursing through her system. The hot, dirty city air had never tasted so good in her lungs and she breathed deeply, loving every inhalation.

She glanced across the mall. Construction lights shone on the White House, and she couldn't tear her eyes off it. So bright, so elegant, so beautiful. So cursed?

She didn't think she'd ever see that building again, for as long as she lived, without her mind trying to paint it red.

As for the monument rising straight and proud, right above her head?

Ronnie turned around in a circle, looking up, seeing the white structure puncture the sky. Lights around the bottom shone up to keep it brightly lit, a symbol of rebirth, renewal and possibility.

She thought about those who had been blown off it, those who had been crushed under it. Those she would never see again.

And for the first time since that day, she felt at peace. Coming up out of that hell here, beside this place that had haunted her nightmares for almost five years, seemed somehow right. It was almost as though her Dad and Ethan had been down there in the blackness with her, urging her through, pulling her along. Bringing her up into the light.

"I love you all," she whispered, staring past the white tip, up into the night sky, letting her heart say the goodbyes she'd found impossible to say until now.

"I miss you. I'll never forget you."

Feeling a warm night breeze blow across her overheated skin, lifting her hair off her neck, she smiled and added one more thing.

"Thank you."

Epilogue

The first rescue crew took off with Johansen within minutes of hauling him out of the tunnel. Sykes and Ronnie weren't far behind in a second ambulance. She felt okay—though she knew she probably needed a few stitches and might have to have her chest taped up. But she wasn't about to let Sykes out of her sight.

Thinking about what could have happened, what *would* have happened if she hadn't found those goggles and seen Williams right before he attacked, made her shiver with revulsion. She'd been devastated about Daniels. If Sykes had been brutalized, as well, she honestly didn't think she would ever have been able to get over it.

The realization that his death would have completely destroyed her made her realize she had a lot of thinking to do. But not now, not tonight. There was too much to be thankful for, and, regarding Daniels, too much to hope for.

She kept her hand entwined with Jeremy's as they rode through the city, sirens and lights blaring. He had started to shake off the electric effects of the stun gun even before the EMT's had arrived, following Ronnie down into the tunnel. The stronger he got, the more angry he became as he realized how helpless he'd been made by the man who'd killed so many. She tried to calm him down, playing down the danger, glossing over the violence and the pain Williams had inflicted on her. She hoped she didn't show that her heart had cracked into a thousand pieces at the thought of losing him. She just wasn't ready to admit that yet…to either of them.

The first person she saw when they pulled up to the emergency entrance was Lieutenant Ambrose. "Sloan!" he barked as they opened the back door and she hopped down, throwing off an EMT's helping hand.

"I'm fine, sir."

He grabbed her and pulled her into his arms anyway, like an overprotective Papa Bear. Considering he'd known her father, she figured that was to be expected.

"What the hell happened?"

"Long story." She wrapped an arm around her aching ribs, trying to physically hold herself together. His hug had reminded her of the pain she'd been trying to conceal. "How's Daniels?"

For the first time in hours, she saw a warm, genuine smile on someone's face.

"He's okay. He's really gonna be okay."

She sagged against a column. "Oh, thank God."

"You're hurt," her boss said, taking her arm and supporting her while they watched Sykes being wheeled into the E.R.

"I'm okay. So's Sykes. Daniels is the main concern. He's really out of surgery?"

"Out of surgery, but not awake yet. Doctors say they think he'll be fine. They're not sure if the reattachment of his hand will work, if he'll ever regain full use of it, but they are very confident that he'll live."

"Can I see him?"

"You'd better get patched up first."

Knowing the lieutenant was right didn't make it easier to find patience for the bustling, hovering treatment of the emergency room staff. They'd apparently heard a bit about what had happened and she'd swear every nurse on duty popped in to check on her, obviously wanting to hear some gossip about what was going on at the White House. It took a couple of hours for them to stitch her up, re-staple her head, x-ray her ribs and determine there was one hairline fracture, which they couldn't do a damn thing about except give her pain pills. Finally, though, she was told she could go check on her partner.

Sykes had recovered from the effects of the electro-shock. While sore, and having shaky muscular control for now, he was going to be fine. He met her at the emergency room exit, asking if it was all right if he went with her to see Daniels.

She hesitated. A few hours ago, she would have said no, absolutely not. Her guilt over what had happened between her and Sykes while Daniels was being attacked would not only have made her be a raging bitch to him, it probably would have made her tell him to just leave town.

But she couldn't do that. Now, having spent those minutes in the dark, desperate to protect him and make sure he didn't share Daniels's fate, she knew she cared much too deeply for Jeremy Sykes to let him walk back out of her life. He meant far too much to her for that.

"Give me a couple of minutes alone with him at first," she said, hoping he understood.

He, being Sykes, did. "Sure. It'll be better if you're the one he sees first. But I do want to thank him—if he hadn't found that key, we never would have cracked this thing."

"The key was the key," she said, trying to make him smile.

He did, at least a little.

They walked together to the ICU, where Daniels was recovering. A nurse saw her—the same one from earlier today—and she gasped at the bandages, bruises and wounds. "Oh, my goodness, honey, were you in a car accident?"

She looked at Sykes. He looked back. They both started to laugh.

Asking the nurse where she could find her partner, she followed the directions down to an open-curtained cubicle. Daniels was lying still and unmoving, monitors beeping beside his bed, thick bandages covering his left hand, all the way up to his elbow. His face was pale, bruised, sunken. His entire body seemed smaller than it had twenty-four hours ago.

But he was alive. Breathing. His heart was beating.

That was as much as she could ask for.

"Mark?" she whispered.

His eyelids flickered, then slowly opened.

She sucked her lips into her mouth, seeing those sad green eyes. Somehow, she knew that he'd been waiting to open them, waiting for hers to be the face he would see. She fought an inner battle against tears and won by reminding herself he would hate to see her cry.

"How are you doing?"

He swallowed, then whispered, "I've been better."

"I'm sure."

"Good thing I'm right handed, huh?" He glanced toward his bandaged left hand.

Ronnie feigned good humor. "Hey, all you ever do with that hand is flip people off, anyway."

A rusty laugh emerged from his throat. "You look like shit," he said.

"Had a little run-in with a friend of yours."

His brow furrowed as he concentrated. "It's fuzzy, damn, I can't remember…"

"Don't worry, there's plenty of time."

She heard the sudden uptick in his heartbeat on the monitor and worried as he tried to sit up on the bed. "Oh, God, Williams? It was Williams, right?"

"Stop it, you'll tear some stitches."

"I remember now—Williams was the one who tried to kill me. Jesus, Ron, did you…"

"I got him," she immediately replied, putting his mind at ease. "Jack Williams is dead and good riddance to bad rubbish."

He sagged back into the pillows. "Thank God. How?"

She quickly explained, telling him everything that had happened since the moment she'd spotted the key on his video download. She glossed over some of the details—including the few brutal blows Williams had landed on her. But she made sure he understood the most important part: that Jack Williams was dead and would never hurt anyone again.

"I'm glad and all, but it's weird thinking you've been inside my head, Ron. You didn't sneak a peek at my junk, did ya?" Easy laughter said he really was on the road to recovery.

"Ha. You wish."

His laughter slowly faded. "How's Sykes?"

"He's fine." She tensed. "He's waiting out in the hall. He wants to thank you."

Daniels shrugged. "Sure. Bring him on in."

She had to wonder if the pain meds were making her partner a little high, because he sounded perfectly sincere. She waited for a second, thinking he might change his mind, but he just settled more comfortably into his bed.

Taking him at his word, she stepped out, nodded toward Jeremy and gestured for him to join them. Once he had, he thanked her partner, insisting he didn't know how long Williams would have gotten away with his crimes if Daniels hadn't found that key.

"Hey, no problem. Just glad you gave Ron some backup. Though, it sounds like she saved your butt."

"She definitely did," Sykes said. "Mine and Johansen's."

"Atta girl."

Ronnie, uncomfortable with the praise, asked, "So, when did you figure out it was Williams? I couldn't see anything that gave him away on your backups. Did he say something?"

He couldn't answer right away, having to think about it, and she realized his memories were still very fuzzy. She almost regretted asking, hoping he *never* remembered some of what he'd been through.

"Yeah, I think…I'm pretty sure I recognized his voice right before he shot me." Another of those painful-sounding, rusty laughs. "Guess you got my message, huh?"

She and Sykes exchanged confused looks.

"Message?" she asked.

"Am I losing it? For some reason I think I tried to spell out his name."

Her mind spun, her thoughts churning as she remembered what she'd seen in that projection booth. Daniels's hand and fingers had been twitching, but she'd definitely seen an I and an L....

"Williams! You were trying to spell Williams."

"Well, yeah, of course," he said.

Relief flooding her, she cast a quick, slightly triumphant look at Jeremy. Daniels had not gone down weak and emotional, torn up because of some feelings he might or might not have for her. He'd been a cop until what he'd thought would be the very last second of his life. Thinking about the case, about justice. Exactly as she'd known he would.

"Yeah, we got the message," she said, so happy she felt like kissing him.

"Glad to hear it." Daniels's voice was getting softer, weaker, and his eyes drifted closed. They'd been in here almost ten minutes, which was the maximum amount of time allowed for visitors in the ICU. Judging by his weariness, that was for a very good reason.

Sykes cleared his throat. "We were a little confused about one thing."

Daniels turned his head slightly, opening his eyes. "Yeah?"

"What was the V for?"

Her partner blinked once. Then again. Confusion was visible in his expression—his tight mouth, narrowed eyes. He was trying desperately to remember something. "The V. The V."

Ronnie lifted her left hand, flashing the sign—pinky and ring finger down, thumb crossed over them. Middle and ring finger straight up. "A V."

Another moment of concentration, then Daniels began to struggle, trying to sit up, his eyes darting frantically about. His mouth opened and closed a few times and the shrill beeps from his heart monitor suddenly began to race

"Mark, calm down. What is it? What's wrong?"

"Not a V," he insisted. "Wasn't a V."

She and Sykes exchanged confused looks. But keeping him calm was far more important than figuring out the last few details of the case.

"It's okay, we'll talk about it later, just rest now." She smoothed his covers over him, taking care to avoid his left hand.

He reached for her with his right one. "Listen. You gotta listen."

She took his hand, bending close. "I'm listening, please, calm down, tell me what's wrong."

Sykes came close, too, and Daniels looked back and forth between them, straining to speak, fighting against the pain and drug-induced fatigue. "It wasn't a V I was making. I figured it out. Williams was with me and Kilgore right before I went down into the tunnel. He was with me, making the list of who knew about it."

She thought about it, considered the scene, began to grasp the timing.

"It was seven-thirty, Ron. He was with me at seven-thirty."

Oh, God. That meant…

"He couldn't have been in Richmond killing Eddie Girardo," whispered Sykes.

"Right." Daniels swallowed again, pushing words out from his tired throat. "That wasn't a V, it was the number two."

Two?

"There were two killers out there, Ronnie. You got Williams. But somebody else killed your Richmond victim. And, I think, Ryan Underwood. It was somebody else…a second killer."

He fell back on the pillow, exhaustion and medication taking him away. Ronnie didn't move, clutching his hand, unable to speak just yet. His words swam in her mind, echoing and repeating.

She'd thought it was over. Thought she'd faced-and defeated— the demon in that dark hole under the ground. But she'd been wrong.

Evil was still out there.

And she had to stop it.

ABOUT THE AUTHOR

Leslie A. Smith is a nationally best-selling author who has written more than fifty novels under various pseudonyms. She lives in Maryland with her husband and their daughters. Visit her online at www.leslieasmith.com or www.lesliekelly.com.